THE FOUR[T
A NICK LASSITER-

TO THE READER

This is the third book in the Nick Lassiter-Skyler International Espionage Series. In Book 1, *The Devil's Brigade*, Mr. Everyman-Struggling Author Nick Lassiter is introduced and goes to New York hoping to confront the second bestselling author in the world who plagiarized his unpublished novel. Instead, he gets caught up in the middle of a CIA operation with his father Benjamin Brewbaker and former girlfriend Natalie Perkins to take down powerful Russian mobsters. In Book 2, *The Coalition*, the *femme fatal* Italian assassin Skyler introduced in Book 1 takes center stage and terminates the U.S. President-elect. As she plays a game of cat-and-mouse with the pursuing authorities, an FBI agent and reporter working together eventually close in on her and in the process uncover a vast right-wing conspiracy to gain control of the U.S. Government. In Book 3, *The Fourth Pularchek*, Lassiter and Skyler appear together for the first time as major characters. They quickly become embroiled in an international case involving Lassiter's newly discovered biological father, the Polish billionaire and intelligence commander Stanislaw Pularchek, and buried secrets from Europe's World War II past. Their perilous journey takes them from the American capitol to the streets of Warsaw to the murderous gates of Auschwitz to the salt mines and snow-dusted mountain peaks of Austria. But can Lassiter, his adoptive father Brewbaker of the CIA, and his Polish biological father Pularchek work together as a team, and are they prepared for the consequences of stirring up the past? Furthermore, will Skyler be brought to justice for her multiple killings on U.S soil, or will she escape yet again?

Praise for Samuel Marquis

#1 *Denver Post* Bestselling Author
Foreword Reviews' Book of the Year Winner (HM)
Beverly Hills Books Awards Winner & Award-Winning Finalist
Next Generation Indie Book Awards Winner
& Award-Winning Finalist
USA Best Book Awards Award-Winning Finalist
Colorado Book Awards Award-Winning Finalist

"*The Coalition* has a lot of good action and suspense, an unusual female assassin, and the potential to be another *The Day After Tomorrow* [the runaway bestseller by Allan Folsom]."
—James Patterson, #1 *New York Times* Bestselling Author

"*Altar of Resistance* is a gripping and densely packed thriller dramatizing the Allied Italian campaign...reminiscent of Herman Wouk's *The Winds of War.*"
—Kirkus Reviews

"Marquis is a student of history, always creative, [and] never boring...A good comparison might be Tom Clancy."
—Military.com

"If you haven't tried a Samuel Marquis novel yet, *The Fourth Pularchek* is a good one to get introduced. The action is non-stop and gripping with no shortage of surprises. If you're already a fan of the award-winning novelist, this one won't disappoint."
—Dr. Wesley Britton, Bookpleasures.com (Crime & Mystery) - 5-Star Review

"In his novels *Blind Thrust* and *Cluster of Lies*, Samuel Marquis vividly combines the excitement of the best modern techno-thrillers, an education in geology, and a clarifying reminder that the choices each of us make have a profound impact on our precious planet."
—Ambassador Marc Grossman, Former U.S. Under Secretary of State

"Samuel Marquis grabs my attention right from the beginning and never lets go."
—Governor Roy R. Romer, 39th Governor of Colorado

"*The Coalition* starts with a bang, revs up its engines, and never stops until the explosive ending...Perfect for fans of James Patterson, David Baldacci, and Vince Flynn."
—Foreword Reviews

By Samuel Marquis

NICK LASSITER-SKYLER INTERNATIONAL ESPIONAGE SERIES

THE DEVIL'S BRIGADE
THE COALITION
THE FOURTH PULARCHEK

WORLD WAR TWO SERIES

BODYGUARD OF DECEPTION
ALTAR OF RESISTANCE
SPIES OF THE MIDNIGHT SUN (JANUARY 2018)

JOE HIGHEAGLE ENVIRONMENTAL SLEUTH SERIES

BLIND THRUST
CLUSTER OF LIES

THE FOURTH PULARCHEK

A NICK LASSITER-SKYLER NOVEL BOOK 3

SAMUEL MARQUIS

MOUNT SOPRIS PUBLISHING

THE FOURTH PULARCHEK
A NICK LASSITER-SKYLER NOVEL BOOK 3

MOUNT SOPRIS PUBLISHING
Trade paper: ISBN 978-1-943593-15-6
Kindle: ISBN 978-1-943593-19-4
Epub: ISBN 978-1-943593-20-0

First Mount Sopris Publishing Premium Printing: June 2017
Cover Design: Christian Fuenfhausen (http://cefdesign.com)
Formatting: Rik Hall (www.WildSeasFormatting.com)
Printed in the United States of America

To Order Samuel Marquis Books and Contact Samuel:

Visit Samuel Marquis's website, join his mailing list, learn about his forthcoming suspense novels and book events, and order his books at www.samuelmarquisbooks.com. Please send all fan mail (including criticism) to samuelmarquisbooks@gmail.com. Thank you for your support!

ATTENTION: ORGANIZATIONS AND CORPORATIONS
Mount Sopris Publishing books may be purchased for educational, business, or sales promotional use. For information, please email the Special Markets Department at samuelmarquisbooks@gmail.com.

Dedication

For the adopted children of the world in search of their biological parents—may you find what you are looking for.

And for Poland.

THE FOURTH PULARCHEK

A NICK LASSITER-SKYLER NOVEL BOOK 3

All Polish specialists will be exploited in our military-industrial complex. Later, all Poles will disappear from this world. It is imperative that the great German nation considers the elimination of all Polish people as its chief task.
  —Heinrich Himmler, March 15, 1940

The Nazis are back—differently dressed, speaking a different language and murdering ostensibly for different reasons but actually for the same: intolerance, hatred, excitement and just because they can.
  —Richard Cohen, August 25, 2014, comparing Islamic State and other Islamic jihadist terrorist groups to Nazi Germany

Nature…is every bit as important as nurture. Genetic influences, brain chemistry, and neurological development contribute strongly to who we are as children and what we become as adults. For example, tendencies to excessive worrying or timidity, leadership qualities, risk taking, obedience to authority, all appear to have a constitutional aspect.
  —Dr. Stanley Turecki, 1985

Adoption begins with the brokenness of loss and trauma, no matter what age the child is separated from their birth parents. It is always a felt loss, even if it doesn't come out until later in life.
  —Christin Slade, 2013

CHAPTER 1

POINT OF VIEW BAR AND ROOF TERRACE
THE WILLARD HOTEL, WASHINGTON, D.C.

NICK LASSITER would never have spotted the assassin—nor would his wonderful new life as a bestselling novelist have been forever altered—if his waiter hadn't accidentally spilled an ice-cold *Mexican Stand Off* cocktail onto his lap.

The time was 9:14 p.m. and violence was the last thing he, or the dozens of other diners on the terrace of The Willard Hotel, expected on this pleasant early June evening.

A fresh breeze blew in from the Potomac, bringing with it the fresh scent of jasmine to mingle with the mouth-watering smell of pan-grilled Maryland crab cakes and shrimp orzo risotto. Patters of lively conversation rippled across the exquisitely appointed patio from the diplomats, journalists, celebrities, power lobbyists, and rubbernecking tourists hoping to catch a glimpse of the rich and famous on the rooftop of the legendary hotel once frequented by Ulysses S. Grant.

On the streets below, the nation's capital, the very seat of the U.S. government, spread out like a picturesque diorama. Sitting at an intimate dining table for two, next to a wrought-iron railing overlooking Pennsylvania Avenue, Nick Lassiter felt as though he could literally reach out and touch the White House's East Wing.

Just before the first gunshot, he and his wife and literary agent, Natalie Perkins, had been talking about their forthcoming honeymoon to Bermuda. Married in Colorado just two days earlier, they were set to fly out in the morning to the British getaway island after a brief stopover in D.C. Now, with all of their wedding responsibilities mercifully behind them, they were eager for two weeks of much needed R&R, scuba-diving, love-making, and rum-tasting.

And then, in the blink of an eye, everything changed.

It all started when the waiter dropped Lassiter's *Mexican Stand Off* onto his lap.

"Good heavens, I'm sorry, sir!" cried the white-jacketed waiter in shock, leaning down with an oversized cloth napkin to mop up the mess.

Laughing it off good-naturedly, Lassiter stood up from his chair, politely took the napkin from the waiter, brushed away the fluid, and artfully directed it to the floor before it soaked into his trousers.

"Looks like I got lucky. I actually think I got most of it," he said with mild surprise, and it was then—the instant he looked up—that his eye caught a thin red beam of laser light piercing a curtain of airborne dust particles. He quickly traced the beam to a silhouetted figure clutching a rifle across Pennsylvania Avenue. Wedged between a pair of mushroom-shaped ventilation turbines, the man was crouched down in the classic shooter's position on the neighboring rooftop.

For a moment, the world seemed to move in slow motion, as the dancing dot of laser light appeared on the forehead of a man sitting at the table next to them. Dark-featured, corpulent, neatly-goateed, the man was impeccably dressed in a traditional Saudi Arabian cotton *thobe* with gold and crystal trim and a red-and-white-checked *ghutra* headdress. The perfectly pressed headpiece was underlain by a white *taqiyah* skullcap and secured by a black circular cord known as an *agal*. The man appeared to be a Saudi royal, or maybe just a wealthy oil tycoon.

The Saudi's dinner companion was a thin, bald-headed man with distinctly Aryan features. He wore a well-tailored gray suit with a silver necktie and rimless eyeglasses. The second man looked like a Swiss banker.

Like something out of a spy movie, the dot of laser light locked onto the well-fed Saudi with eerie calm and held there for a breathless moment that seemed suspended in time. Suddenly, the head of the Saudi jerked back, the rear of his cranium erupted in a violent spray of blood and brain matter, and his all-white accoutrements were covered in a fine crimson mist. As his massive chest and damaged head fell forward onto the table like a toppling Roman bust, the thin Swissman next to him came under attack. He was kicked hard to the left from the force of a bullet that burrowed into his jawbone. His glasses flew from his pineapple-shaped head, and he slumped in his chair like a rag doll, but with a missing lower face. Both unfortunate souls were dead in a fraction of a second; all Lassiter could do was gasp in shock.

Good Lord, didn't anyone else see that?

The answer, he realized belatedly, was affirmative as he heard a chorus of urgent mutterings and screams of astonishment coming from nearby tables. Looking again across Pennsylvania Avenue, he saw the shooter pull back into the shadows.

Then he was gone.

Still unable to believe his eyes, Lassiter wondered why he hadn't heard the report from the rifle. Then he realized that the sniper must have used a silencer, since there had been virtually no sound over the loud dinner chatter when the shots were fired.

"What? What is it?" cried Natalie, whose back was to the victims.

"There was a sniper on the rooftop across the street! I'm going downstairs to help the police locate him before he escapes! You wait here!"

"A sniper? What do you mean a sniper?" She started to turn to look behind her as Senator Davenport, the white-haired majority leader seated at the table next to them, yelled out in alarm and people began taking cover.

"Don't turn around!" Lassiter jumped up from the table and blocked her view. "Just stay here! I'm going down there and help the police!"

"But Nick—"

2

"Just stay here! I've got this!"

Before she could talk him out of it, he darted from the terrace to the elevator and then from the elevator through the hotel lobby and out onto the street. No sign of the police yet, he thought direly, looking up Pennsylvania Avenue in the direction of the Hoover Building. There was still no sound of any sirens either. *Jesus, what does it take to get law enforcement off its ass in this town, a Russian invasion?*

He looked across the street at the Premier Insurance Company building. On the rooftop loomed the two coral-head ventilator turbines where he had caught a brief glimpse of the shooter. Taking his bearings, he darted across Pennsylvania Avenue, heading towards the front of the large insurance building.

He knew he shouldn't be doing what he was doing. Who the hell did he think he was, Jason Bourne? He was a novelist for crying out loud, a keyboard puncher who sat behind a desk all day, not a cop or FBI agent. And what would he do even if he found the shooter? He didn't have a gun, and he had no actual training at stopping bad guys even though he wrote about them in his testosterone-infused thrillers. Well, aside from that incident last summer in New York involving the NYPD and Russian mafia, when he—along with Natalie and his father who, at that time, both worked for the CIA—were almost killed. But did New York actually count as training? It was definitely field experience, and he supposed that was better than nothing.

Crossing the street, he ran to the side entrance of the bank building. He didn't see anyone or anything suspicious, and no sign of a getaway car. It was deathly still and quiet.

He pulled at the door handle. Locked.

He continued on to the rear of the building. Now he could hear shrilling sirens echoing in the distance.

Finally, he thought angrily.

He started to check the rear door.

Without warning, the door burst open and a man plowed into him, knocking him to the pavement. The man's momentum then carried him forward and he tripped over Lassiter, the semiautomatic pistol he had been carrying skittering across the sidewalk as he toppled awkwardly onto the hard concrete surface.

Lassiter jumped quickly to his feet.

Hearing screeching tires, he looked to his left and saw a long, black limousine with German diplomatic flags turn the corner and race towards him.

Jesus, what the hell have I gotten myself into?

Facing the bright headlights, his eyes darted to the gun lying on the pavement. Behind him, he heard a grunt as the man rose to his feet.

He and the man looked at one another.

Then the gaze of each diverted to the weapon. For a split second, they both hesitated.

His adversary was the first to make a move. But he was a generation older than Lassiter and not as spry. He had not taken his second step before the Coloradoan took him out at the knees like a pulling guard and dove for the pistol.

They wrestled for the weapon, straining and grunting, with neither gaining the upper hand until Lassiter was able to clasp his hands around the pistol's grip and begin to pull the handgun free. But as he gave a final jerk to pluck loose the weapon and take it into his hands, his finger accidentally squeezed the trigger.

The gun discharged with a thunderous roar.

The shot, delivered at point blank range, drove into the man's chest like a freight train, searing his suit jacket in a smoldering flash of fire. Grunting in shock and pain, the man grabbed him by the shoulders to steady himself, their faces mere inches apart.

And then, a strange thing happened.

Up close and in the bright headlights, the man's face looked startlingly familiar, and so did Nick's face to the man. They both froze and stared in shock at one another for several seconds, as if each was peering into a mirror at his own image.

"You!" cried the man with a distinctive British accent.

Lassiter continued to stare at him in shock, unable to believe his eyes, as the limousine screeched to a halt and a pair of men in dark suits jumped from the vehicle. He was staring at himself—only twenty years in the future!

There was no mistaking it.

The face was long and narrow at the chin just like his, the cheekbones and jaw line were stubbornly prominent just like his, and the nose was slender and the eyes a distinctive aquamarine blue just like his. Everything about the man was an exact replica of Nicholas Maxwell Lassiter of Denver, Colorado, after taking into account the natural effects of aging. The hair was the same sandy blond color, only thinner and flecked with gray, and the man had the exact same build, but with twenty pounds of additional girth at the midriff. In the bright headlights of the limousine, there seemed to be little doubt that the DNA that belonged to the man was the same DNA that belonged to thirty-one-year-old Nick Lassiter.

It couldn't be just a remarkable coincidence.

"How...how can this be?" gasped the dying man as he started to slip from Lassiter's grasp. In the distance, the sirens were now blaring; the police would be on the scene any minute now.

Suddenly, Lassiter felt two pairs of arms clasping him—the driver and his comrade from the limousine were yanking him violently away—and he dropped the gun and released his grip from the man. Onto the pavement his unexpected double fell like a slab of beef. Lassiter kept his gaze fixed on the man as his two new adversaries jerked him away from the body. The face was now blank, the eyes as cold and lifeless as a stuffed animal mounted on a wall.

"He's dead! You've killed him, you bastard!" snarled the driver in a heavy Eastern European accent, pointing a gun at his face.

But, to Lassiter's surprise, the driver's cohort quickly stepped between them and warned his partner off.

"Stop, there is to be no killing except the targets! Now we must go!" The second man's accent, too, was Eastern European.

"But he has killed the Komandor!"

4

"Our orders are clear. There is to be no killing. Now we have to get out of here, damnit!"

But the driver was no longer listening. He was looking intently at Lassiter. "My God, look at his face."

The second man stared at Lassiter too. "Mother of God, it's the Komandor only younger! But how is it possible?"

"I don't…I don't know."

The sirens were now shrilling from the north and west. "There's no more time! We have to get out of here! The police are coming!"

From the darkness down the street, a woman's voice called out. "Nick, is that you?"

Lassiter felt a wave of panic. "Natalie, get out of here!" he shouted, waving her back.

The driver pointed his pistol at him. "Who the hell are you?"

"I'm Nick Lassiter—I'm just an author. And whoever he is"—he nodded at the body—"I didn't mean to kill him. He's the one that shot those men on that rooftop, isn't he? Why did he do it?"

"That was no murder, you bastard. That it was an execution. And I should shoot you where you stand for what you've done to our Komandor."

"No!" cried his partner. "There is to be no collateral damage!"

The driver shook his head angrily. "Mark my words. You will pay for this, Nick Lassiter. The Komandor's blood is on your hands!"

And with that, he and his comrade picked up the lifeless body, quickly carried it to the limousine, stuffed it in the back seat, and drove off as Natalie came running up.

"Jesus, Nick, are you all right?"

He took her into his arms and hugged her tightly, feeling the adrenaline surging through his body, mingling with relief that it was all over and he had survived. "I don't know what in the hell got into me," he said as flashing lights appeared down the street. "I just killed that guy."

"What?"

"I fucking killed him. He died right in front of my eyes."

"Well, it's over now. Thank God you're okay. I don't know what I'd do if I lost you," she said, tears of relief filling her eyes.

Holding her close, he felt the preciousness of her warmth, the steady rhythm of her beating heart, before pulling away and leaning down to pick up the gun.

"My God," he said regretfully. "I still can't believe I killed him."

As if on cue, a fleet of police cars and pair of SWAT vans rounded the corner and screeched to a halt at the curb. Doors flung open and two dozen hard-looking men in uniform poured from the vehicles, the SWAT team members wearing raid gear and brandishing lethal assault rifles. He and Natalie held up their hands in surrender. Still in a state of shock, Lassiter didn't realize he was still holding the gun in his hand.

A SWAT commander wearing full Kevlar body armor stepped forward with an assault rifle trained on Lassiter's chest. He signaled his men. They moved forward in a phalanx and surrounded the two of them.

He and Natalie stood there gaping-mouthed, stunned, like deer trapped in headlights. They didn't dare move a muscle.

"Drop your weapon—now!"

Still in shock, Lassiter hesitated. *This is all wrong, goddamnit! I'm not the assassin! You have the wrong guy!*

"Put the gun down now, or we will shoot! You have three seconds!" His face was as hard and bleak as granite. "One!"

Slowly and cautiously, Lassiter started to hold out his hand to drop the gun.

"Two!"

He dropped the weapon to the pavement.

The next thing he knew he and Natalie were knocked viciously to the sidewalk and swarmed by cops and SWAT men.

"Don't hurt her! She's not part of this!" he protested.

But with the White House only a few blocks down Pennsylvania Avenue and two corpses on the terrace restaurant of The Willard, the police were in no mood for kid-glove treatment. While part of the team peeled off and searched the parking lot, bushes, and building, Lassiter and Natalie were kneed hard in the spine, their arms were jerked back savagely, and they were cuffed so tightly that Lassiter lost feeling in both hands. Then he was yanked to his feet, searched, and read his Miranda, while the same was performed with nearly equal aggression on his poor, innocent wife, which really pissed him off. The cops then shoved them, Gestapo-like, towards a waiting police car.

For Lassiter, the whole thing was surreal. *How can they think I'm the killer? Don't they know they have the wrong guy?*

"I didn't do it," he said finally in his defense. "There was an assassin on the rooftop. I fought him, and then I accidentally killed him with his own gun. His men picked him up and drove off with the body. I know it sounds crazy, but I think the man I just killed might be my...my biological father."

The two MPDC officers looked at one another—they had never heard such an outlandish story—before shoving him and Natalie into the back seat of the police car and squealing away from the scene.

CHAPTER 2

ST. STEPHEN'S CATHEDRAL
VIENNA, AUSTRIA

WITH HER LEICA CAMERA dangling from her neck, the woman known to the world not by her face but by her murderous deeds walked along the Stephansplatz towards the entrance of St. Stephen's Cathedral. She was of Italian heritage, but with her clever disguise, polyglot mastery of languages, and surgical alteration of her Roman nose, it was impossible to tell. Her given name was Angela Valentina Ferrara, but years ago she had forsaken her real name for aliases. Her current alias was Skyler, no name. She also had a *nom de guerre*—Diego Gomez—a fictitious name created by her control agent. The invented Spanish assassin remained a mystery, a phantom of the files in the hands of the international law enforcement community. For her own security, Skyler was determined to keep it that way, although even she had to admit that her time was running out.

How could it not be after what she had done? Last November, during the U.S. presidential election, she had assassinated not one but four prominent American leaders. President-elect William Kieger and his vice-presidential running mate Katherine Fowler, Louisiana Senator Dubois, and a leading Christian conservative leader named John Locke had vanished off the face of the earth as a result of her talent with a sniper rifle. The only reason she was not being hunted down like Carlos the Jackal was because the FBI, Secret Service, and CIA were in sharp disagreement about the actual person responsible for the killings. No one in a position of high authority believed a *woman* could possibly be behind the multiple, military-style, long-distance shootings that had brought the U.S. to its knees. So the whole sordid intelligence failure was blamed on the most prominent usual suspect: Diego Gomez, a male assassin that did not actually exist. But Skyler knew her real identity could not be concealed forever; it was only a matter of time before the FBI, CIA, MI6, Mossad, German BND, Russian SVR, and every other intelligence outfit in the world hunted her down. Even Carlos the Jackal hadn't stayed anonymous forever.

All the same, she was confident that no one would recognize her in her current disguise. Her blue contact lenses, clear normal-vision glasses, pale makeup, ample tummy padding, and stretchy business pant suit outfit made her look like a pleasantly plump German tourist instead of the olive-skinned beauty with dark amber eyes and hair of like color she normally saw gazing back at her in the mirror. With her Aryan masquerade, camera around her neck, and slight German accent she'd assumed upon her arrival to Vienna, she carried a harmless, pudgy Teutonic persona that bore no resemblance to Italian-born-and-raised Angela Ferrara of Florence. But even without her disguises, to the casual eye she could pass for not just an Italian or ethnic American, but a South American, Mexican, Spaniard, Greek, or even someone of Arabic persuasion as the occasion called for it. The classical Roman profile of her nose had been re-sculpted to conceal her Italian heritage and lend her a more generic look that she could then modify, add to, or subtract from depending on her theater of operations.

She had the uncanny ability to complete the transformation to whatever type of person she wanted to be. Changing physically—not just clothes but hair, eyes, skin, and overall appearance—was easy for her. Facial features could be altered with a simple actor's kit. Height could be added or taken away, as could weight, through the clever application of padding. Though she preferred wigs, hair could be manipulated through coloring, combing, or cutting. From years of experience, she knew how to alter her appearance dramatically to achieve the desired effect. Male or female? Full-figured or slender? Old or youthful? Clothes were definitely a big part of it, but Skyler liked to think her facial expressions, contrived accents, and mannerisms were just as critical. Though people saw what they wanted to see in a person, she preferred to think of herself as an actress given the unenviable task of winning over an audience while handicapped with a horrendous script. She took pride in her own ability to become someone else, to transform herself and fool those around her with sheer skill and cunning.

It was an important part of the game.

Near the front entrance, she paused to check for signs of surveillance. No sign of anyone suspicious or anything out of the ordinary. But then two policemen in dark-blue uniforms swung around the corner of the cathedral and walked briskly towards her from the east. Sensing danger, she shifted her purse containing her Swiss-made SIG-Sauer P228 from her right shoulder to her left. But the policemen just walked on past, showing no interest in her.

Blowing out a sigh of relief, she looked up at the massive cathedral. Built between 1137 and 1160 A.D., St. Stephen's was the most prominent architectural achievement in all of Austria. It also happened to be one of the tallest houses of worship in the world and the mother church of the Roman Catholic Archdiocese of Vienna. Gazing up at the impressive Gothic edifice fashioned from Miocene limestone, capped with a steeply-pitched tiled roof, and accented by a 450-foot-tall south tower affectionately nicknamed *Steffl*, or Little Stephen, Skyler couldn't help but feel the power of God.

The soaring structure standing before her brought a smile to her full lips. It reminded her of growing up in *Firenze* as a little girl—before her world had been turned upside down. Before Don Scarpello and Alberto—the heartless bastards— had killed her inside.

Stepping up to the main entrance to the cathedral, she quietly pulled out her secure, encrypted mobile phone and punched in a number.

"I have been expecting your call," said a cosmopolitan, British-accented voice on the other end. "Any sign of our friends?"

"Not yet," replied Skyler. "I am in position at the cathedral entrance."

"Good. Let me know when they arrive."

"I will."

"And take lots of pictures."

"Of course." Putting away her coded mobile, Skyler took her camera and began taking photographs of the cathedral. At the front entrance was the famed *Riesentor*—the Giant's Door—named for the massive mastodon thighbone that had once hung over the aperture for decades, after being unearthed in 1443 during the excavation of the north tower's foundation. She clicked a photo before turning the camera upon the two Roman Towers standing more than two hundred feet tall on either side of the door. Then she photographed the tympanum above the door, depicting *Christ Pantocrator* flanked by two winged angels.

Skyler was more than just a professional assassin whose true identity was concealed by a fictitious Spanish killer-elite named Diego Gomez. She also happened to be a skilled professional photographer, with an instinctive feel for imagery, subject matter, lighting, and shadow, a fact which her current employer was well aware of. Her photographs of bustling city scenes and pastoral landscapes fetched generous prices from discreet dealers in North America, Europe, and Asia. But she sold her work only rarely, under a pseudonym.

Suddenly, she heard a gunning car engine and looked up to see a Mercedes S-Model wagon pull up along the curb in front of the cathedral. The sleek, jet-black vehicle bore an official German government tag, bullet-proof windows, and tinted glass to conceal the identity of the occupants. She discreetly turned her camera on the new interlopers and snapped off several pictures as the vehicle screeched to a halt.

The car doors opened. A woman and three men stepped from the Mercedes. Skyler took in the chiseled face captured in countless international intelligence dossiers, noting the high cheekbones, perfectly coiffed blonde hair, and gracefully athletic female figure that was too amply muscled to be confused with that of a European fashion model. It was Angela Wolff, second-in-command of the *Bundesnachrichtendienst*, the German foreign intelligence service known in abbreviated form as the BND. Skyler found Wolff a strikingly beautiful woman—but in a cruel, über-Aryan way that somehow harkened back to the dark days of Auschwitz and Stalingrad, when Europe was embroiled in a holocaust of war and destruction and unspeakable inhumanity.

She discreetly clicked another photo of Wolff and then took several in rapid succession of the three men with her, whom she recognized from the complete, up-to-date dossiers she had on them. Angela Wolff's number two was Dieter Franck, reported to be her secret lover, and the other two were her BND lieutenants Johannes Krupp and Arne Bauer. With Wolff in the lead, the group walked to the front entrance of St. Stephen's. There they stopped, looked around impatiently, and waited for more than two minutes. Pretending to photograph the spectacular Giant's Door at the front entrance, Skyler clicked off several more shots before putting away her camera, walking down the Stephansplatz in the opposite direction, and pulling out her secure mobile.

"She's here," she said to her contact, the man with the British accent.

9

"Who is with her?"

"Franck, Krupp, and Bauer."

"Is Hoess there yet?"

"No, not yet. But they're obviously waiting for him. They look tense and anxious."

"Are you getting lots of pictures?"

"A whole wall's worth. A wall of shame."

"Good. Now watch and wait. Hoess should be there soon."

"I'll call you when they leave."

"Ciao, my friend. And get some good pictures when they come back out too."

"I'll make sure of it."

"I can't wait to see the look on their faces. It's going to be priceless."

Skyler allowed herself the faintest trace of a smile. "No, Komandor, it's going to be even better than that. Ciao."

CHAPTER 3

ST. STEPHEN'S CATHEDRAL

"YOU'RE LATE, MONSIGNOR HOESS," bristled Angela Wolff, the number two of the German foreign intelligence service. "But perhaps you didn't know that I despise tardiness."

The monsignor tipped his head and shoulders apologetically. His face was lined with deep fissures like a desert landscape, and he wore steel-rimmed spectacles, a lengthy black cloak, a crimson sash, and a wide-rimmed black hat.

"My apologies, Ms. Vice-President," he said timorously, addressing her by her formal BND title. "This way please. We must hurry."

She fixed Hoess with a sharp look. "Hurry? It is you who are late and yet it is we who must hurry?"

"The Archbishop has been asking questions," he replied nervously. "Now, if you would please follow me."

With a claw-like hand, the octogenarian flicked the joystick on his electric wheelchair and, with surprising alacrity, began racing through the early morning pedestrian traffic of the Stephansplatz towards the front entrance of St. Stephen's. Wolff and her three BND subordinates—Dieter Franck, Johannes Krupp, and Arne Bauer—followed quickly behind Monsignor Hoess and his young aide, Ernst, whose assistance appeared to be unnecessary given Hoess's aggressive navigational tactics as he wove his wheelchair in and out of the crowd. Twice, he beeped a small horn on the contraption to clear a path, taking advantage of people's inherent sympathy for the handicapped. Following the withered but speedy Hoess, they passed swiftly beneath the famed *Riesentor* and through the main entrance to the cathedral. The cathedral's façade, with the tympanum above the door depicting *Christ Pantocrator* flanked by two winged angels, presented a breathtaking sight; and yet, Angela Wolff was too on edge to appreciate its artistic majesty.

There was so much at stake!

Once inside, they made their way quickly though the nave, passing the masterly stone pulpit carved by Anton Pilgram between 1510 and 1550. Wolff felt a shiver as her eyes passed over the carved toads, lizards, and other hideous creatures climbing the spiral rail alongside the steps leading up to the pulpit. Nonetheless, she couldn't help but feel the ethereal power of this holy and historic place. Mozart himself had been married and buried here at sacred *Stephansdom*;

and she would always fondly remember her first visit here as a little girl on holiday back in the early 1980s.

From the magnificent nave, the wheelchair-bound Hoess led them to a locked door. His assistant Ernst swiftly unlocked the door with a card-key, and the group proceeded down a hallway to a bank of elevators. They took one to the second floor of the basement directly beneath the 17th-century tomb of Emperor Frederick III in the Apostles' Choir. Two minutes later, they stood before yet another locked door, into which the assistant again swiftly gained entry using the electronic card-key fastened about his neck.

"Please, I welcome you to my office," said the monsignor magnanimously. "You will find, Frau Wolff, everything to your satisfaction, I am confident."

I had better or you will feel the brunt of my wrath, she was tempted to say. But she held her tongue, noticing that her second-in-command, her younger lover Dieter Franck, was looking at her. She reached out discreetly and gently touched his hand, her three-button Bettina Schoenbach blazer whispering with the movement. He smiled softly at her in reply, as if to say that everything would be all right. He could always tell when she was agitated and knew how to soothe her emotions. She felt all of her pent-up tension about to be released like a typhoon, and, for a brief moment, she remembered back to how sweetly he had made love to her last night.

The group stepped into the room. The assistant closed the door behind them. Hoess's office was furnished with the austere care and restraint of a deeply religious man: a large silver figure of Christ on the cross hung from the wall, presiding over a mahogany desk with pictures of friends and family, a simple Tyrolean rug, a colorful wall tapestry bearing Italian Renaissance motifs, and a pair of mahogany bookcases filled with religious objects, copies of illuminated manuscripts, five leatherbound copies of the Roman Catholic Old Testament Canon Holy Bible, and several books on European Old Masters and Florentine and Venetian architecture. But what caught Angela Wolff's eye was the locked door bearing three separate graphite padlocks.

"Your grandfather died on July 15, 1984, in Prien on Lake Chiemsee, Germany," said Hoess, as if it happened yesterday. "As your grandfather's lawyer, Herr Heydrich, has informed you, your grandfather's dying wish was for you to have, on your fortieth birthday, the contents of what resides in my personal storage room beyond that locked door. That day is today, Ms. Vice-President."

She felt her heart palpitating in her chest, but did her best not to appear overly anxious. "Thank you, Monsignor Hoess. Herr Heydrich has kept me up to date on all the developments. Now please open the door."

"As you wish, Ms. Vice-President. I checked on the contents just last night. I think you will be quite pleased with what your grandfather has bequeathed you."

Just open the door, damn you! I can't believe the time has come at last!

Hoess turned to his assistant. "Ernst, if you would, please?" He held out three individual keys attached to different colored ribbons: one blue and gold, a second crimson, and a third greenish-gray referred to as *feldgrau*, the color of the German World War II Wehrmacht uniform.

Taking a deep breath, the assistant took the keys from him and stepped to the door. Wolff held her breath as the assistant slowly inserted the key on the *feldgrau* ribbon into the top lock. The pin-drop silence of the room was broken by a gentle clicking sound. Ernst paused to look up at his audience, building up the moment. Then he proceeded to carefully open the second and third locks using the key attached to the blue and gold ribbon and the one attached to the crimson ribbon. A moment later, he had opened all the locks and again looked up.

"Would you like the honors, Frau Wolff?" said Hoess in the voice of a gracious host.

She could barely control her excitement. "Yes, yes. Thank you, Monsignor." Her eyes glittered with avarice.

Ernst flipped on the light switch. Then he pushed open the storage room door, but only part way to build the suspense, and stepped aside, allowing Wolff to come forward and claim her prize. As she walked towards the partially open door, euphoria washed over her like a soothing hot shower after a wonderful day of alpine skiing. The supreme moment had come.

Slowly, she pushed the door open all the way.

The treasure is now mine, all—

"*Scheisse*, where is everything?" she gasped, seeing that the storage room was empty except for a wooden table covered with a white linen altar cloth with gold trim.

Hoess flipped his joystick and darted forward in his wheelchair to peer inside the storage room for himself. When he saw that it was indeed empty except for the table, his mouth fell open, his eyes blinked rapidly, and he shook his head violently, as if by his sheer will he could refill the empty storage room with its proper contents.

"My God, they've taken everything!" cried Ernst, prying his way into the room. "But it was all there last night! The monsignor and I checked in preparation for your arrival, Frau Wolff! I tell you everything was there last night! Everything!"

Unimpressed, Wolff had her Walther PPQ M2 nine millimeter with the custom-fitted Brügger & Thomet baffle-type sound suppressor out in a flash. She quickly pointed it at Hoess, as did her three BND cohorts with their own semiautos.

"What have you done, Monsignor? Where are my grandfather's things?"

He just sat there in his wheelchair shaking his head and blubbering to himself. "I don't know...I...I honestly don't know."

"You must believe us, Ms. Vice-President!" pleaded Ernst. "We checked it together last night and everything was there!"

She cocked her Walther and pressed the gun against Hoess's temple. "I'm not going to ask you again, Monsignor. What have you done with what my grandfather has bequeathed me?"

Sweat beaded at his temple. "It was all there, I swear! We didn't touch anything!"

She jabbed the gun into his ear drum. "You are lying, Helmut. Where is my fucking merchandise?"

"It must have been Heydrich! I swear it wasn't us!"

She looked at Ernst. He was nodding his head vigorously, tears pouring from his eyes. "You must believe us, Frau Wolff! We had nothing to do with this!"

She tipped her head towards Dieter. He stepped forward and jabbed his Walther into Hoess's neck. "Who else has keys to this storage room besides you?"

"Just Ernst!"

"Then how could anyone else gain access?" demanded Wolff.

"I don't know!" pleaded Hoess. "But it was not us, I tell you! It has to be Heydrich! No one else knows! I have kept the secret for more than thirty years, I swear!"

She felt herself about to lose control. She pressed the nose of her pistol deep into the folds of his neck. "You are a liar, Helmut. You have betrayed my grandfather, and now you have betrayed me. And now I am going to kill you for it, unless you tell me what I want to know. I am going to count to three, and if you haven't told me by then, I am going to splatter your brains all over this room. And then I am going to do the same with your assistant Ernst here. Do you understand me?"

"But I swear I am not responsible for—"

"One!"

"It is Heydrich, I tell you! It is not Ernst or me!"

"Two!"

"Please, you can't do this! You will burn in Hell!"

"Three!"

"Wait!" cried a voice.

She turned to see her number three, Senior BND Agent Johannes Krupp, leaning down and poking at something lying beneath the wooden table against the wall. Krupp had pulled up the altar cloth to expose some sort of box under the table that was covered with a small blanket. Slowly, he withdrew the covering, and it was then Wolff realized that it wasn't a blanket at all, but a red-and-black Nazi flag. Removing the flag, Krupp leaned down and pulled out a metal lock box concealed beneath it. Wolff estimated that the box had to be at least three feet long by one foot wide, unusual dimensions, to say the least, for a container. The lock box was inscribed with the *Parteiadler* of the Third Reich—an eagle violently clutching a swastika in its claws.

"What? What the hell is it?" she demanded, but already she had a bad feeling about what she would find inside.

Slowly, Dieter opened the box. It was lined with red velvet bearing a single black swastika on a white circular background in the middle of the container.

"If this is somebody's idea of a fucking joke, they are dead," snarled Wolff.

"There's a note," said Dieter.

He pulled a small embossed envelope from the side of the metal lid, carefully withdrew it from the box by its corner with his thumb and fingertip, and handed it to his boss once she had holstered her weapon. The envelope bore her name—ANGELA BETTINA WOLFF—in raised gold lettering in a Renaissance-style font. Shaking her head, she slowly opened the envelope and removed the card inside, careful to only touch the edges so as not to disturb any fingerprints.

She read the card once, twice, then a third time before carefully placing the card back in the envelope and stuffing it into the pocket of her blazer. She recognized the signature. A combination of shock, seething anger, and veneration for her clever adversary's Machiavellian cunning boiled up inside of her. But she kept her expression studiously neutral as she stuffed the envelope in her designer jacket, not wanting to reveal her intentions, not even to her own men.

So it is to be war then, she thought coldly. A war until she had recovered what belonged to her by her inheritance, by her supreme birthright.

It was the *Schatzfund*—the great treasure trove. That was what her grandfather had called it. And now someone had stolen it. Someone she knew. Someone she had been hunting unsuccessfully for years.

They were all looking at her now, desperate to know the answer to the riddle and where they would go next from here. But still, she allowed her face to reveal nothing.

It was the ancient one, Hoess, who broke the silence.

"Who was it, Frau Wolff? Who has done this unspeakable thing?"

Her lip quivered slightly, and she scolded herself for letting her emotions get the better of her. "I can't tell you that, Monsignor," she said, quickly recovering her composure. "But I can tell you that I will be in touch with you soon. Very soon."

He bowed his head. "I understand and offer my profound sympathy, Ms. Vice-President."

"You are not to reveal what happened here today to anyone. Ever. Furthermore, from this point on, you are to report any and all contact with all persons, including Ernst here, directly to me. Is that understood?"

He bowed his head. "Yes, Ms. Vice-President. Consider me your obedient servant in this most unfortunate matter. And as God Almighty is our witness, Ernst and I had nothing to do with this. I made a promise long ago to your grandfather, and I have faithfully kept that promise. I am deeply sorry for this most unexpected development."

"Thank you, Monsignor. I believe you." She turned to her men. "Come, gentlemen, we're returning to Berlin. It's time to pay another old friend a visit."

ψψψ

Five minutes later, Skyler clicked off a handful of snapshots of Angela Wolff and her three BND operatives climbing back into their black Mercedes. As they drove off, she made her follow-up call on her coded mobile.

"They've gone," she said laconically.

"How did they look?"

"Not happy."

"And the pictures?"

"I managed to get several. You're right, they are priceless."

"Nice work. I'll see you in Berlin then."

"Yes, I'll be there, Komandor. Ciao."

CHAPTER 4

CIA HEADQUARTERS
LANGLEY, VIRGINIA

THE CLOCK READ 11:07 P.M. EST. The popular Starbucks in the building had closed down over two hours ago, and Benjamin Brewbaker—deputy director of the agency's National Clandestine Service—had been forced to settle for the lousy break room pot shortly thereafter in an effort to stay awake. He was grappling to come up to speed on a thorny Russian counterintelligence case, when he saw the CNN news flash on the double homicide at The Willard Hotel on the flat screen TV in his office. He instantly recognized the names of the two men killed. In fact, he had a good idea who was behind it—and, for a multitude of reasons, it deeply disturbed him. But what he found most vexing was that the prime suspect in the double murder was not the international operative whom he suspected was ultimately responsible, but his own son Nicholas Maxwell Lassiter.

He could scarcely believe his eyes.

Suddenly, the secure phone on his desk rang, startling him. He looked at the caller ID, recognized it. He picked up the phone.

The voice on the other end spoke without preamble.

"Are you seeing this, Benjamin? That's our son on CNN. *Our son*, Benjamin. Tell me this isn't happening!"

"Now just calm down, Vivian. I'm going to take care of this."

"Calm down? How can I calm down when Nick is in police custody? You know perfectly well he has nothing to do with this atrocity."

"Don't worry. I'm going to get to the bottom of this."

"Do you even know where he's being held?" His wife was a power lawyer and she spoke like one, particularly when she was agitated.

"Not yet. Look, I just saw it on the news myself." To his surprise, he saw his own face appear on the screen as CNN reported that Nick Lassiter, bestselling author and alleged assassin, was the son of the deputy director of the CIA's National Clandestine Service.

"My God, Benjamin, are you seeing this? I'd say you're not only behind the curve—you're behind the eight ball. You're a top CIA official for goodness sakes. Do something about this!"

"I will, Vivian, but first you've got to calm down. I told you I'd take care—"

He stopped right there as his phone started flashing again: another urgent call, this time on Line 2. It was his boss, Richard Voorheiss.

"I'm sorry, Vivian, but I've got to take this call."

"No, you've got to take care of this situation!"

"I told you I will."

"You know that Natalie is in custody too. They're supposed to be on their honeymoon, not in jail. Promise me you'll take care of this before it turns into a fiasco. This can't go on their permanent records. My God, they could be branded for life!"

"I promise I'll take care of it. Now I have to go. The director's on the other line. I'll call you when I have something definite. Goodbye."

"Clear this up and make this right, Benjamin! This is *our* son and daughter-in-law we're talking about here!"

"I said I'll take care of it. Now I've got to go." He calmly punched the flashing red button for Line 2. "Yes, Mr. Director."

"Why the hell didn't you pick up?"

"I'm sorry, sir. It was my wife and she's very upset."

"So you're seeing this on CNN?"

"It's like something out of *The Fugitive*. I can't believe it's actually happening."

"You'd better get down to my office right now, Ben."

"Yes, sir."

He slowly put down the phone, feeling as if the wind had just been knocked out of him. He didn't like his boss's tone; it was as if Voorheiss thought his son Nick was guilty. He took a couple of deep breaths. Then he rose from his chair, opened the door to his office, walked down the hallway to a bank of elevators, took a lift to the sixth floor, and navigated his way down two more hallways until he reached his boss's office. Along the way, he kept abreast of new developments by passing several color monitors tuned to CNN showing what was being called "the shooting near the White House." When he arrived at his destination, he found that the director's administrative assistant had gone home for the evening and the door was open. He knocked gently and poked his head inside.

"Come in and sit down, Ben," said Richard Holyard Voorheiss, Brewbaker's immediate supervisor and the director of the CIA's National Clandestine Service branch known prior to 2005 as the Directorate of Operations. The NCS was responsible for covert action and collecting foreign intelligence, mainly from human intelligence sources, or "humint" as it was known in the jargon of the trade. While the clandestine branch also relied heavily upon signals intelligence, or "sigint," and financial intelligence from electronic computer records of financial transactions, or "finint," the role of the NCS was primarily to serve as the lead in the coordination of clandestine field activities across the globe. It had been created out of good intentions to end years of rivalry between the various competing agencies of the U.S. intelligence community; the new name was supposed to reflect the NCS's role as the principal coordinator of human intelligence activities, while incorporating the increasingly important "sigint" and "finint" components into its own "humint" operations. In reality, the paranoid climate of the post 9/11 world ensured that the NCS still competed furiously with the NSA, FBI, and Department of Defense's newly created global clandestine intelligence unit, the

Defense Clandestine Service. With all of the competing agencies enjoying virtually unlimited budgets and minimal congressional oversight, it was dog-eat-dog and every-redundant-agency-for-itself.

Brewbaker took a seat in the upholstered chair in front of the director's desk. For a moment, they both just stared up in silence at the flat plasma screen on the wall showing the CNN coverage.

"This isn't looking good for the Agency, Ben," said Voorheiss. "They mentioned you by name."

"My son didn't do it, sir. It's as simple as that. He just writes books."

The director's eyes remained glued to the screen. "You know who the targets were." It was not a question.

"Khalid Al-Muraydi, Saudi jihadist financier, and Alfred Kiefer, Swiss banker with a lot of dirty secrets."

"Saudi royals and Swiss bankers are always dirty, Ben. That's rule number one in the intelligence business. You remember the old saying don't you? 'To the Swiss, there is no past. There is only money.'"

And money doesn't lie and can be traced back to its owner, thought Brewbaker, who was well versed in global terrorist banking and money-laundering operations based on CIA "finint" wire intercepts of jihadist financiers. Of the ten thousand wealthiest Islamic business entrepreneurs in the Middle East and Europe, one of every three was funding al-Qaeda, Hezbollah, Hamas, Islamic State, and other prominent terrorist groups to the tune of a million dollars or more per day. That bought a lot of weapons—and a lot of mass murder and terror.

Voorheiss stuck his chiseled jaw forward and rubbed a hand through his shock of silvery white hair, like the plumage of a falcon. "My main question, Ben, is this: are we going to get blowback on this? Is there anything that can link these two bastards to us?"

"They're not ours, sir. We've been following their transactions for several years, but we haven't made any moves to date. Both are on our priority global watch list, but no covert action has been taken against them."

"You're telling me this wasn't done by us? You're one hundred percent sure?"

"Yes, sir. I didn't authorize it."

"What the hell was your son doing there, Ben?"

He groaned inwardly at the accusing tone, but tried not to let his irritation show on his face. "He was having dinner with his wife, Natalie. They were set to leave on their honeymoon tomorrow. They're staying with me and Vivian in Georgetown. They just went out for dinner, sir, and then…well, you know the rest."

"The police found him with a gun in his hand, Ben. Innocent or not, that boy of yours is in quite a bind here."

"He must have taken the gun from the shooter. It's the only reasonable explanation."

Voorheiss said nothing, just stared at him with a non-committal expression on his lean, hawk-like face.

"Come on, Richard, you know damned well he didn't kill Al-Muraydi and Kiefer. That's why I need to get into the city as quickly as possible. I need to clear this mess up."

"Do you really think that's a good idea? This is personal for you, Ben. But we're the Company, and we never let the personal get in the way of our mandate."

He looked up at the screen at the projected images of his son on CNN: a picture of him as a kid riding a bike, a photo of him from a Kenyon College yearbook, and a recent image of him at a book signing for his debut novel, *Blind Thrust*. My God, they already had his whole life laid out, as if everything he had done up until now had led to him becoming today's D.C. killer.

"He's my son," he said, feeling an upwelling of emotion. "I'm going to make sure he's all right and be there for him. He's *my son*, sir."

"I understand, Ben. All right, get your butt down to the Hoover Building. But you are to tread carefully, you hear me?"

Shit, he's being held in the Hoover Building? I didn't know the FBI had him.

His boss was studying him closely. "Do you have a problem with the Bureau that I should be aware of, Ben?"

"Let's just say I don't send anyone over there Christmas cards. I guess I'm just surprised that MPDC isn't the one holding him."

"I'm reminding you again to tread lightly down there. Just get the facts. If your boy is innocent—which I have no doubt he is—then you have the go-ahead to get him the hell out of there. Same goes for his new bride. Jesus, what a terrible place to spend your honeymoon."

He stood up from his chair. "Yes, sir, it most certainly is. I'd better get going."

But Voorheiss held up his hand, not letting him leave just yet. "Now hold on just a minute. Even if you clear this up, we're still going to need to talk to your son. After all, he just witnessed the killing of two high-level targets on our priority list. We're talking about goddamn Al-Muraydi and Kiefer here, not some gangbanger from the projects. Whoever killed them knew they would be at The Willard Hotel tonight, dining on the Point of View terrace. Who do you think could come by such intelligence?"

"I don't know, sir," he said. But he did know, and he was keeping it from his boss, at least until he got to the bottom of this mess.

"I'm sorry, but I think you do know, Ben. This has Pularchek written all over it."

Brewbaker felt a little twitch cross his face, but he swiftly suppressed it. He said nothing in reply. His boss was referring to Stanislaw Snarkus Pularchek, the Polish biathlon champion, former Special Forces officer, billionaire entrepreneur, and alleged assassin of European neo-Nazi and Islamic jihadist practitioners and financiers. The terrace sniper killings had the clever Pole's signature all over it, but he wasn't about to tell his boss that—for one very important and highly personal reason. In any case, he would need to thoroughly review the FBI's ballistics report and the DNA results from the blood samples collected from the crime scene to be certain, and it would be at least a week before the tests were completed, the results compiled, and the final laboratory reports prepared.

"As I recall, Stanislaw Pularchek is your boy, Ben. You've been following his career for quite some time now. Since you were on the Russian and Eastern European Counterterrorism Desk."

"Yes, sir, I know Pularchek. And I concur with you that he could be the one behind this. Nonetheless, I'm going to withhold judgement until all the facts are in."

"You're lying to me, Ben. You've already concluded Pularchek's the trigger man, and yet you're pretending otherwise. I can see it in your eyes."

"Sir?"

"Why are you lying to me, Ben?"

Again, he felt himself flinch inside, but he forced himself not to allow it to show on his face. "Lying to you, sir?"

"You know that Pularchek is most likely behind this, and yet you're pretending otherwise. Why would you do that?"

"I'm not holding back on you, sir. Honestly, I have my doubts about Pularchek."

"Based on what evidence?"

"One very important reason: he's never operated before on U.S. soil. Not once."

"Come now, Ben. Just look at the targets. Two prominent financiers of terror, one a Saudi oil billionaire, the other a Swiss banker who also has dirty ties to Nazi money stolen from the Jews. It's just too much of a coincidence."

"Maybe, sir. But until all the facts are in, I think it's premature to draw any conclusions about responsibility."

"And yet, you've already made up your mind that your son has nothing to do with it."

Brewbaker said nothing. "If there's nothing further, Richard, I need to get down to the Hoover Building."

"All right, but be careful. And for God's sake, don't embarrass the Company. It's bad enough that our name has come up. You should also know that your son was the one who requested that you be contacted. That's why you and I are having this little chat. The FBI called the director, who, in turn, called me."

"Director Brennan knows about this?"

"The whole world knows about this, Ben. It's a bloody disaster, and I mean literally. Two men are assassinated while eating dinner a stone's throw from the Oval Office. It doesn't matter that they're dirty foreigners with a history of supporting the wrong side in the war on terror. Or that they're on every NATO intelligence agency target list. To the rest of the world, it will look like we can't protect the goddamned homeland."

"That may be, sir, but my son has nothing to do with this. And don't worry, I'll be discreet."

"I know you will, Ben. Because tomorrow morning at nine o'clock you're going to be sitting in that chair again giving me a full briefing—and it had better be good. Director Brennan has made it clear that you are to be our eyes and ears over at the Hoover Building."

So that's what their play was. The mandarins at the top of the Company food chain weren't allowing him to retrieve his son out of a sense of altruism, but rather to spy on their rivals at the Bureau while gathering intelligence on the killings. Intelligence that might one day prove useful for the CIA's clandestine operations.

"Yes, sir, I believe I get the picture now."

"There's one more thing."

He raised a brow. "Sir?"

"Remember, I'm going to need to talk to that boy of yours tomorrow morning too. That is, if you manage to secure his release."

"He and I will be here, Richard. You can count on it."

CHAPTER 5

FBI HEADQUARTERS
HOOVER BUILDING, WASHINGTON, D.C.

TONIGHT MARKED THE THIRD TIME Nick Lassiter had been taken into custody—not counting tenth grade when he got busted for smoking weed—and, based on his experience to date, he had come to the conclusion that being handcuffed, fingerprinted, photographed, locked behind bars, and interrogated was something to be assiduously avoided. He had been grilled for over two hours now. He had told the three FBI agents seated at the table the same thing over and over, namely that he was 100% innocent. But they didn't appear to believe him, and he was growing tired and frustrated with their endless questions. But more than anything else, he was worried about Natalie.

She certainly didn't belong in this bureaucratic hellhole—especially when they had been married for only two days and were about to set off on their honeymoon. She had probably looked forward to her wedding since she was a little girl, and now he had ruined everything by stubbornly insisting on playing the hero.

But he wasn't a hero. Not even close, in his mind.

He hadn't caught the sniper and saved the day. All he had done was contribute to more killing by wrestling the gun away from him and shooting him dead. There was nothing noble about killing someone, even in self-defense, he knew from his first-hand experience in New York last summer and now from what had happened tonight in D.C. But what had been most painful for him was seeing the man referred to as the Komandor die before his very eyes; somehow, it didn't seem to matter that he was an assassin.

He had recounted the whole story at least five times, from start to finish, to Special-Agent-in-Charge Jack Forsythe and his two lackeys seated across from him. But they still didn't seem to believe a word of it. To be honest, he wasn't sure whether he believed it himself.

Was it really possible that this so-called *Komandor* could be his biological father? After all, there was not a scintilla of doubt how uncanny the resemblance was between them, despite their age difference. They were precise mirror images—only twenty or so years apart. Their striking similarity could not be attributed to random chance. Even the shooter's two accomplices had been stunned by how much they looked alike. So much so that he and the assassin could have been clones, or identical twins, if not for their difference in age.

But how was such a thing possible? Could it truly be that the man he had killed was his real father?

It seemed highly unlikely. His parents would have told him if he was adopted, right? They couldn't possibly have brought someone else's baby boy back from the hospital and allowed him to grow up for more than thirty years without telling him where he came from. How could they have kept it a secret all these years from friends and family? No one—not his parents, friends, grandparents, aunts, uncles, cousins, counselors, teachers, or coaches growing up—had ever so much as hinted that he could possibly be adopted.

So how the hell was it possible?

He didn't know the answer. But something about the whole thing didn't feel right. In retrospect, it seemed odd that his parents had reportedly lived in London for a year before he was born, and for a short time after, before they had moved back to Washington. That was the story they had told him since he was little, that he was born in London. Could they have adopted him and lived overseas for a time, and then later brought him to the U.S.? Could they somehow have managed to keep his adoption a secret from him and everyone else all these years? But if they weren't his real parents, then how come he bore a strong physical resemblance to them both? People always said he was a chip off the old block compared to his old man, and that he had his mother's eyes and tall, trim physique.

But how was that possible if he had been adopted?

Who were these people if not his real parents, and why had they lied to him all these years? Or was he just imagining it all? Was it coincidence that the assassin looked just like him, only older? And what about the guy's British accent and his accomplices' Eastern European accents? What was their significance, if any?

Beyond the window of the glassed-in interrogation room, he saw a flash of movement in the corridor. Looking up, he saw his father, Benjamin Brewbaker— or was the man really his father?—and another man in a suit standing at the window. FBI Special-Agent-in-Charge Jack Forsythe turned off the digital camera and recorder, rose from his seat, and motioned the other two agents to accompany him. They all got up and left the room.

For the next few minutes, Lassiter watched as his father, Forsythe, and the other two FBI agents had an intense discussion. They turned to look at him several times as they conversed, and by his father's body language, it was obvious that he was agitated.

After a few minutes of back-and-forth, his father pulled out a manila envelope from his briefcase and handed it to Forsythe. The SAC proceeded to look over the contents of the envelope. Then they resumed arguing for a while longer before Forsythe sent one of his subordinates off on an errand, opened the door, and led his father and the remaining agent back into the room.

Lassiter had the feeling that his father and Forsythe knew one another, and perhaps even had some old score to settle. He hoped he wasn't caught in the middle of some internecine FBI-CIA turf war.

"Hello, Son, I'm going to get you out of here as quickly as possible," said his father right off the bat, as if he, not Forsythe, was the one in charge. Lassiter could

23

see the love and the pain on his father's face. That he was innocent in his father's eyes was obvious—and his father's steadfast belief in him gave Lassiter a feeling of strength and determination. "Special Agent Forsythe has briefed me on the situation. He has agreed to let me ask you a few questions so that we can clear all this up. Are you ready, or do you need a quick break?"

"I'm ready."

"Good, Son. Then let's get started."

CHAPTER 6

FBI HEADQUARTERS

"SO, WHY DON'T YOU tell us, for the record, exactly what happened from the time you arrived at The Willard to your arrest by the police. Don't leave anything out. As I'm sure Special Agent Forsythe has made clear to you, even the smallest detail can be important in cases like these."

His father delivered a withering glare to the SAC before returning his gaze to him.

Nodding in understanding, Lassiter spoke into the camera at the far end of the table. It took him twenty minutes from start to finish, with his father and Forsythe stopping him occasionally to pose questions. He deliberately left out the part about the man he had shot—the Komandor, as his two accomplices had called him—and their close physical resemblance. He still wasn't sure he believed the assassin could be his biological father, and he didn't want the FBI or CIA thinking he was making stories up.

The second run-through was easier for him than the first, since his dad was in the room with him this time. The second time around, he also found that Forsythe's partner seemed to be more understanding. The guy nodded in agreement several times when his father raised a point of emphasis, which he took as a positive sign. But Forsythe didn't budge and was still sullen as a clam. Several times, he looked at his watch and out the room's interior window, as if impatient for the agent he had ordered off on an errand to return. Lassiter wondered what the SAC had sent his subordinate off to find out.

"I've got to be honest with you, Nick," said Forsythe when Lassiter was finished with his account. "Your story still sounds far-fetched to me. You expect us to believe that you saw the shooter from across the street prior to the killings because your waiter spilled a drink onto your lap. And that you proceeded to dash down to the street, run behind the insurance building, and tussle with the assassin just as his getaway vehicle with German diplomatic flags drove up. And that you then wrestled his pistol away from him and shot him dead. And then, after all of those heroics, you're stupid enough to just stand there holding the gun when the authorities arrived. Sorry, but I'm just not buying it."

"I don't care if you buy it or not, Special Agent," countered Lassiter. "It happens to be the truth."

"So you tore the gun out of the hand of this professional assassin and killed him with his own weapon. You really expect us to believe that?"

"Yes, because that's how it happened. What can I say? I was jacked up with adrenaline."

The FBI agent's eyes narrowed. "Is there something you're not telling us, Nick? It might just be my gut, but I believe you're withholding something from us. Is there something you want to tell us now that your father's here, something you neglected to tell us before?"

What does he think I'm hiding? Or does he know the answer to his own question? "I shot the guy at point-blank range and saw him bleeding onto the sidewalk. So the FBI has by now collected samples of his blood from the crime scene. And I'm sure you've also recovered the sniper's rifle and know that the pistol I took from him wasn't the same gun that he used to shoot those two guys on the rooftop."

"So what are you saying?"

"If you don't already have enough evidence to release me, you will soon enough. Your crime-scene forensics team is going to figure out quickly that I have nothing to do with this. Which is why I don't understand what I'm still doing here. And I also want to know what's going on with my wife. Are you questioning her? If so, where is she and why won't you let me see her? We're supposed to be on our honeymoon."

"At least two men, and possibly three, are dead, Nick, and there are still a lot of unanswered questions. It's going to take some time to sort everything out. So until then, you'd better come clean and tell us the whole story. I still don't think you've told us everything, and my first instincts are usually pretty—"

His father held up a hand and spoke up abruptly, cutting the FBI agent off. "That's enough of the Boy Scout routine, Jack." He pulled out a stack of photographs from his briefcase and pushed them across the table towards Lassiter. "I want you to look over those photos and tell me whether the man in them is the man you believe you shot and killed. Can you please do that for me? And remember, you're being recorded."

"What are you doing, Brewbaker?" demanded Forsythe. "This isn't going to prove anything."

His father ignored him. "Just look at the pictures, Nick. Is that the assassin who shot the two men on the terrace and also the same man you wrestled the gun away from and killed? Yes, or no?"

The whole room seemed to come to a standstill, the silence as acute as a stiletto blade. Feeling the tension in the interrogation room and the palpable animosity between his father and Forsythe, Lassiter took his time examining the photographs. He wanted to be sure. There were eight photos in all: a distinguished-looking gentleman in a tuxedo giving a speech; the same man laughing at a lavish dinner table with actors George Clooney and Izabella Scorupco; the man getting out of a silver Range Rover; the man shaking the hands of François Hollande and Angela Merkel at some staged business photo op; the man on the cover of *Le Monde*, the *European Business Journal,* and *Scuba Diver* magazine.

"Nick, I'm going to ask you again. Have you ever seen the man in the photographs before?"

Lassiter nodded. "Yes," he said. It was the aquamarine eyes. He would never forget those eyes. It was like staring into a mirror, or peering through a keyhole and seeing himself staring back from the other side.

"Is it the same man you saw tonight?"

"Yes, that's him. That's the man I killed."

"You're sure."

"Yes, I'm positive. His two accomplices called him the *Ko-man-door*."

"The Komandor? With a K, one M, and an O?"

"Yes."

"And is this Komandor you've just identified also the shooter? What I mean is, is he the same man with the rifle that you spotted on the rooftop across the street from the terrace restaurant?"

He studied the pictures again, flipping through them one by one. "I think so, but it was dark."

"But the two accomplices from the limo did verify that he was the shooter, correct?"

"Yeah, both of them verified it." He picked up the photograph of the man with his arm around actor George Clooney and looked it over closely. "I'm pretty sure it's the same guy I saw on the rooftop, but I'm not one-hundred-percent certain. But I am sure it's the guy I shot on the street. He and I were only inches apart and the limo's headlights were right on him."

"Please note, Special Agent, that my son has ID'd the killer with a reasonable degree of certainty."

Lassiter looked at his father. "Who is he, Dad? I mean, one minute he's a European socialite hanging out with George Clooney and Angela Merkel—the next he's an assassin taking out people in the nation's capital. Who the hell does that? This guy is obviously a mover and shaker, yet he's also a well-trained killer. So who is he?"

"That's classified," said Forsythe.

"Like hell it is," declared his father. He held up the *Le Monde* cover. "His name is Stanislaw Pularchek. He's been on various watch lists for the past five years. He is—or rather, was, until his recent demise—a Polish billionaire entrepreneur, playboy, recreational pilot, avid scuba diver, and former Olympic gold medalist in the biathlon. He also happens to be, I mean he was, a suspected international assassin of Islamic terrorist and neo-Nazi financiers who has for years been secretly backed by the Polish government."

Lassiter was rendered speechless. *My God, that's who I killed, a Polish billionaire-assassin?*

Forsythe was shaking his head and glaring at his father. "Come on, Deputy Director, you really expect us to believe that Pularchek was behind this? The man has never worked the U.S. and you know it."

"Is that a belated admission on your part, Jack, that my son the fiction writer isn't the one behind the nefarious plot and acting alone like Lee Harvey Oswald?"

Forsythe frowned. "There are unanswered questions, Deputy Director. And until your son here answers them to my satisfaction, he's not leaving this room.

He's in our custody, not yours, and you are here only out of professional courtesy."

Lassiter looked into his father's eyes. "Wait a second, Dad. If the guy I killed is Polish, how come he spoke to me in English, and with a British accent?"

"Pularchek was privately tutored by an English governess growing up in Poland and was educated at Oxford. He's also spent significant time in England during the course of his professional career. He's fluent in five languages, including English, which he speaks with a British accent."

Forsythe was shaking his head skeptically. "We don't know that the guy your son killed was Pularchek. As a matter of fact, without a body or any forensics yet, we don't know if anyone was actually killed."

"We have my son's testimony." Brewbaker picked up the photograph of the man hobnobbing with French President François Hollande and German Chancellor Angela Merkel. "Nick, I want to be absolutely certain here. Are you one hundred percent sure this is the guy?" He pointed at the older man's handsome, sunburnished face and mischievous aquamarine eyes. "It's very important."

"Yes, it's him. That's the man I shot, I'm sure of it. And for the record, I did kill him. He definitely wasn't breathing when his men carried him to the limo. The driver checked his pulse and actually accused me of murdering him."

His father looked back at Forsythe, this time with a shrug. "Would you like to give him a polygraph, Jack? Would that satisfy you?"

"Don't test my patience, Brewbaker, or I'll have you thrown out of this building onto the street. As far as I'm concerned, without a body we don't have confirmation of a damned thing yet, so you two had better just sit tight. Furthermore, we still don't have even preliminary forensics or ballistics analysis, and the eyewitness accounts are still coming in. So no one's going anywhere until I say so."

Lassiter looked at his father. He had pulled out his smartphone and was scrolling through it. "You know damn well, Jack, that the calibers and rifling characteristics of the bullets pulled from Al-Muraydi and Kiefer won't match the ones from the Glock Nick seized from the shooter."

Forsythe said nothing.

"More importantly, have you seen the traffic camera footage at 9:27 p.m.? It shows images of a limousine with German diplomatic tags passing through Georgetown with three occupants, one of whom is slumped in the back seat. That in itself confirms that my son is telling the truth."

Forsythe glared at him. "Where did you get that?"

"From the same people at NSA who just sent it to you and your boys, Jack. Now quit this bullshit and release my son. You're beginning to embarrass even your own staff."

He tipped his head towards Forsythe's Bureau cohort in the seat next to him, who looked at his boss nervously.

"With all due respect, Jack, you have no further reason to hold my son. You know damn well that this was the work of a professional, not Nick. He's an author for crying out loud, not a sniper."

"He was holding a gun at the scene of the crime. His prints are the only ones on the weapon."

"You're going to look foolish when ballistics confirms that the Glock Nick was holding is not the murder weapon of Al-Muraydi and Kiefer. Are you really doing this just to piss me off?"

The senior FBI agent stiffened. "No one's saying the gun with Nick's prints on it is the same one used by the shooter. In fact, I can tell you and your boy right now that there are two different weapons. But it doesn't matter. There's still not enough evidence to release him, not yet."

At that moment, the door opened and the third FBI man reappeared. Closing the door behind him, he walked directly to his boss and whispered into his ear. After a moment, Forsythe nodded and folded his hands in his lap. The agent sat back down at the table next to him. Lassiter didn't like the smug expression on Forsythe's face.

He glanced at his father, who was looking at the SAC intently. "Is there something you want to tell me, Jack?"

Forsythe's smile widened; the man was unable to resist from gloating. "As a matter of fact there is, Mr. Deputy Director. It seems that Stanislaw Pularchek was not in our fair city this evening after all. He was in Warsaw."

"You don't say?"

"You don't seem surprised. Then I'll wager you won't be surprised to hear this either. Pularchek is at this very moment in his private suite at the Hotel Bristol with a young Polish supermodel named Izabella Sliwinskao."

"And you've confirmed its Pularchek? You're one-hundred-percent certain?"

"One hundred percent. It seems our Polish friend gave a rousing speech on the current state of the global economy to a packed crowd at the National Theater and Opera House several hours ago. And now, he has apparently retired for the evening with his attractive guest. You know that's funny, Nick, because I thought you just killed the man right here in our fair city." He turned to his father. "Now is there anything you want to tell *me*, Ben?"

Lassiter looked at his father, who gave a guilty shrug. "As a matter of fact there is, Jack. I think it's time you and I have a real talk...this time in private."

CHAPTER 7

PULARCHEK AIRFIELD
WARSAW, POLAND

STANISLAW SNARKUS PULARCHEK stepped into the luxury cabin of his Gulfstream G650ER. The $70 million aircraft, powered by two massive Rolls-Royce BR725 A1-12 jet engines, was parked on the tarmac of Pularchek Airfield, named after his grandfather, hero of the Polish resistance during the Second World War. His female flight attendant, Rachel Landau, a black belt computer expert who doubled as part of his Operations-Security Detail, escorted him to his plush white Corinthian leather seat and handed him his usual *espresso macchiato*. He calmly sipped the warm drink while waiting for his right-hand man, the Counselor, to return from the lavatory to deliver a second morning briefing on the American operation.

Normally, Pularchek himself manned the cockpit controls of his business jet, but the current situation demanded his immediate attention. Though he loved to fly as much as he enjoyed womanizing, scuba diving, and competitive shooting, right now he needed to be making critical decisions instead of piloting a 600-mph aircraft into the enemy territory of the former Third Reich.

He stared out the window of the plane into the foggy gloom, taking a moment to be alone with his thoughts. Inside, he felt the agony of the loss of his *Braciszku*. He had genuinely loved the man, loved him as he loved all of his soldiers that had dedicated themselves selflessly to the Cause. Thinking of his death on the streets of the American capital, he felt water come to his eyes, a clotted feeling in his throat. He reminded himself that his *Braciszku* was a professional soldier, a warrior in a noble crusade, and he knew the risks. But it didn't help. Pularchek couldn't help but feel a deep sense of loss at the death of yet another valiant comrade-in-arms.

Another *Braciszku*. Another Little Brother.

He gently wiped away a tear and quietly sipped his espresso. A moment later, the cabin door closed and the pilot prepared for take-off. Pularchek fastened his seat belt and took another sip of his espresso as Aleksander Romanowski—his trusted *consigliere*, chief of security, and closest advisor whom he referred to simply as *Counselor*—took a seat next to him.

"Once again, Boss, I am sorry about our *Braciszku*," said the Counselor. *Boss* was the special term of endearment he used for Pularchek rather than *Komandor*, the name used by the Polish billionaire's other comrades-in-arms, including his special independent contractor Skyler. "All I can say is at least he achieved his objective. Thankfully, Al-Muraydi and Kiefer won't be financing terrorists any longer."

"That is true. But sometimes I wonder if this war can be won at all," said Pularchek gloomily, staring out the window at the business jets lined up next to the runway.

"Don't worry, Boss. I know you loved our Little Brother with all of your heart, but the wounds will heal in time. And if we can't win this epic fight, we will certainly die trying. And that is something we can all be proud of. We are warriors, eh, and for a true warrior there is no better place to die than a battlefield."

"You are a good and wise man, Counselor. Don't plan on dying any time soon. I need you now more than ever."

"Yes, Boss, I promise not to die just yet."

The Gulfstream took off, nosed to the northwest, and held a steady course towards its ultimate destination: the small, inconspicuous Neu-Staaken Airfield in West Berlin. As the jet raced through the cumulus-laden sky, Pularchek took a moment to look over his team. His Operations-Security Detail consisted of eight individuals in addition to himself and Romanowski. The pilot and flight attendant were in their mid-thirties and former operatives with Mossad, the formidable and highly secretive Israeli intelligence service. Not only were they martial arts experts and crack shots with a Beretta, they were first-rate computer and GPS technicians and counterintelligence interrogators. The six other field operatives were men in their late-twenties to mid-thirties with a more rugged soldier-of-fortune appearance. Like Pularchek, they had served in the *Wojska Specjalne*—the Special Troops of the 4th military branch of the Polish Armed Forces—and would, once the team touched down on German soil, be operating as drivers, lookouts, and, if necessary, advance- and rearguard-soldiers.

After a few minutes, Romanowski pressed a remote button and a 24-inch screen popped down overhead. Using a hand-held mouse, he quickly accessed a program using his laptop on his tray table. The Gulfstream's two Rolls-Royce BR725 engines quietly hummed through the soundproofed cabin doors.

"As you ordered, Boss, I have done some digging into our Good Samaritan," he began, as Nick Lassiter's image appeared on the screen. "His name is Nicholas Maxwell Lassiter and he is an American citizen."

Pularchek reclined his seat. "Tell me about him."

"He is thirty-one years old, a bestselling author, and was just recently married and set to go on his honeymoon. His mother and father are Vivian Lassiter and Benjamin Brewbaker. The father is—you're not going to believe this—the deputy director of the CIA's National Clandestine Service. They are quite the dysfunctional American family. The parents were divorced in Washington, D.C. when young Nicholas was thirteen. But they got back together over a year ago and were just remarried in a joint wedding in Colorado with their son and Natalie Perkins, who was Lassiter's college sweetheart at Kenyon College in Ohio. Lassiter has carried his mother's name since his parents were divorced and he moved with his mother from the nation's capital to Colorado. Apparently, at the time, he was angry with his father and he has kept his mother's last name ever since."

"Interesting. Go on."

"It is only in the last year that Lassiter has distinguished himself. You may remember that incident last summer in New York that drew some international media attention. It involved Lassiter, his father Benjamin Brewbaker, Natalie Perkins, the Russian mafia, the CIA, and the Australian bestselling author Cameron Beckett. Lassiter helped uncover a Russian money-laundering operation at a New York literary agency. There was a big shootout and numerous arrests were made. Through it all, Lassiter became the bestselling author of a novel called *Blind Thrust* that Beckett had apparently stolen from him. Meanwhile, Lassiter's father was promoted to deputy director of the NCS for his handling of the CIA undercover operation. The incident was all over the news and led to lengthy prison sentences for a number of CIA officials and members of the Odessa Mafia of Brighton Beach."

"I remember, Counselor. Thank you for the preliminary briefing. But you still haven't answered my main question. Why does this young American look just like me?"

He pointed up at the screen. For several seconds, both men studied the image. The resemblance was amazing despite the obvious difference in age.

"I have made some headway, Boss, but regrettably unanswered questions still remain. I was hoping that you may be able to shed some light on them."

"Ask me whatever you want, Counselor. But before you do, I just want to say that I watched the film footage from my *Braciszku's* microcam, and I spoke to Józef and Gustaw myself after your debriefing with them."

"And now, like all of us, you're wondering if it's just a coincidence that you and Nick Lassiter look exactly alike, except a generation apart. Or if that young man up there on the screen is related to you in some way."

"Precisely. Which is it, Counselor?"

Romanowski licked his lips. "As I've told you, I don't know yet, Boss. But I do have some preliminary intel."

"Please proceed."

"Our team has managed to decrypt Benjamin Brewbaker's dossier from a Russian intelligence report we, ah, acquired this morning. It seems the Russian's are very keen to know more about the NCS deputy director, his son, and his new daughter-in-law after that Russian mob and rogue CIA incident in New York last summer."

"Go on."

"I think a good starting point is Nick Lassiter's place and date of birth. He was born on June 1, 1986 in London, England."

Pularchek felt himself sit up straight. "London, you say?"

"Yes, Boss. He was born at St. Catherine's Hospital near Hyde Park at 4:44 a.m."

Pularchek scratched his chin thoughtfully. "So the boy wasn't born in America at all? Interesting."

"Yes, but that isn't the most important thing. You're not going to believe this."

Pularchek held his breath.

"Vivian Lassiter is not the birth mother."

"She's not? Then who is?"

"Her twin sister Rose. She gave birth to the boy and gave him up for adoption to her sister and Benjamin Brewbaker, who was posted at the London station of the CIA at the time."

"Yes, but what does it all mean?"

"I don't know, Boss. I was hoping you could tell me."

Pularchek pondered a moment, his mind reaching back to his distant past. "All right, so we know who Nick Lassiter's real mother is, but we still don't know the father. But first, why would Vivian Lassiter's sister Rose give the baby up?"

Romanowski nodded slightly. "Because she had terminal cancer and had only weeks to live." He paused a moment to click the mouse. "I have managed to get my hands on a picture of this Rose." A slightly faded photograph appeared on the screen. "Is there a chance that you knew her, Boss?"

He calmly studied the picture on the screen. It showed a beautiful young woman with blonde hair done up in the style of the mid-1980s. She had a rosy complexion and blue eyes with a hint of mischief about them. She also had a long, slender neck that would have made Botticelli proud, and she wore a white laboratory jacket and a stethoscope around her neck.

"Did you perhaps know her, Boss, when you were at Oxford?"

At first, Pularchek couldn't place her. But after scrutinizing the photograph for nearly a full minute, the distant past where his world had intersected with the woman slowly came back to him.

It was the physician's jacket and the hint of mischief in her eyes that brought it all back, like a slowly unfolding dream. He continued to study her ruddy, smiling face. Slowly but assuredly, snippets of another time and place trickled into his mind like drifting snowflakes.

Yes, he had known this British woman Rose. He recalled an abandoned farmhouse in Southern Lebanon. He remembered the ground shaking from the blast of distant shells. And then he remembered struggling to pull off her panties and laughing afterwards about how silly Duran Duran's *A View to a Kill* was and then making love again, only more urgently, a second time because the shells were getting closer and they felt so small and vulnerable and desperately young and alive. It pained him that he hadn't even remembered her name, but he supposed that was often the case in war. It had happened the fall after he had graduated from Oxford. Back when he had naively believed that he could truly make a difference in the world and transform it into a better place.

Letting out a weary sigh, he suddenly knew the answer of where Nick Lassiter had come from.

He felt tears coming to his eyes, a powerful sense of loss. How was it possible that a single burst of passion could produce a living, breathing child that would have such a dramatic impact on his future? And how was it possible he had

33

never known about the boy. *My God,* he thought with a mixture of joy and trepidation, *I actually have a son!*

"Boss…I'm sorry, Boss…are you okay?"

He stared out the plane window, tears pouring uncontrollably from his eyes. There wasn't a damned thing he could do to stop them.

A full two minutes passed before he spoke, after he had wiped away his tears. "Her name was Rose," he said softly.

"Rose the Englishwoman. You are full of surprises, Boss."

"She was a young doctor with *Médecins Sans Frontières,* and I was working for an international relief organization. Hell, I don't even remember the name of it. That was back when people—myself included—actually believed peace in the Middle East was possible. Can you believe that? How idealistic we all were back then."

"So you loved her, Boss?"

He thought back: the truth was he had barely known her. He slowly nodded. "Yes, I loved her," he said. "For a sweet, brief moment during that terrible war that gave rise to Hezbollah, I loved her. But I never knew that she carried my child."

"So you have a son, Boss."

"Yes, it appears I have a son."

"You have always wanted a son, Boss. Even back when Johanna and the girls were still alive, you told me how much you always wanted—"

Romanowski stopped right there, covering his mouth with his hand.

"I'm sorry, Boss. I didn't mean to say that."

Pularchek held up a hand, telling him it was all right. But in his mind, he once again saw the tragedy unfold. It was a nightmare that came to him every single day, but hit him hardest on cold winter nights: Johanna and his three sweet daughters—Lena, Magdalena, and Zofia—blown to nothingness before his very eyes. It had happened in Madrid. He had seen it all from a distance—had felt the searing wave of heat and been knocked backwards ten feet—but he had been powerless to stop it. The suicide bomber had taken them away from him in the blink of an eye, inadvertently sealing both of their destinies.

"It's all right, my friend. I know what you meant," he said to the Counselor in a mollifying tone, struggling to keep his emotions in check. "It is true that even before my poor Johanna and the girls were taken from me, I always wanted a son. But not like this, Aleksy—not like this."

"Yes, Boss, I understand how you feel. But you must look at it this way. You now have the very thing that you have always wanted. You have *a son!*"

Pularchek looked up at the grainy CCTV image frozen on the screen. The young man Nicholas Lassiter was the spitting image of himself in his early thirties, after his brief career as a Special Forces soldier, but before he had made his first million zloties.

"Yes, Aleksy, I have a son," he said ruefully. "But given the present circumstances, what in the world am I going to do about it?"

CHAPTER 8

GRÜNEWALD
WEST BERLIN, GERMANY

FROM THE EDGE OF THE TREES, Skyler brought her Polish Alex-338 sniper rifle slowly to her shoulder. She took a breath of the cool night air as she sighted her soft target through her scope. That target—Berlin power lawyer Bernhard Heydrich—sat upright in his sumptuously appointed bed in his neoclassical mansion that boldly captured the architectural style prevailing in the Third Reich during Hitler's rise to power. He was reading a copy of Nele Neuhaus's police-procedural page-turner *Snow White Must Die* while devouring a jagerschnitzel sandwich sans mushroom gravy. She quietly studied him for several seconds while reciting the *Our Father*. Then she swept her scope one last time to her left and right across her field of fire, examining the perimeter halogen lighting and army of security cameras embedded in the polished granite columns, balustrade balconies, and dense shrubbery beneath the windows.

She was in the heart of Grünewald—the famous Green Woods of the Charlottenburg-Wilmersdorf borough—a landscape of thick pine forests and clear lakes, broken by grassy clearings boasting mansions and villas that were incorporated into Berlin in 1920. The historic neighborhood attracted only the city's most affluent denizens, and the German capital's well-to-do continued to be quite content cosseted within their moneyed sanctuary amid the dark, forbidding forest reminiscent of the Brothers Grimm.

Skyler felt a trickle of trepidation at the sight of the huge ghostly mansion, as if it were haunted by old Nazi ghosts. After all, a mere mile down the road was the location of the old Grünewald freight railway station, where between October 1941 and February 1945 more than 50,000 Jews were deported by Himmler's SS to extermination camps and murdered. All around her, the massive pine trunks and jagged limbs blotted out the light like a black hole, blanketing the Green Woods in a sepulchral stillness.

She continued to study her target through her scope. It was going to be an easy kill, especially with the outstanding military hardware Pularchek had outfitted her with. Her Alex-338 sniper rifle was fitted with a Schmidt & Bender PM II telescopic sight, chambered for special hollow-point .338-caliber Lapua Magnum rimless bottlenecked centerfire cartridges, and equipped with a 5-round detachable box magazine. The weapon had been expertly designed for military long-range sniping operations by the Polish Special Armed Forces, and she had used it successfully on several prior contracts. She snugged the stock of the rifle deeper into her shoulder, placing the crosshairs on her soft target.

The unsuspecting lawyer Heydrich looked so peaceful and innocent lying on his bed reading his German mystery that she couldn't help but feel guilty.

"Holy Father, forgive me for what I am about to do," she whispered aloud.

Suddenly, she saw a flash of unexpected movement at the edge of the bushes on the left side of the house.

What the hell?

She put down her rifle and picked up her Leica range-finder for a better look. There were two interlopers, she saw now. They emerged from the bushes like stalking wolves, passed beneath an exterior halogen light, pulled out firearms and quickly checked them, and then paused for what appeared to be some sort of countdown.

My God, were they going to save her the trouble of taking out Heydrich?

She had better call Pularchek and let him know about the shocking new development. Keeping her gaze fixed on the two silhouetted figures, she quietly pulled out her secure, encrypted mobile phone and punched in the number.

"I thought I might be hearing from you before I touched down," said the voice on the other end. "Is it done?"

"No. There's been an unexpected—"

She stopped right there as she heard rumbling car engines. She looked up through her range-finding binoculars to see a caravan of Mercedes S-Model wagons pull up along the road at the edge of a clearing. The jet-black vehicles were the same make and model as the car she had seen in Vienna, and they bore official German government tags, bullet-proof windows, and tinted glass to conceal the identity of the occupants. The car doors opened, and Angela Wolff and more than ten heavily armed men stepped from the fleet of Mercedes.

She heard Pularchek on the other end. "What is it? What's happening?" he asked.

"It's Angela Wolff," she said to Pularchek. "She has with her a team of at least ten armed men."

"And the others?"

She turned her Leica on Heydrich's. "They've gone inside."

"Is it clear that their intention is to kill Heydrich?"

"Crystal. So what do you want me to do?"

"Watch and wait. Let's see if they do the job for you. You will, of course, still receive your full compensation package."

"I would expect nothing less. But what if they don't?"

"Then take the shot."

"Even with Wolff here?"

"*Especially* with Wolff there. A little unexpected fireworks will no doubt shake things up, which has been our intention all along."

"All right, I'll watch and wait."

"Is Dieter with her?"

"Yes, I see him. Along with Krupp and Bauer."

"Good, keep me posted and take lots of pictures. I'll see you at our next rendezvous at the Berghain."

"I'll be there." Clicking off, she looked again at Wolff and her heavily armed team through the range-finder, which had a built-in night camera.

It was definitely going to be a busy and eventful evening.

CHAPTER 9

GRÜNEWALD

AS THE ASSAULT TEAM reached the edge of the trees, Angela Wolff called a final halt and studied Bernhard Heydrich's neoclassical mansion one final time. Was she mistaken or did she just hear sounds coming from inside the house?

She looked at the mansion and, seeing nothing unusual, scanned the dark woods that enveloped it. The massive pine trees blotted out the light and blanketed the Green Woods in a deathly stillness. It was the perfect setting for an assault—but it was also the perfect place for a counter-ambush.

For an instant, she wondered if operatives from a rival foreign intelligence service might be lurking in the shadows, ready to thwart her plans. But there was no sign of any interlopers, save for a hooting owl in the tree on her right.

But what about the noises inside the house? Were they her imagination?

She gave the order for a final weapons check and inspected her Walther PPQ M2. When finished, she re-holstered the 9mm and gave the signal to move. In addition to herself, her spy team consisted of her three *Bundesnachrichtendienst* subordinates Dieter Franck, Johannes Krupp, and Arne Bauer, as well as eight lower-level BND field operatives whose names she didn't know or care to remember. They moved forward stealthily in accordance with the prearranged plan. Though Wolff had sat behind a desk for the past decade, she had cut her teeth for the first eight years of her intelligence career in Operations. She liked to take charge in the field, especially if it meant she could boss around a bunch of testosterone-overloaded men that had trouble taking orders from a woman.

They dashed through the clearing to a second set of trees flanking the western edge of the mansion. From there, they broke up into the two designated groups. Red Team, commanded by Johannes Krupp, moved clockwise to its assigned position at the front door. Wolff's group, Blue Team, maneuvered counterclockwise to take position at the rear of the house.

At the back door, Wolff and her team paused to wait for the prearranged time, both teams having synchronized their watches an hour earlier. The house was still; not a peep could be heard. She looked at her watch and counted down the seconds to penetration.

It was then she heard a distinct noise.

Was it a snapping twig? Whatever it was, the sound came from the east at a ninety degree compass angle from Red and Blue Teams. She looked at her second-in-command and lover, Senior Agent Dieter Franck.

"Did you hear that?"

"No, what was it?"

"I thought I heard something." She strained her ears and scanned the mansion and the woods beyond. But she heard nothing and saw no unusual movement, nothing out of the ordinary. She took a deep breath to steel herself, suppressing a faint miasma of fear. Now she knew she had not imagined the noises. What she had heard was real and someone was out there. But she felt an even stronger presence than that: she felt like they were being watched.

"It's probably nothing," said Dieter. "Just a squirrel or rabbit."

"Or maybe it's the big bad wolf," whispered Arne Bauer, pointing to the dark, forbidding forest beyond the glowing halogen lights.

She shot the senior BND agent a withering glare. This was no time to joke around. While the forest was the cornerstone of the founding mythology of German culture and identity, it was also a source of deep uneasiness for her and the vast majority of her countrymen. The old fairy tales that she had grown up with warning her of the dangers of the forest, of tempting houses fashioned of sweets and clever wolves in disguise, always made her feel a sense of foreboding whenever she was in the woods, particularly at night. But she didn't want to show any fear in front of her men, so she quickly issued an order to the other team, talking into her radio headset mouthpiece.

"Red Team, we think we heard something. Hold until I give the command."

"What is it?" asked Johannes Krupp on the other end.

"We don't know yet, but you are to hold until—"

She left the words unfinished as she was interrupted by a definite crunching sound. This time the whole team heard. Everyone froze in their tracks, aiming their semiautomatic weapons towards the trees. The thick woods were blanketed in dark shadow at the edge of the lighting, with only faint smears bleeding into the forest. Wolff paused to carefully listen.

Again, her instinct told her they were being watched.

She looked at Arne; with his gaze focused intently on the trees and clutching his Walther in a two-handed grip straight out of the BND Field Manual, he was certainly not making any more Little Red Riding Hood jokes.

For a moment, there was no sound and all was calm. Then, with a suddenness that took everyone by surprise, Wolff heard a thumping sound to their right, followed by a tearing through brush. This time there was no mistaking the source: they were definitely running footsteps. And not just those of one person; she distinctly heard the sound of two pairs of running feet.

"Quick, Heydrich is getting away! And there's someone with him!" she cried. "Blue Team, after them! Red Team, hold your position! And no shooting— we need Heydrich alive!"

With the command given, Blue Team tore into the woods and fanned out with Dieter at the apex of the advance, leading the way, and Wolff right behind him. Feeling her whole body seized with adrenaline, she raced frantically to keep up with him.

The sound of running feet picked up to their right. The team turned and dashed in that direction. She ran as hard and fast as her legs would carry her, ripping through underbrush, stumbling, banging into trees, recovering, running on, her breaths coming in gasps. And then, up ahead, she could make out faint smudges of light where the woods ended and a second clearing, sprouting another mansion, began.

But when they reached the clearing, there was no one there.

"*Verdammt*, they must have doubled back," cursed Dieter, waving his pistol in angry resignation.

"No, they couldn't have," she puffed, struggling to catch her breath. "We would have seen them."

"She's right," said Arne, as the team began fanning out and scanning the area. "They couldn't have gotten past us."

Wolff looked right, left, and then back into the open clearing. Where could the bastards have gone?

And then, off to the left next to a rock outcropping, silhouetted against the lights from the nearby mansion, she saw something. At first, it was only a little blur at the edge of her vision, but then she saw the pair of figures more clearly: not more than thirty feet away, two dark forms poked out from behind a tree and then shrank back from the light into the oblivion of the forest. One of the figures was of medium height and heavily built just like Heydrich, the other tall and thin.

"There they are!" She pointed at the two figures now making a mad dash for the trees on the other side of the open clearing.

"I've got them!" yelled Dieter Franck, who was closest to the fleeing figures, and he started chasing after them again.

"Remember, we need Heydrich alive, Dieter! Alive!"

She and the rest of the team ran after them. A moment later, she was stunned when she heard a gunshot, followed quickly by three more.

Mein Gott, I said no shooting Dieter!

She ducked under a tree branch, leapt over a pile of stones, and ran along a section of flat terrain before racing past the outcrop, beyond the treeline, and into the illuminated clearing.

There, just short of the trees at the far side of the clearing, she saw Heydrich sprawled on the ground with Dieter kneeling over him. Even from a distance, she could tell that the stoutly built man in the well-tailored business suit was the lawyer. She and the others ran up to them. Somehow, the other interloper appeared to have vanished into thin air.

But where could he have gone?

And then she looked closer at the figure on the ground. Her mouth opened with astonishment. "That's not fucking Heydrich!" she cried.

Dieter was rifling through the man's pockets for identification. But it was quickly evident that there was nothing with which to ID the man in his wallet or jacket pockets. Picking up and pocketing the discarded pistol, she pulled out her smartphone and closely scrutinized the man with the phone's flashlight. He was a sandy-blond-haired, Northern European male in his mid-thirties, and he carried a SIG-Sauer P228 with a noise suppressor. A definite professional. But that was all she could tell, at least for the moment.

"Why did you have to kill him, Dieter?" she hissed. "I told you I wanted them alive. You could have just winged him."

"He was shooting at me, damnit. I didn't exactly have time to aim for his elbow or shin. And besides, the son of a bitch got me."

He tipped his head towards his left, non-shooting arm, where a bullet had torn through his jacket and he was bleeding just above the elbow.

"So he did," she said laconically.

"That's all you have to say? Thank you very much for worrying about me. I'm damned lucky the bullet missed bone and tendon."

She leaned in close, so only they could hear one another, and gently touched his hand. "I'm sorry, my love. I didn't mean to be unsympathetic," she whispered.

Their eyes met. He winced in pain and gave a nod. She smiled briefly yet lovingly before turning away to speak into her mouthpiece.

"Red Team, we have one man down and one got away, but neither of the fleeing targets was Heydrich! You need to get in that house now!" she barked to the second team, once again using her command voice. "You are greenlit for entry! Hopefully, the subject hasn't been compromised!"

Inside the nearby mansion, a light came on and dogs began barking loudly.

"We've got to get back to Heydrich's," she said to Dieter. "Take a picture of this man's face so we can ID him. Then have two men carry the body to the woods and hide it there. We'll link up at Heydrich's. And don't forget to have them remove everything from his pockets."

"What about the other one, the one who got away?"

"He's long gone and he definitely wasn't Heydrich. He's too tall and skinny. Our top priority is to find Heydrich."

"All right, I'll catch up with you."

Five minutes later, Wolff and Blue Team were at Heydrich's palatial home as police sirens began to moan in the distance. Senior Agent Johannes Krupp was waiting for them at the rear door.

"We found Heydrich," he said. "He's dead."

"Quickly, show me. We only have a few minutes before the police arrive."

He led her through the kitchen, past a drawing room with a chandelier made of antique crystal, down a corridor decorated with carefully restored antique vases along with the picturesque canvases of German landscape painters from the 19th Century, past a pair of resplendently furnished guest rooms, and finally to Herr Heydrich's master bedroom. Thrice divorced, the renowned lawyer lived alone at the estate, which had been in his family for several generations.

As Wolff entered the room, she quickly spotted the body sprawled on the floor next to the bed. Bernhard Heydrich was wearing ridiculous bedroom slippers and striped pajamas. Lying on his imperial bed was, ironically, an open copy of the popular German mystery *Snow White Must Die* along with a half-eaten, dry jagerschnitzel sandwich, as if the last thing the victim had expected tonight was an intruder breaking into his home.

That in itself was strange. After what Heydrich had done in Vienna, wouldn't he have known that she would come after him? Wouldn't he have, therefore, made himself hard to find? How could he possibly just lay there in bed casually reading a mystery and eating a jagerschnitzel?

Though generally disgusted by the sight of blood, she navigated her way swiftly to the body, kneeled down, and closely examined it, trying her best to conceal her discomfort as Dieter slipped quietly into the room. The cause of death was unmistakable: two gunshot wounds to the chest and one to the face.

"It's Heydrich all right." She silently cursed her bad luck that such a key cog in the wheels of the subterfuge that had begun in Vienna was now dead and unavailable for questioning. Tracing the three entrance wounds, she noted that there were heavy powder burns, so the bullets were fired quickly and with exceptional accuracy from less than three feet. Heydrich must have been taken completely off guard by the two intruders. Either that or he had known them and allowed them to get in close. She realized now that the noises she had heard shortly after their arrival must have been gunshots muffled by noise suppressors. The two operatives must have already been here when she arrived, killed Heydrich, and then retreated to the woods when she and her team had come upon them. She leaned down and touched Heydrich; he had only been dead for a few minutes for his body was still warm.

"Two weapons were used: one nine-millimeter, the other a .45," said Dieter, examining the wounds with a penlight. "I think we can close this one."

"Yes, it would appear so. Grab his hard drive and let's get out of here," she said, feeling suddenly anxious at the sound of the approaching sirens, which were getting noticeably louder.

"I don't see any brass," said Krupp.

"That's because the shooters took them with them," said Dieter. "We got two of them from the pocket of the dead man. These guys were house cleaners. Professional hit, tidy up afterwards. Nothing to match with ballistics."

"We must have come upon them only a couple minutes after they shot Heydrich," said Arne, looking at his boss. "Who do you think they're working for? Is it Pularchek?"

"We'll know once we identify the man we left in the woods and the one that got away," responded Wolff.

"But Pularchek's got to be the one pulling the strings, right?" said Krupp. "The Polish bastard wrote the note we found in Vienna."

Wolff didn't answer at first. The police sirens were shrilling less than a mile away. She looked down one last time at Heydrich; somehow the beefy Berlin lawyer appeared small and insignificant lying dead in a pool of coagulating blood.

"Sometimes, things aren't as they appear. In any case, we're going to need hard proof," she said. "Now it's time to go. I have no desire to try to explain what we're doing here to the damned police."

And with that, the assault team slipped noiselessly from the mansion and disappeared into the dense, dark woods of the Grünewald.

CHAPTER 10

GRÜNEWALD

FIVE MINUTES LATER, once Angela Wolff and her team had driven off and the police cars came racing in, Skyler crept through the woods to her silver BMW parked a quarter mile away and called Pularchek again on her coded mobile.

"They're all gone now," she said without preamble. "They stole away before the police arrived."

"So the police are there now?"

"Yes. They're inside as we speak."

"What happened? Is Heydrich dead?"

"The two gunmen liquidated him and then one of them was killed by Wolff's team. The other one got away."

"So Heydrich is definitely dead?"

"Confirmed kill."

"Any ID on those responsible?"

"Negative. One was stoutly built, the other tall and thin. They were professionals."

"Germans?"

"Polish, I think. But I don't know for sure."

"Which one got away?"

"The thin man."

"Who shot the other one, the one that was killed? Wolff?"

"No, it was Dieter."

"Dieter did it?"

"Yes, and like I said the other one got away. The third man."

"Did you get a look at him?"

"I only managed to catch a glimpse of his face. But he did look Polish to me. Definitely Slavic. As I told you, he was tall and lean, and he was very fast."

"A runner of some sort?"

"In a previous life. But there's no doubt he is, or was, a professional soldier. I managed to get several photographs of him and his comrade running through the woods before the stocky one was killed. I was able to zoom in quite nicely. Very high quality. But he never looked back at me so I wasn't able to get a photo of his face."

"That's all right. Hopefully, we'll still be able to ID him as well as his dead companion."

"What do you want me to do now?"

"Though things didn't go according to plan, Phase One has still been successfully carried out. Now it's time for Phase Two. I'll see you at the Berghain."

"Yes, I'll be there. Ciao."

CHAPTER 11

BREWBAKER-LASSITER TOWNHOUSE
O STREET NW, GEORGETOWN

"SO, ALL THESE YEARS YOU'VE BEEN LYING TO ME? How could you knowingly do that?"

As the accusatory words lingered in the air, Lassiter saw the guilt and pain on his mother's and father's faces, but he was too angry to feel any sympathy for them. After all, they had been lying about his origins since the day they had first set eyes upon him. He seriously doubted that he would ever be able to forgive them. He had been released by the FBI under his father's recognizance over an hour ago, and they were sitting in the living room of his parents' East Village brownstone. It was nearly 4 a.m.

So now he knew. Five days after his thirty-first birthday and three days after his wedding, his parents had finally told him the truth. And that painful and heartbreaking reality was that he had been "adopted" and they were not his real biological parents. He hated them for their silence, for living a lie all these years, for deceiving him about who he was and where he came from and for falsely pretending that his blood was theirs.

Then his mother started crying and he couldn't help but feel badly for her.

He forced himself to try, to truly try to see things from his parents' perspective. Surely, they must have had an important reason to do what they did. Putting himself into their shoes thirty-one years earlier, he suspected that their motivation for withholding the truth from him was complicated. But that still didn't exonerate them. They had deceived him all these years, and there was no going back to the way things were before they had come clean with the truth. What they had done was unforgivable. All the same, he was still curious to hear why they had chosen not to reveal to him that he was adopted.

Please tell me why, Mom and Dad, you chose to make a complete mockery of my life for the past thirty-one fucking years?

"Please stop crying, Mother," he said. "You'll wake up Natalie."

"I can't stop," replied Vivian Lassiter through a pair of sniffles, tears streaming down her face. "I've dreaded this day since the day you were born, and now it's finally happened. I feel so terribly low."

He looked at his father, who was quietly shaking his head. "We are so sorry, Nick," said Benjamin Brewbaker. "We never meant to hurt you like this."

He fixed him with a hard stare. "Then why the hell did you do it?"

His parents looked at one another, but did not reply.

"Why did you do it, goddamnit?"

"Because that's the way my twin sister Rose wanted it," answered his mother. She appeared to have regained a modicum of composure as she daubed her eyes with a handkerchief and sat up straight. "Rose was your birth mother, Nicholas," she went on, using his full Christian name, something she only did when she was angry at him or had something very important to say. "She was a doctor and lived in England. That's where she gave birth to you and we adopted you."

"Somehow, that sounds awfully convenient. If it was Rose's idea, that relieves you from culpability. Well, I'm not buying it. You lied to me, goddamnit—and now I don't even know who the hell I am, or where I came from!"

"She had ovarian cancer, Nick, and died giving birth to you," said his father, who had risen to his feet from the couch and stepped to the window. "Her last dying wish was for us to take you in as our own and raise you without ever telling a soul what really happened. There was no father to help raise you, and she didn't want to make things complicated for you. She wanted for us to be your parents, and she didn't want there to be any...questions about legitimacy. She thought it would be too messy."

"But life is messy. And, in the end, all you've done is make it even messier."

"What we did was wrong," admitted his mother. "But your father and I have loved you more than anything in the world since the day you were born. We were right there, Nicholas. We saw you born and my sister expire before our very eyes. Your father and I made a promise to Rose and we kept it—for thirty-one years. We're sorry, but please know that we love you and will always love you. You are our son, Nicholas. You will always be *our* son."

He looked away, feeling all torn up inside. Did the circumstances of his birth and Aunt's death really change anything? Weren't his parents still liars who didn't deserve to be trusted? More importantly, would he ever be able to forgive them?

He looked at them both. His mother was crying again, and his father stared numbly out the window into the dark night. He couldn't help but feel as if they were imposters.

He shook his head angrily. "You shouldn't have remained silent and deceived me all these years," he said through gritted teeth. "When I was old enough, you should have told me the truth, goddamnit!"

"On your fourth and sixth birthdays, I almost did," said his father ruefully, still gazing intently out the window. "But at the last second, your mother talked me out of it. She had made a promise to her sister Rose."

"You should have been more worried about keeping promises with the living than the dead. It wasn't your place to make a mockery of my origins."

"Is that what this is about?" asked his mother. "You want to know where you came from?"

"You're damn right I do. If Rose is my mother, then who's my real father?" He looked at his adoptive father, Benjamin Brewbaker. "Is it this Polish billionaire-assassin Stanislaw Pularchek?"

His mother shot his father a glance. "My God, was that who Nicholas shot?"

"No, that's not the guy. It's…it's complicated."

"What have you done, Benjamin? You told me that Pularchek was Nicholas's father, but you never told me he was an *assassin*."

"Now just hold on. First off, we're not sure who Nick shot because there is no body. It's true that Nick and the assassin look a lot alike, but that's all we know right now. We don't have any DNA results, and even if we did, we don't have Pularchek's DNA on file for comparison."

His mother was shaking her head. "It's time for you to tell us the truth, Benjamin. Look at what our keeping secrets all these years has done to us."

Lassiter looked sternly at his father. "She's right, you'd better start talking. For starters, I want to know if Pularchek is definitely my biological father or not? Is it one-hundred-percent certain?"

His father hesitated.

"Come on, is he my birth father or not?"

"The answer is yes." His dad's voice was laced with pain and guilt. "Stanislaw Pularchek is your biological father."

"And yet you're telling me that's not who I shot, even though he looks exactly like the guy in the photographs and magazine covers you showed me that is definitely Pularchek?"

"Yes, that's what I'm saying. You didn't kill Pularchek. You killed someone who looks exactly like him."

"What? How is that possible?"

"I don't know, but what I do know is that Pularchek is currently safe and sound in Poland. Five separate reports—from not only U.S. intelligence but friendly foreign sources and even our enemies in the Kremlin—have confirmed it. Now this is strictly top secret, need-to-know information I'm telling you two, so it stays here in this room. I'm only revealing it because I care deeply about you both and don't want to lose you. And this is the indisputable fact: Nick, you are Pularchek's biological son, but he is not the man you killed."

"I don't understand. I saw the guy's face up close, and it was the same face you showed me in the photographs. There's no question in my mind. And I'm sure the video footage from the D.C. traffic and security cameras near the crime scene will confirm the guy from the photos was in town tonight. And yet, Agent Forsythe said that Pularchek was positively ID'd in Warsaw giving a speech around the time of the shooting. So how is that possible?"

"I know you want answers, Nick, but I'm afraid I don't have them. Not yet anyway."

"Well then, at least tell me more about Pularchek. You obviously have a dossier on the guy and so does the FBI."

His father gave a heavy sigh, turned solemnly away from the window, and sat back down in the upholstered antique chair across from him.

"All right, you want to know who we're dealing with here. Your biological father—the Polish national known as Stanislaw Pularchek—happens to be the seventeenth richest person in the world, with a net worth of over forty billion dollars. He's the head of Pularchek Industries, an international investment and holding company, and also owns controlling interests in more than a dozen other companies in mineral resources, the energy and chemical industries, infrastructure, real estate, sanitary ceramics and tiles, and, last but not least, biotechnology. The biotech company that he controls a sixty-percent interest in—Advanced Biosystems—happens to be the world's leading company in advanced cloning research."

"Wait a second, are you suggesting that the guy I killed could be a Pularchek clone?"

"You have to admit it would explain why you two look so much alike and how this guy can be at two places at once. You said yourself that you and the shooter's accomplices were both stunned by your close physical resemblance, despite your difference in age."

"Good heavens, Benjamin," exclaimed his mother. "Do you realize what you're saying?"

"You don't think I know how crazy it sounds? And yet, this very scenario is laid out in exacting detail in two separate CIA internal reports. Basically, the story reads like this: an eccentric billionaire has cloned himself and employs a team of assassin-clones who move stealthily around the world taking out Islamic terrorist and neo-Nazi financiers. As well as the wealthy descendants of Nazis who profited from the Holocaust. In other words, what we're looking at here is a real-world Bruce Wayne, who, instead of dressing up as the Caped Crusader and going after bad guys, has a small army of clones that perform his dirty work for him."

"My God, I've always said that real life is stranger than fiction," said his mother. "But this...this is like something out of a Philip K. Dick novel."

"I agree it sounds crazy. But our video and genetics experts in the Science and Technology division haven't been able to come up with a better explanation. Whoever or whatever these lookalikes are exactly, they cannot be differentiated from one another. Statistically speaking, these...these Pularcheks are all the same. They're identical."

His mom was shaking her head. "Come now, Benjamin. You're telling us that there's a Polish billionaire out there who has managed to clone a small army of assassins and this guy also happens to be Nick's birth father? Is that what you're telling us?"

"We don't know if they're clones, doubles, twins, or something else entirely. But somehow, this guy has managed to recreate himself. We just don't know how yet. Furthermore, we're not exactly sure *why* he's doing it. Is it to confuse his enemies and the police? Is it some sort of game? Is he issuing his own personal calling card? Perhaps he's sending a message by making sure that both the terrorists he takes out, and the world's law enforcement and intelligence community hunting down these terrorists, know that he's the one behind their deaths? Or maybe he has a death wish and doesn't care about his safety. Maybe he's so cocky that he doesn't give a second thought about pissing off the jihadi and neo-Nazi worlds. The answer to all of these questions is we just don't know."

"Good heavens, Benjamin," said his mother. "I feel as though *I don't know you* after all these years. You knew that this Pularchek and these...these doubles of his were out there assassinating people, and also that Nick was his biological son, and yet you didn't tell me? Your own wife?"

"I shouldn't even be telling you now. This is all classified information. Until today, the FBI didn't even know about it."

Lassiter nodded. "So that's why you and Forsythe had to leave the room?"

"Yeah, but he didn't believe me either."

"But you still don't have any actual proof that Pularchek has engaged in human cloning?"

"That's correct. But we do know that his company has successfully cloned not only dogs and cats, but various primates, including chimpanzees. So he definitely has the technology at his disposal. At this point, all we know for sure is that there have been suspicious sightings of Pularchek in several European, Middle Eastern, and African countries at the same time as several highly public assassinations. In each case, Pularchek has given a major speech or guest lecture at a conference in Poland around the time of the killing."

"That way he would have the perfect alibi."

"Exactly. Plus you have to admit it adds to the growing Pularchek legend. Any man who has the ability to make people believe he is at two places at once is pretty damned powerful, wouldn't you say?"

"I suppose it's reassuring to know that this isn't all just wild speculation, and you and your colleagues at Langley haven't gone completely nuts," said his mother. "But what in the world have we gotten ourselves into?"

"I'm the one who got us into this," said Lassiter. "It happened the moment I decided to go after the shooter. If I had known it would lead to this, I'm not sure I would have done it."

"No, you did the right thing, Son."

"Did I? I didn't save those two men on the rooftop."

"To be perfectly honest, they weren't worth saving."

"How can you say that?" countered his mother in disbelief. "Are you telling us they deserved to die?"

"No, I'm just saying they were dirty. They were both on our priority watch list."

"For what?"

"For financing Islamic militant groups. The Swiss banker Kiefer also had ties to Nazi stolen property, money, and valuable artwork from the Holocaust."

"Why haven't they been arrested?" asked Lassiter.

"Politics and priorities."

"Meaning?"

"Meaning the unofficial—read tacit and cowardly—policy of the United States government is not to stir the pot with the House of Saud."

"Okay, that covers the *politics*. What about the *priorities*?"

"Our unofficial—again read tacit and cowardly—priority is to fight the war on terror with the same zeal as our jihadist enemies, but it is not to fight old wars settled more than seventy years ago. In other words, it is not the job of the U.S. to hunt down old Nazi war criminals, follow their dirty money or the money they left to their descendants, or reopen old wounds. That job belongs to our friends the Israelis and the members of the EU."

"And, it would appear, Pularchek."

"Yes, and our Polish friend too."

"My biological father."

"Yes."

"So this man, my biological father, is actually a hero, doing what our own government refuses to do. That's what you're saying."

"No, I'm not saying that. The man is a known assassin and we are going to catch him soon, very soon. That is, if Hezbollah, Hamas, al-Qaeda, or Islamic State don't get to him first. Or the Germans, Austrians, or Swiss. They don't like him any better than the jihadists, although Angela Merkel used to love the guy before he went rogue and started killing her prominent citizens. For the past five years, Pularchek has operated like a king beholden to no one, crossing international boundaries whenever he pleases and taking out those he deems evil. He's made a lot of enemies since he started this little private intelligence and retribution agency of his. It's a wonder he's still alive."

Lassiter had a thought. "But what if he isn't? What if all there is out there are his clones?"

His mother was shaking her head. "Come on, you two, you can't be serious. You really think that this man, this Polish billionaire, is not only an assassin, but has actually cloned himself?"

"Like I said, we don't know what these doubles are, whether they're clones or not," answered his father. "All we know is that there have been several Pularchek sightings around the world when the man was known to be in Warsaw. How can he be at two places at once?"

His lawyer mother shook her head. "I don't know. But is human cloning even possible? I mean, is the technology really there yet?"

"Not in the U.S. But we're talking about Poland. Our research experts in the Sci and Tech Division believe Pularchek may have successfully developed the technology for human beings."

She shook her head in disbelief. "Human clones? Has the world really come to this?"

"It's a brave, new world, Mom. That's why you and dad didn't even bother to tell me that I was adopted."

"That's unfair, Nicholas."

"No, what's unfair is being lied to for thirty-one years and then being told one day that your real father is a Polish assassin. An assassin who very well may have cloned himself so he can fight his own private war against Islamic terror and neo-Nazism. To have all that laid on you in one day—the same day that you killed a guy that looks exactly like you only a generation older—now that's unfair!"

"Nick, is everything all right?"

He turned to see Natalie standing there in her silk nightgown at the bottom of the staircase. He shot a glance at his parents, who looked at each other guiltily.

"I'm sorry, dear, did we wake you?" asked his mother.

"As a matter of fact you did." She looked at her new husband. "What's all this about your biological father, human cloning, the war on terror, and Nazis?"

His father stepped forward. "It's complicated, Natalie. There's no other way to—"

"Bullshit," said Lassiter angrily, waving her to come into the room. "It's not complicated at all."

She looked confused. "Nick, what's going on here? Why are you so angry?"

"I'll tell you why. These two people here aren't my real parents. They have been lying to me and everyone else for the past thirty-one years about where I came from."

Her mouth fell open. "What?"

"I'm adopted, Nat. My birth parents are evidently a Polish billionaire-assassin who looks exactly like the guy I shot tonight, and an Englishwoman named Rose who died giving birth to me."

"You're kidding, right?"

His mother stepped forward. "I'm afraid not, dear," she said, her eyes glistening with tears again. "All we can say is how terribly sorry we are to have kept this from you two."

Lassiter shook his head angrily. "No way, Mom. You can't get out of this that easily."

"Nicholas, I know how hard this must—"

"No, no, no! You and dad are going to start from the beginning and tell her everything—and, I mean, everything."

His father was shaking his head. "Nick, I don't think that's—"

"You're going to tell her the truth, goddamnit! Natalie's part of this family now, although after she hears what you're about to tell her, she may wish she wasn't. Now start talking, Dad. She deserves to know what she's gotten herself into."

"You're right, of course," said his father with resignation, looking guiltily at his mother. "Natalie does deserve to know the truth."

CHAPTER 12

FEDERAL INTELLIGENCE SERVICE
CHAUSSEESTRASSE, BERLIN

THE GERMAN INTELLIGENCE HEADQUARTERS was a monstrosity, reflecting the massive amount of resources dedicated to fighting the global war on terror in the Fatherland in the twenty-first century. The three steel-and-concrete, nine-story office buildings and surrounding grounds comprising the intelligence complex occupied an area the size of thirty-five soccer fields, at a total cost to German taxpayers of one billion Euros. Within walking distance of the Federal Chancellery and Parliament, the headquarters was home to over 4,000 employees and 8,000 supercomputers. In addition to combating the war on terror, the spies cosseted within the sprawling complex had the task of gathering intelligence on global weapons of mass destruction, as well as collecting and evaluating information on organized crime, weapons trafficking, money laundering, illegal migration, information warfare, and foreign military intelligence.

But at the moment, Angela Wolff, second-in-command of the German foreign intelligence service, was not thinking about protecting her country from terrorists or rogue states. Rather, she was wondering what government resources she was going to have to secretly marshal to steal back what had been bequeathed to her by her infamous grandfather. That happened to be the priceless merchandise left to her in the last will and testament of *Polizeiführer* Karl Wolff, the head of the SS in Italy during the Second World War, and now stolen from her by an infuriating Polish billionaire-assassin, secretly protected by his own government, named Stanislaw Snarkus Pularchek. The *Schatzfund*—the great treasure trove, her fortieth-birthday inheritance. Just whispering the precious word under her breath sent shivers of excitement up her spine.

The phone on her desk rang. Turning away from the window, Angela Wolff quickly checked the caller ID on the PBX internal telephone system display. It was her boss, Walther Kluge, president of the BND.

She suddenly remembered. "Oh damn, the meeting." She picked up the phone. "My apologies, Walther—I'll be right down."

"You'd better hurry. Dieter is already here."

"Dieter's there? But I had requested the meeting with only you."

"I have asked him to sit in with us. I wanted to hear his thoughts on the current situation."

She felt a flutter in her chest followed by a stab of anger. This was definitely not good. "Yes, I will be right down."

She hung up the phone, snatched up her notebook, and marched down a hallway displaying moody, Romantic-era landscape paintings by the German Caspar David Friedrich and the Norwegian J.C. Dahl. Did Kluge suspect she was up to something, or had he pulled in Dieter merely to get a second opinion? Could Dieter or someone else have betrayed her? Or was her boss doing all this for show to send her a message or provoke her? Kluge had been known to occasionally bring a third party into private meetings to throw people off balance, or get at the truth. It was a ruthless technique, but even she had to admit that it worked. As her heels clicked across the hallway, she felt her stomach twisted in knots, matching the dark, ominous landscapes on the walls of the corridor.

When she reached Kluge's office, her boss's secretary rose wordlessly from her chair, knocked perfunctorily on his door, and showed her into the room.

Wolff took a deep breath to steady her nerves.

Stepping into the stately office, her gaze immediately met that of her boss, seated next to Dieter Franck at the teakwood conference table in the far side of the room. Kluge was bedecked in a conservative, custom-tailored, dark-blue Dolzer suit with a silver-blue tie and matching pocket square. His cool, ascetic expression matched his outfit, and his gunmetal-gray eyes harbored a competitive hostility just below the surface. It was a look that she had come to know only too well since her promotion to vice-president directly beneath him. Descended from a long line of civil servants extending as far back as the Great War, Kluge was one of many men who worked in the German intelligence service who disapproved of women aspiring to positions of authority within the community. Consequently, their dealings and collaborations together tended to be tense and professional to the point of being frosty. They both looked at one another with politely cool calculation mingled with barely concealed distrust.

"Please take a seat, Angela."

She did as instructed. She had the feeling she was in trouble, but how could Kluge possibly know what she had done, unless Dieter or one of the other team members had betrayed her? When her gaze met Dieter's, he looked at her as if to say, "Don't worry, I have your back." But how could she be sure?

"Dieter here has been telling me about the Pularchek case. Are there any new developments that I should be aware of?"

As she gathered her thoughts, she resisted the urge to look at her lover. "As a matter of fact there are, Mr. President. Our latest intelligence indicates that Pularchek is behind the double-killing that took place last night in Washington. The time has come for us to unilaterally arrange for Herr Pularchek's extradition to Germany."

"You're talking about kidnapping a world-renowned billionaire and intelligence officer from his native—"

"He is not an intelligence officer," she cut him off, using both her sharp staccato of a voice and a crisp chopping motion with her left hand. "Or at least he is not a *legally-sanctioned* officer like us. He's nothing but a freelancer, and a reckless one at that."

"He may do as he pleases, Angela, but there is no question that he has the full backing of the Polish president and the Polish government. As you may recall, it was you and your team that uncovered the encrypted signals intelligence that verified this critical fact four years ago."

"I realize that, sir, but he's become even more dangerous since then. Now he's assassinating targets on U.S. soil. You saw this morning's briefing report."

"Yes, but there's been no official confirmation it was Pularchek."

"It was him, I'm sure of it."

He gave a sardonic smile. "Not one of his clones?"

"That's the Americans' theory, not mine, sir. I happen to believe that he employs lookalikes. Such clever devices have been used since the beginning of espionage and warfare. In more modern times, George Washington, Adolf Hitler, Winston Churchill, Franklin Roosevelt, General Montgomery, Saddam Hussein, and even Bin Laden and Abu Bakr al-Baghdadi all used doppelgangers. In the present case, it's the only plausible way to explain how Pularchek is able to be at two places at once."

Kluge held up a hand for her to stop: his patience only went so far. "This is nothing but conjecture, and I don't want to hear any more about it. This is a pet theory, an urban myth, and nothing more. I'm more concerned about what to do about the Pole. I'll agree to ramp up our surveillance, but I'm afraid kidnapping him and secretly transporting him to Germany as a prisoner is out of the question."

"But he's assassinated four German businessmen in a grisly, highly public fashion. He needs to be taken into custody, brought here to Berlin, and made to stand trial for the murders he has committed on German soil."

"I agree with the vice-president," blurted Dieter, his sudden support taking Wolff by surprise. "How much longer can we allow this man to run roughshod over the international rule of law? Pularchek—or someone that looks just like him acting under his orders—has now killed in Germany, Switzerland, Spain, England, the United States, Poland, Syria, Iraq, Saudi Arabia, and in three African countries. And yet no one has lifted a finger to stop him. Because in every case, he has had the perfect alibi. If we can get the clever bastard quickly and cleanly, the Polish government won't have time to lodge a formal protest."

"But it will still come out and where will we be then? The chancellor has already ruled on this, and I am not about to sit here and revisit it. The Polish government and EU have both expressly rejected our request to take Pularchek into German custody—and right now, that is where things stand."

"So you want us to just hide our head in the sand and pretend that this man is not killing our fellow countrymen, is that it?" she challenged him.

"I have approved your request for increased surveillance. Hell, after what happened last night in their own back yard, a stone's throw from the White House, the Americans will probably greenlight extraordinary rendition protocol and do the job for us."

"They'll never succeed in getting him extradited to the U.S. by legal means," said Dieter. "The Poles won't give him up. The man is a national treasure."

Wolff vigorously agreed. "Which is precisely why, Walther, we need to take him prisoner inside Poland, bring him to Berlin, and make him stand trial."

"Permission is not granted, and I've made it clear why. This witch hunt of yours is growing tiresome, Angela."

"We know he is behind the murder of at least four German businessmen on our own soil. Isn't that enough?"

"That has not been proven conclusively in three of the cases, and you know it. Despite the exorbitant special-ballistics analysis and body-profile modeling your team has conducted."

"The man wears disguises, or his doubles do."

"Yes, and he hunts down Nazi profiteers, Holocaust deniers, jihadist financiers, and ruthless Russian oligarchs, Angela. Which is precisely why some people call him a saint."

"But he disavows the rule of law."

"That doesn't mean that we can just dash into Poland and kidnap him. The chancellor has denied your request, and I don't want to hear any more about it." He raked them both with a harsh look. "From either of you."

"Even though Pularchek has struck again inside Germany?"

He looked surprised. "What do you mean? There's been a new shooting?"

"Before this meeting, we received word from one of our police informants that a prominent Berlin lawyer named Bernhard Heydrich was murdered last night at his home. And that's not all. Also killed nearby was a former Polish intelligence operative named Ryszard Stasiak."

"All right, you have my interest."

She quickly described what she had discovered at Grünewald, careful not to reveal any of the details from last night's events at Heydrich's that had not been revealed by the German police.

When she was finished, Kluge snorted: "That's still not enough evidence to snatch Pularchek and risk creating an international incident. There is nothing to tie him to the crime scene. Just because a former Polish intelligence operative was found dead outside Heydrich's mansion, that doesn't mean Pularchek is behind it. And the police still have no idea who the third man, the one who got away, is."

"Yes, but we should have a positive ID soon. We know that his partner in crime is Ryszard Stasiak, who was with the Polish Special Forces just like Pularchek. So I believe it's only a matter of time before a connection is made between all three of them."

"Did Pularchek and Stasiak serve together at the same time?"

"No."

"Same outfit?"

"No, unfortunately."

"Then the Special Forces link may mean nothing. I believe we're done here. Now get some rest you two, you both look like shit."

Wolff looked at Dieter. In the last few minutes, his face had visibly paled during the questioning from their mutual boss. *Pull yourself together and don't look so damn guilty,* she snarled at him through her glaring eyes.

But she also had another message for him. *Don't you ever consider betraying me, lover—or I will not hesitate to kill you.*

CHAPTER 13

FRIEDRICHSTRASSE, BERLIN

WHILE PEERING OUT at the city from the rear window of his six-seat Mercedes-Benz S-Class Pullman limousine, Stanislaw Pularchek dialed a number he had never called before. Then, feeling a palpable tension in the air like a gathering electrical storm, he waited for an answer.

His transportation was not your average Mercedes limousine. This particular model happened to be equipped with Austrian diplomatic car flags and plates, armored plating, tinted bulletproof windows, and an enhanced-performance engine that enabled the vehicle to attain a straightaway speed of two hundred miles per hour. The limo headed south along the Friedrichstrasse, navigating through the heart of the German capital that had once been the center of Berlin's debauched nightlife during its version of the Roaring Twenties, long before the nightmare of the Third Reich or the partitioning of the fabled city into eastern and western sectors during the Cold War. The vehicle was trailed at a discreet distance by an innocuous-looking silver van containing high-tech electronic monitoring equipment and Pularchek's mobile Operations-Security Detail, armed with enough weapons to start a small war.

The team was a larger one than the one used in America. But, of course, the prize this time was much bigger, and the German intelligence service presented graver risks than the careless Americans. In the U.S., deranged individuals armed with knives and guns traipsed into the White House unmolested and rode elevators with the president. No wonder, Pularchek sometimes mused, 9/11 had been so easy for the jihadist mass murderers that had financed, planned, and executed the terrorist attack that had shaken the very foundations of the modern world. Regrettably, America was often asleep at the wheel when it came to trouble on its own doorstep.

The Mercedes limo knifed expertly through the nighttime traffic on the Friedrichstrasse, cruising effortlessly like a shark. Still waiting for his party to answer on the other end, Pularchek took in the façade of the stately *Friedrichstadt-Palast* on his left, lit up by colorful lights. The largest show palace in all of Europe was where Berliners gathered to enjoy the circus, take in a children's show, or watch a famous guest performance at a festival gala.

As if on cue, a throng of happy children and parents filed out the doors onto the sidewalk after just such an event. He felt a twinge of guilt. In a way, it was a shame that he was about to violently terminate two of Berlin's most celebrated citizens within shouting distance of so many happy children and their parents. But then again, his duty to the Cause demanded it.

Now, he heard the voice he wanted to hear on the other end. "Hello, this is Nick."

He hesitated, not quite believing that he actually had his biological son on the phone. *Should I go through with it?* he wondered, still unsure if he was doing the right thing. After all, his trusted *consigliere* and chief of security, Aleksander Romanowski seated next to him, had already spent the last half hour trying to talk him out of calling Nick Lassiter on the telephone.

"Hello, Nicholas. This is Stanislaw Pularchek," he said, and he felt suddenly ridiculous, especially when he saw Romanowski shaking his head in consternation. "I wanted to talk to you. I hope I'm not disturbing you."

The voice on the other end said nothing. He decided that he had no alterative now except to bull ahead with what he wanted to say, the consequences be damned.

"I wanted to talk to you, Nick, because I…I have just unexpectedly found out that you are my son."

The words hung there agonizingly, the silence so acute that he thought he had lost the connection.

"Nick, are you there?"

Nothing.

Cursing himself, he tried again. "Nick, did I lose you?"

"No, I'm still here. But I'm not quite sure I believe this is happening."

Pularchek smiled at the Counselor, as if he had just scored a point in a sporting contest. He was talking to his very own son! Not only that, his son was talking back to him and they were actually having a conversation! He was especially pleased that his English was so good that it didn't even sound like a second language. He had an unmistakable British accent from his years at Oxford and tutelage under stern British nannies growing up in Poland, but thankfully not the excessive preciseness of one to whom English is a second language.

"Yes, it is a bit unbelievable for me as well, Nick," he said. "But I really am your father…I mean your birth father…and I would very much like to meet you."

"I'm not sure I want to meet you."

The delivery and tone were blunt, but not scathing. He had expected resistance; no doubt by now Lassiter's CIA father, Benjamin Brewbaker, had told his adopted son where he had come from and the young man was still in a state of shock. Pularchek knew that the agency had an extensive file on him. In fact, he had a personal copy of the file, updated through May of the current year.

"Why is that, Nick? Do you have something against me that I should know about?"

"Yeah, you're an assassin and I don't make a habit out of hanging out with assassins."

"Who claims I am an assassin?"

"The FBI, CIA, NSA—and fifty other intelligence agencies. What, don't you read their reports?"

"You impress me, Nick. It appears you have access to top secret intelligence documents that even Edward Snowden couldn't get his hands on. But you're going to have to do better than that. There's no Interpol Alert out for my arrest any more than there is for the agents who work for MI6, Russia's SVR, Israel's Mossad, or your father's CIA."

"You may be the world's seventeenth richest person, but you're still an assassin under investigation by the authorities. You kill people for a living when you're not buying and selling mineral resources, software, real estate, and ceramic companies. Or doubling down on energy futures."

"I can see your father has briefed you quite thoroughly. Now let me ask you something. If James Bond and Jason Bourne were not fictional characters and you could sit down and have a beer with them, would you do it, Nick? What a silly question—of course you would. And they're not even *your father* like me."

"Are you really comparing yourself to the creations of Ian Fleming and Robert Ludlum? In any case, you're nothing like them."

"Is that what your father, the deputy director of the National Clandestine Service, told you? Well then, did he also tell you that, between them, Khalid Al-Muraydi and Alfred Kiefer have financed a dozen bombings and the purchase of eighteen million dollars' worth of illegal arms in the last five years alone? Those two men, if they can be called that, are mass murderers and nothing more. For their crimes against humanity, they have been summarily executed, without trial. But not by me, mind you. I, of course, was in Poland at the time, as you have no doubt been told by your spymaster father."

"What do you want from me?"

"I want to get to know you, Nick. I want to get to know the son I never knew I had."

"Like I said, I don't think that's a good idea."

"Probably not, but since when did you obey the rules? As I recall, you caused quite a stir last summer in New York. Were you not arrested twice by the police when you, Deputy Director Brewbaker, and your then-girlfriend Natalie Perkins uncovered a Russian money laundering operation at De Benedictis Literary Associates? In my admittedly humble opinion, that was quite a piece of detective work. I must say I'm proud of you...*son*."

"Are you trying to win me over by flattery?"

"In my experience, it happens to be a technique that usually works."

"Not with me, it doesn't. The truth is I have no desire to meet you. You may be a billionaire spy protected by the Polish government, but you still kill people—and personally I find that reprehensible."

"I can tell by your vocabulary that you received a sound education at Kenyon College in the tiny hamlet of Gambier, Ohio. But tell me the truth, Nick, doesn't your own government and the Israeli intelligence service kill specific targets? How are your U.S. special forces who killed Bin Laden any different from the assassin who managed to send Al-Muraydi and Kiefer to their Maker? Tell me, Nick, tell me the answer because I would really like to know."

"So you're saying that what you do is justified?"

"I'm not trying to justify anything, Nick. Nor am I admitting to anything. As I told you previously, your father and his task force at the NCS can confirm that I was in Warsaw during the unfortunate incident at The Willard Hotel rooftop. But I have to admit that I did read about it with great interest on the Internet."

"That's bullshit, and you know it. You killed them, or at the very least, you had them killed."

"There's a little thing called proof, Nick. And in this instance, there simply is none. Don't you believe in that most fundamental American axiom, namely that a man is innocent until proven guilty?"

The line went silent.

The Counselor was looking at him. "You shouldn't be doing this," he hissed in Polish in a low whisper. "This can only lead to trouble."

Pularchek covered his cellphone. "He's my son, Aleksander, and I intend to get to know him whether you like it or not."

"Sounds to me like he'd rather rip your throat out."

"It's our first conversation. It was bound to be bumpy."

"Yes, well, the only thing your little reunion fantasy is going to accomplish is to land you in prison. Have you considered that?"

"I'll take my chances."

The long, sleek Mercedes was now in the heart of Friedrichstrasse's major culture and shopping center, purring its way past a Manhattan-like expanse of upscale shops, posh restaurants, and glittering theaters. On his left, Pularchek saw the venerable Metropol Theater, founded by Marxist playwright Bertolt Brecht in 1873 and housed in the *Admiralspalast*. Continuing south on the Friedrichstrasse, they passed Louis Vuitton and Gucci boutiques; the über chic Galleries Lafayette, a European luxury store exhibiting French savoir vivre with a glass façade and striking atrium; and Departmentstore Quartier 205, an Art Deco wonder housing more posh designer boutiques and department stores for the exquisite taste. The Friedrichstrasse was the most legendary thoroughfare in the whole city, combining the tradition of the "Golden Twenties" with the architecture of the new, post-Cold War Berlin.

Pularchek found it strange coming to this town that had once been the seat of power of Hitler's Third Reich. Due to the brutality of Nazi Germany towards his native Poland and the entire Pularchek clan during the war, he had always loathed Germans and would certainly never forget or forgive what they had done to his beloved country. But he did have a grudging admiration for their vibrant artistic culture, intellectual rigor, and unrivaled engineering capabilities.

He spoke again into the phone. "I am sorry if we have gotten off on the wrong foot, Nick. I did not call you to argue."

"You didn't? Well, you're doing a damned good job of it. Maybe we have more in common than I thought."

Pularchek laughed. He looked again at the Counselor, who was frowning like an angry schoolmaster.

"So why exactly did you call me?" asked his son.

"I wanted to invite you and your lovely new bride on a deluxe, all-expenses trip to Poland for your honeymoon. I know it sounds crazy, but I want to meet you and Natalie. I know you were planning on going to Bermuda, but I humbly request that you reconsider. And as inducement, I would also like to offer you a modest wedding present of, say, ten million dollars for your trouble."

"I don't want your money. You can't just buy a son, you know."

"Then give the money to your favorite charity. Since you're a bestselling author now, how about a sizable donation to *The Unpublished Writers of America Guild*, or something like that. I read recently that a man can't even make a living above the poverty line being a writer these days—and yet you just sold a million copies of your debut novel *Blind Thrust*, earning a tidy sum in the first week. So why don't you give my ten million dollar present to all those independent writers out there who can't even feed their own children? You could make a real difference with that kind of money, Nick."

"Okay, that's enough. I don't need you, of all people, to tell me how to run my life."

"Why not, I'm your father. And rule number one is that fathers always meddle in their children's affairs. One day, I hope you'll have the pleasure to learn that firsthand."

"I really don't find this amusing."

"Fair enough, Nick, but just tell me one thing. Don't you want to know where you *really* come from? Don't you have the least bit of curiosity about your *true* origin?"

Silence on the other end. Pularchek could tell that he had struck a nerve as they turned onto the Leipziger Strasse and headed east. The posh boutiques, exclusive offices, fashionable department stores, and art galleries of the Friedrichstrasse had given way to more utilitarian surroundings. Neat, tidy rows of apartments and shops sprouted up on both sides of the street, interrupted by the occasional coffee house and government building.

"Let me put it another way, Nick, since I know all this must come as a shock. Now that you know your true origin, do you not have any desire to see the world you and your ancestors came from for yourself? Come to Poland, Nick. Come and see your family. Find out why you are—and will always be—a Pularchek."

The phone remained awkwardly silent.

He felt a stab of guilt laying it on so thick, but he was determined to prevail. After all, Poles had been doing precisely that for centuries. Prevailing when the odds were stacked overwhelmingly against them. In a way, it was liberating to not hold back his emotions.

"I believe it was your Mark Twain who said, 'The two most important days in your life are the day you are born and the day you find out why.' Come to Poland and find out the answer, Nick. I promise that you and your beloved wife Natalie will enjoy a journey of discovery that will change your lives for the better."

"I still don't believe this is happening."

"I almost don't believe it, either. But I think we both need to consider it an opportunity. A blessing."

"I don't know about this."

"Please just talk it over with your wife and parents. You can tell your father you are doing it just to spy on me. I'm sure he and his bosses at Langley would love the opportunity to do that. Who knows, perhaps they will learn the reason I get my intelligence more quickly and accurately than they do."

"Yeah, I'm sure they'd love to hear that."

"Just think about it. I'll call you tomorrow. And by the way, the name for Father in Polish is *Ojciec*." He grinned at the Counselor, who was shaking his head.

"Father?" repeated Lassiter, as if the word sounded foreign to him. "I don't think I can call you that. That word has to be earned."

"I would have it no other way. Come to Poland and I *will* earn it."

"I seriously doubt that."

"I just might surprise you, Nick. But I can't do that if you won't accept my invitation."

"I'm not going to take that bait."

"But of course you are. Blood is thicker than water and you are your father's son, the son of Stanislaw Pularchek, descended from a long line of great and not-so-great Polish princes and kings. You will rise to the challenge and accept my invitation—you will see."

"Like I said, I wouldn't bank on that."

"You see, that's precisely the problem—I already have. You can't run away from who you are, Nick."

"Oh, yes I can. I can do whatever the hell I want."

"I know you can, but you won't. Curiosity is a powerful motivator. Adios, my prodigal American son. I'll be in touch."

CHAPTER 14

RESTAURANT BIEBERBRAU
DURLACHER STRASSE, BERLIN

PRECISELY ONE HOUR before her contractor Stanislaw Pularchek and his entourage touched down at West Berlin's Neu-Staaken Airfield, Skyler parked her BMW in a parking lot next to the woods along the Prinzregentenstrasse. Turning off the engine, she quietly exited the vehicle and looked around for signs of surveillance. To her relief, she saw nothing suspicious and yet...and yet she still couldn't help but feel a presence in the air. Was someone following her? If not, why did she feel like she was being stalked? Or was it all in her mind?

She began walking south towards Durlacher Strasse. Overhead soared huge oak and elm trees, blotting out the thumbnail moon. She had taken a parking spot next to the thickly forested park so that she had a chance to survey her surroundings en route to Restaurant Bieberbrau. A connoisseur of fine dining, she was famished and wanted a quality meal before her next assignment at the Berghain.

At twenty paces, she thought she heard the snap of a twig followed by the sound of brush being crumpled underfoot. A wave of alarm rang through her whole body. She scanned the trees to her right, like a deer picking up the slightest sound. Again, she wondered if she had somehow been followed here. She still felt a vague presence that was disconcerting.

She continued along the sidewalk running alongside Prinzregentenstrasse. A suspicious-looking man in a gray jogging suit with headphones approached her from the south. Sensing danger, she stopped in her tracks and her left hand slipped into her purse and carefully latched onto her SIG-Sauer P228. But the man walked past her without incident, merely fiddling with his headphones, and resumed jogging to the north.

She started off again, walking at a brisk pace along the sidewalk. Dappled moonlight trickled through the leafy branches of the overhanging trees. But the trees made her feel hemmed in, threatened. Why did she feel like she was being followed? She kept a vigilant eye out, feeling increasingly paranoid.

When she reached Durlacher Strasse, she scanned the well-lit street. There were more people now that she was on a major thoroughfare: two businesswomen walking along the sidewalk; a pair of gay men holding hands as they crossed the street; a pack of twenty-something revelers obviously drunk and talking loudly; an elderly couple out for an evening stroll; and another jogger running up the street towards her wearing the same jogging outfit as the man who had just passed her.

Her body stiffened.

The same jogging outfit? It was too much a coincidence. Again, her hand slid into her purse and reached for her SIG.

But once again, the jogger passed without fanfare. She blew out a sigh of relief. My God, was it Berlin itself that brought out the paranoia, or was it everything that was happening with the Pularchek operation? She felt like she was in a John le Carré spy novel.

She quickly crossed Durlacher Strasse, ducked into Restaurant Bieberbrau, and was cordially seated by the well-coiffed maître d' at a table in the back away from the front window. Once seated, she surveyed the room's broad expanse, looking for prying eyes, someone familiar or threatening. Seeing no one suspicious, she turned her attention to the mouth-watering menu. Two minutes later, a smiling waiter in a stiff white shirt and neat bow tie came by her table. In German-accented English, she informed him that she was a bit pressed for time and ordered the Menu 1 Option: an appetizer of Scottish scallops with Brussels sprouts, chorizo oyster tartar, and almond; a main course of Fläminger Wild Boar Fillet with yellow turnip, common black orchid, champignon, and sloe; and a desert of black poppy seed semolina with elderberry sorbet. The waiter commended her on her selection in a distinct Mecklenburg accent and walked off.

She pulled out her coded mobile to check her phone messages. As she did so, she caught her reflection upon the surface of the cell phone. Her blue contact lenses, clear normal-vision glasses, pale makeup, extra padding around the midriff to make her look tubby, and casual business pantsuit outfit was quite the clever masquerade. With her disguise and slight German accent she'd assumed upon her arrival to Berlin, she looked like just another blandly average Miss Lonely Hearts out for a quiet dinner. No one would be able to even remotely guess that she was a violent Italian assassin codenamed Skyler, or that she had once been a young aristocrat from *Firenze* named Angela Ferrara.

On her phone, she had a new message from her lover Anthony. But did she dare call him? After all, she was on assignment—and the golden rule of field operations was to cease all personal contacts when in the midst of an op. It was standard field protocol, something not to be violated. But she was lonely and wanted to hear his voice. Despite the importance of her current assignment on behalf of Pularchek, she longed to talk to him. It was simple really: she was deeply in love with him.

Anthony Carmeli was a burnt-out yet charming, brilliant, and successful Hollywood film producer responsible for a string of financial and artistic hits that had, for seven years straight, bested even the Weinstein Company during the Golden Globes and Academy Awards season. Following a two-month recovery from her gunshot wounds sustained during the Fowler assassination, she had spent the past five months up until last week alone with Anthony on St. Croix in the Caribbean. But then Pularchek—with whom she had developed an important connection—had managed to coax her out of semi-retirement for the current assignment and put her up at the Hotel Bristol. After a seven-month hiatus, she had no desire to get back into the contract-killer game, but her control agent Xavier had been insistent. Xavier, former ops director of the French intelligence service, was the one who arranged her assignments around the world and her safe house accommodations, depending on where she wanted to live at any given moment and her contractual obligations. But the most important reason she had agreed to jump back into the fray was the special loyalty she felt towards Pularchek. In her view, he was a truly tragic figure who had treated her with exceptional professionalism and grace during their previous stint together. That supremely violent stint, in fact, had bound them together for life.

Their bond was a unique and highly emotional bond forged from tragedy. Five years ago, she had helped him avenge the inadvertent suicide-bombing murder of his wife and three daughters by taking out, on his behalf, the key Islamic terrorist leader who had ordered the attack on Spanish soil. In their mutual suffering in a world that had wrecked them both, Skyler and Pularchek had found common cause. He was one of only three men—the others being her lover Anthony and her control agent Xavier—that she trusted in the world.

There were no others.

She would never forget what Pularchek had said to her shortly after she had assassinated Ahmad Monatzeri, the Iranian paramilitary chieftain who had ordered the suicide bombing operation that had resulted in the death of Pularchek's wife and three daughters. She had delivered a single incendiary bullet to the jihadi commander's chest from five hundred yards outside Tehran, blasting away a goodly portion of his lungs and killing him instantly.

"You and I have a bond forged in the spilling of blood," Pularchek had said to her as the two devout Roman Catholic's had kneeled beside one another in St. Peter's in Rome. "I am starting up a little home-grown intelligence outfit that will rid the world of men like Monatzeri. Would you consider coming to work for me full time?"

"No," she said flatly. "But for the right price, I will help you eradicate evil when you believe my particular skill set is indispensable and you want someone outside your group as a matter of discretion. You can count on me for that."

"That is good to hear. One day, I may very well call upon you then."

"So you're going to be an avenging angel, is that it?"

"You make it sound quaint. I think it is absolutely necessary."

"I can tell you truly believe that. But I have to ask you, is this mission of revenge of yours because Monatzeri took your wife Johanna and your daughters Lena, Magdalena, and Zofia from you?"

"No, it is because I genuinely want to rid the world of evil. No doubt I will not succeed, but I am going to try. Naïve, don't you think?"

"To be perfectly honest, I admire you for it. And I wish you luck and promise that I will be there for you on that day in the future when you may call upon me."

There was a gleam in his eye. "You promise?"

"Yes, I promise."

"I believe you. So it is settled then," he said, and they recited the *Our Father* together, sealing their unusual bond in the sacrosanct language of their Church.

Skyler would never forget that day, just as she would never forget the love she felt for Anthony. Years ago, Don Scarpello and Alberto had ruined her for what she thought would be her entire life—but then she had met Anthony Carmeli and her life had changed for the better. They had fallen hard for one another, the jaded Hollywood film producer and the cold-blooded contract assassin who hated men with a passion. After she had been wounded during the Fowler hit and an underground physician had attended to her for two weeks, Anthony was the one who had nursed her back to health without asking questions, which had only deepened her love for him.

Years ago, she had resigned herself to a life as an assassin, a vagabond mercenary engaged in short episodes of shocking violence followed by long periods of loneliness devoid of love, family, and intimacy. But living first in LA and then on St. Croix in the U.S. Virgin Islands with Anthony, she had rediscovered how to love and wanted something more out of life. And then, just as she was ready to get out of the game for good and permanently retire with her wonderful new lover, Pularchek finally called upon her. Five years after she had made her promise to him, the Polish billionaire finally had the mission of a lifetime for her. He needed an asset outside his organization for an extremely delicate assignment that would involve two weeks of difficult work in Europe and several different potential targets.

He offered her three million U.S. dollars and warned her that it would be a serious challenge. But he simply had to have her since she and Xavier were the only two people he could trust outside his organization. Given her need to lay low after her American operation, she knew she should probably have turned the Pole down, politely but firmly. But she couldn't bring herself to do it. Not after she had made the promise to the man. And not after what those barbarians had done to his family. The fact was she empathized with his pain and suffering, and she admired him for his iconoclastic crusade as an avenging angel operating outside the realm of the world's international intelligence community. And so she had, as a private contractor and with Xavier's blessing, joined his little band of intelligence gypsies, knowing full well that Pularchek was doing the entire world a service by eradicating evil men that humanity would be far better off without.

But even after agreeing to take part in Pularchek's new operation, she still felt uncomfortable and guilty getting back in the game. Since meeting and falling in love with Anthony, she had wanted to quit wet work altogether. He made her feel special and loved in a way she hadn't known since she was young, and the intimacy they shared made the killing seem dirty and immoral. She was also growing tired of it all. Her seventeen years of being an assassin and the two gunshot wounds she had sustained following the Fowler contract had taken a toll on her. Then there was the ever-present danger of being caught. The longer she stayed in the game, the tighter the net became as the world's intelligence forces and her enemies closed in around her. At the moment, Xavier was doing a good job keeping the bloodhounds away, mostly through clever misinformation through the Diego Gomez front, but how much longer could he cover her tracks, especially now that she had come back out into the open?

Her first course arrived. She picked up her fork and began eating her scallops. Her thoughts turned once again to Anthony. Did she dare call him?

Just do it, Angela. If you don't, you'll regret it.

Before she could talk herself out of it, she punched in his number on her coded mobile, reaching him after two rings.

"Hello?"

"It's me," she said in a quiet voice.

"Jesus, I thought you'd never call. I was getting worried," he said with emotion. "God, how I miss you."

"I miss you too," she said softly. "But I am almost finished with my work here. I will be back late next week."

"Let's not kid ourselves, Skyler. It will never be over. You're with the CIA. Now that they've sunk their claws into you again, they'll keep coming back time and time again. It's never going to stop."

The phone fell awkwardly silent. She hated herself for lying to him, but there was no other way. Since they had first met seven months ago, her cover story had always been that she worked as a non-official cover officer in the Domestic Resources branch of the CIA's National Clandestine Service, which meant that she was not officially attached to any U.S. government agency and was, therefore, harder to link to the CIA. Domestic Resources was the branch assigned to gather information on foreign countries using American citizens living or traveling overseas, who reported on what they learned or saw abroad. For Skyler, being a non-official cover officer provided the perfect cover since it could not be checked up on, except by senior CIA officials. However, NOC officers had no diplomatic immunity and could be arrested and imprisoned by foreign governments for spying, or for consorting with spies. Which was a major reason that Anthony was worried about her.

"I told you that I am going to quit the CIA after this assignment is done," she said to him, and she meant it.

"That's what you said when we moved to St. Croix."

"I told you that I had to do a favor for an old friend. There was no way I could get out of it."

"Well, now the FBI wants to talk to you."

She felt her heart lurch in her chest. "What are you talking about?"

"It's the reason I've been calling you. An FBI agent came to talk to me yesterday—about you."

"An FBI agent. What do you mean an FBI agent?"

"His name was Ken Patton. He's with the Denver Field Office."

Skyler felt a wave of panic as she forked another scallop. Ken Patton was the FBI special agent assigned to the Kieger and Fowler assassination cases. He had discovered who she was and that Diego Gomez was nothing but a fictitious assassin, but his 200-page report had been gutted and rewritten to protect the members of the U.S. Secret Service that had been implicated in the conspiracy. Through painstaking detective work and detailed facial recognition analysis, Patton was convinced that Diego Gomez was nothing but a fiction and that Skyler was behind both highly public assassinations as well as two other killings. But no one believed him and he had been promoted and promptly removed from any association with the case. He must have been making inquiries on his own time in St. Croix, which was bad news for her. Apparently, he was reluctant to let go of the case.

"What did you say to this Agent Patton?"

"I didn't tell him anything."

"Are you sure?"

"Yes. How can I tell him anything when I don't know anything?" He sighed deeply. "Skyler, are you involved in something? I feel like you're being less than honest with me."

"You know perfectly well that it's my job to be less than honest. I'm actually breaking protocol by even talking to you over the phone."

"Where are you?"

"You know I can't tell you that."

"I'm not trying to be a pain in the ass. It's just that I care about you."

"I know, and I care about you too. But we both have to be careful about what we say and do. What did this Agent Patton have to say about me?"

"He just asked if I knew you."

"That's it? That's all he asked?"

"He said that you had been working with him, but had gone missing."

"That's a lie!" She scolded herself for raising her voice and looked around the restaurant. One of the waiters was staring at her.

"Why are you getting upset?" asked Anthony.

"Do not say anything more to this FBI man. Agent Patton is a rival of the CIA and will only bring harm to me. Do you hear me? If he comes back, you must refuse to speak to him."

"Yes, I understand. But I didn't tell him anything."

"Good. It's just that I can get into a lot of trouble if you say the wrong thing. Entrapment is the name of the game with the Bureau and Justice Department."

"Don't worry. I won't talk to this Patton fellow if he comes back again."

"Did he indicate that he might?"

"No, but he gave me his card and said to call him day or night if I had any information."

"Have you seen any signs of anyone watching you?"

"No."

"Was he alone?"

"Yes, it was just him. Jesus, what has this guy got on you? Why are you being so paranoid?"

"The FBI and CIA don't like each other. This is a turf battle on a case that we're running and nothing more."

"I wish I could believe that, Skyler. Honestly, I do."

"You don't believe me?"

"Come on, the last time we did this little dance, you got shot in two places, remember? And who was the one who had to nurse you back to health? I've seen the scars. I've seen them practically every day for the last six and a half months."

"I know you were there for me and I appreciate it, but you're overreacting. I can take care of myself."

"Getting shot in the stomach twice and being out of commission for two solid months is not exactly taking care of oneself. And now you're back with the CIA. When is it ever going to end?"

The waiter came with her main course. Skyler looked at the Fläminger Wild Boar Fillet with yellow turnip, common black orchid, champignon, and sloe—and realized that she had lost her appetite.

"I just want to be with you, all right? I thought that we had agreed to quit our high-stress lives and be together. You know that I have plenty of money and want to be with you the rest of my life. I have twenty million dollars, Skyler. Twenty million dollars that I want to share with you and no one else. I thought we had something special away from it all here on St. Croix."

Indeed, it was special. She loved sailing twice a week on their 38-foot trimaran, snorkeling and scuba diving at Buck Island and the Wall, body surfing at Davis Bay, and devouring the best conch fritters and *langusta gratin* in the world at the Club Comanche and Duggan's Reef. St. Croix was truly a tropical paradise, and these past several months with Anthony she couldn't have been happier.

"I love you Skyler," he said to her. "I just don't want you to be in danger. I can tell that being back with the CIA has put you in the crosshairs again."

"Crosshairs? What do you mean crosshairs?"

"It's just a figure of speech. Don't get so paranoid."

"I'm sorry. I didn't mean to lash out at you."

"It's the stress in your voice. I don't just hear it—I can feel it. You're into something, something that frightens you."

Is it that obvious? My God, you're supposed to be a pro. "No, you're overreacting. Everything is fine and I'll be back next week."

"I have plenty of money, Skyler. You don't have to work ever again. And I know you have enough yourself. Look, I just don't know why you continue to do it when some of these people that you've questioned in Domestic Resources have threatened you. That's what you told me. Why do you keep at this job when you're at risk? Together, we don't want for anything financially and I want to be with you and take care of you."

"I can handle the risks, Anthony. Now I have to go."

"I don't want to end like this. I'm sorry. It's just that I love you so much."

"I love you too." She was so moved she thought she would cry. "If by some chance something did happen to me, it's important for you to know that."

"You shouldn't talk like that. Nothing's going to happen to you."

"But if something were to, please remember that these last few months with you have been the best of my life. And that I love you."

"Why are you even saying this? Nothing's going to happen, okay?"

"Just tell me you love me. I want to hear you say it."

"I love you, goddamnit!"

Skyler felt tears come to her eyes as it dawned on her how exposed she was once again. Coming out of semi-retirement to work on behalf of Pularchek put her directly in the crosshairs of the world's intelligence services, especially with

Patton unable to let go of the case and sniffing around like a bloodhound. She might pull off her part flawlessly—or she might be wounded, killed, or captured and never be with Anthony again, or be forced to run for the rest of her life. Anything could happen to her, and these intimate words between them might be their last.

"I have to go now," she said, feeling a deep melancholy. "Goodbye, and if by chance something does happen to me, please know that I love you."

And with that, she clicked off before he could say another word.

CHAPTER 15

BREWBAKER-LASSITER TOWNHOUSE
O STREET NW, GEORGETOWN

"I'LL BE DAMNED if my son and daughter-in-law are going to Poland to be at the mercy of a professional assassin. I don't care if he's a billionaire on the cover of *Forbes* magazine or not. You're not going!"

Lassiter was not surprised by his mother's vehemence, but he was surprised at how flushed her cheeks were as he looked at her, then at his father, then back at her. He had just informed his parents and Natalie about his bizarre conversation with his biological father minutes ago—and he was getting his first taste of their reaction. The four of them were sitting at the kitchen table, sipping early morning cappuccinos and munching croissants with brilliant June sunlight spilling through the diaphanous silk curtains.

But there was nothing brilliant about the tense atmosphere in the room. He knew that he had struck a nerve. All the same, there was no delicate way to talk about his newly discovered father. He had family ties on both sides of the Atlantic now, and nothing could change the new paradigm. Lassiter felt badly for his parents—he knew the sudden change was hard on them—but the new reality had to be addressed. There was no turning back the clock to the time when he only had two American parents.

"I know it sounds crazy, but I'm seriously thinking about taking him up on his offer and going to Poland," he said, choosing to be up front with his mother and father at the risk of upsetting them. "At first I was resistant, but after taking some time to think about it, I actually want to go. But before I agree, I want to know what you all think." He looked at Natalie first. "Would you even consider going to Poland for our honeymoon? Again, I know it sounds crazy, but my gut tells me I'll regret it if I don't do this. I mean, if *we* don't do this."

"My God, Nicholas, I don't believe this! You're actually considering this outrageous—?"

"Just hold on a moment, Vivian," his father cut his mother off. "Let's hear what he has to say."

"Oh, that's just great. You're going to just hand our son over to a professional assassin. I know why you're not stopping them. You'd just love to have a pair of secret spies do your bidding entirely off the CIA's books, just like you did last summer in New York. How convenient for you, Benjamin. Now you can recruit spies, pay them nothing to do your dirty work, and save the federal government a small fortune in the process. Are you really so cold that you would do such a thing to your own son and daughter-in-law?"

"I'm just coming up to speed here like you, Vivian. Believe it or not, I haven't made my mind up about anything."

"You two are both forgetting about one thing," said Natalie in a gently forceful tone. "The choice isn't yours or your husband's to make. The choice belongs to me and Nick."

She inched closer to her husband at the kitchen table and gently took him by the hand. He noted that her hand was soft and warm. He thought back to their lovemaking the night before last, when they had been two simple newlyweds on their way to Bermuda to spend their honeymoon. Lassiter felt as though he had aged a decade since then.

"Oh, you don't know what you're talking about," bristled his mother, giving that overly theatrical gesture she always gave when she didn't get her way, like Daisy Buchanan in *The Great Gatsby*. He had always found such histrionics irritating growing up, but all the same he loved his mother dearly. "There's no reason to have any further discussion on this matter. You two are not going," she concluded emphatically.

Lassiter watched with amusement as Natalie defiantly crossed her arms. "I'm afraid I'm going to have to politely disagree."

"Disagree?"

"Yes, I have decided to go to Poland on my own, even if Nick doesn't want to go. I was invited, too, and quite frankly I'm curious. Call me stupid, call me irrational, call me whatever you like—but it's ultimately my decision. And I'm telling you right now that I'm going. I've never actually visited Poland, but I hear it's wonderful this time of year."

He couldn't help but crack a smile. Goddamn, did he marry the right woman or what! "Welcome to the family, kiddo. Watching you and my mom do battle is like watching Poland versus Germany. And I think we all know that in this particular case, you're the Fatherland." He looked at his mother. "Mom, I think you'd better wave the white flag now and sign the armistice because the Panzers are rolling into Warsaw."

"That's not funny, Nicholas."

His father held up his hands like a referee. "Timeout." He waited a moment for everyone to quiet down before fixing Lassiter with a hard stare. "Natalie is right. It's your decision as husband and wife whether or not to take Pularchek up on his offer. But you and I, Nick, have an appointment in less than two hours with my boss, and he's going to be very interested in what your plans are. Because all indications are that your biological father just orchestrated the assassination of two foreign nationals on U.S. soil three blocks from the White House and in the presence of the senate majority leader. Pularchek has made the U.S. intelligence and law enforcement community look like fools, and there are people that are going to want to do whatever possible to get quality human intel on him. So it is important for me—mostly as your father but also as a senior intelligence officer— to know exactly *why* you want to go to Poland. Your mother and I deserve that much, Son. You want to know why? Because we love you more than anything else in the world and don't want anything to happen to you."

His mother now had tears in her eyes, and it killed Lassiter to see her so distraught. "I honestly don't want to hurt you or mom," he said to them. "But I have to go through with this. I want to know where I came from. I want to meet this man—even if he is dangerous. Actually, maybe even *more* so because he's dangerous. The bottom line is I may never get this opportunity again, and I'm not going to pass it up. And obviously, Natalie feels the same way as I do."

"The man is a killer, Nicholas," said his mother. "It may very well be for an ultimately noble cause, but that doesn't make being around him any more safe. You and Natalie's lives could be in danger from the moment you step off that plane in Warsaw. According to your father, Pularchek is at the very top of more than a dozen Islamic terrorist group kill lists."

"I'm not going to let terrorists decide where I can go in Europe."

"Neither am I," said Natalie.

"Don't you two understand that Islamic supremacism is a worldwide, ideologically connected movement? These people are everywhere in the world now. And their sole reason for living is to cripple the West through acts of indiscriminate slaughter. They care about nothing else except foisting their narrow, primitive *sharia* law on the civilized world and restoring an Islamic Caliphate to the descendants of Allah and Muhammad. These fanatics don't listen to reason, and neither do the neo-Nazis and rogue Russians who have also targeted Pularchek on their kill lists. You two could very well end up being suicide bombed or gunned down by Pularchek's enemies. And, according to your father, he has an awful lot of them."

"I appreciate that you're worried about us, Mom, but this is something—"

"My God, would you just listen to reason for a minute! Is it worth risking your life and your marriage to visit a man who has not been a father to you for the past thirty-one years of your life? A man who only today appeared out of nowhere, after you witnessed a brutal murder that he is likely responsible for?"

"Yes, I think it is worth it," he said. "I'm going to Poland."

"And I'm going with him," said Natalie.

His father nodded in solemn understanding. "I can appreciate why you two feel this way, but I think it's important you know what you're dealing with here."

"You've already told us. Pularchek takes out bad guys."

"It's not that simple and you know it."

"Actually, I think it is. The war he's fighting may never be won, but when confronted by evil on this monstrous a scale, standing by and doing nothing is absolutely not an option. Stanislaw Pularchek, my biological father, understands that and I'd be lying to you if I told you that I don't already respect him for it. Even if I pretended not to when I spoke with him on the phone earlier."

"All right, I can see you've made up your mind on this. But here are some things you should know before you venture down this path. I can't tell you everything, of course. But because Pularchek is your father, too, I'm going to disregard national security protocols for a moment and let you take a peek at something."

He reached down into his briefcase on the floor, opened it, withdrew a four-inch-thick three-ring binder, and set it down on the kitchen table in front of them. Lassiter looked at Natalie; like him, she was intrigued.

"That highly classified document happens to be my personal copy of the Central Intelligence Agency's file on Pularchek. Now I can't give it to you, but you two can take a look at it before the meeting at ten. It's a compilation of FBI case files, Interpol alerts, international police reports, CIA memos, and dossiers from friendly intelligence services around the world. We have developed a computer code that has queried hundreds of thousands of records, using facial and voice-recognition software from international surveillance cameras and signals intelligence as well as data on murder weapons, bullets, firing distances, and tactical elements. The computer has identified our friend Pularchek as the assassin in twenty-eight cases in the past five years, with a correlation coefficient of over ninety-five percent. Twenty-eight cases—now that's nothing to sneeze at—but it could also be more. There are an additional dozen cases with a correlation coefficient between fifty and seventy percent, and nine more between seventy and eighty. All of them have been expertly planned, highly professional, long-distance shots to the head or upper chest with a sniper rifle. But then that's what provides the ultimate mystery: if there are multiple shooters, how come all of the cases are forensically identical? It's just not statistically possible."

"Well, first off, does Pularchek have the kind of shooting ability you're describing?" asked Lassiter, reaching across the table for the thick binder.

"He most certainly does. He did a three-year stint as a sharpshooter and officer in the *Wojska Specjalne*, the Polish Special Forces. But more importantly, he had a gun in his hands regularly growing up in Poland. He was a crack shot with a rifle and cross-country skier as a boy, and he went on to even greater success in the Olympics. He won the gold three times and the silver twice in the biathlon. At the 1984 and 1988 Winter Olympics, when he was eighteen and twenty-two years old. Apparently, he was something of a prodigy. But then, to the surprise of his family, he gave it all up and went into business. Over the next twenty-five years, he rose up to become the seventeenth richest man in the world. And he didn't even go to college."

A real self-made man, thought Lassiter. *How could I possibly not want to meet the son of a bitch, even if he is an assassin?* "Tell us more about his targets. Who are these people and why were they targeted?"

"Most, but not all, are Middle Eastern jihadists on the U.S. State Department's list as 'specially designated global terrorist financiers.' These are people guilty of what is legally classified as 'providing material support to a foreign terrorist organization.' But, as you're aware, he has a fixation on Nazi Holocaust profiteers and neo-Nazi financiers. And he doesn't much care for dirty Russian oligarchs and Soviet mass-murderers from the Second World War either."

"Okay, so give us a rundown."

"His two most recent targets, as you know, were Al-Muraydi and Kiefer, both of whom financed terror. Before that was a Jordanian businessman known as *Al Sheikh Al Fateh*—the Conqueror Sheikh in Arabic. He was the chief bankroller of the *Jabhat al-Nusra*, an al-Qaeda spinoff group in Syria, before he was shot twice in the head outside a mosque in Raqqa. Before that were German industrialists Günther Bormann and Edward Volcker and the Dutch entrepreneur Anton Corbijn. All of whom had the misfortune of being sons or grandsons of SS generals and inheritors of more than forty million dollars' worth of French and Dutch art, jewelry, and gold stolen from Holocaust victims. Then there was Abu Musab al-Baghdadi, the Saudi monarch who provided funding to the tune of more than twenty million dollars to both al-Qaeda in Iraq and Islamic State, as well as the 'general emir' of the *Nusra Front*, one of the most powerful rebel groups in Syria. The financial disbursements were handled discreetly through a Vatican-owned bank. Before that was Andrei Varlamov, a Soviet colonel who played a key role in the 1940 Katyn massacre. Soviet forces killed over twenty thousand Polish officers and political leaders and subsequently blamed it on the Nazis. Then there was Christian Escher, Senior Asset Manager with Credit Suisse. He was responsible for distributing more than seventy million in stolen Jewish Holocaust funds over the past two decades to the descendants of several Nazi war criminals who managed to escape persecution. Before that was Chechen oligarch-jihadist Grigori Karpov, killed with a single hollow-point round to the head outside a Budapest nightclub. Should I go on?"

"No, I think we get the point," said Lassiter. "The dude kills bad guys. Maybe that's why I want to meet him."

"Me too," agreed Natalie.

"Look, this isn't some game you two," said his mother. "With a man like this, anything could happen. Half the world wants him dead."

"Your mother's right, Nick. Islamic State has put out a bounty in the amount of five million Syrian pounds on his head."

"Islamic State has put out the same bounty on our own president's head."

"That's different."

"Is it?" He opened the CIA intelligence report and began looking through it along with Natalie. "Is Pularchek actually being sought by U.S. authorities?"

"He's on our domestic and international watch lists."

"But he's not even wanted by the FBI and CIA for what happened last night on the rooftop. How bad can he be?"

"The FBI wants him, all right. But we've told them to show restraint because of his potential value as a foreign asset."

"What does that mean?" asked Natalie.

"That there are people in high places who are privately happy that Al-Muraydi and Kiefer are dead. These people want the whole thing to blow over quickly before too many questions are asked about what they were doing in the U.S. They apparently have connections to a rather reputable bank as well as a gold-plated investors' group here in the nation's capital."

"What about the Polish government? What do they think of their billionaire assassin running around bagging bad guys on U.S. soil?"

"Privately, they're not pleased with their protégé, but publically they deny he had anything to do with it, since he gave a speech in Warsaw nine hours before the shootings. Given the eleven-hour flight time from D.C. to Warsaw, they claim he couldn't possibly have been responsible."

Lassiter paused to examine a photograph in the report. "If Pularchek's so bad, I'm wondering what he's doing standing next to the Polish president and U.S. secretary of state in this picture here. It was taken at a ceremony at the Tomb of the Unknown Soldier in Warsaw just last year to honor World War Two Polish soldiers. If I didn't know better, I'd say the man was a Polish national treasure—not a wanted criminal."

Lassiter continued flipping through the report. His wife moved her chair closer to have a better look, her eyes filled with equal fascination as they came upon photograph after photograph of the subject hanging out with celebrities at gala events, including George Clooney, Helen Mirren, François Hollande, and Angela Merkel. In one photo, Pularchek appeared to be engaged in a playful, drunken wrestling match with Clooney next to a Lake Como poolside bar with a crowd of onlookers laughing uproariously.

"Whoever this guy is," said Natalie, "he's definitely a puzzle."

"You can say that again," said his father. "Which brings us to another key theme of our little intelligence briefing here. You and Nick might actually be able to help me and my colleagues at Langley get a better handle on our mystery man."

His mother shook her head adamantly. "My God, Benjamin, don't tell me you're actually *recruiting* them to go now?"

"No, I just want them to understand what they're up against. People with a lot higher pay grades than me are going to have an interest in what they choose to do here, and it will be out of my hands. Seldom does the agency miss out on an opportunity for the big coup *a la* Bin Laden—or the big screw-up like the Bay of Pigs."

"Please don't tell me that those mandarins at Langley are going to hide bugs in their clothing and ask them to play secret agent over there in Europe?"

"I honestly don't know what they're going to do, Vivian. But my motto is hope for the best, plan for the worst."

"Good words to live by," said Lassiter. "But I still don't understand why the U.S. and Polish Governments are willing to cover for this guy. I mean, in all likelihood he just had two people executed a stone's throw from the Oval Office. If Pularchek is behind it, he's created a major international incident. I also don't understand why he would take such a risk. From what you told me earlier, this is the first time he has struck on U.S. soil."

"There are a lot of questions we need answered about this guy, Nick. And you've just raised another one. Why has he chosen to cross the Atlantic at this time? What was so special about these two targets that he would take such a chance? Or is there something else going on?"

"Oh, stop it, Benjamin. Now you truly are encouraging them." She turned towards her son and Natalie, her expression pleading. "Please don't do this, you two. Please don't go through with this."

He met his mother's gaze. "Are you saying that because you're genuinely fearful for my life? Or because you don't want me to spend time with my...my birth father?"

"Both," she admitted, and he now saw tears in her eyes. "We love you so much, Nicholas. We just don't want to lose you."

Feeling guilty for making her tear-up again, he looked at his father. "What about you, Dad? If you were in my shoes, what would you do?"

"It doesn't matter what I think, Nick. You're going to go your own way, like you always have. And so will Natalie. But before you go through with this, finish reading the dossier. It may change things a bit."

CHAPTER 16

FEDERAL INTELLIGENCE SERVICE
CHAUSSEESTRASSE, BERLIN

"YOU'RE NOT GOING TO BELIEVE THIS."

Angela Wolff looked up from her desk at her number two, Dieter Franck. "What is it? What's happened?"

"Remember that new, experimental voice recognition software we installed last week?"

"You're talking about at our Joint Sigint Activity Facility in Bad Aibling?"

"At a range of five-hundred kilometers, we can penetrate virtually any encryption coding as long as smartphone devices are turned on."

"Yes, what about it?"

"We've gotten our hands on our first major sigint intercept and managed to decrypt it. We got lucky: the sound is crystal clear, and the matrix interference and background electronic chatter are within tolerance criteria. But more importantly, you're not going to believe who we think we've managed to intercept."

"It had better be Pularchek."

He nodded. "This may allow us to go on the offensive, instead of sitting here waiting for the phone to ring."

She stood up from her chair. "I'll show more enthusiasm when I know for sure. Where is Pularchek now, and what are the correlation parameters?"

"You're not going to believe this. He's right here in Berlin, and the voice correlation index is over ninety-five percent. It's got to be him."

At this positive news, she felt her heart rate click up a notch, a frisson of sudden energy. "*Du lieber Himmel*, how close is he?"

"He just passed through the Friedrichstrasse twenty minutes ago. Should we notify Walther?"

"Why not notify *Der Spiegel* while we're at it?" she said scornfully, referring to the popular German weekly news magazine known for digging up controversial stories on intelligence community overreach and government corruption. "Don't you understand? We are in a situation here. We need to catch the bastard ourselves, interrogate him, find out what he's done with the merchandise, recover it as quickly as possible, and then terminate him."

"Terminate him? Is that really necessary?"

"The last thing we want is anyone sniffing around asking questions once we've recovered what rightfully belongs to us. Or, I should say, belongs to *me*."

"But I thought you wanted to keep Walther in the loop. At least for show."

"If we are forced into a situation where we have to arrest Pularchek and extradite him to Germany, yes. In that case, Walther could prove useful. But as far as recovering the merchandise is concerned, we cannot allow anyone in this building to know a damned thing." She was referring to not just her boss, Walther Kluge, the president of the *Bundesnachrichtendienst*, but her domestic intelligence counterparts and frequent rivals in the *Bundesamt für Verfassungsschutz*—the Federal Office for the Protection of the Constitution, or BfV. The sometimes fractious relationship between the country's foreign spy agency, the BND, and its domestic equivalent, the BfV, was similar to that of the American CIA and FBI, or the British MI6 and MI5.

"I hear you loud and clear, Ms. Vice-President. But my gut feeling is we won't be able to deceive Walther much longer. He's bound to figure out we're up to something after Vienna and Grünewald. Our time is running out."

"That is why we must take Pularchek into custody as quickly as possible."

"That's proving more difficult than we had anticipated. Once the inevitable questions start coming over Heydrich's death, someone is going to become suspicious. There is nothing we can do to prevent that."

"Heydrich's death will be blamed on Pularchek. And that Polish assassin you shot and killed outside his home—Ryszard Stasiak—will eventually be linked to him too through their Special Forces connection. So what's the problem? This has Pularchek's fingers all over it, and that's what the police will see. Once Pularchek stole the merchandise, he killed the man who gave him the information. Only Heydrich and Hoess knew about the letter and my inheritance—and now one of them is dead. I think it's clear who betrayed me and my grandfather."

"It's true we know that Stasiak was with the *Wojska Specjalne*. But as Kluge pointed out, that still doesn't mean that Pularchek's the one that hired him to kill Heydrich."

"You think there's a third party involved?"

"That's what my instincts tell me. There's also the matter of the third man, the one that got away."

"He had to have been working with Stasiak. Or why else would they have fled the murder scene together?"

"I don't know."

"You let me worry about third parties and loose ends. Have you triangulated Pularchek's last known position?"

"Yes, but unfortunately once he punched off his cell we lost him. He was last heading east on Leipziger Strasse."

"Were you able to record the conversation?"

"Most of it."

"Well, who was he talking to?"

"You're not going to believe this either: his son."

"His son? But Pularchek doesn't have a son."

"He does now, and apparently by a stroke of luck, the young man witnessed those killings in Washington, D.C."

"Are you telling me we can tie Pularchek to the D.C. murders?"

"Doubtful."

"Why not?"

"As usual, he has an alibi. He was in Warsaw giving a speech yesterday and couldn't have been in two places at once, right? Once again, he has hundreds of reliable witnesses."

Clever bastard, thought Wolff, grinding her teeth with irritation. Pularchek was proving to be a far more dangerous adversary than she had suspected. Was this renegade billionaire actually going to get away with stealing her *Schatzfund* from her and ruining her life? What had he done with what he had stolen from her? And what the fuck was he doing in Berlin?

"What do you think he's up to here in Germany?" wondered Dieter aloud, echoing her troubled thoughts.

"I don't know, but we have to find him. The situation has escalated. You do realize what's at stake, Dieter?"

"Yes, you don't need to remind me again," he said, as she reached out and touched him softly on the hand. "We can be together—filthy rich and retired on a beach in Skopelos—instead of languishing here fighting a war on terror with no end in sight. That's why the Israeli's euphemistically call it 'mowing the lawn.' It's routine and it's never going to fucking end."

"Which is precisely why it is absolutely critical that we find this Polish rogue elephant, interrogate him, find out where he has hidden the merchandise, retrieve it, and then liquidate him. Do you really want to be chasing after bearded jihadi fanatics the rest of your life?"

"No, I don't."

"Neither do I. I've seen enough of these mindless Neanderthals to last a thousand lifetimes. I mean, what kind of people are so violently fanatical that they murder cartoonists over doodles in a magazine and run over women pushing strollers in the streets using heavy trucks?"

"I'm tired too, Angela. And there's no denying that you and I have more in common with Pularchek than these zealots. He actually does our dirty work for us by eliminating these Islamic extremists. Sometimes, I can't help but find myself quietly rooting for the bastard."

"The man has stolen from us, Dieter. He is a thief and nothing more. You must never forget that."

"Do you want to activate the mobile unit?"

"Yes, immediately. I want three surveillance vans and a full tactical assault team. Also, I want a surveillance alert issued for vehicles with diplomatic plates from our closed-circuit television cameras throughout the city. We're probably only going to have a small window of opportunity to grab him. We need to keep our eyes and ears open for his video signature and radio chatter. Round up the unit and give them the usual briefing. But first I want to listen to the audio recording. We need to know where he's going and what he's planning to do. He must have come to Berlin for a reason."

"Or, he could be toying with us."

She smiled truculently. "If he is, it will be for the last time."

CHAPTER 17

BERGHAIN
AM WRIEZENER BAHNHOF
FRIEDRICHSHAIN, BERLIN

FROM THE FIFTH FLOOR WINDOW of an abandoned Cold-War-era apartment complex, Stanislaw Pularchek raised his Leica range-finding binoculars and scanned the post-modern industrial façade of the Berghain. His position provided a clear line of sight to the front door of Berlin's most legendary nightclub. He could hear the technopop bleeding into the night from the ear-splitting sound system that pumped music onto an 18-meter-high dance floor, where every evening a 1,500-strong crowd raved itself into a hedonistic frenzy until daylight beckoned. It was an unusual spot for a double killing; but then again, his two soft targets gyrating inside on the dance floor at this very moment were very unusual men.

His mind reached back to his last Winter Olympics in Calgary, Alberta, in February 1988. He had shot well in the biathlon that year, better even than in '84 in Sarajevo, winning a pair of gold medals as well as a closely-contested silver despite formidable opposition from strong Norwegian and East and West German challengers. He hoped to shoot as well tonight in Berlin.

With his Leica range-finder, he surveyed the grounds around the building and the surrounding neighborhood for signs of police. He didn't need to worry, for he had his Operations-Security Detail acting as his eyes and ears on the ground. Whenever he carried out an assignment or moved about in enemy territory, they never let him out of their sight. At the moment, they blended seamlessly into their surroundings, so much so that he couldn't spot any trace of their presence or their vehicles on the street below.

There was also no trace of his coveted private contractor and guardian angel for the current ongoing operation, the quietly competent female assassin Skyler, whom he had coaxed out of semi-retirement. She was in her appointed position on the rooftop of the three-story office building a quarter mile to the east. But there was no visible sign of her. *Of course not,* he thought; *she is a true professional.*

He also saw no sign of the opposition. Not a single green-and-white police car or surveillance van anywhere in sight. All the same, he couldn't help but feel a rising tension as he mulled over the trajectory of the shot and his escape plan.

The line to get into the club was long. More than three hundred people were waiting impatiently along the dusty track leading from the street to the entrance. A queue of taxis a dozen deep stood along the front curb outside the heavy-chain link fence, waiting to ferry home revelers and those unfortunate enough to be refused entry at the door by the detail of grim-faced bouncers wearing matching black leather jackets. Standing as supreme gatekeeper at the graffiti-framed entrance was Sven, the club's terrifying head doorman. Studying him through his Leica binoculars, Pularchek thought he resembled a post-apocalyptic, bearded version of Otto Skorzeny, the Waffen-SS colonel who had led the daring rescue mission that had freed the deposed Italian dictator Benito Mussolini from captivity during WWII.

Suddenly, Pularchek's radio headset crackled to life. "The targets are on the move," he heard the Counselor say from his hidden command post on the street below. "They're with the same women they entered the club with and their two bodyguards. They'll be in your line of sight in three minutes."

"I copy," replied Pularchek, sitting upright and snapping to attention.

"Komandor, the team is in position, airwaves are clean, and there's no sign of unfriendlies," reported another voice through his headset. It was Janusz Skrzypek, his counterintelligence chief and radio operator as well as sometimes driver. His nickname was Janu.

Now Pularchek checked on his private contractor. "Skyler, are you in position."

"Yes, I'm ready. Clear to the front door."

"Good. Happy hunting then." Now he spoke to the rest of the team. "All right, it's a green light. When it's over, everyone proceed to the rendezvous quickly, mingling with the fleeing crowd. I'll see you there."

"Happy hunting to you too, Boss," said Romanowski.

"Yes, good luck, Komandor," added Skyler.

"You know I don't believe in luck. I believe in preparation. Over and out."

As he reached for his range-finder, he thought with a measure of satisfaction: *Vice-President Wolff, you and your lover boy are about to get a very blunt message. And just so you know, there will be no collateral damage. These are going to be clean kills.*

He locked the laser-ranging dot of the Leica binoculars once again on the burly Sven-the-Gatekeeper's head to triple check the distance. The invisible ray of laser light struck his simulated target and bounced back instantaneously, and he read the red digital readout superimposed, in standard metric units, in the upper right hand corner of the image.

Two hundred ninety meters.

He re-shouldered his Alex-338 sniper rifle. Fitted with a Schmidt & Bender PM II telescopic sight, it was Pularchek's weapon of choice. He had outfitted his whole team as well as Skyler with the high-performance Polish sniper rifle. He quickly re-computed the elevation angle, bullet drop, and bore angle correction with his pre-programmed smartphone calculator plugged into his range-finder. There was no breeze, so fortunately he wouldn't have to correct laterally for windage. With his field computations complete, he adjusted the gun sight up by 3 feet in order to compensate for the bullet drop over its flight path to the kill zone.

As if on cue, the two soft targets appeared at the door along with their retinue of protectors. Peering at the bland, unremarkable faces of the twins Wilhelm and

Friedrich Shottenbruner, Pularchek was reminded of political theorist Hannah Arendt's widely misinterpreted catchphrase "the banality of evil" used to describe SS mass murderer Adolf Eichmann. With their blandly ordinary faces, pencil-thin mustaches, wire-rimmed spectacles, and diminutive frames encased by black hipster outfits and ties, the pair of Shottenbruners looked like a pair of über-rich, metrosexual, Euro dotcom multimillionaire clones out enjoying Berlin's debauched nightlife. But what the two lookalikes happened to be was far more interesting.

They were the biological grandsons of SS Lieutenant General Franz Shottenbruner, Commander of the Security Police in Poland and the Netherlands, a man directly connected with the Holocaust in two countries and implicated in the murder of more than 250,000 Jews. By testifying at the Nuremberg trials and cooperating with the U.S. Office of Strategic Services and Army to ferret out remaining Nazi agents, the Shottenbruners' grandfather had been fortunate enough to escape prosecution for war crimes and set himself up nicely in postwar Austria, peddling intelligence to various spy agencies, including the Soviet Union. More importantly, his respectable cover allowed him to live in comfort from plundered Jewish assets, which after his death fifteen years earlier he had left to his remaining heirs—his prodigal, carousing grandsons Wilhelm and Friedrich—both of whose net worth Pularchek had discovered was over seventy million Euros. The grandsons were indeed chips off the old block: together, they routinely gave large sums to a host of anti-Semitic causes and neo-Nazi organizations, and both were staunch Holocaust deniers. Most importantly, they were both unmarried with no wife or children: the Shottenbruner seed would be eradicated with the two young neo-fascists. And because Pularchek's team of cyber gurus had hacked into their computers and those of their lawyers and redone their wills, including forging perfect signatures, upon prodigal Wilhelm's and Friedrich's deaths all of their assets would be given to various Holocaust foundations.

The Shottenbruner twins started down the walkway leading to the limousine and taxi queue and the parking lot beyond. On their arms were the same curvaceous, flaxen-haired women with the giant breasts that had accompanied them into the Berghain. Their two private bodyguards took protective positions, one in front and one behind, after scanning the area for signs of trouble.

Watching the scene unfold, Pularchek calmly brought the stock of the rifle to his shoulder, placing the crosshairs on his soft target, Wilhelm Shottenbruner. The weapon was chambered for special hollow-point .338-caliber Lapua Magnum rimless bottlenecked centerfire cartridges and equipped with a 5-round detachable box magazine, both developed for military long-range sniping operations by the Polish Special Armed Forces. He wore ultrathin leather gloves to ensure his fingerprints would never be found on the weapon.

Peering through the Schmidt & Bender PM II telescopic sight, Pularchek held on his soft target with the icy sangfroid and collected discipline of an experienced long-range sharpshooter. His right index finger slid forward and curled around the trigger. His hands were steady, his muscles tense but precisely controlled.

After tracing Wilhelm's movements, he was confident he could take down the target without harming the women or bodyguards. Ensuring no collateral damage was a strictly observed professional code of honor for Pularchek. In the present case, the downward trajectory and use of expanding, soft-nosed hollow-point cartridges would ensure a mushrooming bullet upon impact that would maximize internal damage, limit over-penetration, and guarantee lodgment inside the target, thereby preventing collateral damage.

He took one last moment to study his target's face. The image through the scope was as sharp as a winter night.

A perfect hold: no tremble or wobble, unwavering.

A clean kill.

His nerves hardened. He regulated his heart rate to a slow, steady rhythm.

He raised the rifle a hair. Once again, he locked onto the soft target's face.

Then he drew a final, deliberate breath.

Held it.

And gently squeezed the trigger.

CHAPTER 18

BERGHAIN
FRIEDRICHSHAIN

TEN MINUTES BEFORE THE FATAL SHOTS WERE FIRED, Skyler took out her rosary and kneeled down to pray. Closing her eyes, she pressed her hands together into a steeple and brought the string of crimson beads to her lips with her fingertips. There was no need to ask forgiveness for what she was about to do; she knew that it was unforgivable, that righteousness was little more than a stepping stone to hypocrisy. Nor did she plead for a keen eye or steady hold, or pray for a clean escape. Instead, she surrendered herself unconditionally before God, in all her imperfection, and gave Him praise. She concluded her supplication by kissing the rosary again and declaring, in a soft voice, "Glory be to the Father."

Now she felt cleansed, purified, but not absolved. She knew that, as a professional assassin, she would never be absolved.

The preparations were now complete: mind, body, and rifle were ready.

Tonight would mark her nineteenth contracted kill. Yet surprisingly, even after all the killing she didn't think of herself as a murderer. She was simply an extension of her gun, a mechanical robot that pulled the trigger. The ones ultimately responsible for the killings were the powerful men who hired her, men like Stanislaw Pularchek. She wasn't the one who gave the orders; all she did was execute them, and if she didn't, someone else would. But with Pularchek, it went even deeper than that. The men that he liquidated with his own hand and that she dispatched on his behalf deserved to die for their crimes against humanity, and she knew that what they were doing was not wrong. All the same, she couldn't help but feel guilty inside.

It was at night when the self-torment overwhelmed her. When the nightmares came—and they always did—she would quake with shame. With sweat pouring from her body and teeth grinding, she would see the faces of her victims, one after another. They always came through clearly, framed in the perfect circle of her sniperscope with the crosshairs centered on the forehead. When she squeezed the trigger, the faces would explode in a spray of blood and she would gasp for air and leap up in her bed, covered in sweat.

It was strange how she always saw the faces blowing open when it was her custom to shoot for the heart. She thought it was to remind her that the people she killed were actual human beings, tangible and alive. Real people with real faces, real emotions, real lives.

The bad dreams usually came the first evening after a contract and gripped her for two or three nights. It was on those nights that she hated herself for what she did and wished she had never become an assassin. And it was on those nights that she prayed to the Holy Father—not for her own redemption, but for the souls of those she had killed.

Suddenly, her radio headset crackled to life. "The targets are on the move," she heard Romanowski, Pularchek's number two, announce to her and the rest of the team. "They're with their two bodyguards and the women they entered the club with two hours ago. They'll be in your line of sight in less than three minutes."

"I copy," she heard Pularchek say and then he issued orders to her and the others. At the end, she wished him luck in their joint operation.

"You know I don't believe in luck," he said good-naturedly to her in a final flourish. "I believe in preparation. Over and out."

She smiled as she took a knee to make her final scope adjustments. Two minutes later, the two targets appeared at the front door with their entourage next to Sven-the-Gatekeeper. She sighted her soft target, Friedrich Shottenbruner, Wilhelm's twin neo-Nazi brother, through the scope. His head looked like a ripe cantaloupe ready to be pulverized into oblivion. She gritted her teeth; it was easy to hate him and his brother for who they were and what they and their grandfather had done. The heavy black lines of the duplex reticle converged from all sides of her circular field of view. The thick lines pointed to a thinner crosshair centered on Friedrich, who came through so clearly, Skyler could see his lips moving, his gray-blond forelocks riffling in the breeze.

She lifted the rifle until the crosshairs were centered on his face. All reservations were pushed aside, leaving her with perfect concentration. There was not the slightest tremor in her grip, only supreme confidence.

She took a moment to study the lines and curves of her soft target's face. The image through the scope was clear, unwavering. The plan was for Pularchek to shoot Wilhelm first, and she would quickly follow up by taking out his twin brother Friedrich before he could take cover.

Her nerves hardened and her breaths came in a steady rhythm as she awaited Pularchek's opening salvo.

She raised the rifle a hair and the third-mil dot locked onto the soft target's face.

The perfect hold: no anger, no guilt, no doubt, no fear. Killing the evil descendants of a Nazi mass murderer was as easy as shooting rats.

The mil-dot became one with the target as she entered her own private world, the sniper's cocoon.

The field of fire turned noiseless. No one and nothing moved.

And then she saw Pularchek's bullet strike. There was only the tiniest puff of smoke, followed by a wet pink cloud of spurting blood, brain-matter, and bone as Holocaust profiteer Wilhelm Shottenbruner's head was literally pulped by the hollow-point .338-caliber Lapua Magnum bullet. The body was driven back, the arms flung out helplessly, like someone being thrown off a cliff, and the victim collapsed to the pavement. It was a gruesome sight that would be indelibly etched into her mind for as long as she lived. But there was no time now for emotion.

Her gloved right index finger curled softly around the trigger. All her resolve, all her professionalism, all her energy, would go into her own shot.

"Bless me Father, for I am about to sin once again," she murmured in her native Italian tongue.

And then she squeezed her own trigger.

She saw Friedrich Schottenbruner's body twitch once and his arms fly out helplessly, as if he were groping through the darkness. The blood from the two shots sprayed over the two slinky blonde women and the bodyguards standing nearby, like crimson paint spattered across an empty white canvas. And then the two brothers were both down on the ground, dead.

She heard a collective shriek of horror and saw people recoiling from the scene in panic, running in every direction, staggering, colliding, the pandemonium spreading like a contagion as it moved through the frenzied crowd in front of the historic nightclub.

And then, as the scene turned to total chaos, Skyler—alias Diego Gomez— slipped quietly into the night along with Stanislaw Pularchek and his band of avenging angels.

CHAPTER 19

HOLOCAUST MEMORIAL
CENTRAL BERLIN

FROM THE EASTERN EDGE of the Tiergarten, Angela Wolff looked out wearily at the Memorial to the Murdered Jews of Europe. She and her team had spent the past four hours crisscrossing the city with the surveillance vans, following up on lead after lead about Pularchek's whereabouts, but they still had not pin-pointed his position. The city's CCTV cameras had ID'd his vehicle convoy—cleverly brandishing Austrian diplomatic flags and plates—at multiple locations east of the meandering Spree. But each time they had followed up, there had been no sign of the elusive Pole or his team. Growing tired and frustrated, Wolff had called a break for the team to replenish itself with some much-needed sandwiches and coffee from the Starbucks at Pariser Platz.

Now, while waiting for developments, they sat quietly munching their turkey rustic paninis and sipping their vanilla white mocha frappuccinos on a line of park benches looking across the Ebertstrasse. The brightly-illuminated white marble columns of the Brandenburg Gates to the north contrasted sharply with the stark Holocaust Memorial to the south. The memorial consisted of more than two thousand drab-gray, rectangular boxes of varying sizes, arranged like coffins in a grid pattern. The *stelae* were designed to produce a discomfiting yet strangely orderly atmosphere, with the overall configuration of the coffin-like boxes meant to represent the systematic extermination of six million Jews. Whether one was a supporter or detractor of Architect Peter Eisenman's memorial, there was no denying its raw power. The memorial brought to mind a vast field of nameless tombstones, capturing the anonymous horror of the Nazi death camps.

Angela Wolff hated the memorial. She was sick and tired of hearing about Germany's Nazi past, sick and tired of feeling guilty for the deeds of her ancestors. It wasn't her fault that six million Jews had been murdered, along with millions of others guilty of nothing more than being communists, gypsies, cripples, homosexuals, or Poles. What Hitler and his henchmen had done was a horrendous thing, and she sympathized deeply with the plight of the Jewish people and all the others who had been sacrificed for the Führer's demented Thousand Year Reich. But it wasn't her generation's problem. It was time for Germany to stop feeling guilty, to stop tormenting itself by reliving, over and over, its evil past. The country of Frederick the Great, Goethe, Kant, Bach, and Mozart was a world leader and Europe's greatest economic powerhouse, and nothing good could come from constantly agonizing over its role in the Holocaust.

By the same logic, there was no reason for her to feel guilty about accepting the merchandise her grandfather had bequeathed her, once she recovered it from Pularchek, of course. Why should she not accept what rightfully belonged to her? After all, her flawed but ultimately heroic ancestor had honorably earned the *Schatzfund* by securing peace in Italy with the Americans at the end of the Second World War, an extraordinary feat. *Obergruppenführer* Karl Wolff had, in fact, detested Hitler and Himmler both, and he had risked life and limb to sign an armistice surrendering all forces along the southern front with American spymaster Allen Dulles in Switzerland. Did he not deserve something for his monumental efforts? If he was so bad, why had the Allies protected him and refused to try him at the Nuremberg War Crimes Trials like Göring, Hess, von Ribbentrop, and all the other Nazi mass murderers? And as a German intelligence officer who had for seventeen years made her country safe from its foreign enemies, didn't she too deserve just compensation? The treasure trove stolen by that bastard Pularchek was not only hers by birthright, it had been *earned* based upon years of devotion to the Fatherland by both herself *and* her grandfather.

She pictured the man: tall, blond, blue-eyed with a strong chin, long blade of a nose, and the regal bearing of the elite of his day. All in all, an exquisite specimen of Aryan perfection before the term had been twisted by Hitler into something monstrous. With his closeness to the Führer and longstanding service to SS headman Himmler, her grandfather had been a deeply flawed man, true, but he had still risked his life on multiple occasions to effect an early surrender agreement in Italy, saving countless military and civilian lives on both sides. And despite being third only to Himmler and Kaltenbrunner within the SS hierarchy, he had never authorized the killing of a single Jew. Most tellingly of all and to his eternal credit, he had not even been indicted at Nuremberg and was on record, from credible sources, as having been revolted by Eichmann and the other Nazi "desk murderers." Based on available records and by his own design during his tenure in Italy, he had only been peripherally involved in "the solution of the Jewish problem," choosing to distance himself from the vilest designs of the Third Reich. Nonetheless, his legacy was still a tainted one. During the war, the SS troops under his command had committed beastly atrocities against Italian partisans and he had been the senior Nazi officer ultimately in charge of transporting by rail 300,000 Jews to labor and death camps, including Treblinka.

When she looked in a mirror, she saw a feminine version of her grandfather, who hadn't passed away until 1984 when she was nine and with whom she had spent considerable time growing up. *Like him you are both noble and despicable,* she often thought when she was alone and feeling vulnerable. *Blut ist dicker als wasser.* Blood is thicker than water.

Her musings were interrupted by the opening of the nearest van door. "We've spotted Pularchek!" cried Johannes Krupp.

Wolff tossed her half-eaten sandwich into the bushes and jumped to her feet. "Where?"

"He's headed west on the Französische Strasse. We can cut him off."

"Do we have time to set up a roadblock?"

"Yes, at Franz Strasse and Ebertstrasse—if we can get into position in the next five minutes."

This is our chance! "Quickly to the cars!"

"Wait, that's not all. Just before we picked him up on the CCTV camera, someone reported a shooting outside the Berghain."

"Who was the target?"

"We don't know, but apparently there are two men down. The police are headed to the nightclub."

Looking at Dieter, she motioned the team back to the cars and vans. "All right, let's go!"

They dashed for the vehicles. "There's one more thing," said Krupp, running alongside her and Dieter Franck. "Pularchek's convoy now has German diplomatic markings and a German police escort."

"What the hell?" cried Dieter. "They can't be real police."

"I wouldn't be so sure about that."

It would be just like the clever Pole to pull a trick like this, thought Wolff. "Are you positive it's him and not someone else?"

"Yes, I'm sure. We were able to match the two drivers from before. They must have hidden out somewhere and made a switch after they crossed the river. That's where we lost all sign of them."

Wolff called a halt in front of the vehicles. "All right, this is our opportunity, people. We're going to set up a blockade at the intersection of Franz Strasse and Ebertstrasse." She pointed up the street. "Now we won't get a second chance, so we have to, I repeat have to, take him now. I know I don't need to remind you again that this is our op and we do this alone. We can't have any police involved in the arrest, so we're going to have to force the vehicles to stop, seize control of Pularchek and his team, and take them into custody by ourselves. Alive. We need Pularchek alive. That means if I authorize us to open fire to slow them down or take them, we target tires, drivers, and their shooters only—and definitely not Pularchek. If they have bullet-proof glass, fire for effect, but try and take out their tires first. Dieter and I will set up the blockade with Red Team. Arne, you take Blue Team, drive slowly east on Franz Strasse, and swing in from behind to trap them just before they reach the intersection."

"Got it!"

She looked at the determined faces, all male. "Any questions?"

There were none.

"All right, let's move!"

CHAPTER 20

TIERGARTEN

"I DON'T THINK THIS IS A GOOD IDEA, BOSS. I think we should have skirted north of the city and avoided downtown Berlin like the plague."

Pularchek gave a thoughtful smile as his black, six-seat Mercedes-Benz S-Class Pullman limousine darted in and out of traffic along the four-lane Französische Strasse. "Yes, well, I want to pay my respects to my dead ancestors."

"You can visit the Holocaust Memorial any time, and right now is not one of those times."

"The police will not be looking for us in the heart of the city. This is part of the escape plan, remember?"

"It's your escape plan, Boss. I never approved it. Seriously, you take too many risks, and right now I have a bad feeling about this. As your chief of security, it is my official duty to tell you that."

"You worry too much, Counselor. Though I know worrying is part of your job description."

Suddenly, their radio headsets crackled.

"Komandor, we've got trouble up ahead!" came the voice of Jerzy Gagor. He was the driver of one of the two green-and-white German police cars out front, though Gagor was neither German nor a policeman. Taking up the rear and second-to-last position of the now five-vehicle convoy, with the addition of the two new German green and whites as part of their cover, was Skyler in her silver BMW and the surveillance van.

"On the contrary, there's no trouble," pronounced Pularchek calmly into his radio headset, having rolled down the driver's side window and stuck his head out to assess the situation firsthand. Up ahead he saw a fleet of sleek, black Mercedes S-Model wagons and vans arranged in a quickly improvised road block. "Take a right at the memorial, and then drive parallel to the Ebertstrasse to the east of the trees along the avenue. There's no reason to stop for one measly German patrol."

"This is going to get hot, you know that, Boss."

"I thought you told me that gunfights and car chases only happen in the movies."

"That was before you picked the return route. This one is on you, Boss."

"Looks like I'll just have to get us out of this then."

"Don't worry, you've got me as a guardian angel," said Skyler over her headset.

"You don't know how encouraging it is to know that, my friend."

One hundred feet before the roadblock, one of Pularchek's police cars out front veered hard right up onto the curb, and then shot north along a sidewalk that ran parallel with the Ebertstrasse and the trees lining the avenue. The bullet-proof limo, van, and Skyler in her BMW followed suit along with the second police car pulling back and taking up the rear. At the memorial, the four vehicles swung hard to the right and followed closely behind the lead police car.

At Behrenstrasse, the convoy quickly turned onto the Ebertstrasse, heading north with the Brandenburg Gate on the right. The 18th century neoclassical triumphal arch, one of the most well-known landmarks in all of Germany, was lit up with bright lights, somehow lending an air of historical significance to the current contest of Poles versus Germans.

"All right, as expected they're following in pursuit," said Pularchek, peering out the rear window as the limo bounded down the street, feeling a little rush at the thrill of the chase.

"Like a swarm of locusts," said the Counselor, who, like his boss, had a fondness for biblical references when it came to espionage activities.

"Do you think we can make it to the airfield?"

"We'd damn well better. Otherwise, I'll never listen again to one of your crazy ideas."

"For what it's worth, Counselor, I'm sorry. I shouldn't have insisted on coming this way."

"They must have been listening in and picked up a signal from your mobile. Turn it off."

"It's supposed to be a secure, encrypted phone."

"Not anymore. Turn it off!"

"*Tak, oczywiscie.*" He immediately did as requested.

The convoy tore through a red light and continued racing north on the Ebertstrasse, skirting the eastern fringe of the park. The convoy then took a hard left at Schneidemannstrasse, the five vehicles screeching and burning rubber as they entered the Tiergarten. Passing the Reichstag Building on the right, they scattered a group of pedestrians that had started to cross at the crosswalk.

"Be careful, damnit!" Pularchek yelled into his radio headset. "There can be no collateral damage, and that's an order!"

"Don't worry, Komandor, we know the drill," shouted Gagor in the police car up ahead, his voice nearly drowned out by the roaring engines. "But do we have permission to shoot these bastards?"

"Only if they shoot at us fir—"

His voice was cut off by a thunderous explosion of gunfire, coming from behind them. Looking out the rear window, he saw several men in suits firing semiautomatic weapons from the windows of the four Mercedes-Benz wagons following in pursuit. *So much for no gunfights or car chases,* he thought. He saw another flash of gunfire, heard the echoing staccato. The Germans were aiming low: they were apparently trying to shoot out the limo's tires.

But their bullets would have no effect. The tires on all of his Operations-Security Detail's vehicles were self-inflating and could not go flat. When a tire was punctured, an internal pressure regulator opened to allow air to flow into a pumping tube, and as the wheel turned, the flattened part helped squeeze air from the tube through an inlet valve into the tire. Once the air pressure reached an optimal level, the regulator closed and the tire was fully inflated. The last thing Pularchek wanted was his team's tires deflating and escape vehicles put out of action in enemy territory.

"All right, let them have it," he said. "But first, has anyone ID'd them yet?"

"They're not cops, that's for sure," said the Counselor. "I'm thinking BfV."

"Domestic intelligence? I don't think so. I smell Angela Wolff. But if that's the case, how did the BND manage to find out we were here from a secure mobile intercept?"

"I don't know, but they're listening in somehow. I have to give the bastards credit."

Another round of gunfire cut through the air, mingling with the roar of the revving engines. This time a spray of bullets ricocheted off the armored glass as well as the lower part of the limo near the tires. The pursuing vehicles were taking up two lanes and coming up fast, as his team returned fire from the van and rear police car and Skyler opened up from the driver's side window of her BMW.

"Please speed it up, Janu," he said calmly to his driver, Janusz Skrzypek. "These bastards mean business."

Suddenly, they were rammed from behind by one of the Mercedes that had managed to squeeze in between the limo and the van.

Pularchek felt his neck whiplash violently forward and saw Romanowski thrown hard to the floor of the limousine. Janu accelerated away from their pursuers, but within a matter of seconds, the fleet Mercedes wagon again rammed them from behind. Then it began to flank them on the passenger side as they struck west onto John-Foster-Dulles-Allee, deep within the Tiergarten. Like Central Park in New York and Hyde Park in London, the Tiergarten was the oldest and largest park in Berlin, an oasis of green in the big, bustling city.

But right now, it was a Polish vs. German battlefield in the heart of Berlin, where the Third Reich had once ruled all of Europe.

Now Pularchek could see his adversaries up close and he knew for certain they were BND. Several armed men in suits were leaning out the windows of the vehicles, and he recognized one of them as Dieter Franck, Angela Wolff's top deputy at the German foreign intelligence agency. He had a complete dossier on the man and knew that Franck and Wolff were secret lovers, carefully concealing their relationship from not only their coworkers at the agency, but their friends and family. With no sign of Wolff in the car with Franck, he wondered if she was in another vehicle, or perhaps not among the enemy.

With the wind flapping the collar of his suit jacket, Franck gritted his teeth and fired his pistol. The bullets were deflected harmlessly astray by the bullet-proof windows of the limousine. The tinted windows shielded Pularchek from view from his adversary, but the Pole could see Franck. His face showed frantic desperation. No doubt he was in on his boss Angela Wolff's plan to recover the inherited fortune she believed she was due. The magnitude of the stakes showed on his determined face.

Here was a desperate man willing to take extreme risks to get Wolff back her *Schatzfund*. If her lover was this desperate to recover the stolen property, he thought, how desperate must Wolff herself be right now? Again, he wondered where she was at this moment. Was she in the car with Franck, or back at headquarters impatiently waiting for him to take care of the job?

The Mercedes wagon again swung towards them like a Tiger tank. Gripping the wheel tightly, Janu swerved hard to the right to avoid the impact, but it wasn't enough as the wagon struck the limo a hard blow. The air was filled with the sound of scraping metal as the two vehicles ground into one another.

"Go into the park! It's the only way we're going to be able to lose them!" shouted Pularchek, as Franck and his cohort shooting from the rear passenger side window unloaded another clip, this time striking the limo's tires, which instantly re-inflated after initially losing air pressure.

Janu cut hard left and knifed into a gap in the thick forest of the Tiergarten. The rest of the team followed his lead, both police cars and the van dashing into the open clearing. The terrain was uneven and the limousine bounced across the grass-covered landscape, its powerful engine gunning.

Their pursuers were only momentarily fooled. They quickly regrouped, darted through a stand of giant oak and beech trees, and came upon them once again, this time from the right.

Now, through the Mercedes wagon's open window, Pularchek saw Angela Wolff in the back seat along with Dieter Franck, who began to open fire with his semiauto along with the BND operative in the front passenger seat.

"Screw this—I'm fighting back!" cried Pularchek.

He rolled down the rear automatic window and opened fire with his Glock 9mm. Romanowski did the same in the seat in front of him. Both sides were delivering a blistering fire now from multiple vehicles.

The chase had escalated into a full-fledged, roving gun battle. He saw one of the enemy take a round in the shoulder and fall back into his vehicle. He saw glass explode from one of the Mercedes, which didn't have armored windows like his fleet of vehicles. He saw Angela Wolff recognize him firing from the window and scowl at him. He saw one of the Mercedes crash into a rhododendron tree. And then suddenly, Janu managed to navigate the limo back onto a road again—this time the Strasse des 17 Juni—and they were driving straight towards the Victory Column, actually pulling away from their enemies.

Until they came upon a traffic jam in the road.

Switching lanes and driving straight into the incoming traffic, they were forced to zigzag dangerously through the myriad cars going in both directions. Weaving through the heavy traffic, they nearly bowled over a pair of late night lovers out for a stroll. The young man and woman barely managed to dive out of the way at the crossing in front of the *Siegessäule*, a towering statue of a golden-hued goddess, and then Janu had to break hard and dart right to avoid a collision with two older couples. After taking the roundabout around the brightly-illuminated Victory Column, they continued west on the Strasse des 17 Juni. As the traffic thinned, the convoy quickly closed ranks and returned to its standard defensive formation with one police car out front, the limo and van behind, and the second police vehicle and Skyler taking up the rear, forming a protective rear guard.

"Was anybody hit back there?" he asked the team through his radio headset.

"I got nicked in the arm," said Andrzej Kremer. "But I'll be fine. I took out one of them, so I gave as good as I got."

"That's good to hear. But unfortunately, it looks like we're not going to be able to shake them. I believe it's time for the countermeasures."

"It's about time," said Skyler from her silver BMW. "I was beginning to think you'd lost your nerve."

"Me—never! Obviously, Angela Wolff and her rogue BND unit don't want the police involved in this op of theirs. They are acting on their own and are all alone out here, so we're not going to have a better chance than right now. Skyler, pull back a hair so that your vehicle is alone in the rear position. The countermeasures should cut a wide berth, so that Wolff and her cohorts are put out of immediate action and cease all pursuit. Gagor, you'll maintain the lead of the convoy. All right, good luck."

"I thought you didn't believe in luck," said Skyler.

"I don't, but I still like to say it. Good luck!"

"Hold on, everyone!" then said the beautiful and dangerous Italian assassin through her radio headset. "This is going to be quite a scene!"

CHAPTER 21

TIERGARTEN

IN THE LEAD OF THE PURSUING PACK, Angela Wolff would always remember the moment *just before* it happened. She knew something was up when she saw the silver BMW slow down and take up a position directly behind the fake police car it had been driving beside only the moment before. She knew her team was in serious trouble when the BMW began to weave into all four westbound lanes at the same time that a rear panel opened up and disgorged hundreds of shiny, spiked metal objects.

"Watch out! Stay right!" she screamed to her driver.

But it was too late as the first wave of caltrops instantly punctured the front and rear tires of her Mercedes-Benz. The spiked weapon had first been used by the Roman army in the time of the Caesars to slow the advance of footsoldiers and cavalry mounted on horses, camels, and war elephants—caltrops were noted to be particularly effective against the soft feet of camels—but in modern times, its primary function was to deflate the pneumatic tires of fast-driving wheeled vehicles.

To her horror, Wolff saw instantly that there was no way for the rest of her team to avoid the four-pointed contrivances; there were too many of them and they were spread all over the four driving lanes and the break-down lane as well. Looking in her side-view mirror, she saw that the tires on all four of the remaining vehicles had been deflated and instantly shredded. The two vans had been ravaged so badly that they were spinning out of control on the metal rims.

This was a disaster!

But then things went from bad to worse.

Her driver slammed his feet down hard on the brakes, struggling to control the Mercedes as the mangled tire completely detached from the rim. Suddenly, they were rammed from behind by the two vans, which had collided, locked up, and somehow managed to couple together to form a single massive vehicle. Wolff's Mercedes wagon was knocked out of the way, as if by a freight train.

The vans detached for a breathless instant. But their momentum was too great. They veered hard to the right towards a large brown UPS Deutschland truck that had parked along the roadside, where the driver was changing out a flat. Wolff felt the impact propagate through her entire body as the pair of vans collided with the UPS truck, the one to the left driven by senior operative Arne Bauer exploding on contact.

"*Nein! Nein!*" she yelled as a hubcap went sailing across the front windshield of her Mercedes like a flying saucer.

Instinctively flinching, her driver swung the wheel hard to the left to avoid the impact, but at that precise instant the vehicle struck another pocket of caltrops. The vehicle gave a convulsive shudder, banked even harder to the left, and then, as her driver overcorrected, it fishtailed to the right, leapt the curb, and closed in on a large oak tree at the edge of the thick Tiergarten woods. Still fighting mightily to control the vehicle, the driver merely sideswiped the tree. But the force of the blow was enough for the Mercedes to career hard left, smash into another tree, roll over once, miraculously right itself, and come to rest in the shadow of a third tree.

With the front and rear airbags turned off, Wolff and everyone else in the vehicle felt the full brunt of the crash. Then everything went terribly still as the Mercedes lay crippled along the side of the road, no longer part of the chase.

After a moment, she heard Dieter's voice.

"Are you all right?" he asked, and she felt his warm hand take hers, a reassuring presence.

Wolff quickly checked to see if she was hurt. No blood, but her right wrist was numb from slamming against the car door. "I'm fine, I think." She gently touched his hand. "How about you?"

"I'll live," he said.

"I love you, Dieter," she said, softly touching his cheek with her fingers. "Thank God you're all right. I don't know what I'd do if I lost you."

He nodded and gave her a hug of affection and relief that she was okay. When they pulled apart, she looked up front at the others. Both the driver and armed operative in the driver's seat were unconscious, but breathing. She glanced in her rearview mirror to see what had happened to the rest of her team.

She couldn't believe her eyes: Arne Bauer and the others in his van were trapped inside the vehicle with roiling flames coming up through the engine block!

Mein Gott, she thought in horror, *they are being roasted alive!*

"Quick, we have to help them," said Dieter, echoing her thoughts. He helped extricate her from her seat belt and they jumped from the car.

It took them a moment to get their bearings. On the road, the caltrops had caused a dangerous chain reaction and thrown everything into disarray. Beyond the burning van, dozens of cars had collided and created a pileup in all four driving lanes as well as the break-down lane. The wreckage was so bad that the traffic along the entire westbound portion of the Strasse des 17 Juni was backed up. The hundreds of four-pointed nails had snared some twenty vehicles, ripping the tires of several cars to shreds and causing drivers to abruptly halt, which in turn led to pileups and complete gridlock.

They moved quickly to the burning van. It was crumpled like an accordion, the front and rear windshields were shattered, and a flaming inferno raged inside the vehicle. She saw at once that at least four people were trapped inside the van. Not one of them was moving.

"What should we do?" she asked Dieter.

"I don't know that there's anything we can do," he said. "They look to be dead."

"But we have to do something. We can't just let them burn."

Taking off his jacket, he used it to protect his hand while trying to open the van's door handle. "Damn, that's hot!" he cried, jumping back.

She shook her head worriedly. "This is a disaster, Dieter. And it's all my fault."

"I'm not going to disagree with you," he said, and she felt the familiar hurt of his disapproval.

He made another attempt to open the door using his jacket to keep his hand from burning, but again the door handle was too hot.

She stepped forward, reached out, and touched him on the cheek. "I love you, Dieter. I am sorry this has happened, but you must understand that I am doing all this for us."

He said nothing, and again she felt the sting of his disapproval. She took off her own jacket and started forward to try and pry open the door herself. But he took her by the arm, forcibly, and held her back.

"You don't need to do this. They're all dead and there's nothing more that can be done."

"I just want you to know how much I love you. And I don't want all hope to be lost."

"Are you talking about us or them?"

"Both."

He reached out and gently touched her hand. "I know what you're trying to say, Angela," he said with the faintest trace of suppressed anger. "But there has to be a better way than this."

He nodded his head towards the inferno. The unfortunate crash victims in the front seat were tilted forward with their heads resting on the dashboard, as if peacefully sleeping while the flames roared and crackled all around them.

"I'm sorry," she said. "I'm sorry for everything."

"So am I."

Smelling a pungent waft of gasoline, she saw Johannes Krupp and others coming on the scene. He came running up to them waving his arms. He had a huge gash on his head and was bleeding.

"What the hell are you still doing here?" he shouted at them. "She's going to blow any second!"

He pointed to a stream of gasoline leaking from the ruptured gasoline tank. All of a sudden, a little burst of flame leapt up from the little river in a burst of blue and orange, taking her by surprise. *My God, he's right,* she thought, as she felt her arm grabbed suddenly by Dieter.

"Everyone out of here, now!" he cried, as the fire quickly surged laterally towards the van's ruptured fuel tank.

They couldn't run towards the roadway, which was total chaos, so they made a mad dash for the trees.

They only made it halfway.

There was a tremendous explosion, a fiery flash of yellow that hurt Wolff's eyes, followed by an eruption of noxious black smoke and a wave of searing airborne heat. A second explosion rocked the Tiergarten as the UPS truck, too, became engulfed in flames. Both vehicles quickly disappeared behind expanding plumes of fire, in front of a disaster-film-like background of piled-up cars. Hunks of molten metal, glass, and rubber blasted in all directions, whizzing past Wolff's ears like flak. She and Dieter covered their heads as glass and dangerously sharp shards of metal shot past them. Luckily, they were far enough away to avoid the heaviest chunks and were low enough to the ground to avoid the flying metal. But it was as if they were under heavy enemy fire back in the Second World War during the Battle of the Bulge.

When the worst was over, they stared out at the wreckage. Flames poured from the confused jumble of charred metal and rubber on the ground, rumbling like a storm. Thick black smoke billowed up from the flames. By now a stupefied crowd of people had stepped from their cars and gathered along the perimeter to gaze upon the blaze in awed silence.

"Pularchek's going to pay for this," snarled Angela Wolff with tears in her eyes, staring at the roiling flames with the Victory Column as an incongruous backdrop. "If it's the last thing I do on this earth, I swear I'm going to kill that Polish bastard."

CHAPTER 22

CIA HEADQUARTERS
LANGLEY, VIRGINIA

"IT APPEARS THAT both the president and CIA Director Brennan like your crazy idea. But I'd be lying to you if I said I share their enthusiasm."

Nick Lassiter stared into the fierce gaze of NCS Director Richard Voorheiss, top dog of the operational arm of the world's fourth most proficient spook agency—after the Israeli, British, and Russian intelligence services. Once that intimidating task was finished, he looked appraisingly at his father, seated to his right next to his wife Natalie, and received a nod of approval before looking back at Voorheiss. The second floor conference room remained silent and smelled of an unusual mixture of freshly laid carpeting, stale Starbuck's coffee, recently eaten Cantonese food, and astringent cleaning fluids.

Lassiter calmly folded his hands in his lap. "Could you please just brief us on exactly what you'd like us to do, Mr. Director? Because we're going to Poland, whether you or anyone else likes it or not."

Out of the corner of his eye, he saw a hint of a subversive smile on Natalie's face. In that instant, he was damned glad he had married such an adventurous, intelligent, supportive, and, when the occasion called for it, mischievous woman.

Voorheiss snorted condescendingly, "My, my, you certainly are a chip off the old block."

"Yes," agreed his father Benjamin Brewbaker. "But the question is *which* block?"

Lassiter suppressed a grin. He hadn't meant to be flippant; he was hungry and tired and it had just come out that way. But he meant what he had said: he and Natalie were going to Poland whether the CIA, his parents, or anyone else wanted him to or not. He had spent the morning talking it over with his wife and parents; and, over the past six hours he, his father, and Natalie had been in and out of meetings here at Langley to go over the events of last night and this morning's phone conversation with his biological father. He and his wife had read Pularchek's dossier over twice, and although it contained some graphic details that had horrified them, they had still reached a decision to accept his all-expenses-paid invitation to visit him in Warsaw. Having made their decision, they wanted to get the agency details over with, for it was clear that the CIA would have to have some level of involvement. Having gotten little sleep last night, they were physically exhausted and in no mood to drag out their stay here at Langley any longer than necessary.

"If you would please, Mr. Director, can you tell us what the CIA wants us to do in Warsaw. My father's already explained that if we go through with this, we'd be operating off the books, so to speak. That way the agency has complete deniability and no involvement if something goes wrong. My wife and I are fine with that."

"Very well," said Voorheiss. "Since I can't talk you two out of this, I suppose I shall turn the briefing over to your father. He will be running this operation and acting as your control officer in the field. I might add that decision was not mine, either."

"I believe we're all clear on where you stand, Mr. Director," said Benjamin Brewbaker. "But I think before we get into the details, I should make it clear to Nick and Natalie exactly where *I* stand as well." His eyes narrowed on them. "For the record, I have always been and still am vehemently opposed to you two going to Poland when you are supposed to be in Bermuda on your honeymoon. In my estimation, the Bay of Pigs is what you get when you insert ordinary civilians into clandestine operations in foreign countries. And that little fiasco down in Cuba cost Allen Dulles—the greatest director this agency has ever known—his job. But since you two stubbornly insist on going through with this fiasco-in-waiting, not to mention security nightmare, I have made it clear to CIA Director Brennan and NCS Director Voorheiss here that you are absolutely, one-hundred-per-cent not going unless I'm running you both.

"So here's the deal. The director here will be holding me on a short leash, and in turn, I will be running you two on an *extremely* short leash. You will be bugged, equipped with undetectable micro-cameras, and under constant electronic and visual surveillance. More importantly, you will do exactly as I say at all times—or I'm sending you back stateside on the first available flight with no questions asked. Do you understand me?"

Lassiter looked at his wife, who nodded. "Yes," he said. "We copy you loud and clear. You're in charge."

"You are not James Bond, Natalie is not Pussy Galore, and this is not a joke. This man—you're, ah, birth father—is a world-class marksman and professional assassin. He is to be regarded as extremely dangerous at all times. Our contacts in Germany have just informed us that last night Pularchek struck again outside a Berlin nightclub. I don't know what his game is, but he is up to something. According to our voice analysis unit, we have no reason to believe that his invitation to you to come to Poland isn't genuine and that he has any reason to threaten either of you. But don't think for one second that you don't have to be extremely careful at all times in the presence of this man. Now do you copy *that* loud and clear?"

Lassiter had rarely seen his father so intense. He wondered if his dad didn't want him and Natalie to go because he was worried about their safety, or because he was upset that his son would be spending time with his biological father and might actually end up liking him.

"So here is what we want from you," his father continued in that stern, patriarchal tone Lassiter usually only heard when he was in trouble. "You are to be flies on the wall and nothing more. Don't forget, Pularchek may not be doing all this out of the goodness of his heart, but rather to lure you in and use you as an asset so he can acquire information."

"What kind of information?" asked Natalie.

"He may be trying to use you and Nick to get intelligence that might be embarrassing to the CIA: deals we've made with the Russians, the Arab world, the Germans, and other EU countries to secure information of our own in the global war on terror. Sometimes we have to partner up with, or look the other way from, some unsavory individuals or governments. He may not like that, or he may want to take advantage of it somehow. He obviously struck in our nation's capital and Berlin for a reason, and we want to know what that reason is. We believe he may be trying to send a message."

"For what reason?" asked Lassiter.

"We don't know. That's what the director of the CIA and president of the United States want you to try and find out."

"I don't see why Pularchek would think Natalie or I have information. We know very little about what goes on here at Langley."

"But Pularchek doesn't know that. For all we know, he may think you two are working for us here at the CIA as private contractors. The whole world knows what happened last summer in New York, Nick. And now you're a bestselling author. He may think that, like other celebrities, you have access to the intelligence community—like Tom Clancy did before he died or like Skunk Baxter, formerly of Steely Dan and the Doobie Brothers. Or, based on last summer, he may think he can plug into me through you. Maybe once he found out who you were, he decided to try to open a channel into the American intelligence community. After all, you two did help take down the biggest Russian mafia network in New York and one of the biggest money laundering operations on the East Coast. That may be worth something to Pularchek."

"Honestly, I think he just wants to get to know me, Dad. You know, he *is* my father too."

Benjamin Brewbaker showed no visible reaction. But as soon as the words left Lassiter's mouth, he wished he could take them back. He knew that he had unintentionally hurt his father's feelings.

"You'll be given information on a need-to-know basis," his father continued. "That's what will keep you safe and ensure that the operation isn't blown. You are non-official cover assets acting under my orders, and you will brief me nightly. This is not going to be a picnic or a stroll through the park."

Now Voorheiss cleared his throat to speak. "Remember, Pularchek has a home-grown intelligence network in place. Our sources tell us that even though it's small, it's as good as the Mossad or the Polish intelligence service. The latter happens to turn a blind eye to his work as long as he doesn't get in their way or embarrass them. He goes wherever he pleases and does all of their off-the-books work for them, while continuing to mete out his own brand of frontier justice."

"Hang 'em high. That appears to be his motto," echoed his father. "Or rather, shoot them down from long-distance."

Voorheiss nodded. "His network consists primarily of former operatives from the Polish and Israeli intelligence services, including their special forces. They are highly unorthodox, but extremely well trained, and they will be lurking in the shadows wherever and whenever you are in his presence. They'll be the ones with the hands-free mobile phones doubling as secure radios attached to their ears. Like us here at Langley, he has field operatives and office analysts. The latter are breaking down every email, phone call, and financial transaction from Riyadh to Tokyo as we speak. I hate to admit it, but they're better at what we do than even we are."

"Pularchek pays extremely well and has a first-rate benefits program," said his father. "That's how he's able to recruit the best of the best. And you should know that these men and women he hires for his special operations team are true believers in every sense of the word. I don't want to use the word 'fanatic.' But they are no less dedicated to fighting terrorism than the jihadis they go up against are to killing the infidel and destroying the West."

Natalie was looking at Voorheiss. "I'm wondering why you want Pularchek so badly? His methods may be unorthodox, but it seems to me that his interests coincide with those of the United States."

"We don't want to take him into custody," said the director. "We just want to know more about him, and we want to make sure he stays more or less friendly and doesn't jeopardize our overseas assets. The man is too much of a loose cannon to be trusted, or to form an alliance with. He does whatever he pleases anywhere around the globe, even in the Middle East. But you are correct when you say that his interests coincide with ours. Our primary concern at the moment is to figure out how he does what he does. As the president said, and I quote, 'This man is an extremely valuable intelligence source. We need to know everything about him.' Well, Nick and Natalie, apparently you two are our chance to do just that."

"What are the main things you're missing from his profile?" asked Lassiter.

"The top priority is to find out how he can be at two places at once," said his father. "And number two is to find out where he gets his human intelligence from, because this guy is as well-briefed as WikiLeaks. But while you're trying to get information about him, you have to constantly keep in mind that the man is dangerous and not to be trusted."

"You have to remember that you will have the real Polish intelligence service keeping an eye on you as well," said Voorheiss. "Poland is one of our country's most important allies, second only to our British friends. The country is our most important buffer to counter the hard liners in Russia. So your trip is, in another sense, a diplomatic visit. That's why the president himself has taken an interest in this case."

"Great, no pressure there," said Natalie. "Can someone please buy me a new wardrobe?"

A ripple of laughter filed the room, easing the tension. Voorheiss looked at his watch.

"I have a meeting to go to. I'll let your father finish the briefing. As I've made it clear on the record, I think it's a risky enterprise given that you're untrained, non-Agency personnel. But perhaps it will bear fruit. Just be careful out there and follow your father's instructions. I don't think I need to remind you that it may very well save your lives."

He rose from his chair.

Lassiter knew he shouldn't say what he wanted to say next, but he did anyway. "Why do I feel, Director Voorheiss, like you're not giving us the full story?"

"Your father and I get that a lot, Nick. And our stock answer is that's need-to-know and *you* don't need to know." He stuck out his hand. "Good luck, you two." He shook first Lassiter's hand and then Natalie's. "Now, all you have left is to sign the confidentiality agreement and take your polygraphs."

Lassiter felt himself cringe. "We have to take polygraphs?"

Voorheiss gave a bloodless smile. "You didn't think we'd let you be Uncle Sam's eyes and ears overseas without a polygraph, did you?"

"Gee, I can't wait," said Natalie. "And then we get to go on our honeymoon."

"Yeah," said Lassiter sardonically. "To Poland."

CHAPTER 23

FEDERAL INTELLIGENCE SERVICE
CHAUSSEESTRASSE, BERLIN

"YOU'VE MADE A TERRIBLE MESS OF THINGS, ANGELA. I'm afraid I have no choice but to put you on two week's unpaid suspension."

For a moment, Angela Wolff struggled to breathe. But one would not have known that by looking at her carefully-composed face. Her mind was already churning forward at a furious pace, trying to calculate her next move in response to her boss's startling revelation. Going on a two week's unpaid suspension was positively out of the question when she had to have a team in the field to recover what rightfully belonged to her. There had to be a way out of this.

Kluge was staring at her almost fearfully, she noted with some satisfaction. She liked that she could intimidate powerful men with a simple mask of aplomb.

"Don't think for one second, Angela, that you are going to talk me out of this," warned the president of the BND, as if reading her thoughts.

"But it wasn't my fault Arne and the others were killed," she countered. "It was Pularchek who did it."

"Pularchek? Really? How can that be when he was giving a speech in Poznan commemorating his grandfather the partisan fighter and war hero? Three hundred people were there, Angela, including a dozen reporters. Tomorrow there will be a full-page article on it in that paper there." He pointed to the copy of *Gazeta Wyborcza*, the top Polish newspaper, lying on his cluttered desk along with intelligence briefs and today's editions of *Süddeutsche Zeitung*, *Le Monde*, *The New York Times*, *International Herald Tribune*, and *The London Times*.

"We've already been through this, Walther. He has a small army of clones that allow him to be at two places at once. Our voice recognition analysis shows that the voices are exactly the—"

"An army of clones, is it? You need more than a two week vacation, Angela. You need to have your head examined."

"All right, I meant to say doubles. But I tell you, there is more than one Stanislaw Pularchek out there. Perhaps as many as a half dozen."

"This is the real world, goddamnit, not a science fiction movie. Now get a grip on yourself."

"An hour ago, Pularchek was here in Berlin, Walther. We have nine CCTV cameras and voice recordings captured by our signals intelligence task force in Bad Aibling to prove it. His presence in the city is an indisputable—"

"Why did you not report Pularchek's presence in the city to me *before* you went after him and got five people killed and a dozen badly injured? You caused a major traffic accident in the Tiergarten and lives were lost, Angela. There were news vans everywhere, and the chancellor is screaming for answers. My God, people think this was a terrorist attack. Why did you not report to me that you were going after Pularchek?"

"We didn't know for sure it was him. We only had his voice."

"I have been told that the reliability factor was over ninety-five percent."

"That's true, but we still didn't have him on camera. I wanted to be certain."

"*Kuhscheisse!* You deliberately kept me out of the loop."

"Who told you that? Johannes? Dieter?"

"Do you think I'm stupid, Angela. You are fixated on Pularchek and I want to know why? What is your obsession with this man?"

"I am not obsessed with him. I simply want him brought to justice. We believe he is responsible for three murders here in Berlin in the past two days."

"You are talking about Bernhard Heydrich's murder as well as this incident at the Berghain?"

"Yes."

"That's interesting, because I received a call from Günther Meier an hour ago," he said, referring to the director of the *Bundesamt für Verfassungsschutz*, or BfV—their intelligence rival in the Federal Office for the Protection of the Constitution, the Republic of Germany's domestic security agency. "Günther had some rather unsettling questions for me about the Heydrich murder. It seems there were enough footprints around the area to indicate a small army had been there. Both satellite imagery and tire-mark analysis reveal that there were half a dozen vehicles with government tags parked in the woods nearby. He didn't come out and accuse us, mind you. But he doesn't need to because he knows he has us by the balls. He's going to wait and play his card when he wants something from us." He banged his hand hard on his cluttered desk. "I want to know what the hell you were doing there, Angela. And I want to know now!"

Normally Kluge was restrained and his banging his balled-up fist onto his desk caught her by surprise. She took a moment to compose her thoughts, keeping her face as inscrutable as possible. Did she dare lie to him, or would that make the situation worse?

"Speak up, Angela, and don't even think about lying to me."

My God, she wondered, *can he actually read my thoughts?*

But still she said nothing.

He shook his head angrily.

"All right, we were there, Walther. Are you satisfied? We received a tip from one of our informants that Pularchek would be there."

"But, of course, he wasn't."

"When we arrived at the house, we found Heydrich dead. We must have missed the murder by no more than a few minutes."

"And what about this Ryszard Stasiak that was found by the police in the nearby woods? The assassin formerly with the Polish Special Forces. Who killed him?"

"We don't know. He, too, must have been killed before we got there."

"So Stasiak killed Heydrich, and then he was shot by a third party?"

She nodded. "One assassin killed by another to destroy the link in the chain. I would call that a reasonable theory. There was another man there too, a third man. But he got away."

"A third man? Why is there always a third man? And your theory is that Pularchek's the one behind all this because he was once in, and recruits heavily from, the *Wojska Specjalne?*"

"That would be the most logical conclusion. We don't have official confirmation yet, but Pularchek has to be the prime suspect. The man behind the curtain, so to speak."

"Why have you kept me in the dark about all this? You are the vice-president of this agency, not a field operative. What have you been doing running around like a cowboy with bodies piling up everywhere? This has to end now, Angela. We have a domestic intelligence agency that deals with internal threats, damn you. Do you realize how badly you have stirred the pot with your ill-conceived clandestine activities? As the Americans like to say, you have gone off the goddamned reservation. For that, there will be hell to pay."

"I don't particularly like American clichés. But more importantly, I don't care what you think. I am going to go after Pularchek myself. He is the cause of all this—not me."

"Oh, so you're going rogue on us, is that it? How original!"

"We can't let him get away with this, Walther. He's made a mockery of us."

"And you're making a mockery of this agency. We have to answer to the chancellor and the Parliamentary Control Panel, Angela."

"We also have to answer to the people, and Stanislaw Pularchek has just murdered three of our citizens. Heydrich was a reputable Berlin lawyer. Wilhelm and Friedrich Shottenbruner may not have been good men, but they were still German citizens and didn't deserve to be gunned down outside the Berghain."

"I want to catch Pularchek as much as you. It's your methods that I object to, Angela."

She rose from her chair and went to the window. The flickering lights of the city winked through the black gloom, making her feel cold and alone. "You can't suspend me, Walther. I'm the only one motivated enough to catch him."

"What do you mean *motivated?*"

It was a Freudian slip, and she forced herself to compose her face into a mask of innocence. "I'm sorry, bad word choice. What I meant to say is that I can get him, but you have to give me another chance. You have to let me operate off the books."

"I already told you we have to answer to the Chancellor's Office and the PKGr. That's under Article 45d (1) of the German Constitution. I know you've read it. Remember the part where it says the *Bundestag* shall appoint a panel to scrutinize the intelligence activities of the Fed—"

"Yes, I know what the Constitution says, Walther. Don't talk to me as if I am a damned farm girl from Holstein."

He stood up abruptly from his desk, signaling that the meeting was over. "I'm done with this conversation," he said sharply, making it clear that he would brook no further opposition. "As of this moment, you are on a two-week suspension without pay."

"You can't do this, Walther. I'm the only one with enough balls in this office to catch Pularchek. That was what I had originally meant to say."

"I said I want you out of my office right now—and out of this building five minutes after that!"

"Please, you can't do this, Walther. Who will take over for me in the interim?"

"Dieter can handle it. I've already spoken with him."

She felt as though she had been punched in the stomach. "Dieter?" she gasped, unable to believe what she had just heard. "You talked to Dieter?"

"Yes, he just left my office ten minutes before I summoned you."

So her lover and subordinate had lied to her; he had said that he was merely stepping outside for a smoke, which he typically did when he was stressed out.

"You and Dieter had this all planned out *before* I came to your office?"

"Oh, hush up, Angela. This isn't some sort of conspiracy against you. You've overstepped your authority, damn you."

She felt herself gritting her teeth, and took a deep breath to calm herself. My God, she was so angry she wanted to shoot her own boss and lover both!

"Don't look at me like you want to poke my eyes out, Angela. I've had enough of this. I told you I want you out of my office and now you're forcing me to call Security."

He started to reach for his phone.

"Don't do this, Walther. I can capture Pularchek, bring him back to Germany, and make us both look good."

His fingers clasped the phone and he was poised to dial. My God, was she really done for? How would she be able to recover the *Schatzfund* now under the guise of her Pularchek investigation? A two-week suspension would be a severe blow to the entire operation; there was no way she could allow it to happen. She needed her official position and her team intact and under her command to recover the merchandise. Damn the clever Pole for putting her in this compromised position!

Suddenly, Kluge's phone on his desk rang, startling them. At the same moment, they recognized the name on the caller ID.

"You'd better leave now, Angela. This isn't going to be pretty."

She folded her arms and sat back down in the chair in front of his desk. "I'm not going anywhere, Walther."

He delivered a smoldering glare. "This is flagrant insubordination," he seethed.

But she had called his bluff and he had to answer the phone. Still glaring at her, he picked up the phone and answered it. "Good evening, Chancellor," he said in his most ingratiating voice. He made a brisk stabbing motion, instructing her to keep absolutely quiet and then went to the window, his ear to the phone.

Wolff impatiently waited, still feeling like a condemned prisoner about to face the whooshing blade invented by Frenchman Joseph-Ignace Guillotin. Kluge and the chancellor talked for several minutes, with the chancellor doing most of the talking and the BND president quietly voicing surprise and objecting every so often while Wolff looked on anxiously. When the conversation was finished, Kluge hung up and turned around slowly, his expression one of stunned disbelief. Was it her imagination or had the blood drained from his face?

"What? What is it Walther?"

He sat down in his high-backed leather executive chair. Anxious to know what had happened, she inched forward in her own chair.

"You must be the luckiest person in the world," he said. "It looks like you are going to get your wish."

She felt herself about to burst with relief, but forced herself to remain calm.

"The Polish authorities have refused to issue a European Arrest Warrant, on the grounds that Pularchek was known to be in Warsaw at the time of the shooting and could not have taken part in the Berghain killings. The chancellor wants you to go to Warsaw, capture Pularchek, and bring him back here to Berlin."

"My God, the chancellor said that? What changed her mind?"

"The German diplomatic tags from Pularchek's vehicle convoy have been identified. They belong to our ambassador in France, Karl Bomblies. The chancellor feels that Pularchek has crossed the line. Not only has he potentially murdered as many as six of our fellow German citizens on our own soil in recent years, he's committed the even more egregious sin of political fraud by masquerading as one of our top diplomats. She wants him apprehended as soon as possible. Since the Polish government refuses to cooperate and is filing a formal complaint to the EU extradition authorities, the chancellor wants him rounded up before he can cause further problems."

"I won't say I told you so."

"Don't gloat, Angela. It's unbecoming. And don't think for one second this gives you carte blanche." He looked at her sternly. "You have authorization to assemble a team, go to Warsaw, and capture Pularchek. But you are to keep me in constant contact and will be operating on an extremely short leash. Furthermore, the chancellor has authorized me, not you, to make the call of when to make the grab. Success has to be guaranteed, or we don't take him. Is that clear?"

"Crystal."

He waved a finger. "I'm warning you. One false move on your part and I shut you down. Do you understand?"

"I understand."

"The chancellor's gone out on a limb for you and put everything on the line on this one. You won't get another chance, Angela. She made that abundantly clear."

"Did she say anything else?"

"As a matter of fact, she did. She said that if you fail to capture Pularchek cleanly, don't even bother coming home to Germany."

CHAPTER 24

WARSAW, POLAND

THE LOT POLISH AIRLINES BOEING 787 DREAMLINER touched down at Warsaw Chopin International Airport three minutes early, at precisely eleven minutes before seven p.m. local time. Exhausted from lack of sleep and being cooped up for the past ten hours, Nick Lassiter and Natalie Perkins wearily removed their carry-on bags from the overhead luggage compartment, deboarded the plane's forward cabin, and took the walkway to passport control, where they were ushered through an unmarked door. Their tired eyes immediately popped wide open at the sight of the huge reception committee assembled in the private lobby to greet them.

"Welcome to Poland, my son and beautiful daughter-in-law!" cried Stanislaw Pularchek ebulliently, his voice carrying a trace of an aristocratic British accent, catching them off guard as he lunged forward with both arms outstretched.

Looking larger-than-life—like something out of Tolstoy but with a distinctly Polish flair—the big man took them in a crushing bear hug as cameras flashed and the crowd cheered. Lassiter was awestruck by the unexpected turnout. He estimated that there had to be at least fifty people waiting to greet them in the large lobby, including several holding up huge *Welcome Nicholas and Natalie* banners and copies of his debut thriller *Blind Thrust*, as well as a few who looked like news reporters. Flanking the group was a small army of surprisingly cheerful-looking security personnel bedecked in formal wear and wireless radio headsets.

"Thank you so much for coming!" Pularchek continued to gush, addressing not only them but the gathered crowd with animated gestures. "I know this is probably more than you were expecting. But there are so many family members that wanted to meet you, and I couldn't keep the devilish reporters at bay!"

The crowd roared its approval. Lassiter was still unable to speak, so stupefied—and moved—was he by the magnanimous reception. He looked at Natalie for words, but she was as surprised and powerless to speak as him. The whole thing was unbelievable! Seeing their reaction, Pularchek gave a hearty laugh and, taking them each by the arm, he spun them around to face the cameras.

"Nicholas and Natalie, from all of the Pularcheks, Onyszkiewiczs, and Romanowskis, we welcome you to Poland!"

The cheering rose to a crescendo and was punctuated by a flurry of clicking sounds as the reporters and extended family members took photographs and videotaped the much-anticipated father-son reunion. Lassiter was still so stunned, he just stood there blinking and smiling into the cameras, unable to speak. Again, he looked at Natalie for help, but all she could do was shrug, smile, and wave helplessly at the large group of well-wishers. Everyone appeared so genuinely excited to see them, they had no idea what to say or do. Even the reporters and bodyguards didn't seem like reporters or bodyguards at all, but rather part of the extended Pularchek family.

Lassiter wondered if he was dreaming. How could this possibly be the same guy he had read about in the CIA file? Pularchek was like a Polish Bill Clinton—a charismatic but unassuming rock star that made you feel like you were the most important person in the room. Despite all the dangerous things he had read about the man in the file, he found himself utterly mesmerized by him in person.

For the moment, he forgot that the whole spectacle was being captured on both audio and video by his and Natalie's iPhones and by the transmitters carefully concealed in their clothing. Or that at this very instant, the transmissions were being clandestinely received by Benjamin Brewbaker and his CIA team on the seventh floor of the Hotel Bristol in downtown Warsaw. The Bristol was the luxury hotel where the two young newlyweds would be staying courtesy of Pularchek. In addition to monitoring and receiving the secure broadcast of their arrival to the airport, his father's team was also busy sweeping their hotel room. Brewbaker had decided not to put them under physical surveillance until they had checked into their hotel.

For the next ten minutes, Lassiter and Natalie were introduced to dozens of people with unpronounceable Polish names. They were hugged, pumped with handshakes, and smothered with kisses while plump babies were shoved into their arms. Reporters asked them what they thought of Poland, and how Lassiter felt being reunited with his long-lost father. Choosing his words carefully, Lassiter said he was excited to be here and glad to finally meet his birth father—which was, surprisingly after what he had learned about the man from the CIA file, the actual truth. He and Natalie were introduced to crinkly-faced grandparents, aunts and uncles, brothers and sisters, and a swarm of pimply-faced teenage descendants, all bedecked in their Sunday finest for the occasion. Lassiter was blown away by the gracious reception; he had never met a nicer or more genuine group of people in his life. He wondered if all Poles were this friendly.

It was as if he and Natalie were movie stars or war heroes returning home after years of being away.

The celebration literally took over the entire terminal and was like something out of a Norman Rockwell painting, except it was a distinctly Polish affair. Finally, once everyone had greeted them individually, they were given a sumptuous offering of *kielbasa* from one of the Aunts Pularchek—there were at least four of them by Lassiter's count—and then sent on their way with best wishes and a reminder that they would be reuniting with everyone again at tomorrow night's family gathering at Pularchek's resplendent Warsaw home.

Just who in the hell is this guy really? Lassiter found himself wondering over and over again as he hugged babies and kissed a gaggle of female blood relations of various ages, shapes, and sizes. But more importantly, why was he so excited to be here? Why did he feel so comfortable and relaxed when he should have been anxious? After all, despite Pularchek's intriguing combination of Polish family man and urbane Brit, the guy was still reportedly a killer wanted by intelligence agencies around the world.

Or, was that just what his father was telling him? Was it possible that Pularchek wasn't even wanted by Western intelligence services at all? Maybe they didn't care what he did. Maybe they were secretly standing by and cheering him on while the intelligence services of the former Nazi strongholds, Germany and Austria, as well as the jihad-supporting countries like Iraq, Iran, Syria, Saudi Arabia, Afghanistan, and Pakistan, privately stewed and plotted their revenge?

From the lobby, they were escorted along with their collected suitcases to a black limo. Once seated, they were handed a glass of French Veuve Clicquot Ponsardin champagne and hors d'oeuvres of beluga and sevruga caviar from an assistant, and then chauffeured into the city accompanied by a sizable security detail stuffed into three separate black Mercedes sedans. It was early June and a sunny, breezy day so the noxious brown cloud of pollution that sometimes hovered above the city wasn't visible above Old Town Warsaw to the north.

"I know you two had to take a leap of faith in coming here," said Pularchek after they had made a few minutes of small talk and were approaching Wawelska Street. "I want to thank you for taking the chance. I know it wasn't easy, and I promise to make your honeymoon something that you will treasure for the rest of your lives."

"We're glad to be here," responded Lassiter, and he meant it.

Suddenly, his host's face lit up with an idea. "Do you want to go straight to your hotel, or can I show you something? We have over an hour and a half until dinner."

Lassiter looked at Natalie. "It's up to you," he said.

She gave a shrug. "Sure, let's take a look."

Pularchek smiled. "I think you will enjoy it."

They passed the giant National Stadium on their right, where Warsaw's professional soccer games and outdoor concerts were held. Then they took a right onto Wawelska and a left onto Wiejska until they reached the *Pomnik Armii Krajowej*—the Monument of the Polish National Underground State and Home Army. They parked by the curb. Doors flew open. Hands reached in and politely pulled them from the limo as if they were a visiting prince and princess attended by royal servants. To his surprise, Lassiter found himself enjoying all the lavish attention, and he could tell that Natalie felt the same way.

"Come, my son. Come and see your history," said Pularchek with a gleam in his eye.

Lassiter looked at Natalie and they both smiled.

And then, the burly Polish billionaire-assassin took them by the hand and they walked with him.

CHAPTER 25

MONUMENT OF THE POLISH NATIONAL UNDERGROUND STATE AND HOME ARMY WARSAW

HE LED THEM down a pathway to the base of a towering obelisk nearly a hundred feet tall. Fashioned out of grayish-white slabs of polished Strzegom granite and capped by Italian quartz-rich granite, the abstract sculpture was curved in a shape that most closely resembled the wing of a bird. Behind the monument was a four-foot wall bearing dozens of inscribed names. The early evening sunlight shone down resplendently upon the memorial, with the Parliament building in the background and the meandering Vistula River to the east.

"This monument was built to commemorate the *Armia Krajowa*, the secret forces of the Polish Underground during World War Two," he said as they approached the giant sculpture. "It is a special gift of the Polish nation. It pays tribute to all the veterans of the Home Army, the strongest and most well-organized resistance movement in Europe during the war. But more importantly, it is a reminder of the heroism of the men and women who sacrificed everything for freedom during the Warsaw Uprising and the other battles waged in Poland during the war. We Poles are a particularly stubborn people. We value our freedom above all else. And believe me, it isn't easy winning your freedom when you have to go toe-to-toe against Nazi and Soviet brutes."

Lassiter smiled. "'A Pole is born with a sword in his right hand, a brick in his left. When the battle is over, he starts to rebuild.'"

"Ah, you've read your Michener."

"I needed a good book and a crash course on Polish history, and *Poland* happened to fit the bill. Thankfully, it was a long plane ride. I finished the book just before we touched down. It's a six-hundred and forty pager, but it seemed like it could have been longer."

"The book was written in 1981 and the best and last chapter of our country's history wasn't yet written back then. Since 1989, we have been free for the first time in half a century. Here, let me show you something."

He motioned them towards the wall behind the monument, while the security team quietly took positions all around the perimeter of the memorial. They stood impassively behind impenetrable sunglasses with their hands neatly crossed in front of them, the faint bulges beneath their armpits signifying concealed handguns.

"Inscribed in that wall are the names of all the institutions and leaders of the Polish Underground during the war. Recognize any of the names?"

Lassiter leaned down and felt the smooth surface of the granite wall as he read the list of names inscribed into the rock. There were four Pularchek's in all listed on the wall: Mikolaj, Maciej, Józef, and Stanislan.

"Mikolaj Pularchek was the commander of the resistance forces during the Warsaw Uprising. He also happens to have been your great-grandfather. He was killed at this exact spot."

As he continued to feel the smooth granite, Lassiter felt something—something powerful—come over him: a connection to the sweep of Polish history. And also his own personal family history.

"And the others?" he asked solemnly.

"Maciej and Józef were your great-uncles. Stanislan would have been your great-cousin, I believe. They were resistance leaders. They all died in the summer of 1944 during the uprising. This monument you see before you was dedicated to the resistance fighters by Pope John Paul II a decade and a half ago."

"I've heard of the Warsaw Uprising," said Natalie. "But I don't know much about it. What happened?"

"It was at the end of the war when the Polish Resistance Home Army was trying to liberate Warsaw from the Nazis. The uprising was timed to coincide with the Soviets approaching the eastern suburbs of the city and the retreat of the German forces. But Stalin ordered his advancing Red Army to stop at the outskirts of the city. Halting the advance sealed the fate of the Polish resistance. It allowed the Nazis to regroup and then, over the next sixty-three days, they demolished the city and annihilated the non-communist Polish partisans, who had no outside support from the Allies. Only then did Stalin take Warsaw. The Warsaw Uprising was the single largest military effort taken by any European resistance movement during the war. But the only result was the killing of two hundred thousand residents, the destruction of eighty-five percent of the city's buildings, and nearly a half century of Soviet dictatorship. That was a high price to pay by our ancestors, wouldn't you agree, Nicholas?"

Lassiter looked into his biological father's eyes, felt the understated power of his emotions. This wasn't just another war memorial in a city that had once been razed to the ground by the Nazis and had dozens of monuments commemorating the fallen. Instead, this was the place where the blood of his ancestors had been spilled. Not across the street, not in Old Town a mile away, but right here where this memorial stood.

Lassiter's mind harkened back to the past—*his* past. He heard the exploding shells from the German's 88's, the *rat-tat-tat* of the Mausers, the grinding mechanical squeals of the approaching Panzers. He heard the commands being shouted by the partisans and the *crack-crack* of their bolt-action rifles as they struggled to defend their threatened positions from being overrun. He heard the plaintive screams of the wounded and the anguished cries of the women and children whose fathers had been killed in action rising up to defend their city. And now, in the present, he looked into the eyes of this man, who yesterday had been nothing more than a sperm-donor and an assassin, and he saw...he saw a father.

A father just like Benjamin Austin Brewbaker. And yet different.

In this new father, he saw a heroic past, an ancestral history, a lineage of Pularcheks marching inexorably to the present day. In this father, he felt the sacred power of his Polish past that he had never known existed. Unbidden, tears came to his eyes. Overcome with emotion, he suddenly felt lightheaded.

He started to stagger.

He saw his father—*my God, am I really already calling him that?*—reach out with a pair of strong arms, keeping him from falling.

Then, the big bear of a man pulled him in close.

There were tears in his eyes too.

"I am sorry, my son," he apologized. "I didn't mean to...I didn't mean to hit you with all of this so suddenly. I have overdone it, and I am sorry."

"No, no," cried Lassiter, tears flowing freely as he felt himself suddenly part of something bigger than himself, a link in the chain of Polish history. "I want to know about all this. I want to *know* everything."

"Then I will show you, Mikolaj."

"Mikolaj?" asked Natalie, who now had tears in her eyes too, tears that each of them were now, in embarrassment, struggling to wipe away.

"Mikolaj is Polish for Nicholas," said Pularchek, daubing his eyes with a linen handkerchief. It bore the red-and-white striped colors of the Polish flag with the national coat of arms in the middle of the upper white portion of the handkerchief.

"Are you telling me that my great-grandfather, the head of the Polish resistance, was named *Nicholas* too?"

Pocketing his handkerchief, Pularchek wrapped a muscular arm around his shoulder. "Yes, Mikolaj, that's exactly what I'm telling you. But that's not all."

Lassiter raised an inquiring brow. "What else?"

"You and I both look exactly like the old war horse. He was a great hero of Poland."

CHAPTER 26

HOTEL BRISTOL, WARSAW

BUILT IN 1901, the Hotel Bristol—formerly known as *Le Royal Meridien Bristol*—was not only an architectural icon and top destination resort for Europe's rich and famous, it was one of the few buildings in the Polish capital to survive the Second World War. Situated on the celebrated Royal Route, next to the Presidential Palace and a pleasant stroll from Old Town, the Royal Castle, and the National Theater and Opera House, the hotel owed its survival to the fact that, following the German invasion in 1939, it served as the Occupation Headquarters of the chief of the Warsaw District and provided housing for German officers until the 1944 Nazi evacuation. The landmark cream-colored building stood alone like an orphan amid the rubble of its razed neighborhood until 1945, when the war thankfully ended and the hotel was renovated, reopened, and once again made available to clientele not wearing Wehrmacht *feldgrau* or jet-black SS uniforms.

In the stately Paderewski Suite—named after the illustrious Polish politician and pianist Ignacy Jan Paderewski—Benjamin Brewbaker was briefing his son and daughter-in-law on the bugs he had found in the room. He and his team had swept the entire suite and detected a grand total of seven: two in the living room furnished with a plush golden sleeper sofa, encrusted mirrors, gilded escritoire, and crystal chandeliers; two in the master bedroom with the king-size royal bed; one in the master bathroom with the oversized Art Deco-style washbasin, and another in the second full bathroom off the living room; and the seventh and final one carefully hidden outside along the Secession-style railing of the private balcony, which overlooked the most esteemed boulevards in all of Warsaw: the Royal Route, King's Walk, and *Krakowskie Przedmiescie.*

"I don't believe it," said Lassiter. "He actually bugged our room?"

Brewbaker looked at his son and could tell something had changed since he had last seen him in the United States. "We don't know if it was Pularchek, or his friendly rivals in the Polish intelligence service. But we removed them."

"Won't they know then that we have CIA guardian angels watching over us?" asked Natalie.

"We want them to know. If they know we're watching, you will be safer. They wouldn't dare strain U.S.-Polish relations any more than they have already been strained by what happened in D.C. Pularchek was summoned to the Polish intelligence office this morning. Normally, he is the one that does the summoning, not the other way around. The Polish president is apparently not happy with

Pularchek's extracurricular activities when reporters are asking questions about two U.S. rendition sites in Poland that are not supposed to exist."

"But do, in fact, exist," said Natalie.

"You didn't hear it from me."

His son was shaking his head. "So, you're telling me that right now some Polish intelligence techies are scratching their heads wondering why their surveillance bugs aren't working?"

"Yep, that's what I'm telling you."

"I don't believe that Pularchek would actually bug our room."

"Why not? You read the man's file. He's capable of anything."

"I know what's in the file. I just don't think he would do such a thing, that's all."

"You mean because he's your *father*?"

"Don't you mean my *birth father*? But yes, I thought that after the *Pomnik Armii Krajowej* things were different and maybe—"

"The Pom-nik what? Don't tell me you're fluent in Polish now?"

"There's no need to get testy," interjected Natalie. "Nick's just trying to tell you that they have a connection between them. I thought that's what you wanted, so you can get intel on this guy."

He kept his gaze fixed on his son. "A connection, is that what you two have now?"

"I guess that's what you'd call it. On the way from the airport, we stopped at this monument for the Polish resistance fighters. The *Pomnik Armii Krajowej*."

"So you're telling me that you've already bonded with your Polish Daddy Warbucks in the short car ride from the airport?"

"You really are jealous," said Natalie. "At first, I thought you might be just needling him, but now I can see you're serious. Nick's ancestors were war heroes in the Polish resistance. Pularchek just wanted to show him the monument to his great-grandfather and the Polish resistance."

"That's wonderful."

"And now they have a connection. An important one. It's in the history of this country—and it's in the history of this once demolished city. A city that had to be reconstructed, brick by brick, after a defeated Hitler, in his last epic act of hatred, ordered the systematic destruction of Warsaw. Did you know that this city was burned, bombed, and dynamited to rubble? Because I didn't. I knew that Poland was attacked without provocation in 1939 and that millions of Jews were gassed in the concentration camps. But I didn't know that Warsaw was the main staging area for the genocide. Nor did I know that the city was completely destroyed and had to be rebuilt by architects—as I said, brick by brick—from old photographs. Six million Poles were murdered in the war—with Jews and non-Jews killed in equal numbers—and their ghosts are everywhere in this city. The streets all around this old hotel are graves. Graves where Poles gave their lives for freedom. Nick is part of all that now."

He bit his lip, grappling to hold back his irritation. "I think that's great."

"No, you're jealous. Nick has another father now and the two of them are hitting it off, and that bothers you."

"Stanislaw Pularchek is a cold-blooded killer and a very dangerous man. Those are the indisputable facts. But I'm glad to know that you all are bonding."

"He may be an assassin, as you say, but he has good reasons for what he does. Reasons that you and I can't even begin to understand because we're not Polish. But Nick is."

"All right, you two, that's enough," snapped Lassiter. "Dad, I'm sorry. I didn't mean what I said to come out the way it did. But Natalie's right about one thing. All of this history here, it's...it's created new feelings in me, opened my eyes to things I never knew about or considered before. But it doesn't change the way I feel about you or mom. I love you both, and you're still my...my primary parents. Okay?"

He was embarrassed. *My God, Natalie is right, I really am jealous.* Not knowing what to say, he went to the seventh-floor window and stared out at the stunning red brick facade of the Royal Castle and King Zygmunt's Column. "I'm sorry, Son," he said, staring at the imposing façade, the square towers at each end with the bulbous spires, and the huge clock tower in the center of the main façade, flanked on both sides by the castle. "Natalie's right. I guess it's just hard for me to accept that you have another father. Especially since I didn't do the best job as a dad for you growing up."

"You were with the CIA. You did the best you could. Just remember, I love you, Dad, and I'm here as much for you as I am to find out about my past. I'm not just your son, I'm your *asset*."

They all laughed. "You're a hell of a lot more than that, Nick. That's why I have to ask you one more time if you're sure you want to go through with this. I know it may not seem like it, but things could get ugly. I'm not joking when I say that just being around Pularchek is dangerous."

"You don't really think he'd harm us?"

"No, I'm talking about his enemies that want him dead. He has a lot of them."

"We know what happened to his wife and daughters," said Natalie. "But that was a random attack, right? He wasn't the target."

"You're right, he wasn't the target, and neither was his family. But the suicide bombing is what set him down his current path as an avenging angel. And since then, he's had three attempts on his life."

"But the only thing in the file was the attack in Turkey," said his son.

"Attempts were made on his life in Rome and Brussels too. But there were reasons to keep those two quiet."

"What reasons?"

He turned away from the window. "Remember what I said about need-to-know. It's not just an operational protocol, it actually saves lives. So, I'll ask you one last time. Are you two sure you want to go through with this, because we can shut down and pack it in at any time? There have been three attempts on Pularchek's life, and I don't want you two to be around for a fourth."

"Sorry, but we're still a go, Dad," said Lassiter after making eye contact with his wife. "We'll just have to be careful."

"All right, but I had to ask. Now remember, you are nothing more than flies on the wall. All you need to do is closely observe everything you see and commit it to memory. The size of Pularchek's security detail, the number of vehicles, who is closest to him, what their names are, other people you notice watching Pularchek. And don't worry, we'll have two separate teams close by watching and listening at all times."

"Where are the bugs besides in our phones?"

"Your clothing has been equipped with microphones. As far as cameras go, we've had them sewn into your suit, blazer, and gray sports coat. Natalie's purse also has a camera. And don't worry, they'll never find any of the electronic devices."

"And just who exactly are *they* again?"

"We don't know. Could be Pularchek, could be Polish intelligence. But it's definitely one of the two."

"So you're saying that regardless of who it is, you'll be able to track us at all times via audio and video."

"As long as you're within ten miles. Your smartphones are equipped with a homing beacon to track your movements. Just keep them on at all times and we'll be able to track you. Also, whenever you enter a new building or go to a different room or floor, nonchalantly say out loud to one another where you are to help us track you. Try and act natural, but make it loud enough that we can hear. We'll be following your movements from two surveillance vans, Charlie #1 and Charlie #2."

"What if Security asks us to power off our iPhones or remove our SIM cards? What do we do then?"

"Do as you're told. We'll still be able to track you by the cameras and transmitters in your clothing, as long as we're in range."

"And if you're not?"

"Then say a prayer, Mr. Bojangles. Just kidding. That's not going to happen." He stared out the window again. "But I'm not kidding when I say that Stanislaw Pularchek is a dangerous man to be around. So keep your eyes and ears open at all times, and never let your guard down. This guy saw his own wife and three daughters taken from him before his very eyes in Madrid. Now he kills to avenge their murders. Death seems to follow him wherever he goes and don't you ever forget that. You need to be constantly on the alert. Do you understand me? Constantly."

"Are you trying to scare us, Dad?"

"No, I just want you to be on your toes at all times." He paused. "Look, I didn't tell you this before because I didn't want to alarm you unnecessarily, but today marks the fifth anniversary of the death of Pularchek's wife and daughters. It happened on June 7, and the suicide bomber who murdered his family did not choose that date at random."

"What's the significance of the date?" asked Natalie.

"June 7 was the date that the Muslim sultan and war leader Saladin won a great victory over the Knights Templar army at Marj Ayun in 1179 A.D. He took nearly three-hundred Christian infidel knights captive and beheaded every one of them. That was the same date in history that Pularchek's family was murdered, only nine centuries later. And tonight marks yet another anniversary of that legendary battle and the suicide bombing."

"So you think someone might try and take him out tonight on the anniversary?"

"I highly doubt it. But all the same, you must keep your eyes open at all times. Muslim fanatics don't pick their mass murder dates at random. Their obsession with numbers and dates is exceeded only by their lust for vengeance against the infidel."

"Okay, I think you've succeeded in scaring the crap out of us," said Natalie.

"I didn't mean to. Just be alert at all times. That's all I'm saying. I'm sure nothing's going to happen, but it pays to be cautious. Remember, you two haven't been officially trained and you're in enemy territory. After last summer, this is only your second field op, so don't try and do more than we're asking of you. You are flies on the wall and nothing more. All we want to know is how Pularchek's home-grown intelligence operation works. Got it?"

"Yeah, we got it. Is there anything else, because we have to get ready for dinner?"

"As a matter of fact there is one more thing. You need to keep a close eye out for German intelligence too. I wasn't supposed to tell you because it's strictly need-to-know, and I didn't want to lay too much on you. But I don't want you walking into this unprepared."

"German intelligence? So you're telling us we have to worry about Germans too?"

"We've received word from our sources that they're ramping up their surveillance in Warsaw."

"What's the reason?" asked Natalie.

"It has to do with the double shooting last night at a nightclub in Berlin. It seems the Germans are worked up. We received a tip from our British friends."

"Who was killed again?" asked Lassiter.

"Wilhelm and Friedrich Shottenbruner. They were German neo-Nazis, Holocaust profiteers, and supporters of anti-Semitic jihad. The Germans believe Pularchek is behind the shootings. We don't know exactly what they're up to, but we do know they have doubled their surveillance of him. So keep your eyes and ears open, all right? This doesn't change anything."

"Jesus, we really are spies. Now that you've scared the holy crap out of us, is there anything else you want to tell us?"

"Actually, there is one more thing. I want to remind you to keep a special eye out for any Pularchek doubles. It has been confirmed by numerous sources that Pularchek was in Warsaw the whole time during the attacks in D.C. and Berlin. For obvious reasons, we want to know how in the hell he can be at two places at once."

"You don't really believe he has clones?"

"We don't know what to believe. All we know is this guy is clever as hell. He's developed his own first-rate intelligence operation that respects no international boundaries and allows him to do whatever he wants. We want to know how he does it and who his key lieutenants are."

"More likely, the Pentagon brass wants to get its hands on the next generation of super soldier. That would explain why the U.S. government is so interested in Pularchek and his potential clones."

"Stuff like that only happens in the movies or your suspense novels, Nick. Now you two had better get ready."

They just stood there, neither of them moving. He saw the conflicted emotions on their faces. After all, he was not just asking them to venture into the lion's den. He was asking Nick to betray his biological father, a charismatic figure who he obviously admired despite spending only an hour with the man.

"When will we see you again, Dad?"

He looked at his watch. "We'll hold a debriefing at midnight, right here. After we've swept the room again for bugs. By the way, where is he taking you for dinner?"

"U Fukiera, in Old Town Square."

Brewbaker delivered a reassuring nod of approval, hoping to make them feel more comfortable. "That's the best restaurant in all of Warsaw, maybe even all of Poland. Pularchek certainly has good taste."

"He can afford to. He's a billionaire."

"Well, I certainly can't compete with that. Have fun tonight, you two, but keep your eyes open and be careful."

"Don't worry, Dad. We will."

CHAPTER 27

HOTEL BRISTOL

IN A SPLENDID ROOM JUST DOWN THE HALLWAY from Nick and Natalie's, Skyler stared out from her seventh floor balcony. She had just taken a refreshing shower and wore only a soft, monogrammed terrycloth robe. To the north loomed the handsome red brick facade of the Royal Castle and King Zygmunt's Column. Once the official residence of the Polish monarchs, the castle suffered extensive damage during WWII and, like much of the city, was rebuilt like a Hollywood movie set.

Gazing out at the spectacular structure, Skyler found it hard to believe that it was a mere reproduction of the original that had been destroyed by the vengeful Nazis during their withdrawal from the city, while the Red Army stood by and watched without lifting a finger. She imagined the Polish partisans and Germans battling street by street, and felt a pride in the stubborn resistance of the Poles. They were indeed fierce fighters, having been repeatedly attacked and plundered by Swedish, Brandenburgian, German, and Russian armies over the centuries.

She sniffed contentedly at the salubrious early June air. Ornate spires and domes loomed majestically in all directions, like emeralds against the pastel dusk. It was impossible not to be inspired in this historic city rebuilt brick by brick, or to feel the power of God watching over these people that had endured such hardship, both Jew and Gentile alike. She pulled out her rosary, leaned over the railing, and, staring out at the city, began to pray.

Hail Mary full of grace, the Lord is with thee...

It was a simple prayer, as much a vestige of her Roman Catholic upbringing as a supplication to a higher authority. But Skyler truly believed in the words as she recited them from long memory. She accepted Jesus as Lord and Savior and sought, in quiet moments like these, to draw closer to Him. She knew that all true believers endured to the end, that only through faith could a person, even someone who had committed terrible sins like her, remain in a state of grace. She also knew that she needed to turn away from sin towards God, to show genuine repentance, if she was ever to be accepted into His kingdom upon her death.

But it wasn't a quest for God's acceptance that she was worried about on this evening. It had to do with the feelings in her heart. Despite the importance of the current assignment on behalf of Pularchek, she was lonely and missed her lover Anthony Carmeli terribly. Years ago, after Don Scarpello and Alberto had broken her and made her hate the world, she had resigned herself to the life of a loner instead a world filled with love, family, and shared intimacy. But now, with Anthony, she wanted to get out of the game for good and gain something more out of life.

But most of all, she hated lying to him about what she really did for a living. It made her feel dirty and shameful, like a cheating wife. Even though she had to keep her professional career as an assassin private for her own safety, the constant deception grated on her. It was true she had been deceiving everyone around her for seventeen years and lying about her past and present had become second nature. But somehow, with Anthony, it made her feel ashamed.

He made her feel special and loved in a way she hadn't known since she was young. The intimacy they shared made the killing seem ugly, reprehensible. For years now, since she had become an assassin, she thought of herself as simply an extension of her gun and the men who hired her as the real killers. It had been easy to rationalize what she did, and she had considered herself no different from the sharpshooters under the employ of the CIA, Mossad, or Russian intelligence. In fact, she had long believed herself superior for she had always been far better paid and took on only those assignments she desired. In her field, no man was her equal or left investigators in a greater state of confusion. But now all the old arguments seemed feeble and she wanted out for good.

She thought of how she felt when she was with Anthony. When he kissed her, she got goosebumps. When he looked her way, she lost her concentration. When she was alone with him, she felt a sense of inner peace. And when she lied to him about her job, her life, her past, she felt miserable. The excitement on the one hand and the guilt on the other were but different sides of the same coin. She was achingly and desperately in love with the man, and knew that if she lost him, she might never find another like him.

After finishing her *Hail Mary*, she rose from her kneeling position and stared out at the imposing façade of the Royal Castle. She marveled at the graceful artistry of the square towers at each end. Staring out at the dusky skyline framing the historic city, she felt a powerful sense of irony. On the one hand, she felt inordinately blessed to have found Anthony; on the other, she felt unworthy of such good fortune. What had she done to deserve God's blessing when she had spent half her life as a killer? Was He giving her a second chance? If so, why had she been chosen? Surely there were many others more deserving of a second chance than her? Was she ultimately going to blow her chance and be captured by the authorities? One day she knew they would come for her; she could not remain under the radar forever. But how long could she hold out?

With her eyes and her heart, she continued to take in the sacred city destroyed by the Nazis. Though she felt deeply conflicted with the idea of continuing on in her role with Pularchek, she knew that he was doing the right thing in destroying the destroyers, in taking the fight to the enemies of human decency. The men he tasked for liquidation were genuine evildoers who corrupted the world absolutely, and Balzac would no doubt have appreciated what the Pole was doing and why. In a world gone mad with violence, violence was the only antidote for those who committed crimes against humanity by their very presence on earth. From that standpoint, she knew her only choice was to put aside her misgivings, honor her promise to Pularchek, and finish the operation.

Once she had done that, she could quit the game for good. And then she and Anthony would be free at last.

CHAPTER 28

OLD TOWN WARSAW MARKET PLACE

ANGELA WOLFF stared out the Land Rover's front passenger window at the entrance of U Fukiera. The restaurant was located in the famous *Rynek Starego Miasta*, the oldest part of the Old Town of Warsaw, which had been faithfully reconstructed after the war. She had kept Pularchek under surveillance for the past hour now, and was going over scenarios in her head on how she was going to take him. Given the Pole's vast and sophisticated security apparatus, it was certainly not going to be easy. When the time came, she would most likely need a diversion. But what could she do to create one?

She rolled down her window, took a breath of air redolent with the smell of potato pancakes, roasted venison, and baked sturgeon, and heard her stomach growl. My God, was she hungry. Not only that, she was having her monthly and was in a foul mood. How long was she going to have to be in this town? More to the point, how long was it going to take to snatch Pularchek?

She hadn't even been here a full day and already she was growing annoyed with the Polish capital. She had been to Warsaw several times before, of course, and she always enjoyed the sights and authentic Polish cuisine. But what she resented was how practically every square inch of the damned city served as a memorial to what the "evil Nazis" had done. It was as if every German who had worn the uniform had been a National Socialist Party member and murderous SS storm trooper.

The Warsaw Rising Museum, Mausoleum of Struggle and Martyrdom, Monument of the National Military, PAST Building, Tomb of the Unknown Soldier, Little Insurgent Monument, Warsaw Uprising Monument—the whole city was like a theme park that paid tribute to the "brave" Poles and vilified the "evil" German oppressors in stark, black-and-white terms that reduced both sides to caricature. But that was only the tip of the iceberg. Every direction she went, she came across plaques in the sidewalks detailing the number of people murdered by German soldiers in that precise spot during the war; or strips of cement showing the remnants of the Warsaw Ghetto's walls; or bullet holes preserved in the original walls of a market or corner store and, next to the holes, plaques representing the Polish citizens who had died in that spot.

She was well aware of the extreme vengeance Hitler had exacted upon this poor country and this historic city—and yes, she too admired the Poles for their resilience—but she resented having to be reminded at every street corner, every sidewalk, every wall about how evil her country had been three-quarters of a century ago. The past was past; there was no sense in being bombarded by its ugliness every day in the present. She didn't have to be reminded every five minutes that the city had been destroyed by the withdrawing German Army. She didn't need to be told over and over again how the city had been painstakingly rebuilt using paintings and photographs as an architectural blueprint. Why it was as if the Germans had been the only barbarians during the war. But was it not true that the Allies—most notably the Big Red Army—committed atrocities too, atrocities which successive generations of historians had only grudgingly acknowledged? Didn't anyone remember that the Russians murdered ten million people, more than the Holocaust, during the course of the war? And how could anyone forget that the Russians raped more than a million German women in 1945 alone—including little girls younger than ten and great-grandmothers in their seventies—while the Americans, British, and French looked the other way and even committed rape and plunder themselves on a far lesser, but still significant, scale?

Closing her car window, she purged her mind from these bitter thoughts. She knew that her situation was becoming desperate, and that was the main reason she was in such a foul mood. If she didn't capture Pularchek soon and force him to talk, she might never get her merchandise back. And if she couldn't get back what rightfully belonged to her, how would she and Dieter ever be able to live the life together that they dreamed about?

She stared again at the front entrance of the restaurant. U Fukiera was, in fact, her favorite dining establishment in the city. Whenever work compelled her to visit Warsaw, she made a point of eating at the restaurant during her visit. Occupying one of Old Town's restored townhouses, U Fukiera was an eccentric grotto that served traditional Polish peasant cuisine, but with the mouth-watering panache of a five-star European restaurant. Wolff remembered back fondly to her last meal here two years ago: the herring lathered in cream sauce, chopped onions and capers, and veal dumplings sprinkled with pig cracklings had been divine. And it had cost her only 110 zloties.

Suddenly, her radio earpiece chirped with a voice. "Blue Team, this is Krupp with Red Team! We've got a situation!"

She snapped to attention and looked at Dieter, seated next to her in the driver's seat of the Land Rover. "What? What is it?" she said into the mouthpiece of her radio headset.

"Look to your right, three o'clock. There's a man standing beneath the street light north of the restaurant. Do you see him?"

Discreetly, she raised her Zeiss binoculars and peered through the front passenger side window. Yes, she saw the man standing just off the cobblestone street on the sidewalk. His face and upper torso were well illuminated by the street lamp. He appeared to be in his mid-twenties and was talking inconspicuously into a cell phone, which he held to his ear with his left hand. But what wasn't inconspicuous was that he was wearing a heavy Italian-style trench coat. The jacket was at least two sizes too big for him and was not a piece of clothing normally worn in hot summer. Not only that, but beneath the heavy jacket he had a noticeable bulge around his midsection. That, in itself, might not have been extraordinary had it not been that he also happened to be Arabic with a pale complexion along the jaw line where, if he was a devout Muslim, his beard would have been. Which meant that he had cut his beard only recently. He also appeared inordinately nervous and was gripping something tightly in his balled-up right hand. If she wasn't mistaken, she would say that he was screwing up his courage to perform some act.

"So you're telling me, Johannes, that this man is a suicide bomber?"

"Look at the bastard. He doesn't just fit the profile—he *is* the fucking profile."

"He's right," concurred Dieter, also looking through his high-powered binoculars. "Look at the son of bitch. He's not even talking into that phone. He's reciting verses from the Koran."

"How do you know?"

"Because I'm reading his lips."

"Well, what the hell is he saying?"

"I can't make out everything, but it's something like, 'Allah is the helper of the oppressed. With faith and…and weapons…I shall defend Islam. And the light of truth will shine on…no, shine *in* my hand.' I don't know for sure if that's from the Koran or not, but it sure as hell sounds like it to me."

"Dieter's right. *Allahu Akbar*, we are fucked," said Krupp, reciting the invocation shrieked by Islamic suicide bombers the whole world over before they detonated their murderous midriff devices. "He's invoking the will of Allah, and his trench coat is definitely concealing an explosive vest. Look how tightly it's buttoned up. He doesn't want anyone to get in there."

She studied the man more closely, searching for confirmation that he truly was a suicide bomber and her men weren't overreacting. The Mossad—the Israeli intelligence service—was la crème de la crème when it came to the documented tendencies of Islamic suicide bombers. At this very moment, the man across the street exhibited many of the telltale signs she had learned about in the counterterrorist training courses she had been taught by Israeli experts over the years. The wearing of long coats and heavy clothing, especially in warm weather, to conceal explosive belts and devices. The blank thousand-yard stare and reciting of prayers just before the attack. An unnaturally pale, freshly shaven face, evidence that a thick Muslim beard has just been hastily removed so as to allow the suicide bomber not to attract attention and blend in. Signs of irritability, sweating, tics, or other nervous behavior. A hand in the pocket or tightly gripping something, possible evidence of clutching a detonator or a trigger for an explosive device.

"All right, you've convinced me," said Wolff. "The question is what are we going to do about it? We can't call the Polish police. That will take too much time and they'll ask questions."

"We have to take him ourselves," said Dieter. "The square is packed with people. Look at all the diners in the outdoor tables. He'll kill dozens of people."

"And how do you propose to stop him?" she asked him. "We're not trained for this sort of thing."

He had pulled out his Walther PPQ M2 nine millimeter. "One shot to the drill stem will do the trick."

"Are you insane?" she cried. "With all the explosives that bastard has strapped around his waist, the blast radius is more than fifty feet. You'll never be able to get close enough to—"

"Jesus Christ, he's on the move!" Krupp cut her off. "If we're going to take him, we have to do it now!"

"No, wait! No one moves until I say! I want one last look to be sure!"

"But he's reciting his final prayers! We've got to move now!"

"I said wait, *verdammt!*"

She held up a hand for Dieter to hold on and peered one final time through her Zeiss binoculars. In the street lighting, the suicide bomber's image was crisp and clear, and his intentions now seemed clear as well. The eyes had taken on that tunnel-vision look, signifying that the bomber was fixated on his target and dreaming pernicious thoughts of his hand-picked harem of dark-eyed virgins in Paradise. Based on the subject's movements, his target appeared to be the Old Town Market Place. It was packed with more than a hundred people at the restaurant tables along the margins of the cobblestone street. His lips were indeed moving as if he was talking to himself: the man had to be reciting his final prayers. He also had an unusual, almost robotic gait, as if compensating for extra weight that was bogging him down. It was the bomb, she realized. Carrying the equivalent of a very large backpack around one's waist filled with high explosives, ball bearings, bolts, and nails pre-soaked in cyanide or rat poison provided a challenge even to a physically fit fanatic bent on martyrdom. And then there was the final tell-tale sign. As the man stepped across the cobblestone drive, his foot caught on one of the stone's and he was thrown off balance. In that instant, Wolff saw his right hand bunch into a fist with the thumb at a right angle, and just visible at the sleeve of his overcoat was a thin wire at his wrist. No doubt the wire led to a detonator switch linked to the explosives bound about his waist.

She had seen enough. She had all she needed.

"Dieter, Johannes, take him now!"

"We're on it!" cried Dieter.

"Don't either of you get within fifty feet of the bastard, and that's a fucking order! I'm not going to lose any more good men, especially not to a fanatic!"

"Fifty feet! We got it!"

The front doors of both Land Rovers flew open. Both men were out in a flash, Walthers gripped tightly in their right hands inside their jackets, and moving quickly towards the target, who thankfully was so entranced with fantasies of the virginal delights awaiting him in Paradise that he hadn't noticed them.

With her heart racing, Wolff held her breath, quietly praying for success. One shot to the brain-stem and the suicide bomber would be dead. But from a distance of fifty feet, the chances of either one of them being able to pull that off were no better than a hundred to one.

But a one-percent chance was better than no chance at all.

The detonator would be stiff and resistant enough so that it could not be triggered accidentally. Which meant that if they could get lucky and actually shoot the bomber in the brain-stem, even his twitching thumb would not be able to apply the force necessary to activate the bomb. But they had no chance at all if they couldn't get to him while he was still outside in the open marketplace.

"God, please help them," she murmured under her breath as she saw Dieter and Johannes striding forward, like lions moving in for the kill.

And then, to her horror, the suicide bomber turned and saw them.

They ran towards him.

The bomber picked up his pace and ducked inside U Fukiera.

She jumped out of the car and waved Dieter and Johannes off. "No! No! Don't go in there!" she screamed.

But she was too late.

They dashed in after the suicide bomber just before the door closed. It was then she understood who the jihadi was really after.

"My God, this isn't random! The target is Pularchek! I repeat the target is Pularchek!" she shouted into her radio headset again. "Get the hell out of there, or you'll die!"

They didn't respond.

And then she saw something else.

Another suicide bomber was approaching from the northeast. *If at first you don't succeed,* she thought with horror, *then try, try again.*

Taking a deep breath to steel her nerves, she pulled out her Walther and quietly stepped from the Rover.

128

CHAPTER 29

U FUKIERA RESTAURANT

"SO, NICHOLAS, WHY DID YOU ACCEPT MY INVITATION TO COME TO POLAND?"

"That's easy," replied Lassiter, smiling conspiratorially at Natalie. "We came here to spy on you for the CIA."

Pularchek grinned; already he liked them both and was taken by what a handsome couple they made. "Well then, I appreciate your candor."

"Actually, I think it's more because we wanted a little excitement in our lives and were willing to take a chance," said Natalie. "And so far you haven't let us down."

"Excitement, eh? Don't you two lovebirds know that Warsaw can be a dangerous place?"

"So we're learning," said Lassiter. "With warmongering Germans to the west and Russians to the east, simply *existing* in this embattled country has been an epic struggle for the past five centuries. And yet the Polish people have endured."

"Remember, the Polish people are your people too, Mikolaj. Poland is in your blood."

"Yes, I almost forgot. I am half Polish."

"If I had to guess," said Natalie playfully, "I would say that Mikolaj here would have been quite handy at bushwhacking Nazi patrols back in the day. In fact, I would go so far as to speculate that he would have actually enjoyed it."

They all laughed. "Yes, I'm sure of it," roared Pularchek happily. He sipped his Pototcki rye connoisseur's vodka, gave an appreciative sigh, and glanced around the room. It was filled with vases of colorful flowers, flickering candlelight, original Polish artworks, antique silver and crystal, and brothel-red lamp shades and birdcages containing chirping parakeets. He felt genuine warmth sharing this extraordinary restaurant with his newfound son and daughter-in-law. Despite the fact that U Fukiera catered unabashedly to European tourists, he loved coming here and made a habit out of dining at Magda Gessler's tasty *restauracja* at least once a month.

The waiter reappeared to take their dinner orders. Pularchek opted for the Matjes Herring tartare on honey and rye bread for an appetizer; Warsaw-style tripe on veal shanks with dumplings for his soup; Sturgeon enveloped in caviar with chives and champagne for his first course; Milky Veal liver with balsamic sauce and Antonov apple, potatoes, and dill for his main course; and a Tsar's Russia with Chatka crab and thick, velvety smooth dressing of tomatoes and cognac for his palette-cleansing salad. Nick and Natalie were unsure what to order so he ordered them a sampling of authentic Polish appetizers and small plates that would be specially prepared for them: herring and tenderloin steak tartare, pigs' trotters, smoked eel and salmon with red caviar, freshly prepared wild game pâté, veal cutlet with quail eggs, duck breast on blackcurrant mousse, and roasted venison in cream sauce. The waiter, whom he knew personally and was also named Stanislaw, commended him on the choices and shuffled off.

As he snapped his leatherbound menu shut, he looked up and saw a shocking sight. An Arabic man with a pistol in his right hand and a tightly balled fist in left rushed into the dining room, scanned the tables, and quickly recognized him.

He did not recognize the man. But he knew what he was here to do.

The suicide bomber charged.

Pularchek felt the breath leave him all at once. The man seemed like an apparition from a nightmare, a demon possessed. Now that the suicide bomber had identified him, he was moving faster, his face and his churning legs filled with singular determination.

Pularchek quickly and calmly removed his Glock 9-mm "man-stopper" from his waistband. He knew the instant he gripped it in his right hand that, despite the weapon's heralded stopping power, he stood virtually no chance of putting down the suicide bomber before he detonated his bomb. He was well-trained in counterterrorism tactics, and he knew right away the odds were severely against him in U Fukiera's tight quarters. The man was already forty-five feet away and closing and the blast radius would undoubtedly be greater than that.

His only chance was a perfect shot to the brain or throwing down some barrier before the bomber closed the distance to within twenty or thirty feet. For if the killer did that, Pularchek knew that nothing could save him or his son and daughter-in-law. The man was a holy warrior bent on murdering him, in exchange for his own life and martyrdom in Paradise with willing virgins in the afterlife. He was as close to an unstoppable force as existed on earth, and he didn't care a lick that he would probably maim and kill fifty other innocents in fulfilling his jihadist mission.

The Pole's eyes shot quickly to Romanowski and his security team. The team had broken into two separate groups: one seated at a far-away table near the entrance, the second at a nearby table. His men were already up on their feet with their weapons pointed at the intruder, but his security chief was nowhere to be found. Where the fuck had Romanowski gone, the men's room?

O, kurwa! he thought as he locked onto the maniacal eyes of the suicide bomber and cursed his bad luck. He couldn't believe that he was going to die just like Johanna and the girls on the fifth anniversary of their death. Mother Mary, he should have seen this coming. He should not have allowed himself to be caught flat-footed when he knew perfectly well how important historic dates, especially those involving the ancient Muslim sultan and war leader Saladin, were to Islamic holy warriors.

But it was even worse than that: his son—the very Polish blood and Pularchek seed that would continue on after he left this world—would die right along with him, as would his son's wife. That was the real tragedy.

The suicide bomber ran towards him.

"*Allahu Akbar!*" he cried, raising his arms up in triumph and exposing a wire detonator in his right hand. Behind the jihadi, Pularchek saw Angela Wolff's protégé and lover, Dieter Franck, dash into the restaurant carrying a gun along with another German intelligence officer.

"Get down!" he cried to Nick and Natalie, but they had already alertly spotted the suicide bomber and had ducked down.

His security team and the Germans opened fire simultaneously, quickly riddling the suicide bomber with bullets. But still the terrorist didn't go down, his forward momentum and visions of martyrdom in the arms of a dozen *houris* propelling him inexorably forward.

Suddenly, his son and Natalie rose up, knocked the heavy wooden table so that it was on its side, and yanked him down behind it. In his peripheral vision, he saw Romanowski stepping out of the men's room, his gun drawn.

Pularchek peered over the top of the wooden barricade. The suicide bomber was now twenty feet away, staggering but still moving forward, his hand on the trigger mechanism.

"You bastard! You're not going to Paradise!" he shouted angrily at the jihadi as he rose up six inches to fire.

"*Allahu Akbar!*"

He took careful aim at the bomber's forehead with his Glock and fired. Then, he ducked behind the heavy wooden table with his American son and his son's wife.

The last thing he felt was a searing wave of molten heat as he was shot like a cannon into the kitchen door.

CHAPTER 30

U FUKIERA RESTAURANT

ANGELA WOLFF slowly raised her Walther and trained it on the second suicide bomber's chest. He hadn't noticed her yet, as he moved quickly towards the front entrance of U Fukiera, where his fellow *shaheed* had just entered. But he had spotted Dieter and Johannes hurriedly entering the restaurant shortly after his co-conspirator, so the second suicide bomber knew that someone was on to them. Wearing a baggy jogging outfit, he had drawn his pistol in his left hand and accelerated to a brisk walk, gripping the detonator of his device in his right hand, the opposite of his partner already inside.

The second bomber was older and more confident looking than the first attacker, possessing a calm and professional bearing and a steady gait to match. Even though he had drawn his gun, he kept it carefully concealed within his baggy sleeve and pressed up against his dark jogging suit so that it was hard to see. It was only because Wolff's team had identified the first bomber that she was on high alert and had been able to spot the more seasoned professional mass murderer moving through the Old Town Market Place.

From her counterterrorism training, she knew that terrorist organizations carefully selected and prepared the martyrs who carried out suicide attacks. Those recruited were given extensive training on how to blend into the target population and carry out their mission. Their farewell videos were an act of celebration for the afterlife, and arrangements were made to compensate their families with cash payments in "martyr accounts" after they carried out their deeds in the name of Allah. Besides the prospect of carnal delights, this was one of the incentives that drove the suicide bomber to follow through with his mission, knowing that he was going to die. But even taking all that into consideration, this second suicide bomber was a more formidable attacker than the first.

So how in the hell was she going to stop him?

"Blue Team and Red Team, this is Group Leader," she said quietly over her radio headset. "We've got a second bomber coming in from the northeast. I have protection behind the Rover and am going to try to take him, but I need backup. Do not let him reach the restaurant alive. I repeat, do not let him reach the restaurant alive. At this point, all we can do is minimize casualties. But that is what we must do."

"We copy, Group Leader. We're on it."

She took a deep breath, crouched behind the hood, and steadied her aim.

The suicide bomber spotted her and opened fire.

Scheisse! She ducked down as a pair of bullets whistled past her head. Then she returned fire as the terrorist started to run.

At that moment, a blinding flash of white light erupted from the front window of U Fukiera.

Even tucked safely behind her massive land Rover, Wolff was knocked to the ground by the blast wave. The explosion battered her eardrums and she dropped her pistol to the cobblestones. For a moment, she couldn't hear at all, as the fiery flash of white turned to a tidal wave of searing airborne heat and a murderous mélange of flak—a mixture of glass, metal, wood, plaster, lamps, silverware, and bloody body parts—blasted out the window. The violence was so great that the row of plants and trees gracing the front entrance of the restaurant, as well as the first row of outdoor dining tables across the street in the square, were wiped out. She covered her head as the debris whizzed past her ears like spitting machine gun bullets.

It was as if it was 1944 all over again and Old Town Warsaw was being blown to bits by the German army.

When the worst was over, she picked up her gun and stared in awe at the devastation. The front door, window, and decorative trappings near the entrance of U Fukiera had been blasted into nothing. The cries of the dying and severely wounded rose up into the air like a dirge. A stunned crowd began gathering along the eastern and southern quadrants of the square, their eyes fixed on the devastation in stunned silence.

Out of the corner of her eye, she saw the second suicide bomber stagger to his feet, shake off the dust, and look around for his pistol.

Mein Gott! He survived the blast?

It made sense now that she thought about it. He had been up the street, a hundred feet north of the restaurant entrance, when the bomb went off. Like her, he had not been directly in the blast zone. It was a miracle he hadn't triggered his detonation switch when the explosion had knocked him to the sidewalk. But there he was, alive and still prepared to fulfill his holy mission and become a martyr. He would finish off whoever had survived the initial blast inside the restaurant.

The second suicide bomber looked at her and started to run.

She took aim with her Walther on his chest again and fired, making sure to maintain her crouch behind the protective Land Rover.

The shot missed the mark.

The bomber dashed for the fiery, smoking entrance. Another Suicide IED–Improvised Explosive Device—on the move, this time ready to finish the grisly job. Here before her eyes, she realized, was the most dangerous and effective weapon system facing civilized society. The terrorists themselves called it a "bomb on human platform," as if it were nothing but a new software product. Eyeing the second suicide bomber and all the wreckage around her, she cursed these mass-murdering zealots inside with all her being.

She fired again, this time catching him in the leg.

It was then she saw the American Benjamin Brewbaker and several more U.S. government agents to her left. They opened fire on the jihadi with pistols from a hundred feet away.

But it wasn't Brewbaker and his team that took him down.

It was a woman armed with what looked to be a Modular Small Arms System Radon-B Bullpup Assault Rifle. She appeared seemingly out of nowhere with the compact 30-round semiautomatic exquisitely equipped for close-quarters combat by the Polish Military Technical Academy. Shockingly, she was a pudgy redhead with a pasty face and a floppy maternity dress that looked completely out of place on her because she moved like a panther and snugged the lethal weapon against her shoulder with the precision of a world-class commando.

My God, who is this woman? Is she with Pularchek or the Americans?

With striking calm, the woman took careful aim with her bullpup rifle and put a bullet in the center of the second suicide bomber's forehead. He staggered and fell, but as he struck the ground, his thumb pressed down on the detonator.

This time, a brilliant burst of white light filled the western half of *Rynek Starego Miasta.* Wolff ducked down behind the Rover as the explosion mowed down a swarm of people struggling to escape the outdoor tables in the square next to the street. It was as if they were toy soldiers knocked down by a great gust of wind.

The bomber had been about fifty feet north of U Fukiera when his device detonated so, fortunately, the two empty shops next to the restaurant received the brunt of the blast. Shards of broken window glass showered the street, along with smashed dishes, furniture, and dislodged stucco. The violent blast of air pushed the Land Rover backward, and only by a stroke of luck was she able to get out of the way as the vehicle was knocked onto its side.

A second cloud of dust and smoke now spread over the Market Place.

Rising to her feet, she looked where the suicide bomber had been the moment before.

He had completely vanished.

The area was devastated; all that was left was a huge hole in the wall of the building next to U Fukiera, and a large crater in the cobblestone street. She scanned further to the south where she had seen the female sniper in the odd-looking maternity dress and Brewbaker and his CIA team. They had disappeared into thin air too. *My God, did they take cover, or were they all blown to bits?* She turned her gaze towards the gutted, burning entrance of U Fukiera, as well as the street and square where the outdoor dining tables had been. There lay scattered bodies and body parts. She had no idea how many had been killed, but it had to be at least thirty, with an equal number or even more dead inside the restaurant. There were also many wounded screaming in terror and moaning in agony. The devastation was more than she could have possibly imagined.

The gruesome reality of it all made her feel nauseated; for a moment, she thought she might vomit. But she was able to steel herself and started towards the entrance to help the survivors.

Suddenly, her radio squawked to life. "Team Leader, Angela, it's me, Dieter. Are you okay?"

She felt a bolt of relief. "Dieter, you're alive! Thank God!"

"Yes, and so is Johannes. We ducked behind the heavy oak bar in the restaurant. We got lucky, but there is something I need to tell you."

"What? What is it?"

"We have Pularchek."

"What do you mean you have Pularchek?"

"He was knocked into the kitchen door by the blast and we were able to locate him. He hit his head hard and was unconscious for a moment, but not anymore. He's giving us an earful."

Wolff could hear cursing in Polish in the background. "Good Lord, will you be able to extract him?"

"I think so. We're bringing him out of the kitchen now. It's on the west side of the restaurant. Johannes has already sent Albert to direct both teams to meet us there. We lost radio contact for a minute, but we're back now."

"But...but how did Pularchek survive the explosion?"

"You're not going to believe it. He was saved by a heavy wooden dining table. It took the brunt of the blast."

My God, the lucky bastard. Just like Hitler at the Wolf's Lair, she thought. Then she heard the first police sirens shrilling to the north. They had little time.

"You know, this is the will of God, Dieter. This could never have happened without divine intervention."

"You give God too much credit. We and Pularchek both survived because of sturdy Polish oak."

"All right, I believe you. But now we have to get out of here. The police are coming. Unfortunately, my Land Rover is out of commission. I will have to come to you on foot."

"You'd better hurry. And by the way, I have a surprise for you."

"A surprise?"

"Perhaps I should call it insurance."

The shrieking sirens were growing louder. "I will be there in one minute. You wait for me, my love."

"I will, but you must hurry."

CHAPTER 31

U FUKIERA RESTAURANT

LASSITER FELT as though he had ducked below the surface of a raging river. His eardrums were still ringing: it sounded like turbulent white water sweeping past his ears. He saw his father Benjamin Brewbaker's lips moving, but no sound came out. His vision was still fuzzy, the bright white light from the explosion rending its own trauma. He saw his father's arms reach down to lift him, but they didn't seem like human appendages, more like the blurry tentacles of an octopus.

His father helped him to his feet. But he still felt lightheaded, ethereal. He staggered and nearly collapsed. The sensation reminded him of a lacrosse game versus Wooster when he was an All-American attackman at Kenyon College a decade earlier. After driving hard to the net on an inside roll and delivering the game winner, he had been hit late and driven hard to the turf by a snorting 220-pound defenseman named Trent Douglas, a divisional opponent that he had come to hate over the years. The game had been played on a biting day in late February, on a still-frozen field. He had, according to his teammates, laid there on the frozen ground, in a catatonic state, for three straight minutes without moving. And then slowly, the world had returned, and he had felt like he had awoken from a deep sleep.

That was how he felt now. The world around him seemed curiously surreal and he felt only semi-conscious. His sensory intake was coming in fuzzy, like a weak radio signal.

"You're going to be all right, Son," he heard his father say. "Just take a minute to get your bearings."

He looked around the restaurant. It was a wilderness of devastation. A huge hole had been blasted out of the floor and there were blown-apart corpses, scattered body parts, and splatters of blood everywhere, along with the splintered remains of wooden furniture. The air was filled with the cries of the wounded and dying, mingling with the shriek of approaching police sirens, fire trucks, and ambulances.

He made a rough count of the bodies: there had to be at least twenty dead with another thirty seriously wounded. It was like a horrible reenactment of the Warsaw Uprising, only this time featuring radical Islamic terrorists instead of Nazis. Among the ruins, he saw the body of an adolescent boy. The child lay on top of uprooted concrete flooring near a huge hole caused by the explosion of the bomb. It broke his heart.

It was only then that he realized that his wife and Pularchek were missing.

"Dad, where the hell is Natalie?" he asked, beginning to regain his bearings, though his ears were still ringing.

"I'll tell you in a second, Son, but first I have to get that thing"—he pointed to his arm—"out of you."

His father reached through his torn shirt just above the elbow and yanked out a jagged sliver of shrapnel. Lassiter groaned in pain. His father then tore a strip of cloth from one of the battered table cloths, wrapped it around the wound to fashion an improvised field dressing, and quickly tied it off. Lassiter realized he had been lucky. It was just a flesh wound and could have been a lot worse, though it hurt like hell.

"Thanks, Dad. But we need to find Natalie."

"I'll tell you where she is, but first we have to get moving. The police are coming, and we can't be here."

"I need to find my wife first."

"That's going to be tough, Son. The Germans took her. In fact, they took Pularchek too."

"The Germans?"

"Angela Wolff and her storm troopers. She works for the BND, the German foreign intelligence service."

"Are you telling me the Germans are behind this?"

"No, they're not terrorists. They're just taking advantage of this suicide bomber diversion. I suspect they were looking for an opportunity to kidnap Pularchek and take him to Germany for trial, but they wanted some insurance. So they took Natalie too. She must have been lying nearby. But at least we know they're both alive."

"What? How do you know all this?"

He held up a device that looked like an ordinary iPhone except bigger. The screen showed a stationary blue GPS beacon and a separate red beacon that was slowly moving. Both the blue and red dots were superimposed on a crisp, satellite-image background that looked like an unusually high-resolution Google map. The red beacon was also flashing.

"That's us in blue and the bad guys in red."

"You're getting that from Natalie's transmitter in her clothing?"

His father nodded. "But we don't have any video. Just audio and the GPS beacon."

"Thank God we have that."

Outside, a pair of police cars screeched to a halt in front of the blown-up restaurant. Armed officers began jumping out of the cars. Next to the vehicles stood a tubby, red-haired woman in a baggy maternity dress; the woman had a butch law enforcement look about her that was oddly incongruous with her clothing and overall manner. She carried no weapon but she looked like she should have. Lassiter studied her a moment through foggy eyes and the woman stared back at him.

"We have to go. That means now, Son."

He tipped his head towards the police, who were now dashing towards the jagged, bombed-out front entrance with their semiautomatic weapons pointed up and away in two-handed holds. As they swept forward, the red-headed woman in the maternity dress disappeared.

"Did you see that woman?" he asked his father.

"No, what woman?"

"She was standing there staring at me and then she suddenly vanished."

"You mean she was killed in the blast?"

"No, she was alive standing next to the police—and then poof she was gone. I wonder what she was doing there?"

"You're not making sense, Son. We need to get out of here."

He looked down at all the bodies and body parts on the floor. He was sickened by the carnage and devastation. "No wonder Pularchek does what he does," he said. "Look at what these bastards have done. And to think you saw this coming and even warned us about it."

"I know, it's a tragedy. But we need to get the hell out of here now."

"Which way?"

"Out the kitchen, or what remains of it. That's the way the Germans went."

They started off. "I can't lose Natalie, Dad," said Lassiter as they ran. "We have to get her back. We have to get them *both* back."

"Don't worry, we will. We will get them back."

"How can you be sure?"

He held up his GPS tracker-smartphone. "Because I know where they're going."

138

CHAPTER 32

BND SAFE HOUSE
URSUS, POLAND

THE GERMAN CONVOY swept into the town of Ursus from the northeast. With flashing police cars, fire trucks, and ambulances racing past in the opposite direction, Angela Wolff and her BND team roared down the aleja Solidanosci and then Wolska at over seventy miles per hour before turning right onto Dzwigowa, taking the exit onto Swierszcza, and navigating a series of left hand turns that led to the BND safe house at Stanislawa Wojciechowskiego 9. A bank of heavy garage doors opened up like a drawbridge to a Medieval Castle. The fleet of Land Rovers drove inside and screeched to a halt. The doors rumbled closed again, leaving no evidence of their entry, as if the convoy had been swallowed by the jaws of Jonah's whale.

"Take them to the holding room," snapped Wolff to Dieter as she stepped from one of the Rovers. "I have to take this call from Walther."

She held up her vibrating secure mobile as, one after another, car doors slammed shut and Stanislaw Pularchek and Natalie Perkins were escorted from the Land Rover at gun point.

"You shouldn't be doing this, Angela my dear," said Pularchek. "My people will come for us, which means you and your men have only a few minutes to live."

The face of Johannes Krupp and two other of her team members showed visible alarm. "Don't listen to him. He's just trying to scare you," she snapped. Then into her phone, she said, "I apologize, Walther, but I'm going to have to call you back." She punched off abruptly to her boss's vehement objections.

Pularchek laughed derisively. She stepped up to him and fiercely met his gaze.

"I can't believe your boss Kluge and the chancellor have authorized this insane scheme of yours. Surely, they realize that it is illegal for a state to abduct an individual from the territory of another state without requesting permission, or following normal extradition procedures. In fact, this kidnapping is not only a violation of Polish law, but a violation of international law—in particular the prohibition against arbitrary detention. You can't use kidnapping to circumvent the formal extradition process, Angela my dear. You know that, and so do your bosses."

"Are you finished?"

"Not quite. You are in Poland now, not Germany. You should have thought this through before you rushed into that restaurant. Kidnapping me was a serious mistake, but not nearly as bad as taking young Natalie here."

"You weren't kidnapped. You are a criminal and will be tried in Germany for crimes committed within our borders."

"I can see the pressure is getting to you. As a matter of fact, if I didn't know better, I would say you look a bit like Herr Goebbels at the Chancellery at the very end. Not a pretty sight, I must say."

"You are going to give me what I want, and if you do I will let you live. That is my promise to you. But what I can't guarantee is what shape you'll be in." She turned on a heel and looked sharply at Dieter. "Now get him out of my sight! *Schnell! Schnell!*"

Her men promptly did as instructed. Feeling her blood boiling, she punched her boss's automatic number into her secure mobile and waited a moment for him to answer.

"Yes, Walther, what is it?" she said curtly.

"Tell me you have nothing to do with that bombing in Old Town! Tell me, Angela, because I can't believe what my eyes are witnessing at this very moment on BBC and CNN!"

"Calm down, Walther. We had nothing to do with it."

"Are you telling me you were actually there?"

"Of course we were there. We were watching Pularchek when two suicide bombers showed up. One of them was able to infiltrate inside and blow up the restaurant. The other bomber we were able to take down before he could detonate inside."

"Good Lord! So I take it Pularchek is dead then?"

It was time for the grand lie, if nothing else to buy time. She took a deep breath. "Yes, Walther, he's dead. He was killed by the first suicide bomber."

"The media is going to be all over this. Did anybody see you?"

"No," she lied, thinking of the American Benjamin Brewbaker's face when their eyes had met. "We saw no one except the suicide bombers and they are both dead. We're clean."

"Where are you?"

"The safe house?"

"You're in Ursus? How do you know you haven't been made and weren't followed there?"

"Because I'm a professional intelligence operative like you, Walther. Now if you don't have any critical intel for me, I need to get back to work."

"Who do you think you are, Angela? You don't talk to me in that dismissive tone. I'm your goddamned boss, and I have some more questions."

She shook her head in disgust. How a by-the-book bureaucrat like Walther Kluge had ascended to the pinnacle of the German foreign intelligence hierarchy, she would never know. "All right, Walther, what do you want to know?"

"I just got an interesting call from our friends at the BfV. They know that you were in Vienna three days ago and that you were at Bernhard Heydrich's the night before last."

140

"We were performing our jobs."

"You didn't tell me about Vienna, Angela. I want to know why."

"I was following up on various Pularchek leads."

"Like hell. I want to know why you've been keeping me in the dark and operating as a lone wolf. What is going on?"

She gnawed her teeth with frustration. Her time was running out and she had to get Pularchek to talk. She was jeopardizing her entire career before she had her prize in hand, which could prove to be a fatal mistake.

"What happened in Warsaw tonight is a major international incident. There are CCTV cameras all over the place, and this had better not come back to haunt us. If the Americans get wind that we were there, they're going to want to have a serious talk with us. And if Polish intelligence knows you were there, we are just as fucked. So let me ask you one more time, Angela. Did anyone see you?"

"No. Will that be all?"

An excruciating silence.

Then, in agitation: "I don't know what in the hell you're up to, Angela. But whatever it is, it had better be over with the suicide-bombing death of Stanislaw Pularchek. Do I make myself clear?"

Her secure phone suddenly vibrated, another caller on the line. She checked the caller ID: it was a ten-digit U.S. number with an unfamiliar area code, and she didn't know who it belonged to. "Sir, I have another call. It's urgent."

"You had better not be fucking with me, Angela, or your career is over. This time, do I make myself clear?"

"Crystal. Goodbye, Walther."

She accepted the second call, curious as to the identity of the caller, and spoke in English.

"This is Angela Wolff. Whom may I ask is calling?"

"The second-in-command of the German foreign intelligence service has just kidnapped a Polish national and an American citizen. I can't wait to see your arrest by the Polish police on BBC International."

She gritted her teeth. "Brewbaker. How did you get this number? This is a secure phone."

"Not for the United States government. Remember, we listen in on your own chancellor just for shits and grins."

"That's not funny."

"Neither is kidnapping American citizens, especially when they happen to be my daughter-in-law. You were always overzealous, Angela, but now you have truly crossed the line. I told you once before that you screwed the pooch when you accused us of spying on your chancellor, Kaiser Wilhelm, and the Holy Father himself when your own agents were spying on us in Turkey. But now you've gone totally off the reservation. Talk about the pot calling the kettle black. You had to backtrack one hundred eighty degrees on that diplomatic snafu, and now you have a true international crisis on your hands."

"What's your point, Brewbaker?"

"You free my daughter-in-law and her admittedly dangerous Polish billionaire friend, right now, and the American government will pretend it never saw you prowling around the biggest walk-in suicide bombing in European history. Do you have any idea what the death toll is up to?"

She said nothing.

"Over eighty. Fucking eighty, Angela! You can count that high, can't you?"

"It is indeed a terrible tragedy, but we had nothing to do with it."

"Tell that to the Internet bloggers and folks at the BBC and CNN. Do you have some private, personal agenda that I don't know about because it sure as hell seems like it? What's your obsession with Pularchek?"

"You know perfectly well why we want him. After all, you listen in on our phone conversations and hack into our computers every day. He's murdered German citizens and completely flouts the rule of law."

"That may be, but in Poland that makes him a saint."

"I don't appreciate your sense of humor."

"And I don't like it when people kidnap American citizens. You're going to hand Natalie and Pularchek over to me, and thereby avoid becoming entangled in a career-ending international incident and public relations nightmare."

"Pularchek is not going anywhere. He stays with us. When I know you are no longer following us, I will release your daughter-in-law. So you had better stay the hell back. Way, way back."

"You're going to regret this."

"I'm going to regret a lot of things. But negotiating with you isn't one of them."

"I'm only going to tell you this once more. You need to let Natalie go—she has nothing to do with this."

"I told you my terms. If you want to get her back, then you had better do as I say."

"You are hurting U.S.-German relations as we speak. Does your chancellor or your boss Walther Kluge know what you're really up to? I don't believe they would authorize you to kidnap an American citizen."

"Who says I need their permission?"

"I thought Pularchek was the rogue elephant in the room, but you are one audacious bitch, Angela Wolff. But you're making a serious mistake. So what are you really after, because what you did tonight smacks of desperation?"

"Pularchek is an international criminal. We have been trying to extradite him for years, as you damn well know."

"He hasn't even been on your nation's watch list until today. I've seen the files, Angela. He's not even tracked by Interpol. The Polish Prosecutor General's office has denied all requests for extradition to Germany. In fact, that office has stated repeatedly that they have no grounds to even hold him in temporary custody while Germany seeks to extradite him. The matter has never been sent to any court that could impose even a temporary arrest, because the prosecution has never found a basis for that."

"After what your own son went through in Washington, I would think that you, of all people, would not be defending Pularchek."

"I'm not defending him. I'm merely pointing out a simple fact. To most intelligence agencies in Europe, he's Robin Hood. He kills the terrorists and saves their agencies significant time, effort, and capital expense just as the man in green tights robbed the rich to feed the poor. Now what are you really up to, Angela? What's your game, because my gut tells me this is about more than obsession?"

"How do you Americans like to say it? Let sleeping dogs lie, Deputy Director. That is, if you want to see your daughter-in-law again."

"Are you threatening me?"

"Take it however you wish."

"I'm coming for you, Angela. I'm coming for you with the full weight of the United States government behind me."

"Is that so? Then you might want to check with your own boss, because I have a feeling he might have a different perspective on all this than you."

And with that, she punched off the phone and stepped from the garage into the safe house.

CHAPTER 33

BND SAFE HOUSE, URSUS

LOOKING INTO the eyes of his son's new bride, Pularchek felt as if he had utterly failed. He should never have taken her and Nicholas out tonight of all nights, on the anniversary of his wife and daughters' murders and Saladin's ancient victory. But even worse was that he had allowed himself and Natalie to be captured by the Germans.

Then again, perhaps he should count his blessings that all three of them were still alive. They had been spared from the blast by the heavy oak table, which had served as a gigantic protective shield against the pressure wave and burst of shrapnel. For him, it was supremely ironic. He had been saved from the bomb blast by a heavy oak table just like the Nazi he hated above all others: Adolf Hitler, at the Wolf's Lair on July 20, 1944, during Colonel Claus von Stauffenberg's failed assassination attempt as part of Operation Valkyrie.

"I'm sorry, Natalie. I shouldn't have brought you and Nick here to Poland. It is too dangerous."

She shook her head. "It's not your fault. We both wanted to come."

"I'm still sorry."

"Like I said, it's not your fault. The terrorists did this. I still can't believe all of those bodies though."

"If I hadn't been at U Fukiera, no one would have died." He felt a savage stab of guilt rock his body. "I know everyone there: the owner, the maître'd, the chef, the waiters, even the dishwashers. It was a bloodbath and I am to blame."

"You didn't know that suicide bombers were going to strike on the fifth anniversary of your wife's and daughters' murders."

Her words took him by surprise. "You know about that?"

"Yes, and I am very sorry. Knowing what they did to your family and seeing the mass murder they performed tonight, I understand now why you do what you do."

"And what is it that I *do*?"

"You know perfectly well what you do. You take the fight to international terrorists instead of sitting by and waiting for them to attack us. To be honest, I admire you for standing up to them. And so does Nick."

He made no response, neither acknowledging nor refuting her.

"Don't bother trying to deny it. It's in your classified CIA file. But what I'm trying to say is I get it now. I think most sane people can agree that these Islamic fanatics are pure evil. There's no other way to describe them, and there's no rational excuse or justification for what they do. And there never will be."

He quietly nodded. "What they represent is evil returned."

"Evil returned?"

"Yes, both the Nazis of the past and the Islamic extremists of today represent evil that can be understood only as something beyond understanding. To actually comprehend such evil is to almost be complicit in it. The jihadist monsters of today represent Nazi-like *evil returned*. I believe it was an American reporter from your *Washington Post* who coined the term."

She gave a sober nod, and they fell into a brief silence. They were seated at a wooden table in a glass-enclosed conference room that had been turned into a temporary holding room. Two armed guards stood outside the room staring in at them. The table contained stacks of files and was surrounded by six plastic chairs. The walls were hung with framed prints of famous paintings by the 19th-century German Romantic landscape painter Caspar David Friedrich. The pictures showed allegorical landscapes and contemplative figures silhouetted against night skies, morning mists, barren trees, and Gothic ruins. Pularchek much preferred Italian Renaissance and Dutch masters, as well as the later French Impressionists. He found Friedrich's paintings celebrating Germanic culture, customs, and mythology to be too bluntly patriotic for his more nuanced tastes. He was only too well aware that Hitler—a failed painter of mediocre talent—had worshiped Friedrich's jingoistic work.

He said, "We were lucky you both weren't killed. I saw Nick. He was unconscious, but breathing, when the Germans grabbed us. He's going to be okay. I know that much."

She nodded ruefully. "I saw him too. But it's still not your fault."

Gently touching her cheek, he pushed aside a loose strand of hair in front of her left eye. "I can see why my son married you. You are a strong woman—and, of course, you also happen to be brilliant and gorgeous as well."

"Okay, stop it. Charm is something that actually works with me."

They both laughed and he took a moment to study her. She was an enchanting young woman. After a moment, she became embarrassed and glanced away, and he felt guilty for watching her so closely. She rubbed her arm. He could tell she was still hurting despite the makeshift bandage he had made for her, a linen napkin he had managed to grab on the way out of the restaurant. But at least it was just a flesh wound. The heavy oak table had saved all of their lives.

"Are they watching us in here?" she asked him. "I mean somebody besides our two guards?"

"I don't think so. I don't see any cameras, and this is their primary safe house. I don't think they even have an interrogation room."

"Why do the Germans want you so badly?"

"Now that is an interesting question and one that deserves an honest answer. The truth is I took something from Angela Wolff and she wants it back."

"You *took* something from her."

"Something that she erroneously believes belongs to her. Something valuable."

"Can you tell me what it is?"

"Unfortunately no. But I can tell you that, right now, we're playing a dangerous game of cat and mouse. Honestly, the less you know the better."

"Are they going to hurt us?"

"You, no. Me, well, let's just say the odds aren't good."

"You mean Wolff might actually torture you?"

"Put it this way: I wouldn't put it past her. She's German and we all know how Germans are when it comes to torture. They make Torquemada look like Mother Teresa. The ironic thing is what I've taken doesn't belong to her. It *belongs* to the world."

"So what is it?"

"Oh, you are a naughty girl. You just won't take no for an answer. But I am telling the truth when I say the less you know the better. It's for your own safety."

"I suppose I can buy that. And I'm sorry that Angela Wolff might go all Torquemada on you."

"Don't be. I'm Polish. We're used to being tortured, especially by Germans."

"I'm surprised a senior intelligence officer would risk doing something like this. Isn't Wolff operating outside the law?"

"There are no laws in the intelligence business. The only rule is don't get caught."

"I don't necessarily believe everything that's in a government file, but it says in yours that you've killed like thirty or forty bad guys. Is that true?"

"So you've read my classified CIA file cover to cover, eh? It's ninety pages long. You must be a very patient person."

"You make for interesting reading. In fact, Nick wants to write a book about you."

"Does he now? What a generous son. Will I be playing an unapologetic villain like Captain Bligh, a sympathetic baddie like Hannibal Lector, or a courageous anti-hero like Bruce Wayne and his alter ego Batman?"

"I don't know. How many bad guys have you really killed?"

"That's not making very polite conversation. Didn't your mother teach you that that is not the type of question to ask a person, especially not your father-in-law?"

"I grew up in Chicago. There were a lot of Polish people in my neighborhood. I think they were a bad influence on me. What do you think of that?"

He looked her in the eye and smiled. "I think you are a clever, clever girl and my son Nicholas is very fortunate to have married you. Seriously, you know my reputation. I don't like neo-Nazis or Islamic terrorists. Or Russians—I almost forgot about them. Isn't it enough to know that making their lives miserable is what I do when I'm not making oodles of money, through *mostly* legitimate means?"

"Mostly legitimate? And what about the other times?"

"It's business. And business is, by definition, at least a little bit unsavory. Unfortunately, the world has to have winners and losers. But I do give tens of millions of dollars a year to a variety of global charities. That allows me to sleep well at night."

"What about the killing? Does that keep you up at night?"

"Polite conversation, Natalie. It's an art form, even if you come from Chicago and spent considerable time growing up with what you Americans disparagingly like to refer to as 'Polacks.' By the way, do you know any good Polack jokes? I haven't heard any good ones lately."

"I don't do Polack jokes. They're politically incorrect."

"Oh, is that how you feel? Well then, you'll really like this one. A guy walks into a bar in Chicago, sits down, and orders a beer. He says to the bartender, 'Hey, want to hear a good Polack joke?'"

"In reply, the bartender says, 'Tell you what...I'm Polish. See those two big guys playing pool? They're Polish. See those other two tough-looking fellows sitting at the end of the bar? They're Polish too. You still want to tell your Polack joke?'"

"The man replies, 'Not if I'm gonna have to explain it five fucking times!'"

They both laughed. Then they again fell into silence. Was that rain he heard on the rooftop? He wasn't sure, but he thought he could hear the gentle pitter-patter of raindrops.

"You are a living dichotomy, aren't you?" she said to him after a minute had passed. "Nick said that when he first met you, he couldn't believe you were really his father. He said you were like something out of Tolstoy, except Polish."

"I get that a lot. Usually from Russians and Ukrainians." He let out a small groan; his lower spine still hurt like hell from smashing into the kitchen door. "So, tell me the truth, Natalie. What is my son Nick really like?"

"He's like you: stubborn as hell."

"A characteristic Polish trait. I am quite proud of him, you know. That New York affair...nailing that Russian Mafia crime lord and that literary agent for that money laundering operation, sticking it to those rogue CIA bastards, and then at the end of it all becoming a bestselling author. A young man like that would make any father proud."

"Or a wife. But right now, I'm more worried about how we're we going to get out of here." She looked at him. "You don't seem particularly worried."

"That's because my team will be here to rescue us any minute now."

"Oh, they will, will they? How do you know?"

"Like you, I have a transmitter implanted in my clothing so that my security team knows where I am at all times."

"How do you know I have a transmitter?"

"The same way I know that Benjamin Brewbaker had the bugs removed from your hotel room."

"So it *was* you. I thought you were supposed to be a simple, semi-legitimate businessman."

He winked at her mischievously. *Tak*, he truly liked her. "Like you, I am not so simple."

"These friends of yours. Do you think they will be here soon?"

"If I were a betting man, I would say that the odds are—"

He stopped right there as he saw a metal canister crash through the second floor window and emit a cloud of red smoke. Five more smoke grenades quickly followed, creating a co-mingled plume of red, green, and blue-colored smoke. Shouts of alarm and stomping footsteps echoed down the hallway as Pularchek felt his eyes begin to water from the gaseous cloud.

He smiled at Natalie. "I told you they would come. It was only a matter of time."

"These are your men? But how do you know?"

"Because we always use smoke-and-tear-gas grenades. You'd better cover your eyes."

The floor and walls rumbled as a giant explosion shook the building. It was difficult for Pularchek to tell what was going on, but he suspected that some sort of projectile had been launched at the front door and blown it to bits. Now he could hear yelling and gunfire down on the street.

The Germans shouldn't have brought us here, he thought. *That was their first mistake. And it most certainly won't be their last.* In fact, he was banking on it. Then he would be back on track again and everything would proceed according to his meticulous plan.

"Get down on the floor," he commanded her. "It will protect your eyes, at least for a minute or two."

She did as instructed, and he lay down beside her.

Suddenly, the door burst open and Angela Wolff was standing there with the two bodyguards armed with semiautomatic pistols.

"On your feet!" she snarled in a harsh, guttural staccato, shielding her eyes with her jacket sleeve. "Let's go!"

"Why, Angela my dear," said Pularchek, "I thought you'd never ask."

CHAPTER 34

BND SAFE HOUSE, URSUS

SITTING IN SURVEILLANCE VAN CHARLIE #2, a mildly inconspicuous Volkswagen Atacama, Nick Lassiter stared across S. Wojciechowskiego at the apartment window of the German safe house. He couldn't see inside. The windows of the two-story, Polish bourgeois-style building bore double-paned reflective glass. But he knew Natalie and Pularchek were being held inside a room on the second floor of the safe house.

His wife appeared as a stationary red dot on the transmitter beacon on his father's smartphone, and both Natalie and Pularchek were visible based on their thermal-heat signatures and backscatter-electron-imaging profiles. They were being tracked by Jackson Glover, the van's dedicated surveillance technician, and Michael Webb, a junior CIA officer, also seated in the rear of the vehicle, which served as a mobile virtual-intelligence station inside Poland. All the same, Lassiter wished he could see them in the flesh, and he was growing increasingly worried with every passing minute.

The stillness of the night only added to his sense of foreboding and gloom. A dead calm had settled over the suburban neighborhood, the only sound the yapping of a dog down the street. A light rain had begun a few minutes earlier, drumming down on the roof of the van in a steady rhythm. The droning pitter-patter served to increase the restless tension Lassiter felt inside, and he cursed himself for allowing the Germans to take his wife and biological father in the first place. Damnit, why hadn't he been able to stop them?

"You were right, Dad, we shouldn't have come to Poland," he said to Benjamin Brewbaker, seated in the driver's seat next to him and wearing a radio earpiece. "You warned us, but we wouldn't listen. And now the Germans have taken Natalie."

"It's not your fault, Nick. You can't blame yourself."

"Why not? You tried to tell me and I wouldn't listen. You even warned us about going out to dinner tonight and look what happened. I mean, you totally called it."

"Blaming yourself isn't going to do any good. We just need to get Natalie and Pularchek back."

He shook his head. "If anything happens to Natalie, I don't know what the hell I would do. I really don't."

"You've got to settle down. There's nothing we can do right now except sit tight. The Germans are going to have to make a move, and when they do, we're going to be right on top of them. They crossed the line by taking her and Pularchek hostage, and they're going to pay for it."

"Yeah, but what if they find the transmitter in Natalie's clothing? Then we won't even be able to track her."

"You're worrying too much. You've got to stop."

"How do we know they aren't torturing her at this very minute? And what about Pularchek? Are you going to just let the Germans kidnap him and take him back to Germany without following due process? They should be following formal extradition protocols, not grabbing people after a suicide bombing attack. What the Germans are doing can't possibly be legal."

"I understand you're upset, but you've got to settle—"

He stopped right there as a series of swooshing sounds echoed down the street. It sounded like mortar shells, but Lassiter quickly realized they were smoke grenades. The first- and second-story windows of the safe house began cracking open from grenades launched in from multiple directions. Lassiter counted more than a dozen of them, colored red, green, and blue. For the first time, faces appeared at a pair of windows that didn't have reflective glass.

There's the bastards!

Now, at least, he could see the faces of his enemies.

Suddenly, the van shook from a violent explosion. Looking out the window, he saw the front door of the safe house disappear in a burst of flame. From out of nowhere, a small army of twenty or so men dressed in full riot-gear, Kevlar body armor, and tear-gas masks suddenly materialized. Armed with light machine guns, they charged towards the blown-open front entrance and the four metal parking garage sliding doors on the east side of the safe house.

"Jesus, who *are* those guys?" Lassiter asked his father.

"Pularchek's men." Then loudly into his radio mouthpiece: "We are in a hold, Charlie #1 and #2! No one moves without my order!"

"Sir, the subjects are on the move!" cried the technician in the back of the van.

Brewbaker held up his smartphone, which now showed two stationary blue GPS beacons, representing the two CIA surveillance vans, and a flashing red beacon that was moving, representing Natalie from the transmitter in her clothing. As before, the dots were superimposed on a satellite-image background showing streets, buildings, and foliage in miniature.

Lassiter and his father both looked back at Pularchek's men. "They look like they know what they're doing," observed Nick.

"They were trained in the Polish Special Forces. We'll wait and let them do our work for us. I certainly wouldn't bet against them."

Neither would I, thought Lassiter as he saw one group pour through the demolished front entrance, and another take position outside the garage to prevent the Germans from making a getaway in their vehicles. Creeping up in support of this second group were three idling, jet-black Land Rovers with tinted windows.

The attack was coordinated and professional, but Lassiter knew something could still go wrong, and Natalie and Pularchek might very well get hurt or killed.

Hurry up and get them the hell out of there!

There was a rattling sound down the street and surge of movement on their left. Suddenly, Pularchek's men were under attack from automatic weapons fire and smoke grenades by a third party. He saw the two closest guards standing in front of the garage clutch their chests and fall to the pavement. A staccato of gunfire erupted from the two opposing forces through a curtain of red smoke. Like the Polish team, the new interlopers had full Kevlar body armor, gas masks, and automatic weapons. But instead of dark blue police uniforms, they wore actual combat fatigues.

"Who the hell are those guys?" cried Lassiter. "Are they German soldiers?"

"No, they're mercenaries contracted by the Germans," responded his father. "Angela Wolff is no dummy. That way the guys in the camo can't be linked to her." He now issued orders into his radio mouthpiece. "Charlie #1 and #2, stand by! We're still in a hold! No one moves until I give the order!"

"Copy that, sir!"

At that instant, all four garage doors opened up. A pair of the German Land Rovers burst through the two openings on the left, while two more Rovers dashed through the open doors on the right. But they were cut off by Pularchek's fleet of Land Rovers—which were also black and looked identical to the German vehicles. The Germans were quickly hemmed in and fired upon by the Poles. At the same time, several fresh smoke grenades landed amid the tangle of cars, causing confusion by throwing up a dense cloud of red smoke that made it virtually impossible to differentiate the combatants.

And then an even stranger thing happened. The pudgy red-haired woman in the maternity dress he had seen at U Fukiera appeared with a compact assault rifle and opened fire on the Germans.

"Jesus, there she is—that woman!"

"What woman?"

He pointed. "There! It's the woman I was telling you about at the restaurant!"

His father stared at her closely for several seconds, and Lassiter thought he saw a flicker of recognition on his father's face.

"Do you know her?"

"I...I'm not sure."

"Come on, Dad, I just saw the look in your eyes. Who the hell is she?"

"I'm going to get a picture." His father quickly snapped off three photographs of the woman with his smartphone.

"Dad, what the fuck are you doing? Who is that woman?"

"I don't...look...it's a longshot, Nick, but I'm going to have our facial recognition experts check her out. It could be someone we're looking for, but like I said, it's a longshot."

"Well, longshot or not, I'm going in there! I'm getting Natalie!"

"No, Nick! You stay here and that's an order!"

But Lassiter was already out the van, carrying a Smith and Wesson M1911A1 .45 semiautomatic with a seven-round magazine that he had managed to coax from his father en route to the German safe house. If he was actually going to be a spy like his two crazy-ass fathers, he was going to have a goddamned gun.

He ran across the street into the melee. There was ferocious combat all around: charging men, rattling firearms, cars ramming one another, bullets breaking glass and ricocheting off metal, dreadful screams, and meaty thumping sounds as soldiers were shot and fell to the pavement. The tires of one of the German Land Rovers had been shredded from the gunfire, and another German Rover had become immobilized after being rammed by the Poles. Suddenly, the Germans from the two incapacitated Rovers were switching into the other two vehicles. Lassiter thought he caught a glimpse of Natalie and Pularchek among this group, though through the skein of crimson smoke he couldn't be certain. But then he positively ID'd them. They were being prodded in the back at gunpoint towards one of the Rovers.

He charged forward, shooting one of the German mercenaries dressed in camo in the leg. For a moment, the smoke cleared and a blonde, fiercely beautiful woman in a stylish business suit came into view.

Angela Wolff!

He fired at her.

The shot missed, but was enough to drive her back behind one of the Rovers. Dashing ahead through the smoke, he started to round the corner of another vehicle as a group of Pularchek's men that had stormed the safe house entered the fray, forming up quickly into a firing line. With military precision, they dropped to their knees in unison and delivered a devastating blast with their machine guns, knocking two German mercenaries to the ground as two more smoke grenades landed on the pavement just a few feet away from Lassiter.

It was then he saw a sight that he would never forget.

Like something out of a dream, he saw his birth father, Stanislaw Pularchek, step from one of the Polish vehicles and dart to the right, towards the German position, as the female sniper in the maternity dress expertly covered him with her bullpup rifle. At the same time, three Polish soldiers shoved a man who looked exactly like him, down to the last wrinkle and stitch of clothing, into a waiting Land Rover.

What the hell?

Shaking his head in disbelief, he looked around to make sure that his eyes weren't playing tricks on him and to see if anyone else had witnessed what he had just seen. But there was no one except Pularchek's plainclothed team and the female sniper. The nearby Poles in the firing line were preoccupied with the battle, and the other possible witnesses—a plainclothed German intelligence officer and one of Pularchek's soldiers in navy blue—were busy fighting hand-to-hand behind the Rover with the bullet-shredded tires.

It was like D.C. all over again: a Pularchek clone on the field of battle, only this time he was fighting German intelligence operatives and mercenaries instead of Saudi and Swiss jihadist financiers.

The car doors slammed. The Range Rover bearing Pularchek—or a man that looked exactly like him—drove off. The tires screeched and burned rubber as they found traction on the pavement. A second Rover peeled away from the curb and followed closely behind the first vehicle, sending up another odoriferous plume of seared rubber.

Now, he heard the sound of police sirens, coming from the east up S. Wojciechowskiego. Again, he scanned the area desperately for Natalie, but he couldn't see her anywhere through the slowly dispersing curtain of smoke.

He sprinted up to one of the trapped German Rovers, bullets pinging and ricocheting all around him, but he was unable to get a look inside because of the tinted windows.

"Natalie! Natalie!" he shouted.

There was no reply.

He shouted out again. "Natalie!"

A burst of gunfire forced him to take cover behind one of the cars. A second barrage compelled two Poles to hide along with him, as they were now being fired upon from a window in the safe house. They let loose with return fire, instantly shattering the window and driving their attacker to take cover himself. The gunfire rattled all around Lassiter, echoing off the walls of the building and mingling with the roar of engines. At that moment, a pair of German Land Rovers managed to detach themselves from the tangle of cars and drive off down the street.

The sound of the approaching police sirens was now deafening.

"Damnit, they're getting away!" he cried.

He fired at the retreating vehicles, but to no avail as they raced down the street and disappeared from sight. His eyes were now red and watering from the smoke, and he wiped them with his hand.

As the sound of the engines faded away, he turned to look at the Polish soldiers all around him. They had stopped firing and were jumping into their vehicles and driving off. To Lassiter's surprise, they weren't even trying to follow the German vehicles.

"Why aren't you chasing them, goddamnit!" he yelled at three men approaching him.

But the Poles didn't respond. Instead, their expressions hardened and they closed in around him. He knew then that he was in trouble.

"Nick, I've got Natalie!" he heard a voice cry.

He turned to see his father leaning down and pulling his wife from the thick bushes next to the driveway the Germans had just vacated. Inside, his heart rejoiced, even as he felt hands grabbing him from behind and a half dozen police cars raced in from the east.

"Natalie!" he cried.

But before she could reply, the red-headed woman with the bullpup rifle and two of the Poles shoved him inside a waiting Rover and he was driven off into the night.

CHAPTER 35

URSUS

BREWBAKER STARED IN DISBELIEF as the Land Rover disappeared around the corner and a caravan of police cars zoomed towards them from the opposite direction. "Come on!" he cried to Natalie, taking her by the hand. "We have to get the hell out of here!"

"Why aren't they following?" She pointed towards Pularchek's men, who were driving away from the Germans instead of giving chase.

"They got what they came for: Pularchek," he said as they dashed to the surveillance van. "And now the police are coming, and they don't want to have to answer questions. And neither do we!"

"But we have to get Nick!"

"Don't worry, we will! But we have to get out of here first!" Now, he spoke into his radio headset as they jumped inside the van along with Jackson Glover, the van's dedicated surveillance technician, and Michael Webb, the junior CIA officer that had accompanied Brewbaker to the safe house. "Charlie #1, move out now! This is Charlie #2, and we're in pursuit of a black Land Rover bearing Nick. They're headed north on Traktorzystów. We're tracking him with the GPS beacon."

"What about the Germans?" asked Glover, as Brewbaker fired the engine and Natalie took her seat in the back next to the technician.

"They're no longer our problem." He pulled away from the curb. "Remember, we need to keep within ten miles of Nick. That's the secure range of the GPS."

The two Volkswagen surveillance vans tore off down the street and turned the corner in pursuit, just as the first police car screeched to a halt in front of the safe house. Suddenly, Brewbaker's smartphone rang. He looked at the caller ID, but all it said was PRIVATE CALLER - SECURE.

"This is Brewbaker."

"Goddamnit, Ben!" he heard Richard Voorheiss, his boss and director of the CIA's National Clandestine Service, yell. "What the hell is going on over there? We've heard reports that there was a major suicide-bombing attack and Pularchek is dead. Why didn't you report in like I told you?"

"We were in pursuit, sir, and there wasn't—"

"Watch out!" yelled Webb from the passenger seat.

A traffic spike strip lay across the road in their direct path.

Brewbaker instantly slammed on his breaks, swung the wheel of the van hard right, and tried to go around the strip, but he was going too fast to avoid it. The van gave a sudden shudder when it struck the barbed metal teeth and, with only one hand on the steering wheel, he almost lost control of the vehicle. All four tires were instantly punctured and shredded by the dark-painted device. Fortunately, he was able to correct from swerving into a parked car and pull over safely to the side of the road. But he was out of commission. Looking in his rearview mirror, he saw that Charlie #1 van had suffered the same unfortunate fate.

"Damnit!" he yelled in frustration. Covering his phone, he yelled to Webb and the other Volkswagen through the radio: "I want these vans up and running in the next fifteen minutes! Call in the backup team! And keep an eye on the GPS! I need to know the exact final position and bearing of the vehicle Nick is in when we lose their position! Move it!"

Voorheiss had been yelling at him over his cell phone throughout the incident, and his angry boss now said, "What the hell is going on, Ben? You'd better talk to me!"

Brewbaker spoke again into his phone. "Pularchek was not killed in the suicide-bombing attack in Old Town. We were in pursuit of him only moments ago, but we hit a tire spike strip. We're immobile, sir."

"Where's Pularchek headed?"

He looked at the moving red dot on the GPS beacon. "Southwest. But we can't follow him. Our goddamned tires are shredded."

"Well, it doesn't matter anyway. I'm relieving you and your team and taking over command of the operation personally."

Brewbaker wasn't sure he had heard correctly. "You're relieving us? But Pularchek has my son. His men just busted him out of a German safe house, and now he's kidnapped Nick and taken him with him."

"German safe house? The Germans are involved?"

"After the suicide attack, they grabbed Pularchek and Natalie and drove them to their Ursus safe house. I saw Angela Wolff of the BND myself."

"Wolff was there?"

"Yes, sir. The Germans had Pularchek under surveillance and were waiting to make a move to snatch him. They obviously want him badly."

"Where is Wolff now?"

"The Germans escaped. They are likely regrouping to take another run at taking Pularchek into BND custody."

"Why would Pularchek kidnap Nick? He's the young man's father, the same as you. It doesn't make any sense."

"It doesn't have to make sense. All I know is I'm going to get my son back, sir."

"Are you disobeying a direct order?"

"No, I'm going after my son."

"Like hell you are. This is bigger than you, or that boy of yours. You're going to stand down and disengage immediately. Team Alpha is taking the football from here."

"No way, my son is out there and I'm going to get him."

"I command you to stand down, Ben. Team Alpha is taking over."

"I'm afraid I can't do that."

"Your transportation has been compromised. Your orders are to pull out immediately. You are out of the ballgame. What part of that do you not understand?"

"My son is in the hands of an assassin. I am not standing down until I have gotten him back."

"Your orders are to pull out. You have ruined this operation from the get-go. Team Alpha will be taking over and I am ordering you to disengage immediately and pack it in. I want you and everyone else on your team on a plane out tomorrow. You have twelve hours to get your affairs in order."

"Why are you doing this, Richard? This sounds like overkill."

"This is not overkill, Ben. You're blown, damnit. The Poles know you're there. They have you and your team captured on multiple CCTV cameras. And as far as your son goes, this disaster was brought about by your incompetence. You should never have allowed him to be kidnapped. If you'll recall, I was opposed to this operation from its inception, and now you know why."

"But both the president and director authorized it."

"Yes, well, they don't want anything to do with it anymore. I'm carrying the football now. Either stand down, or hand in your resignation. Now which is it going to be?"

His phone vibrated from another call. He instantly recognized the number.

"I'm sorry, but I have to take another call, sir."

"Have you fucking lost your mind? You don't hang up on—"

"Sorry, sir, but I have to take this!" he cut him off. "It's my son!"

He punched off Voorheiss and accepted the second call. As he did so, Natalie leaned in closer to the phone from the back seat.

"Nick, where the hell are you?"

"I'm fine, Dad. I'm in good hands."

He jabbed angrily at the steering wheel. "That's not what I asked, Nick. Where the fuck are you?"

"That's not important. I need you to listen and do exactly as I say. I will be in touch with you later with more detailed instructions."

"What the hell are you talking about? What's going on?"

"Nothing's going on."

"Are you with Pularchek? Let me talk to the son of a bitch!"

"Dad, you're not listening. I am one hundred percent safe, and now I need you to listen."

"You're not making any sense. How can you be okay if you've been kidnapped?"

"I haven't been kidnapped. I need you to stop asking me questions and do as I say. First of all, I want you to tell Natalie that I'm safe. Second, forget about Wolff and the Germans. Just let them go. And third, when you've refitted your two vans with new tires, you need to head south to Vienna."

"Vienna? Why Vienna?"

"Because that's where we're headed. You've just got to trust me. I'll call you in a few hours with further instructions."

"What the hell is going on? Why has this man kidnapped you, and why are you driving to Vienna? What's in Vienna, Nick?"

"I don't know. But it's important."

"Is he holding you hostage against your will and forcing you to say these things? You've got to talk to me, Son!"

"Dad, I'm fine, really I am. Now turn around and tell Natalie what I just told you. Go on."

"Wait, what the hell?" He looked around the street. "Pularchek has us under surveillance?"

"What did you expect? He's no different than the CIA."

"Nick, you've got to listen to me. I need you to tell me—"

"Dad, you've really got to stop and listen. He's also instructed me to tell you that in the next two seconds my GPS beacon will no longer be operational."

"I can't track you if…" But he stopped right there, aghast, as the moving red GPS dot dissolved into the satellite image background and was gone. "Nick, you can't let him—"

"Goodbye, Dad, I've got to go. Make sure to tell Natalie that I'm okay and that I love her. Everything will become clear very soon. Just drive to Vienna and wait for further instructions."

"Wait, Nick, wait—"

"I love you, Dad. Bye."

CHAPTER 36

EUROPEAN ROUTE E67
SOUTHWEST OF WARSAW

"WHERE ARE YOUR MEN NOW, HERR PULARCHEK? It appears they have abandoned you."

Angela Wolff allowed the smirk on her face to linger while her words continued to resonate. Her adversary's eyes narrowed, but he made no reply as the Land Rover roared southwest on E67. A second vehicle driven by Johannes Krupp took up the rear of the two-vehicle caravan. She couldn't help but feel triumphant. Not only did she have Pularchek firmly in her mitts, but by a stroke of luck, she had managed to lose both her Polish and American pursuers. With the timely arrival of the police at the safe house, both enemies had been forced to drive off in the opposite direction, allowing her and her men to escape with their prize captive. Finally, her luck seemed to have turned.

She was so close to success now that she could taste it.

"My men will come for me," replied Pularchek with his usual defiance. "You just wait and see."

"I don't see how," she said, glancing over his dark blue jumpsuit that had replaced his impeccably-tailored business suit. "Using our safe house was a miscalculation on my part, but now that we have removed all of your clothes and thrown them out the car window, the situation has changed. Your GPS beacons are gone and your compatriots no longer have any way to track you."

He conceded this point with a nod. "Yes, but they are very resourceful, Angela my dear. And I wouldn't underestimate Benjamin Brewbaker and the Americans, either. By the way, I thought the United States was Germany's ally. Is that no longer true?"

"Times and situations change."

"For you, loyalty and honor are malleable, is that it?"

"Don't play the holier-than-thou card with me. You're nothing but a ruthless businessman and cold-blooded assassin."

"To radical Islam, the German neo-Nazi world, and Soviet mass murderers, perhaps. But not anywhere on the planet where sanity prevails."

She said nothing in retort, ignoring him. She was beginning to realize it was the only technique that actually worked to get him to keep quiet.

"The exit's coming up," announced Dieter from the driver's seat.

"I can see. Take it," she said brusquely.

"May I inquire where we're going?" inquired Pularchek.

She sat up in her seat alertly as she read the next road sign. "You'll be telling us the answer to that question soon enough."

"I wouldn't count on that if I were you."

She gave a bloodless smile. "We'll see about that."

They turned off the exit ramp into a light industrial area that looked as though it had fallen on hard times, took a right onto a frost-pitted street, and headed west for two more blocks before coming to a parking lot in front of an abandoned warehouse with a large aluminum sliding door.

The door was open.

"Go in," she commanded Franck. "Quickly now."

They drove inside the warehouse and parked next to a sparkling new Land Rover. Next to the luxury SUV were two articulated semi-trailer lorries with a dozen roguish-looking men standing next to the vehicles. They were heavily armed and smoking cigarettes.

"It's time for you to meet your new friends," she said to her prisoner.

He showed no visible reaction except a ghost of a smile. For a flicker of an instant, she wondered if he knew something that she didn't and was somehow manipulating her. But she quickly dismissed the thought. She was the one in control—not Pularchek.

"They don't look very friendly," he said, looking them over. "Obviously, they're not Polish."

"You're right. They're Austrian."

"So the hills *are* alive—with nincompoops."

"Watch your tongue, or I'll cut it out."

"You can try, Angela my dear. You can always try."

The Land Rover came to a halt. "Escort our guest out of the car and put him in that chair there." She pointed with an abrupt stabbing motion. "It's time to play a little game."

"Why Angela, I always knew that in your heart you were Gestapo."

She couldn't help a little smile of triumph: despite his insolent tone, he was genuinely frightened of her and knew that she was the one in charge. Her men dragged Pularchek out of the vehicle, stuffed him into the folding chair in front of the two lorries, and duct taped him into the chair. She inserted a fresh, single-stack 10-round magazine into her Walther PPQ M2 nine-millimeter semiautomatic pistol and took steady aim.

"You are going to tell me what I want to know, or I am going to shoot off a piece of you every thirty seconds for the next hour until every inch of your body is covered in bloody scabs. That's one hundred twenty shots. I doubt you would survive."

He grinned defiantly. "I just hope you're a good shot."

"I am not half-bad. But unfortunately for you, I am not Olympic caliber like yourself."

She trained her 9mm directly on his right ear.

"Is that really necessary?" he said, as if the gleaming barrel pointing at him were nothing more than an irritating insect.

"I'm afraid so. You Poles are stubborn bastards."

She shifted her sighting down a hair to his right earlobe and squeezed the trigger.

The shot struck his ear dead on, detaching it instantly from his head. Blood sprayed onto the clean white paint of one of the lorries. After destroying his ear, the bullet drove into a wooden tool cabinet behind Pularchek with a dull thud.

It all happened so fast that he didn't even have time to flinch.

He grimaced in pain, but made no other sound. "You're fucking crazy!" he snarled. "Just like your murderous Nazi pig ancestors that came before you!"

She didn't like the way he was talking to her. Why did he have to make it personal against the German race? Why did non-Germans always have to bring up the Nazis when they got into a heated argument? It was like a crutch.

He glared at her defiantly. "You can shoot me a hundred times, but I won't tell you a bloody thing."

She fired again, this time taking off a sliver of his left kneecap.

He screamed in agony.

"Welcome to your own personal Holocaust, Herr Pularchek. Are you ready to tell me where you have hidden my merchandise?"

"Fuck you!"

She noticed Dieter and several of the others looking at her uneasily. "Angela, is this really the best way to do this?"

"You should listen to your lover boy, Angela my dear," said Pularchek, struggling to fight through his pain. "He knows what he's talking about."

"Unfortunately for you, Dieter is not the one in charge." She drew a breath. "Everyone talks in the end. No one can withstand torture indefinitely."

"I don't think you want to try me."

The room went deathly silent. Her men were still looking at her fearfully. A blink of tension crossed Dieter's and Johannes' faces. She trained the muzzle of her Walther once again on Pularchek, this time on his left arm. Keeping his eyes warily on the pistol, he slowly raised his hands above his shoulders in surrender.

"You can shoot me, Angela. But know this. What I have in my possession will never belong to you. It belongs to the world."

"Tell that to my grandfather."

"Your grandfather was a butcher just like Himmler, Eichmann, Höss, and Kaltenbrunner."

"My grandfather brokered the deal with the Americans to end the war in Italy, saved hundreds of Jews, and rescued thousands of priceless works of art. He was a hero."

"You really are quite mad, aren't you? But now that you have put two bullets into me, I do believe that you do have my full attention. But I still have to ask you one question: are you going to let me live? Because if you're not, you might as well get it over with and kill me now."

"If you tell me what I need to know and take me to retrieve my merchandise, I promise you will live. I will even allow your security chief Mr. Romanowski and two of your men to be present for the exchange. But first you have to talk to me. Are you ready to do that?"

He said nothing, stared back at her defiantly.

She fired her gun again, this time blasting off a nub of his left forearm.

He struggled to tear himself out of his duct tape. "You crazy bitch! Have you no sense of honor?"

"Normally, yes, but today I am growing impatient. Where is my merchandise? I know that you think I will just kill you once you divulge the information, so to ease your concerns you don't have to tell me exactly where it is just yet. You just have to point me in the right direction. And then we can make at least preliminary arrangements with your *Counselor* for your safe return."

He grimaced in pain. Blood oozed from his three bullet wounds.

"You want antibiotics, I will give you antibiotics. But first you have to talk to me." She tilted her head towards the two twelve-wheel lorries. "As you can see, we've come fully prepared. Now where is my inheritance, you Polish bastard?"

Pularchek said nothing, didn't move a muscle.

"Do you really want me to shoot you again?"

His caterpillar brows knitted together in a frown. Something about his face looked different, and she wondered if this was the real Stanislaw Pularchek or one of his doppelgangers. No, she told herself, he hadn't been out of her sight all evening, except for the brief moment during the smoke-filled attack outside the safe house garage when the American girl Natalie Perkins had managed to escape. Was it possible the Poles had somehow made an exchange then?

Stop it, Angela, she scolded herself. *You're letting your imagination get the better of you. Look at him: it's Pularchek!*

She narrowed her eyes on him. "Just do as I ask and I won't kill you," she said in as reasonable a tone as she could muster, given her extreme anger, frustration, and impatience at the moment. "This trigger finger of mine is very unpredictable, I'm afraid. So you had better just tell me what I want to know. And once I have the merchandise in hand, I promise I will release you to your devoted Counselor. At the moment, he is probably very worried about you and no doubt feels responsible for your having been taken."

"Your greed knows no bounds, does it?"

She pointed her pistol at him again, this time aiming for his left foot.

"Talk to me, you Polish bastard. Tell me what I want to know, or I'll shoot you again and again until your entire body is one big scar. I'll find out where you've taken the merchandise anyway. All you're doing is saving me time."

She steadied her aim.

He looked at her. His expression was filled with defiance and hate. A part of her couldn't help but admire him for his tenacity. So very, very Polish.

Slowly, she started to squeeze the trigger.

His eyes narrowed with loathing.

She applied more pressure, feeling the gun about to kick.

"All right, all right!" he cried suddenly, taking her by surprise by capitulating. "I will tell you what you want to know. But you have to promise to let me go once you have the merchandise in hand."

"I already promised you that."

"No, I mean, you need to promise on a book of God."

"That is ridiculous. We don't have a Bible."

"Then promise to God. You're Catholic, right, like me? Swear in the name of the Holy Father that you will release me, and I will give you what you want."

"Very well. But you must also swear before God."

"And what am I supposed to swear to?"

"That you will walk away and never pursue me or any of my men for as long as you live, once I have what I want and release you, of course. Do you swear on your honor and that of our mutual Roman Catholic God?"

"Yes, I do."

"Then so do I. I swear to the Father, Son, and Holy Spirit that I will release you upon obtaining my merchandise. I am also giving you my personal assurance as a professional intelligence officer."

"And you have mine as well."

"Good. Now where is my merchandise? Remember, in a gesture of my good faith, all I need is a general location to start with."

The room fell silent. Every member of the team inched forward a hair, ears pricked alertly. But her men were also scared, which pleased her since it meant that they would think twice before double-crossing or challenging her.

"Austria," he said. "Your merchandise is in Austria."

"Where in Austria?"

"West of Vienna."

"I figured as much. But are you telling the truth? Because if you're not, the consequences will be very dire for you."

"I am telling the truth."

She scrutinized him closely. "Very well, I believe you. But before we leave on our little journey into *Österreich*, I need to verify one last thing." She looked at Johannes. "Remove the duct tape."

"What?"

"Just do as I say and remove his binds. I need to perform a physical inspection."

He did as requested. She stepped forward and pointed her gun at Pularchek. "Now take off your jumpsuit."

"I'm bleeding like a stuck pig and you ask me to undress?"

"Just do it, or I'll shoot you again."

He stared at her as if she were insane.

She took two steps towards him and pointed her Walther at his privates. "I said take off your fucking jumpsuit!"

"All right, all right."

He was in so much pain from the gunshots that he struggled to remove the jumpsuit, but after two minutes he managed to pull it off. He stood there in his boxer shorts, grimacing in agony and bleeding onto the floor from his wounds.

"Now remove your undergarments."

"What the hell are you doing, Angela?" cried Dieter.

"Yes, what are you doing?" demanded Johannes. "We didn't sign up for this."

She shot them both a fierce glare before returning her gaze to Pularchek. "Do as I say, or I will shoot you again."

Slowly, he lowered his boxers. She stepped up closely to him, so closely that she could smell the vodka and Polish dumplings on his breath. Then she knelt down and examined his groin area. Next to the V of his grayish-brown pubic hair was a purple splotch perhaps an eighth of an inch in diameter. Having located what she had been searching for, she gave a nod, clicked on the safety, and said coolly, "You may put your clothes back on."

"Before I do, would you please be kind enough to give me some bandages and antibiotics for these wounds? After all, you don't want me to die. At least not until after I've led you to your merchandise, as you call it."

She snapped her fingers at Johannes Krupp. "Get him antibiotics and dress his wounds. Now!"

"But what was it?" asked the subordinate. "What did you see in his groin?"

"His birthmark," answered Dieter. "She needed to confirm that she had the right Pularchek."

"So it's him?" said Johannes. "We have the right one?"

Wolff smiled thinly. "Yes, we have the right one. Now get Romanowski on the phone, so he knows his boss is safe and we can fill him in on our deal. Then we'll promptly hit the road, gentlemen. We're heading south for the Austrian border."

CHAPTER 37

EUROPEAN ROUTE E67

TO THE QUIET HUM of her BMW's engine, Skyler navigated the vehicle to the south, forming the rear guard of Pularchek's caravan. Once again, she missed Anthony, and imagined what he was doing in St. Croix right now. She longed to be with him again, strolling along the beach at Davis Bay, feeling the wet sand between her toes, holding hands with the silvery Caribbean moonlight on their shoulders like a glittering coat of protective armor. Don Scarpello and Alberto may have stolen her youth and turned her towards a life of crime, but she was deeply in love now and that was the only thing that mattered to her. Though she was dedicated to Pularchek's crusade and would fulfill her contract, deep down she couldn't wait to be free and back in the arms of Anthony. She reminded herself that she only had a few days left until that would become a reality with the final, climactic phase of the operation now set in motion.

Skyler—or Angela Valentina Ferrara as she was known upon her entry into the world—was not born an assassin. Nor did she show any early warning signs of one who would pursue a life of violence. The daughter of one of Florence's finest families, she grew up in a climate of aristocracy—a world of resplendent art, influential personages, and second homes. It wasn't until her teenage years that her stable cosmos began to unravel and she was drawn—most would say pushed—towards a darker side.

Her father was a reputable architect, her mother a noble marchesa and art collector known for throwing the most lavish parties in all of Tuscany. Angela, her two brothers, and three sisters grew up in a happy close-knit Roman Catholic family, with every comfort unlimited resources could provide. Art, like religion, was central to the family. The city of Florence was perhaps the world's most prestigious art institute, and the Ferraras took great pride in its colorful history. Seldom did a month pass when Benedetto and Constantina Ferrara took Angela and their other children to study the deft brushstrokes of Botticelli and Da Vinci, the chiseled wonders of Michelangelo, the architectural grandeur of Giotto and Brunelleschi.

But just as important to Papa, as Angela affectionately called her father, was that his children gain an appreciation of the natural world. Papa loved the ocean, mountains, volcanoes—and knew that no artist in the world could convey the palpable spirit of nature as well as nature itself. He often took his children on exciting outdoor adventures around their native land and neighboring countries. From her father, Angela learned to appreciate the wonderfully feral side of God's kingdom.

Mama Ferrara too played a significant role in shaping her daughter's character. It was from her mother's influence that Angela developed an abiding interest in reading and helping out the disadvantaged. The family supported the underprivileged of Florence in a wide variety of ways: sponsoring food drives and art auctions to raise money for the homeless, providing academic scholarships to indigent students, and donating generously to several Catholic charities.

This was the world in which Angela was raised: a world of generosity towards those less fortunate, piousness, and an idealistic faith that people were basically good. By her fifteenth birthday, she was a charitable Catholic girl, an exceptional student, an accomplished pianist, and a talented athlete.

Then, within the next six months, Angela's perfect world began to fall apart.

ψψψ

It began the night of her parent's big gala. She had just finished greeting her parents' guests and returned to her bedroom to finish her homework. The room was on the second floor of the palatial home, at the end of a long hallway and away from the party. Unbeknownst to her, Don Scarpello studied her movements closely as she went upstairs, then followed her. He was a wealthy banker who did business with her father. Both were much respected men in Florence, though it was well known that Don Scarpello had a wandering eye.

When he entered her room, he politely asked if he could use the *gabinetto*. The downstairs bathrooms were occupied, he said, and he had imbibed a little too much wine and needed to relieve himself urgently. Angela knew Don Scarpello was a powerful man in Florence, and though his request seemed peculiar, she had been taught by her parents and Catholic schooling to be obedient to her elders. She showed him to the bathroom and returned to her desk.

It was a bad night to be alone. Her two older brothers and sisters were away at college, her younger sister was staying at a friend's house, and the house servants were busy with the party.

Suddenly, she heard a groan and the bathroom door swung open. Don Scarpello filled the doorway, clutching his chest and crying out for help. *My God,* she thought, *he's having a heart attack!* She rose from her chair and rushed to his aid.

At the moment she reached out to help him, she realized something was terribly wrong. There was a look in his eyes like a wild dog.

He grabbed her in a bear hug. As she struggled to pull away, he spun her around and clasped a hairy-knuckled hand over her mouth. Then, using his thick arms, he carried her into the bathroom.

She tried to fight him off, but he was too strong, his grip like a vise.

Keeping his hand cupped over her mouth to keep her from crying out, he pushed her to the sink and doubled her over. A meaty hand slid up her skirt and jerked down her panties.

"Yes, I am going to hurt you," he leered. "But you will like it."

He shoved his way inside her and began thrusting violently. In and out. In and out.

She tried to break free, but he pinned her against the sink, crushing her.

In and out. In and out.

God, help me! God, please! she cried out in a silent plea, tears pouring from her eyes.

In and out. In and out.

Her mind swam with despair. It seemed unfathomable that this could be happening to her. But the pain she felt was physical too: it was like a fist was punching up inside her. Yet, what tortured her most of all was the sound of Don Scarpello's heavy panting. It made her feel sick to her stomach.

For a moment, she wanted to die.

Finally, her rapist let out a low bovine groan and she saw his face in the mirror, grotesquely contorted in a rictus of pain and pleasure.

Then the brutal shaking stopped.

He removed his hand from her mouth slowly, then whispered to her in a voice that sent chills down her spine. "You wanted it, didn't you? You wanted me badly."

Terrified out of her mind, she didn't answer.

He jerked her head back. "You must speak when you are spoken to."

"Yes, yes!" she cried. "I wanted you!"

"Not so loud, girl," he whispered harshly, slipping his meaty hand over her mouth again. "You can never tell anyone what happened here tonight. Do you hear me—never!"

She nodded, staring at her own helplessness in the mirror, the hairy hand cupped over her mouth.

"No one would believe you. They'd call you a little whore. So you won't say anything."

She tried to nod again, but he pulled her head back sharply before she could.

"If you tell, I will strangle you with these strong hands. Do you hear me, girl? I will strangle you. Then I will come for your father and mother."

She nodded again, praying desperately he would just leave her alone.

"There is no evidence, you see. I wore a condom. Thoughtful of me, wasn't it? You won't get pregnant from Don Scarpello's seed."

He withdrew himself, and in the reflection of the mirror, she saw him pull off the soggy, dripping condom. Flushing it down the toilet, he turned back towards her with a smirk of triumph.

It was a look Angela would never forget for the rest of her life.

ψψψ

The atrocity left her feeling angry, guilty, and powerless. But what it did most of all was undermine her faith in humanity and plant the seed of hate and distrust towards men she would carry to the present day. If an important businessman and leading figure of Florence like Don Scarpello could rape her and get away with it, what did that say about other men? Surely there were others in the world far worse than Don Scarpello.

She vowed revenge. Yet she was too ashamed, and frightened of what Don Scarpello might do to her and her family, to tell her parents about the incident. Instead, she kept her feelings corked inside. Over the next few months, her suffering began to manifest itself in a variety of ways. Her grades dropped, she became more withdrawn, her concentration in sports and other tasks tapered off. Her attempts to steer clear of the boys in her class became so obvious they began to taunt her. Her girlfriends abandoned her, claiming she was no fun anymore. Her parents tried to help, sending her to Father Colucci and a child counselor, talking with her teachers, devoting extra attention to her, but their efforts were in vain. She became more withdrawn, moody, and rebellious.

By her final year in secondary school, Angela was a bitter outcast, well on her way to developing a strong antisocial personality. Compounding her problems, her parents let go Gina, a house servant and one of her only friends, when the young woman became pregnant. Angela was furious at this cruel and heartless act, and grew even more distant from her parents.

In the fall, Angela went away to college. Despite her mediocre performance in school compared to her former standards, she had managed to do above-average work and was accepted to the University of Rome. It was there she met Alberto and was drawn to a life of crime.

ψψψ

She saw him for the first time at one of the cafés near the campus where the arm-chair anarchists, socialists, and revolutionaries hung out. Despite her burgeoning hatred of the opposite sex, she couldn't help but notice him. He moved on the balls of his feet in a way that was beautifully animal-like, and his eyes sparkled with passion. He spoke knowledgeably about the cruelty of the ruling classes, the *polizia*, the government. But most important, he was kind, so different from the perverted boys that had tormented her in school and the overweening men of her father's upper-crust circles.

He didn't approach her at the time. It was only after she had begun frequenting the café on a regular basis that they met. Despite her animosity towards the male sex, she was taken in by Alberto Como's powerful charisma, as if under a spell. They soon began spending a lot of time together, attending protests, meeting in secret with underground revolutionaries. Disillusioned with the world, rebellious and impressionable, young Angela was ripe for manipulation and indoctrination.

Within two months, she had dropped out of school, was living with Alberto, and had joined People for the Liberation of the Proletariat (PLP), a newly formed offshoot of the Italian Red Brigade. Undergoing extensive training, she was soon proficient in the use of small arms, surveillance, basic explosives, disguise, and photography, the latter at which she particularly excelled. Over the next two years, PLP proved as capable as its mother cell, pulling off the assassination of Italian Prime Minister Paolo Volpe and blowing up a police station and several government buildings. Angela was not directly involved in any of the attacks; at this point she spent her time on photographic surveillance and research, with the occasional courier assignment. She was not bored with the work; on the contrary, by the end of her second year, she felt a great sense of accomplishment. She genuinely believed she was fighting for a noble cause, and saw herself not as a terrorist, but a freedom-fighter. Her emotional attachment to Alberto grew; he and the PLP became her new family.

It was in her third year that she was called upon for violent action. The target was Gustavo Testa, a high-ranking public official who was launching a crusade against the Mafia and various terrorist cells. It was rare that PLP and the Mafia joined forces, but they had agreed to put aside their differences for a common goal. Testa would be vacationing in Monaco for the week and the hit was to take place in front of his hotel, when he left to dine out for the evening.

Angela had demonstrated exceptional accuracy with a long-range rifle in target practice, and it was her job to cover Alberto's retreat after he swept in on his motorcycle and killed Testa at close range. She was to pour a hot fire into Testa's three bodyguards from the heights to the west, enabling Alberto to race away safely after completing his assignment. As it turned out, nothing went according to plan and Angela was forced to improvise.

The scene would always unfold like a silent motion picture to her. She remembered Testa and his bodyguards stepping cautiously out the front door, the sunlight catching their faces. Suddenly, their expressions changed as they heard a sound down the street. Like startled prey animals, they turned in unison towards the motorcycle, fifty meters away and closing fast. There was a split second of uncertainty as the bodyguards tried to gauge whether the man racing towards them posed a threat, then, erring on the side of caution, they went for their guns. Angela felt a momentary sense of panic as she realized the element of surprise was lost and Alberto might be killed.

Summoning a calm she didn't know she possessed, she placed the crosshairs on the first bodyguard, just as he withdrew his gun, and squeezed the trigger. There was a spurt of blood, his gun hand went limp, and the semiauto dropped harmlessly to the sidewalk. She swung the rifle over and locked onto Testa. The first bullet pierced his heart; the second, as he fell, drove into his brain, killing him before he hit the ground. Sighting the bodyguards again, Angela poured in heavily concentrated but harmless fire at their feet as they dove for cover behind a nearby Citröen. Her final image was of Alberto blazing past the hotel, his body crouched down low like a Mongol horseman to avoid counterfire that never came.

Within the PLP, Angela was heralded as a hero. The killing brought her a feeling of satisfaction for all the wrongs done to her. She wanted to kill again, and she chose as her target the man who had originally set off her anger at the world: Don Scarpello. She didn't ask for permission from, nor was the hit sanctioned by, PLP. She performed the surgical strike alone at night, zooming in on her motorcycle just like Alberto, shooting Don Scarpello twice in the face at point-blank range.

When she told Alberto and the other PLP chieftains what she'd done, they were furious at her. Field operatives were not allowed to carry out lone-wolf actions that might expose the group to the police. In the wake of the Testa assassination, PLP was being pursued with a vengeance and putting the group in jeopardy was considered an egregious offense. The fact that, for a second time, a motorcycle had been involved only made things worse. Angela's apologies to the group and promise to never make such a mistake again fell on deaf ears.

Less than a month later, they tried to bump her off.

In retrospect, she should have realized she was being set up when she drew the assignment to deliver a bomb to a police refueling depot in Naples less than a month after killing Scarpello. The bomb was supposed to explode five minutes after she activated the timer, but instead went off after only thirty seconds. If not for the protection afforded by a heavily armored urban assault vehicle parked at the depot, she would have been blown to bits.

She knew the instant it happened that Alberto had betrayed her.

ψψψ

After the incident, she secluded herself at her parents' vacation home on Stromboli. In the torrid heat of August, they were not expected for six weeks. Every day she walked along the black sandy beaches, swam in the azure blue water, and tried to make sense of what had happened.

Slowly, it dawned on her that Alberto had used her and considered her expendable all along. She knew that terrorist cells often preyed on angry students like herself to achieve their political ends, but she had never suspected that Alberto would betray her like this. She wished she had not given so much of herself to him. She had shared his bed, cooked his meals, loved him as much as any woman could love a man. And yet, through it all, she had been nothing more than a pawn in his eyes.

She tried to figure out what to do with herself. At twenty-one, she was young enough to put her past behind her and go on to lead a productive life. The only problem was, now she posed an unacceptable security risk. Alberto and the others were sure to come looking for her. They would hunt her down and kill her like a dog.

There was another problem: she found she liked being an assassin. She was beginning to think of herself as a professional. More importantly, her job allowed her to take revenge against men. They were the ones to blame for setting her down this path—and now she had the opportunity to make them pay again and again for what they'd done to her. She didn't need to get out of the game; what she needed were some new male targets—and protection.

As luck would have it, she was given both.

ψψψ

His name was Charles Xavier and he ran operations for the National Defense General Secretariat, better known as the French intelligence service. He came to the villa one afternoon, accompanied by three heavily armed men, and surprised her in the kitchen.

He was not here to arrest or kill her, he said, but to strike a business arrangement. He told her that Alberto Como and several high-ranking members of PLP had been arrested in connection with the assassination of Gustavo Testa, as well as the bombing of a government building. From a discreet source, he had learned that Angela was the sniper in the Testa incident. He was impressed with her shooting skill and was interested in taking on a woman of her obvious talents under his umbrella. In an eerily calm voice, he gave her a choice: come work for him, and gain all the protection and anonymity a man in his position could offer, or go to prison for life.

He gave her five minutes to decide.

Despite her distrust of the Frenchman, she had no choice but to accept. She went to work soon after as a non-official cover asset of French intelligence, which meant that if caught, the general secretariat would deny any association to her. Xavier outfitted her with the latest James Bond gadgets and computer hardware. Her first target was a German industrialist who had stolen important nuclear fusion secrets from a French R&D firm. She made the long-distance hit when he was riding his horse in the Austrian Alps. Afterward, Xavier lowered his commission from fifty to twenty-five percent and set her up in a safe house in Paris. This was just the beginning, for he had big plans for her.

Over the years, Xavier fed Interpol and the world's intelligence community misleading tidbits of information on his prized assassin. The fictitious Diego Gomez, reportedly a medium-built Spaniard in his late-thirties to mid-forties, became the man sought for the majority of her hits. He was purported to be an independent contractor working mostly for the Basque separatist movement Euskara. For years, the mystery man appeared on the international watch lists, but there was not a single high-quality photograph or police artist's sketch of him. Over the same period, Angela was never brought in for questioning and no photograph or sketch of her face appeared on any Interpol alert. As a contract killer, she simply didn't exist.

Xavier eventually retired from his post and went into private practice, becoming Angela's control agent. Despite her hatred of men, she found him a fair person and their business partnership proved beneficial to both parties. He set her up with false passports, credit cards, and identity papers and continued to supply false clues to the growing Gomez legend, keeping her safe from the authorities. His contacts on both sides of the law brought in steady work. Meanwhile, she performed her assignments with methodical coolness.

Over the years, as the body count steadily grew along with her numbered Swiss bank account, Angela's hatred of the opposite sex never waned. In the face of every man she was about to kill, she always saw first Don Scarpello, then Alberto. And then she squeezed the trigger.

The trigger of hate and revenge.

And then one day she met a burnt-out but wonderful Hollywood film producer named Anthony Carmeli—and she rediscovered how to love. He had changed her life and made her want to return to humanity for good.

But most importantly, he had made pulling the trigger more difficult than she could ever have imagined.

CHAPTER 38

OSWIECIM (AUSCHWITZ) DEATH CAMP
SOUTHERN POLAND

THE NEXT MORNING, Nick Lassiter's biological father pointed up at the cold steel entrance gate inscribed with the words *Arbeit Macht Frei*—Work Makes Freedom—and solemnly shook his head. "Over one million people were murdered by the Nazis here at Auschwitz," he said, the lines of his middle-aged face visible in the radiant sunlight. "Four hundred thousand of them were Poles, and three-quarters of those were Jews. Unfortunately, work meant anything but freedom for the innocent men, women, and children who were shipped in cattle cars to this nightmare on earth."

Lassiter nodded softly, saying nothing. After a brief pause, Pularchek continued.

"Your great-grandmother Sara, her identical twin sister Rachel, your great-uncle Victor, and several other of your great relatives were all sent to this camp. Your great-grandmother is the only one who survived. But, even she had terrible nightmares until the day she died. I used to comfort her when she'd wake up screaming in the night. Your great-grandmother, Mikolaj...your great-grandmother lived and actually survived at this death camp where you are standing now." He shook his head sadly. "She survived, Mikolaj, but she was never the same. She was a wonderful woman. She loved Chopin and hated Wagner. God, that's why I loved her so."

Lassiter looked up at the meaningless, pithy words—*Work Makes Freedom*—and felt a mixture of anger and physical revulsion. But he was also curious. Curious about his past written in the deeds of his ancestors. Curious about his great-grandmother Sara who had miraculously survived this terrible place. Until two days ago, he had had no past, no blood family, no definitive history. But since coming to Poland, he had found that his history was literally everywhere. Still, he was a bit frightened by it all; everything was happening so fast that he was still struggling to catch up.

His father patted him on the shoulder. "I know this is a lot to take in," he said, as if reading his mind. "I am sorry that we had to do it like this."

"So, you're finally conceding that kidnapping your one and only son is not the ideal situation for male bonding?"

"I have not kidnapped you. I just wanted to spend some quality time alone with you before we take care of this ugly business with the Germans."

"We?"

"Yes, we. Father and son. Actually, Benjamin Brewbaker and your wife Natalie will be there for the closing act too, so I should say *fathers, wife, and son.*"

"So for quality time you decided to bring me to Auschwitz?"

"Yes, well, nuance was never my strong suit."

"You think? After a suicide bombing attack, the second coming of the Warsaw Uprising at a German safe house, and now Auschwitz? I don't know how you became a billionaire, but it certainly wasn't through your people skills."

"I am a Pularchek, what can I say? But you do have a way with words, Nicholas. I can see now why you are a bestselling author."

"Sorry, but flattery will not lead to more father-son bonding."

"Okay. I apologize for not being a very good host. I have put you and Natalie in danger, and for that I am truly sorry. How was your call to her and your father this morning by the way?"

"Good, but it could have been a little longer."

"Again, my apologies. But there are so many eavesdroppers listening in these days—particularly the American, German, and Russian intelligence services—that I had to make you keep the call short. Now, will you please let me give you the tour?"

"All right, but you're going to have to tell me who that man was last night your Polish team exchanged you for. And why in God's name he looks exactly like you."

"There are some things that are best left a mystery. Trust me on this."

"You're really not going to tell me?"

Pularchek shrugged.

"I want to know why that man exchanged before my eyes is willing to risk his life for you. What kind of power do you hold over these doubles of yours?"

Again, he said nothing. There was a hint of pain in his eyes, but his expression was still inscrutable, yielding nothing resembling an answer.

"You're really not going to tell me what the hell is going on?"

He waved his head gently at his surroundings. "Not here, Nicholas. Not in this hallowed place where our ancestors died. It would not be fair to them."

"Then where? And when? When are you going to tell me what I want to know?"

"I have already told you: when the Germans get their comeuppance and you and I have avenged our ancestors not with bullets, but with our brains." He tapped his temple. "Then Mikolaj—then I will tell you what you want to know."

"You promise?"

"I promise. Come now, let me now show you the camp. The camp where our Polish ancestors lived—and died."

CHAPTER 39

OSWIECIM (AUSCHWITZ) DEATH CAMP

THEY PASSED BENEATH the main entrance and walked along the former electrified fence that enclosed the perimeter of the camp. Pularchek's chief of security—whom Lassiter had learned was named Romanowski though his boss called him simply Counselor—and a security team of eight armed individuals walked behind them at a discreet distance. Though solemn and taciturn, they were all friendly when he spoke to them. He had managed to talk to four in particular and even to learn their virtually unpronounceable names: Janusz Skrzypek, nicknamed Janu, was Pularchek's personal driver; Jerzy Gagor and Andrzej Kremer were his two primary bodyguards; and the quiet but intense-looking Rachel Landau, a young Jewish woman that he had learned had worked for the Mossad. She was Pularchek's counterintelligence-electronics expert and the only woman in the group, except for the one called Skyler.

The dark-eyed, sad, and uncommonly beautiful loner was no longer in disguise and seemed to be keeping an eye on things from a distance, as if she was an added layer of protection or some sort of guardian angel. He found her intriguing and wanted to know more about her. But every time he made an inquiry, Pularchek quietly requested that he refrain further from doing so, which only added to his sense of intrigue. There was something captivating about her and as an author, he couldn't help but feel a mini-obsession over her mysterious backstory.

They walked parallel to a double-cordoned barbed wire fence for several minutes before heading towards a crematorium. Situated at the edge of the camp, it was a small nondescript structure built into the ground that included a gas chamber, iron body carts, and furnaces. This wasn't a sanitized Hollywood version of a Holocaust concentration camp like in *Schindler's List*—this was the real thing—and it tore Lassiter up inside to witness it firsthand.

"The older women and young children were often murdered immediately upon arrival and were never even registered," said Pularchek as they stopped to gaze upon the gas chamber. "So the estimate of 1.1 million people killed here is the minimum number. Many scholars put the number closer to 1.5 million."

"How did my great-grandmother Sara survive?"

"By sheer luck, if you can call it that. She and her twin sister Rachel were only eleven when they were first brought here. Because they were twins, they drew the interest of Dr. Joseph Mengele. The *Todesengel*."

"The Angel of Death."

"You have heard of him. He was a true monster of humanity. Mengele conducted horrendous medical experiments on the two girls and Rachel ended up dying. The maniac actually believed he was contributing to scientific research on heredity. But his experimentation on the inmates was complete quackery and had no regard for the health or safety of the victims. As I said, he was particularly interested in identical twins. But he was also obsessed with people with eyes of two different colors, dwarves, and those with physical abnormalities. My grandmother would never speak of what Mengele did to her, but I will never forget her screams in the night. They were unearthly howls of torment that didn't seem human."

Lassiter was rendered speechless as he took in the long-abandoned death camp. Auschwitz was such a staggering display of inhumanity that he could scarcely grasp it. And to think that his very own Polish ancestors had starved, suffered, been brutalized, and died here made it even more depressing and close to home.

"Surprisingly, Sara lived to be an old woman. I heard her screams for most of my childhood because she lived with my family in her final years. She said that the Angel of Death used to give her candy and cookies. Can you believe that? One minute the good doctor would feed children goodies, the next he would carve them up like a slab of butcher's meat. But worst of all, Mengele firmly believed that he was doing it in the name of science."

In the silence that followed, Lassiter could understand now where Pularchek's deep-seated anger came from. Looking at this horrible place, he couldn't help but empathize with the man and have a better appreciation for why he was so adamantly and violently opposed to evil in the world. That Lassiter's own ancestors, his own flesh and blood, had been part of this nightmare tore him up inside. He felt a kind of weary anguish work its way into his soul. But it also made him feel angry. It was both traumatic and enraging to see up close, firsthand, what the Nazis had done to other human beings.

Though more than seventy years had passed since the camp had closed, he could still hear the tramping of the SS jackboots, the shouting and cursing and macabre laughter of the guards, the barking of the German shepherd attack dogs. And he could still see the roving searchlights, the armed snipers up in the towers, and the innocent being marched into the ovens.

Today, all that was left of what could only be described as hell on earth was a mass grave site. He looked into his father's eyes and he saw the pain and suffering of their ancestors emblazoned on his face like the Star of David. This place held incalculable meaning to him, but it was so inhumane that it touched something deeper. Auschwitz was a part of the greater human experience, an experience that tapped into the most shameful window in the history of mankind. In that moment, Lassiter couldn't help but feel he had a deeper understanding of the man who was his father and what that man was all about.

He sighed deeply, his gut twisted with conflicted feelings: moral outrage, sadness, anger, disbelief, hope that something like this would never be allowed to happen again.

Ever.

"I know, my son, I know," said Pularchek in an assuaging tone. "You're wondering how this could possibly happen? And you're also thinking we have to make sure it doesn't happen again."

"How did you know?"

"Because that is what everyone with an ounce of humanity feels when they come to this terrible place."

They continued on to the cell-block-like barracks and saw inmates' clothing and a huge storage bin filled with footless shoes—the victims remembered only by their absence. They walked through the Wall of Death, an execution plaza where an estimated 20,000 inmates were murdered, most by being shot from behind while standing naked. They made their way to the Birkenau unloading ramp, where train transports from twenty-three countries had arrived and delivered more than a million human beings with loved ones and families to their death. It was here that new arrivals—starving, exhausted, and terrified—were cut out like cattle into those chosen for slave labor in the work camp and those who would be marched to the gas chambers, the latter falsely told that they were going to take disinfecting baths and be rewarded with a warm meal. From the unloading area, Pularchek led him past spindly guard towers; wagons used to transport the countless dead bodies; the ruins of several crematoria; the barracks of the *Sonderkommando* slave labor squads; a delousing center called "the sauna" where inmates selected for work were disinfected with cyanide; and finally to the "Pond of Ashes," where the powdery remains of tens of thousands of the Auschwitz Holocaust victims from Crematory IV were deposited.

They stood there in silence, staring out over the pond, for several minutes as a gentle wind chased through the nearby trees. With the early morning sunlight slanting off the surface of the pond, Lassiter found the setting oddly serene. How many once-happy families had been destroyed by this ghastly place? he wondered as he gazed at the lightly rippled surface where the ashes of thousands of people had been dumped without ceremony.

He felt an arm slip around his shoulder.

"Have you seen enough, my son?"

It took several seconds before he could get any words out. "Yes, I think so. But I don't know that I can ever understand why any of this happened."

Pularchek nodded sadly. "There was a great Italian writer of the Holocaust named Primo Levi. During the war, he was sent to this terrible camp. One cold winter day, he was literally dying of thirst and he broke off an icicle so that he could have a few drops of water. But an SS guard brutally snatched it away from him and tossed it to the ground. Shocked by the guard's cruelty, Primo Levi queried the Nazi in his poor German, "*Warum?*" To which the guard sternly replied, "*Hier ist kein warum*"—there is no why here. You see, my son, there will never be an answer to the question of why Auschwitz happened. Nonetheless, there is still a lesson that can be learned from this horrible place."

"What is that?"

"That we have a most sacred duty as human beings on this planet: to make sure that something like this never happens again. *Never.* That is the thing to take away from this concentration camp where our ancestors were unceremoniously and unwillingly cremated and buried. We must not let evil such as this ever gain a foothold in this world. We must stop it—violently if necessary—before it comes to pass. That is our duty to God Almighty and to humanity."

A lengthy silence fell between them.

"I understand. I understand...now," Lassiter then said softly.

Pularchek gave a patriarchal smile and shook his head. "No, you don't understand yet, Mikolaj. But soon, my son—very soon—you will."

CHAPTER 40

NORD AUTOBAHN (E461)
NORTHEASTERN AUSTRIA

IT WAS THE FRAGRANCE OF THE WILDFLOWERS that reminded Benjamin Brewbaker that they had crossed over from Poland into Austria. With the van's windows rolled down and a stiff breeze coming off the mountains to the west, he smelled a hint of comingled arnica, alpine rose, heather, and hyacinth wafting pleasantly through his nostrils. The scent of wildflowers and the rolling green landscape made him feel rejuvenated and filled the air with renewed possibility.

He knew the reason why. He had cut loose most of his team and now only the genuine diehards remained: himself, Natalie, Glover, and Webb. He had held a briefing late last night and reiterated that Voorheiss intended to suspend him and every one of his CIA team members if they didn't promptly stand down, get on a plane, and return to U.S. soil. It was a direct order from the director of the NCS, who had made it clear that to disobey the order could very well result in more than a suspension; it might cost them their jobs and government pensions. Despite the threat, Glover and Webb had agreed to stay on with him, as had Natalie, who was not an official agency employee but was acting as a temporary, unpaid non-official cover officer. They were all committed to getting Nick back and finishing the assignment.

He thought of Nick. He was still worried about him. But for some reason, the new sense of possibility in the air now that they had crossed over into Austria made him feel as if everything was going to be okay. It was funny, but the fragrance of the alpine flora and verdant landscape seemed to have a healing effect. After a minute more of blissful contemplation, he rolled his car window up and Natalie broke through his thoughts.

"How soon until we reach Vienna?" she asked him.

"Less than an hour now."

"Good, I'm getting hungry." Her fingers were fluttering across her laptop keyboard in the front passenger seat next to him. "By the way, did you know that Pularchek's biotech company—Advanced Biosystems—earned over three billion dollars in revenue last year?"

"Actually, I did know that. I read the PR brochure too."

"Then I'll bet you also know that Advanced Biosystems successfully cloned four Rhesus monkeys in 2005, two chimpanzees in 2011, and Sir Alfred, the celebrity mountain gorilla, in 2016?"

"I know all about the experiments. The formal scientific name is 'somatic nuclear transfer cloning.' It's the same technology that was used to clone Dolly the sheep back in the late 1990s."

"And it doesn't strike you as odd that Pularchek is cloning primates whose reproductive development systems are extremely close to humans, while at the same time he has physical doubles appearing in Europe, the Middle East, and United States?"

"There's still no firm proof."

"What about the photographs in that file you let Nick and I see? And what about the video footage from a half dozen CCTV cameras over the years you were telling us about?"

"The footage is not one hundred percent conclusive. The images are all black and white and partially blurry. The visual match coefficient from our facial recognition software ranges from less than sixty percent to just over ninety percent. They may be clones, but we just don't know. Not with one hundred percent certainty. We need DNA confirmation, and the results won't be in from the blood samples collected in D.C. until next week. Then we'll still need a DNA sample from Pularchek for comparison."

"A facial recognition match of sixty to ninety percent sounds like a high probability to me."

"But it's not one hundred percent. And there also happens to be an international ban on human cloning."

"You think Pularchek actually cares? The guy does whatever he wants. You said so yourself. International laws and boundaries don't mean anything to him."

"You and Nick like that about him, don't you?"

"I didn't say that and Nick's not here to defend himself, so don't put words in either of our mouths."

"I wouldn't dream of it, Ms. Touchy-Daughter-in-Law." He stepped on the gas and changed lanes, passing a BMW on the left. "But our Sci and Tech people at Langley have looked in detail into this human cloning idea that you've just described."

"And?"

"And we've come up blank. We have nothing, nada, no proof one way or the other. And believe me, our top people have been looking hard for evidence of wrongdoing."

"Then why don't you explain to me how he's able to be at two places at once?"

"I've told you we don't have the answer to that question. That's what you and Nick were supposed to find out."

"Looks like it's up to my husband now. Who knows, maybe he's managed to coax Pularchek into telling him the old Polish secret family recipe for cloning?"

They both laughed, and somehow the laughter made him feel better. Though he kept his emotions close to the vest in front of Natalie and the others, he was well aware that they knew he was on edge because of the situation with Nick. His son had been taken from him by his birth father, and Brewbaker was supposed to drive to Vienna and await further instructions. Was he riding on a magic carpet of hopeful illusion? It was true that Nick had not sounded like the typical kidnap victim, but that didn't mean that he wasn't being held against his will and might be in danger. These days, trouble seemed to follow Pularchek like a bloodhound, and Brewbaker had no doubt that Nick's life could be in jeopardy in the coming days if he was left in the hands of the Pole. But what nettled him most was Pularchek—not he—was the one in control of the situation.

His secure phone rang. He gulped when he realized it was his boss Voorheiss again.

He laid out his defense without preamble. "Richard, I'm not packing it in and returning on a red eye. My son is still out there and I'm not leaving until I have him back."

"I've reported your insubordination to both the director and Office of the CIA Inspector General, Ben. Your career with the Company is in serious jeopardy. You might as well just come home now and save yourself further embarrassment. And that goes for Glover and Webb too. They are hanging on by the slenderest of threads as well."

"You already filed a report with OIG?"

"I'm sorry, but you left me no choice. You disobeyed a direct order and you coerced Glover and Webb to do the same. It's one thing to throw away your own career, but to ruin it for those two young men. And your daughter-in-law, she's in a boatload of trouble too. She'll be lucky to find a job again after this fiasco goes on her permanent record. She was ordered to stand down like the rest of you, and yet she refused."

"You bastard, I'm calling the director myself."

"He won't take your call, Ben. He feels guilty for allowing the op in the first place, but you made the most grievous error a field officer can make: you let the locals catch you on their home turf."

"That's not true. No one even saw us."

"The Polish ambassador has requested a meeting with the president. Now the noose is around your neck, not the director's or president's. Polish intelligence knows you were at both Old Town and the German safe house. They have you on video, damnit. You got caught and the director, president, and I aren't going to take the hit for your lapse in security. If you'll recall correctly, I was opposed to the op from the beginning."

"But no one except Pularchek's men saw us."

"That's enough to seal your fate. Pularchek may be a renegade, but he's at least a semi-official one. Polish intelligence may not interfere with him, but you can bet they have eyes and ears in his organization and know where he is and what he's doing at all times."

"They track his doubles? They don't have the manpower."

"Do yourself a favor, Ben, and get yourself and what remains of your team on the next flight out of Warsaw. You need to come in and put an end to this game of yours. If you play your cards right, you and those two irresponsible kids can still salvage your jobs. I promise to put in a good word for you at your hearing. But you have to get out now. Disobeying a direct order once is inexcusable, but doing it twice is suicidal. And don't worry, I'll make sure to get Nick back to you and Natalie in one piece. I'm taking personal command of the operation from here on out."

He stared out at the massive, snow-capped Austrian Alps to the West. Somehow they looked inviting, as if they possessed secrets and were summoning him forward to investigate. And then he pictured the corpses and body parts from the suicide bombing and the rattle of the machine guns at the safe house, and he knew that he couldn't just pack it up and leave his son behind, no matter the consequences. What Voorheiss was asking him to do defied logic, and he suspected that his boss was up to something. He realized that he needed more information—but to get more information he had to pretend as though he was agreeing to come in.

When he next spoke, he made sure that his voice carried a note of resignation. "You promise that you'll get Nick back, sir?"

"I'll do my damndest, Ben. I promise you."

You're a fucking liar. "All right, I understand the situation. I shouldn't have disobeyed you. When are you landing in Warsaw to take charge of the operation?"

"I'm not going to Poland, Ben. I'm landing in Innsbruck in the next..." He stopped right there, as if realizing that he had disclosed more than he should have.

Brewbaker looked at Natalie and smiled.

"Innsbruck, sir. Why are you going to Innsbruck?"

"That's none of your damned business. Now are you coming in or not?"

"What are you up to, Richard? Why are you doing this?"

"I'm not *doing* anything. If anyone's done anything, it's you, Ben. You sealed your fate when you disobeyed my direct order."

"You're overreacting, Mr. Director. You're sending in a cruise missile when all you need is a hand grenade. The question is why?"

"I've heard enough of your insolence. I am informing you that, as of this moment, you are officially on a two-week suspension. And so is every member of your team. You are all being notified by text, phone, and email message as we speak. Your operation has been shut down, Ben. Now get the hell out of there before you lose your pension too."

"Why are you going to Innsbruck, sir? What's in Innsbruck?"

"You're on a two-week suspension, Ben. You can't be asking questions."

"Why don't you just answer me?"

"There's nothing to answer. Goddamnit, you've forced me to do something I didn't want to have to do. You're not on a two-week suspension, Ben. As of this moment, you and your team are fired. Hand in your creds and sidearms at the embassy in Warsaw."

"I'm afraid I can't do that. But I promise I'll try to talk Glover and Webb into turning themselves in. But I wouldn't bank on that happening if I were you."

"I'm talking to a dead man. As of right now, you don't exist. Your career in the Company is over and you are nothing but a ghost."

"I guess the term 'spook' is an accurate term for us after all."

"You're in a lot of trouble, Ben. Just get the hell out of there and you may be able to salvage some semblance of a life from the wreckage you've created."

"So you're going after Pularchek? You're going to take him down, is that it?"

Voorheiss laughed scornfully. "We're not interested in Pularchek any longer. This is much bigger than some renegade Polack billionaire. But I will do my best to get your boy back. You and he deserve that much."

"You bastard."

"No, Ben, I'm not a bastard. I'm about to become the next director of the Central Intelligence Agency."

CHAPTER 41

MIKULOV
SOUTH MORAVIAN REGION, CZECH REPUBLIC

PEERING DOWN UPON majestic Mikulov Castle from an öolitic-limestone-capped overlook, Angela Wolff tossed a SIG-Sauer to Stanislaw Pularchek. He dropped his *smažený sýr* sandwich with the delicious *tatarská omácka* sauce, caught the semiautomatic pistol with both hands despite his plastic zip-tie police handcuffs, and pointed the pistol at her, before realizing, belatedly, that something wasn't right. That something was that the weapon was light. Ejecting the magazine, he quickly verified that the gun had no bullets and tossed it back to her, shaking his head in disgust.

"Do you genuinely enjoy fucking with people?" he asked Wolff through angry eyes.

"Sometimes. But I enjoy obtaining incriminating fingerprints even more."

He stared down at the pistol. Realizing he had been duped, he gave her a look of grudging admiration. "Clever girl. An untraceable backup piece. And your plan is to frame me for murder?"

"That would be the logical conclusion, considering that the laser serial number has been removed and the barrel has been re-grooved."

"So the police cannot make a ballistics match to the original weapon. Who am I supposed to kill?"

"That's to be a surprise. Assuming it is even necessary."

"So I may get a possible reprieve?"

"I wouldn't count on it. But maybe."

With his bound hands, he picked up his fried cheese sandwich with tartar sauce wrapped in butcher's paper from the grass and took a bite with a haughty expression on his face. "You're a first class bitch, Angela my dear. No wonder you've never been married. No one could possibly be willing to live with a royal cunt like you."

She gave a bloodless smile. "Dieter and I get along quite nicely, thank you," she said, glancing over her shoulder at her lover and the rest of her team to make sure they were out of earshot. "As you can see, I like younger men. They have such stamina."

"I hate to tell you this, Angela my dear, but what you and your Dieter have is most certainly not true love."

"What do you know about love? Your wife and three daughters are dead. You couldn't stop them from being suicide-bombed, just like you couldn't save those innocent diners at U Fukiera last night. So who do you have to love, Herr Pularchek? No one but your supermodel tramps who share your bed only because of your vast fortune—that's who!"

She wished she hadn't become quite so emotional, but it was too late now. She looked at him crossly. He showed no visible reaction, except a slight twitch at his left eye. She had hurt him, she could tell, but he wouldn't let it show on his face.

"I know that was cold, but you should hush up and finish eating that fatty Czech sandwich of yours. We'll be getting on the road again soon."

"Why should I do anything you say? You're just going to kill me once you get what you want."

"If that's the case, you might as well enjoy your last few hours on earth rather than indulge in morality lectures. Quite frankly, they're growing tiresome."

"As are you, Angela my dear. As are you."

He turned away from her and stared out at the exquisite, red-roofed Baroque chateau of Mikulov Castle. Like an eagle sitting on a lofty perch, the chateau formed the elevated centerpiece of the sleepy Czechoslovakian hamlet, presiding like a sentry over the stunning countryside strung with wine vineyards and an undulating sea of gently-dipping, cream-colored limestone cliffs. Angela Wolff knew the story behind the quaint little village; it was an often-told tale in this portion of Eastern Europe that had been touched by the Armageddon that was the Second World War.

Mikulov had originally been granted to the Austrian noble Henry I of Liechtenstein in 1249 by Ottokar II of Bohemia. By the time the castle was completed near the end of 13th century, German citizens had been called in to populate the growing region. The settlement steadily grew in importance and by the 16th century, Mikulov was home to both ethnic German and Jewish populations and became the seat of the regional rabbi of Moravia, thus becoming a cultural centre of Moravian Jewry. In 1938, prior to the German occupation of Czechoslovakia, the town's population consisted of 8,000 mostly German-speaking inhabitants that included five-hundred Jews. Only 110 of them would survive the Holocaust. The castle was burned to the ground in late April 1945, a few days before the end of the war by the retreating German Army. Shortly thereafter, the town's German population was expelled. As was the case with Old Town Warsaw, the town and its remarkable castle were rebuilt after WWII through the sweat and sacrifice of the surviving inhabitants.

"Everywhere I go, it seems," said Pularchek, staring down at the castle, "I see towns that have been rebuilt, stone by stone, after you Germans destroyed them."

"It's not good to dwell on the past, Herr Pularchek. You should eat your sandwich—it may very well be your Last Supper."

"You're never going to get away with this, you know. The merchandise you so zealously covet will be your curse for what your ancestors did to the civilized world."

"Oh, so you're giving Stalin and his murderous Russians a free pass, are you? That just proves that you don't know your history."

"I'm afraid there is no moral equivalency between Katyn and Auschwitz," he said, referring to the 1940 massacre in which the Big Red Army, at the time an ally of Nazi Germany under the Ribbentrop-Molotov Pact, murdered over twenty-thousand Polish military officers and political leaders. Later, Stalin and his cronies in the Kremlin tried to blame the mass murder on the Germans, while the Allies remained conspicuously silent in order to preserve their increasingly fragile alliance with the Soviet Union.

"The war has been over for more than seventy years. It's time for you and your fellow Poles to move on."

"No, the war still rages on today. Just look at you and me, Angela my dear. Now the grandchildren of the enemy combatants are the ones carrying on the fight. And it will, in all likelihood, continue on for another century without being properly settled."

Her secure mobile suddenly rang. She looked at the caller ID. Damn, it was Kluge!

She waved a dismissive hand at Pularchek, turned away, and took the call. "Yes, Walther, what is it?"

"What is it? You have the gall to ask me that question when you've just made complete fools out of our intelligence service?"

She covered her phone and gave Pularchek a sharp look. "You even think of trying to escape, me and my men will shoot you down like a mangy dog. Understand?"

When he nodded defiantly, she walked away from him towards her Land Rover so she could have more privacy.

"I'm afraid I don't know what you're talking about, Walther."

"Where are you?"

"I'm afraid I can't tell you that. There have been attempts on my life, and I believe our security has been compromised."

"You need to come in, Angela. I know you have Pularchek."

"I'm not coming in until I know it's safe."

"Damnit, Angela, you have created an international incident. The Polish president has summoned the German ambassador to demand what the hell we were doing prowling around his backyard in Warsaw. The safe house is blown and they know that you took Pularchek. This incident has stoked tensions between our two countries that I haven't seen the likes of since before the Wall came down."

"You and the chancellor both wanted Pularchek, and I've gotten him for you. Don't you dare go soft on me now."

"You don't talk to me like that. I'm your boss, damnit. Somehow *Der Spiegel* is already on top of this story too. I don't know how it got leaked, but it did and now the chancellor wants it all to go away. She's washing her hands of it."

"Are you telling me you no longer want Pularchek?"

"Yes, that's exactly what I'm telling you. He is to be released immediately."

"I'm afraid I can't do that."

"Why the hell not?"

"Because he's the only thing keeping me and my team alive right now. After the safe house attack, Pularchek's men and Polish intelligence wouldn't dare risk getting him killed by another ill-fated rescue operation. They want to avoid collateral damage like the plague."

"Listen to me, Angela. We are in damage-control mode here. This whole operation has brought about unwanted media scrutiny and seriously jeopardized our ties to an important NATO partner. The Polish foreign minister is incensed with what he calls our 'autocratic, kidnap first, ask questions later intelligence style.'"

"I had to go to hell and back to catch this Polish bear. I'm not just going to release him back into the wild."

"You're not listening, Angela. We are faced with a situation that needs to go away, and I mean quickly. Our foreign minister is meeting with his Polish counterpart this evening. The Polish foreign minister has already made it publically clear that snatching its citizens off the streets and dragging them to covert safe houses is an act of aggression. It is certainly not something that can be tolerated in a relationship between supposed friends and allies."

"That's just propaganda for the press."

"No, it's a disaster, and right now we need full damage control. You are to release Pularchek and return to Berlin immediately. Where are you right now?"

She had to buy herself some time. "I'm not coming in until it's safe. I'm sorry, Walther, but that's the only way. I lost several men last night, and I'm not going to lose any more. My team and I need to lay low for our own safety."

"Where are you, Angela. You must tell me, damn you!"

"I can't tell you because I'm not sure who to trust."

"This is madness. Through your mismanagement of the operation, you have created an international incident!"

"No one but Pularchek's people and Polish intelligence knows that we were the ones who took him."

"You need to come in, Angela. If you don't, I will have to send another team in after you!"

"I wouldn't do that if I were you. Unless, of course, you want this to turn into an even bigger international incident. Goodbye, Walther. And for your information, my team and I will no longer be answering our mobiles."

She clicked off, took a deep breath, and stared down at the sprawling castle nestled on the hill below. With its distinctive red roof and graceful ramparts illuminated by the morning sunlight, the chateau called to mind the chivalry of the grand duke of Austria—Albert II of Germany—and the princes of Liechtenstein that had once held court here. It was hard to believe that a village of such sweeping architectural grandeur had been put to the torch by her retreating German ancestors, and then rebuilt stone by stone by the Czechs, after the war. Somehow, the sight of the castle and knowing its infamous history made her feel as if she was losing control of her own situation. And she knew precisely why she felt that way.

It wasn't Kluge she was worried about. It was the damned Americans.

CHAPTER 42

NORD AUTOBAHN (E461)
NORTH OF VIENNA

"WAIT A SECOND," exclaimed Natalie Perkins. "You're telling me that Angela Wolff and Richard Voorheiss actually know each other?"

Brewbaker nodded in the affirmative as he stepped on the van's gas pedal, bombing down the gently rolling hills of the *Weinviertel* wine country and the verdant forests of the *Hochleithen* woods. As he had expected, Natalie, Glover, and Webb had refused the NCS director's request to turn themselves in at the Warsaw embassy and were pushing forward with the operation.

"Voorheiss was the Station chief in Berlin when Wolff was cutting her teeth as a field operative," he said. "They met on numerous occasions, which are well-documented in the files. But that's where the paper trail ends and the speculation begins."

"But the two of them are definitely connected?"

"It would appear so."

They fell into silence, both of them thinking. He could see her mind trying to put the pieces together. She reminded him of his wife Vivian when she was young, and he was glad his son had such a smart, wonderful woman in his life. Looking at her, he felt an intense need to get Nick back so the two newlyweds could be together again and get on with their lives. Jesus, they had been married less than a week and already their world together had turned frightfully dangerous. And it was all because of him. He still blamed himself for allowing them to come over here to Europe. But hopefully, soon Nick would call and the danger would pass. Or was that just wishful thinking?

"Could Wolff have been, or could she currently be, a double agent?" wondered Natalie aloud after a thoughtful silence.

"I don't know. But what I do know is that she's worked closely with the CIA on multiple counterterrorism fronts since 9/11. She's also moved rapidly up the BND ladder—bypassing a dozen of her male colleagues—to get where she's gotten. She didn't rise to second from the top of the German foreign intelligence service by being a shrinking violet."

"Could they have been lovers?" asked the techie Glover, sitting in the back of the vehicle. He and Webb had taken a break from looking over satellite footage of last night's safe house battle and were poring through classified documents.

"That would be a major violation of agency protocol," said Brewbaker, passing an Audi on their left. "But it's certainly within the realm of possibility."

"It says here that Angela Wolf's grandfather was Nazi General Karl Wolff," said Glover. "Has anyone looked at it from that angle?"

Brewbaker was intrigued. "What are you suggesting?"

"Well, Pularchek is a notorious Nazi hunter and he seems to have it out for Angela Wolff, whose grandfather was an *Obergruppenführer* and General in the Waffen-SS. That was the armed combat division of the SS. Karl Wolff also happens to have been the sole negotiator of the surrender document between the Allies and German forces in Italy. It was signed by Allen Dulles of the Office of Strategic Services, the precursor to the CIA. When you consider the connection between both Angela Wolff and her grandfather and the OSS/CIA, and then you throw in Wolff's connection to Voorheiss when he was Berlin Station chief, it raises interesting questions. I don't think the connections between all of these people are just a coincidence. Do you, sir?"

"As a matter of fact, I don't." Brewbaker was impressed with the young technician's logic as he stared off at the forested landscape dotted with cycling and hiking trails and the impressive *Wolkersdorf* castle in the distance. "So give us the quick-and-dirty biography on SS *Obergruppenführer* Wolff. I'm interested to know where you're heading with this."

"Yes, sir, give me one second here." He took a moment to pull up a second classified document before minimizing the screen. "Karl Wolff—Angela Wolff's grandfather on her father's side—was born in 1900 in Darmstadt, Germany, to middle-class parents. He was educated in Catholic schools growing up and became well-versed in literature, music, and the arts, which placed him among the high-society youth of his hometown. He joined the Imperial German Army at the age of sixteen and served as an infantry officer on the Western Front during the First World War. He received two Iron Crosses for bravery and served on the protection detail for the Grand Duke of Hesse alongside other promising officers from aristocratic families. This added to his growing self-image of nobility even though he came from humble beginnings.

"Following the war, he studied law, trained as a banker in Frankfurt, worked for Deutsche Bank and in the advertising business in Munich, and then started his own successful advertising firm. His experience in banking and advertising helped him hone his political skills and his ability to sell himself and his ideas. When he joined the Nazi Party and SS in 1931, some of his peers sneered at the new cultivated Wolff. They considered him a "Septemberling," the derogatory term for those who hadn't joined the Nazi Party until after Hitler took power following the successful elections in September 1930. But even though he was a reluctant Septemberling, Wolff rose quickly through the SS hierarchy. His classical Aryan features—he was six feet tall with blond hair and grayish-blue eyes—suited him well for the SS. Motivated by his ambition to be a member of the elite, he embraced Nazism as a calculated choice in contrast to many of his fanatical colleagues. He soon became a close confidant of *Reichsführer* Heinrich Himmler, commander of the SS.

"From 1936 to 1939, Wolff served as Himmler's chief of personal staff and representative in Hitler's military headquarters, with responsibility for several departments of the SS. In July 1941, Wolff accompanied Himmler on a visit to an SS command post near the Soviet city of Minsk. Here he witnessed the shooting of one hundred innocent Jews. According to available records, he was shocked and repulsed by this traumatic event. Shortly thereafter, he was ordered to Italy to serve as 'Highest SS chief' with headquarters in Fasano, forming a diplomatic link between Kesselring's forces in southern Italy and other German Army groups in the north. Hitler and Himmler both trusted him. They considered him a true specimen of noble German blood, a veritable knight in shining armor. Wolff had also won favor with Mussolini while acting as an honorary escort during the Fascist dictator's state visit to Munich in 1937 and on numerous subsequent trips to Italy.

"Once in Italy, one of his first assignments from Hitler was to invade the Vatican and seize Pope Pius XII, who the Führer believed was not adequately supportive of Nazi Germany. Wolff managed to talk Hitler out of the misguided mission, which he knew would be a public relations disaster. He argued that the occupation of the Vatican and kidnapping of the Pope would turn the entire Catholic world and Italy against Germany, including German Catholics at home and at the front. He advocated a compassionate policy that he called the 'easy hand' with Italy and convinced a reluctant Hitler that such a policy was in his best interest.

"Wolff then served as the head of all SS forces in Italy until his surrender in Bolzano on May 13, 1945. By that time, he had spent nearly fourteen years in the SS—including six years as chief of staff to Himmler—and was the second ranking SS member taken into custody following the war, once Himmler committed suicide. And yet, he was not tried at the Nuremberg Trials."

"Why not?" asked Natalie.

"Because he single-handedly negotiated the surrender of German forces in Italy," replied Brewbaker, keeping his eyes on the autobahn. "Allen Dulles—OSS chief in Switzerland and future director of the CIA—managed to quietly and secretly get him a Get-Out-of-Jail-Free card."

"It was called Operation Sunrise," said Glover. "Wolff met with Dulles on two occasions to secure the surrender six days before the final German capitulation of its northern forces in Berlin. I have a quote here from British Major General Terence Airey, a military adviser present at the second meeting with Dulles on March 19, 1945. He said: 'The surrender of the German armies in Italy was due to the initiative of Karl Wolff, who contacted Allied Forces while the war was still in progress and consequently against the wishes and declared policy of the Nazi government and at great risk to himself, his actions led to the abandonment of a fighting withdrawal into Northern Italy and Austria and must necessarily have saved the lives of a large number of German soldiers, Austrian and Italian civilians, and avoided useless destruction.'" He looked up. "That's a pretty strong endorsement from an Allied general, considering that the man was a top Nazi general."

"Are you telling us this SS prick was a good guy?" asked Webb.

"He did risk his life on multiple occasions to bring about the early surrender of German forces in Italy. It says right here that his actions saved thousands of lives, and spared the destruction of roads, buildings, and other important infrastructure. At the time, the Allies obviously thought what he did was significant. They wouldn't have allowed Dulles to cut a deal with the man and would have tried him at Nuremberg if they thought he was a truly bad apple."

"Wolff was also instrumental in preserving thousands of priceless works of art," said Brewbaker. "Or at least that's the prevailing myth."

Natalie's eyebrows flew up from the passenger seat next to him. "Are you saying that he worked with the Allied Monuments Men?"

"Wait, are you talking about those guys that were brought in to safeguard European art collections?" asked Webb. "Like in the George Clooney movie?"

"That's what it says in this report," said Glover.

"Okay, now this is really getting interesting," said Natalie.

"From December 1944 onward," continued Glover, "*Obergruppenführer* Wolff made sure certain art treasures were not moved out of Italy to the salt mines of Altaussee in Austria despite significant resistance from other German officers. Apparently, he even ignored Himmler's order to transfer the Florentine works to the mines. Furthermore, because of his direct orders and disobeyance of Himmler's orders, the *Kunstschutz* art protection representatives were at both repositories to deliver the works of art to American forces—and the Monuments Men—once they arrived in 1945. In short, he was instrumental in saving Italy's art and making sure it didn't get in the hands of his fellow looting Nazi officers."

Brewbaker smiled inwardly; he knew the actual truth was far messier than that. "So Karl Wolff—Plenipotentiary General and Highest SS and Police Führer in Italy—acted altruistically to preserve Italy's art treasures, rather than selfishly placing them at great risk to buy his freedom. Sorry, kiddos, but I ain't buying it."

They were all looking at him, waiting for more.

"Whatever the good deeds of General Wolff may have been, they have to be considered within the context of who he truly was. The man you just described was an aspiring elitist and social climber, a man who was always looking out for his own interests first and foremost. And our rudimentary conceptual model must also take into account his role in facilitating the Holocaust and more than a decade of devoted service to the SS, including serving six years as Himmler's right-hand man. And then there's one more nugget of information in that file of yours that is damaging to Mr. Altruistic *Obergruppenführer*."

"What's that, sir?" asked Glover.

"Shortly after his arrest in May 1945, the Bourbon-Parma private art collection was discovered in the Castle Dornsberg, one of Wolff's residences."

"Are you saying he was an art thief like Göring and Rosenberg?" The CIA technician was referring to the Nazi Reich Marshal and the Aryan Supremacy Racial theory ideologist, the two most prominent Nazi art looters during the war. Both were found guilty of war crimes and sentenced to death at Nuremberg.

"The answer is *maybe* or *we don't know*. But what we do know is that our boy Wolfie wasn't among the defendants at Nuremberg. In fact, he wasn't even indicted. So the question, boys and girls, is not how or why *Obergruppenführer*

Karl Wolff eluded prosecution? No, the real question is what was he offered in return for his *services* in helping terminate the war in Italy?"

"Are you suggesting that Allen Dulles gave him some kind of financial reward or gift?" asked Natalie.

"Thanks to Mr. Glover's excellent doctoral thesis here, the thought was beginning to cross my mind."

Glover said, "Dulles maintained to his grave that there was never any deal between him and Wolff, and that the general received no immunity from prosecution. After he was fired by Kennedy in 1961, Dulles wrote several books and he always denied having protected Wolff. But his private correspondence undercuts that contention."

"It says that in your file there?" asked Webb.

"As a matter of fact it does." He performed a quick search and highlighted a paragraph on the screen. "It says here that Wolff angered Dulles by seeking reimbursement for his property and financial losses incurred through the handling of the Italian surrender. This was in 1950. Dulles wrote a subordinate in Switzerland about Wolff seeking reimbursement from the U.S. government for brokering the surrender deal. In the correspondence, Dulles states, 'Hasn't Wolff gotten enough? Doesn't he realize what a lucky man he is not to be spending the rest of his days behind bars? Doesn't he know that the wisest policy would be to keep quiet? Very quiet.'"

Natalie was shaking her head in wonderment. "So you're saying that Allen Dulles—who, at that time was the future head of the CIA, and is now an American icon—gave Wolff a major war prize and told him to shut up? And no one has come forward with this conspiracy theory until us hammerheads came up with it two minutes ago?"

"It looks that way," said Glover with a shrug.

They all looked at Brewbaker. He knew that they were on to something here. At the same time, he couldn't help but feel that they were digging up skeletons that might very well be better off remaining buried. His gut told him that the path they were headed down was a slippery slope that would inevitably lead to danger for him and his renegade team. And for Nick as well.

"I don't know. Perhaps the reason us hammerheads have come up with this is because we now have a common thread, a chain that links all of these people together. And that thread is the OSS and the CIA."

"Yeah," said Webb. "But if all of this is true and Director Voorheiss is involved or covering up some old OSS-CIA secrets, who the hell can we trust?"

Brewbaker had to confess that he didn't know the answer to that one as he stared through the windshield at the historic Austrian city of Vienna coming into view. He remembered an old Napoleon maxim: "If you start to take Vienna," the legendary French field commander had said, "then take Vienna." Which was another way of saying that timidity was ruinous. He pictured his tyrannical boss Voorheiss. Something was still missing in all this—he could feel it in his bones. Still stumped, his only recourse was to pose another question.

"If Wolff was given a substantial gift from Dulles, why would Wolff later complain about his losses suffered during the Italian capitulation? He would thank his lucky stars that he was still alive, lay low, and keep his mouth shut, don't you think? Unless...unless the gift was something he couldn't have access to right away. Something he had to wait to collect until the coast was clear and he wasn't being watched."

Natalie's eyes lit up. "You mean, like something that might be left to future generations?"

Glover was nodding vigorously. "Like a granddaughter. But how does Director Voorheiss fit in then?"

Brewbaker smiled. "Perhaps he has discovered what Angela Wolff has been bequeathed, and he wants it for himself."

"How?" asked Natalie.

"Someone told him. The same person that told Pularchek."

"Oh shit, now I see where this is headed," said Webb. "This is going to end badly for us all, isn't it? The director of the National Clandestine Service is certainly not going to go quietly into the night."

"We don't know for sure that Voorheiss is dirty. But he definitely wants us out of the way. Which means that either he wants to recover the prize and return it to its rightful owner—as in do the right thing and get the credit—or he's dirty and he wants to keep it for himself."

"After meeting the guy, I wouldn't bet on the former," said Natalie worriedly. "And now he's coming to Austria."

"Jesus, this is way above my GS-7 pay grade," lamented Webb.

"It's above my pay grade too," admitted Brewbaker. "But we still have a job to do."

The van went silent, as the realization dawned on them that they were in for a tough and potentially dangerous battle, a battle that involved one of their own. Just like New York, thought Brewbaker, remembering back to when Natalie had been shot in the stomach. Jesus, he didn't want that to happen again. Suddenly, he felt the oppressive burden of the operation. Once again he was questioning the integrity of one of his own superiors. And that, he knew from hard experience, always led to trouble. But at least now he understood why alarms had been going off in his head when he had last spoken to his boss. Voorheiss was definitely up to something. And that something, whatever it was, had to do with Angela Wolff and did not bode well for Brewbaker and his team.

"What are we going to do now, sir?" asked Glover.

"We're going to wait to hear from Nick. I have a feeling that he and Pularchek are going to help us answer a few questions."

"You think we can actually count on Pularchek?" asked Webb.

"Before I was skeptical, but now I think I'm beginning to understand the man. You see, he's been toying with Angela Wolff all along, playing a game of cat and mouse."

"But what does that mean for us, sir?" asked Webb.

"It means that soon, very soon, we're going to be strapping on our helmets, coming off the bench, and joining in the ballgame. And this time, we're going to make the most of it."

"I like the gridiron analogy, sir."

"Good. Then I'm sure you'll appreciate a military one even more. If you start to take Vienna, take Vienna."

"Who said that?" asked Natalie.

"Napoleon. And right here and now, on this historic occasion, that's us, boys and girls. We're Napoleon."

Glover looked confused. "We're Napoleon? I'm not sure I understand, sir."

"It means that when we link up with my son and Pularchek, we're going to have to take the offensive and kick some serious ass. Just like *Le Petit Corporal*."

CHAPTER 43

ST. STEPHEN'S CATHEDRAL
VIENNA

"THIS IS MONSIGNOR HOESS. He's going to tell us a little story about the Nazis, Nicholas. Or, I should say, one Nazi in particular."

Taken off guard by his father's brusque demeanor towards the Catholic priest, Lassiter looked from Pularchek to Hoess before cordially extending his hand. The monsignor's deeply-fissured face had darkened with something that looked like shame. He was strapped into a high-tech electric wheelchair with joystick controls, and his apparel consisted of steel-rimmed spectacles, a broad cloak the color of ebony bound by a crimson sash, and a wide-rimmed black hat. With his rutted face, stooped shoulders, and cadaverously thin legs like sickly tree branches, he looked like he had barely survived the Holocaust. But Lassiter knew better: Helmut Hoess, respected monsignor of St. Stephen's Cathedral, looked like a man who had once straddled the precarious line between both sides—the Axis and Allies—during the global conflagration that had claimed the lives of more than sixty million people.

"It's a pleasure to meet you, Monsignor. I am Nick Lassiter, Mr. Pularchek's prodigal American son," he said, hoping to ease the tension and perhaps even draw out a little smile.

But the monsignor's lips remained tightly compressed, like welded steel.

"This way, gentlemen," he said curtly in English that carried a heavy Austral-German accent. Using his claw-like hand, he flicked the joystick on his electric wheelchair and took off through the cathedral at a pace that Lassiter found alarming.

His biological father smiled mischievously as they hurried after the speedy octogenarian. The interior of St. Stephen's was packed with intricate altar pieces, stone canopies, masterful Gothic sculptures, and other iconic works of art that many of the finest museums in continental Europe could only dream of possessing. Lassiter took it all in wonderment as they passed the stone pulpit of the nave, a self-portrait of the artist Anton Pilgram looking out a window with a sculptor's compass, and a series of intricate wood carvings and sculptures that made him feel the sacrosanct yet frightening power of the Roman Catholic Church. Hoess parked his wheeled contraption on the left side of the Middle Choir, in front of the Wiener-Neustadter Altar with an angled view of the shimmering High Altar. Staring out at the majestic scene, Lassiter's mind harkened back to the days of his youth at St. Peter's Catholic School in Denver, Colorado, as he took in the mingled fragrance of votive candles, religious oils, and holy water.

"This cathedral almost didn't survive the Second World War, Mikolaj," said Pularchek in a subdued church-voice as they took their seats next to Hoess. "During the German retreat in April 1945, the commandant of the city ordered a certain heroic captain named Gerhard Klinkicht to fire a hundred shells and leave the cathedral in a heap of stone debris and ashes. But Klinkicht disregarded his orders and spared the wanton destruction of Vienna and its treasures. Unfortunately, as fate would have it, civilian looters lit fires in nearby shops as the Soviet Red Army entered the city from the east. The winds carried the infernal blaze to the cathedral, where it severely damaged the roof, causing it to collapse and gutting the choir vaulting and the south *Heidentürme* tower. Fortunately, protective brick shells built around the pulpit, Frederick III's tomb, and other treasures minimized damage to the most valuable artworks. The reconstruction of the cathedral took nearly fifteen years. It wasn't until 1962 that she was restored to her former glory. It was a communal effort, involving the whole of Austria: the new south bell and floor were paid by Upper and Lower Austria, the pews by Vorarlberg, the windows by Tyrol, the candelabra by Carinthia, the communion rail by Burgenland, the tabernacle by Salzburg, the roof by Vienna, and the portal by Styria." He tipped his head towards the High Altar. "Magnificent, isn't it?"

"It certainly is," replied Lassiter as he took in the polished black marble, the statues of Austrian patron saints, and the Gothic stained glass framing the High Altar.

His father cleared his throat. "Well, now that you've had your history lesson, it's time for another." He made eye contact with Hoess. "Monsignor, if you would be so good as to tell my prodigal son here the story you and I recently discussed."

The aged priest's eyes narrowed, and the guilt that Lassiter had observed when they first met returned to his deeply lined face. "Is it absolutely necessary? What I mean is you and I have discussed this already, Herr Pularchek."

"I'm afraid I'm going to have to insist. You see, Monsignor, I want my son to hear it from the horse's mouth, so to speak. Or—should I more aptly say—the *sinner's* mouth."

The words cut like a serrated knife. The old man's expression, already dark and miserable with shame, turned a shade darker. Lassiter tried to imagine what the Catholic priest had done that would make him feel so ashamed and warrant such harsh treatment from his father. It had to have been something terrible.

"Very well," said the old priest reluctantly, his expression one of regret and sorrow. "As you no doubt know or have guessed, the story your father is referring to happened during the war. In 1944, I worked in the Vatican. I was a young assistant to Father Pankratius Pfeiffer, the Vatican Superior General of the Salvatorians. Fluent in German, Pfeiffer was Pius XII's personal liaison with the German occupation forces. He dealt with the German diplomats and military officers, as well as the SS, on issues of importance to His Holiness. My work for Padre Pancrazio, as he was sometimes called, brought me into contact with General Wolff, head of the SS in Italy, and his second-in-command, Dr. Eugen Dollmann. Wolff's actual title was *Obergruppenführer*—Highest SS chief—and both he and Dollmann were erudite men of culture and refinement. They also had a taste for Italian wine, women, and art. Wolff met with the Pope in the spring of 1944, just before the fall of Rome. He and the Supreme Pontiff were both anxious to be the magnanimous peace negotiators to the warring Allied and Axis powers.

"But while I was assisting Father Pfeiffer in dealing with the Germans, I was also working secretly for the Allies. I helped run the Escape Line for British and American prisoners of war with Monsignor O'Flaherty, an Irish Roman Catholic priest and senior official of the Roman Curia. The Irish monsignor was an important figure in the Roman Catholic Resistance in the Eternal City. I worked with him in hiding hundreds of escaped Allied soldiers, Jews, anti-Fascists, and other enemies of the Third Reich in various Vatican properties surrounding the Holy See. We'd help hide them and find them food and lodging in Vatican-protected extraterritorial properties. We also arranged for disguises and false identity cards and supplied the men with money. Everything was going fine—until the day I got caught."

"By who?" asked Lassiter, feeling his curiosity already piqued by the unusual story.

"Dr. Dollmann. Unfortunately, he brought me to his boss, General Wolff."

Lassiter looked at his father, who, though he had already heard the story, appeared equally captivated. Lassiter wondered why his father wanted him to hear the story firsthand from Hoess. Was he trying to make some kind of point? Was this another part of his journey of discovery, like Auschwitz? Or was this all some sort of elaborate game? A part of him was angry at Pularchek for keeping him in the dark about his motives; the other was intrigued by the prospect of hearing an important tale from the past, back when the whole world had been gripped with war.

"Tell him, Monsignor, what *Obergruppenführer* Wolff did next," said his father, prompting the Austrian to continue.

"General Wolff surprised me by striking a deal," said Hoess. "Normally, a man in my precarious position would have been hauled before an SS firing squad, shot, and tossed into an unmarked grave that I would have had to dig myself. But instead, the Highest SS chief offered me a deal. It is a deal that I have regretted making for the past seventy odd years."

Now, Lassiter was on the edge of his seat. "What…what was this deal with the devil, Monsignor?"

"He knew that the Vatican controlled a property—owned by the prestigious Bellomo family outside Florence—that was filled with a priceless Renaissance Old Masters' art collection. The family was an old one, from the so-called 'black' nobility consisting of Rome's wealthy Roman Catholics loyal to the Vatican. This aristocracy had supported the Italian monarchy and the papal authority vested in the Bishop of Rome—represented by black-colored priestly garb—since the time of Garibaldi. But Princess Bellomo, as it turned out, had Jewish ancestry on her mother's side. The family was forced to flee Italy in September 1943, once Italy had surrendered and the German occupation began. The Germans were rounding up Jews and those Italians with Jewish lineage, or that had supported the Badoglio government, which was now in exile. The Bellomo family settled in England, taking a great deal of money with them, but leaving behind their art collection to be administered by the Holy See. The estate was locked up, cordoned off, the road to the property was shut down, and warning placards, printed in both Italian and German, were posted next to every entryway by the German occupiers. They read: 'This building serves religious objectives, and is a dependency of the Vatican City. All searches and requisitions are prohibited.' The notice was signed by Wolff himself. Such placards were also posted by General Stahel, the German Military Commandant of Rome, on all ecclesiastical buildings in and around the Eternal City. But, by the winter of 1944, Wolff secretly had a change of heart. He was no longer willing to protect the Bellomo estate, or its priceless art collections. But he needed a pretext for his next move, and that pretext was me."

Lassiter leaned towards the old priest in his wheelchair, anxious to hear what he would say next. "Then what happened?" he asked, scarcely able to contain his excitement.

"He had me forge the signature of Father Pfeiffer, relinquishing the art collection to Reich Marshal Göring and his Hermann Göring Division for a pittance of two hundred thousand lira. That's around two thousand American dollars. Then he had me bury the supposedly legitimate sales document in the Vatican archives, which are still sealed from that terrible time to this day. He seized the collection the very next week. He had me attend the thievery in person as an official Vatican witness and transport the canvasses by heavily-guarded SS trucks to St. Stephen's here in Vienna, where they have remained safely hidden away since the war."

"So he offered you your life in return for looting the paintings that belonged to the Bellomo family and were under the care of the Vatican?"

"No, he did more than that. He also agreed not to pursue Father O'Flaherty and the Escape Line. Or to take any additional measures than those that were already being performed to hunt down the Allied POWs trying to find refuge in Rome and the outlying provinces. He said he would tacitly leave the matter in the hands of the head of the Rome Gestapo, Colonel Kappler, whom he despised. Shockingly, he told me that I could once again take up with the Catholic Resistance movement and support O'Flaherty and the Escape Line. But he warned me that I would eventually be caught by the dogged Kappler and should stop. Truthfully, at the time I was stunned by his magnanimity. He reminded me that he was a Catholic too, and he was doing this to find the most reasonable solution for all concerned parties. He also acknowledged that he had to protect himself for the future since the Allies were demanding 'unconditional surrender.' FDR and Churchill had made it clear that high-ranking Axis leaders like Wolff would suffer severe punishment and retribution for the misdeeds of Nazi Germany. He told me the war was lost and further resistance by Germany was pointless."

Lassiter said, "Why do you regret what you did then? It seems to me you were in an impossible situation."

"Because I sinned against Father Pfeiffer, against my church, and against God to save my own skin. True, it wasn't just to save my own skin, but that of Father O'Flaherty, British Major Sam Derry, and all of the other men and women who were risking their lives for the Escape Line in Rome. But what I did was still a sin. Even worse than that, I covered up the original sin with another far worse."

The monsignor shot a quick, furtive glance at his father. Pularchek smiled knowingly, a dangerous glint in his eyes that was a prompt to continue, but seemed more like deliberate punishment. He was making the priest admit what he had done in a house of God, right in front of the High Altar. Hoess gave a heavy sigh, withdrew a handkerchief with the official crest of the Vatican, blew his nose into it, and placed it silently back into his pocket.

"Wolff made me swear to the Holy Father," he continued, "that I would never tell a soul what I had done and that I would protect the art treasures for his descendants."

"His descendants?"

"His grandchildren to be precise. As I said, by the spring of 1944, Wolff had begun to doubt that Germany could win the war and he was concerned for its future. He wanted desperately to find some way that Germany could end the war in such a way that it could honorably dictate the terms of the peace that would follow. He hoped that words instead of bullets and bombs would end the bloodshed. He wanted to ensure that Germany would not become a pauper state after the war, as it had after the Great War with the unfair Treaty of Versailles. That way both he—and his beloved Fatherland—would have a chance of surviving the judgment day that he knew would surely follow. Remember, the Allied leaders had made it clear that the leaders of the Axis nations would suffer severe punishment and retribution for pushing Germany into conquering most of Europe, and for the Holocaust."

"It sounds to me like he just wanted to avoid a lengthy prison sentence or the hangman's noose."

"That is partly true. But the most important thing to him was that his grandchildren had a better world. So he asked me to swear to secrecy that I would never tell a soul, and that I would keep the art until after his death, which was in 1984. Specifically, he made me promise to hold the collection if I was alive and to bequeath it to his oldest surviving grandchild on his or her fortieth birthday for disbursement to all of the grandchildren. Well, he ended up having three grandchildren, but two of them died before the age of thirty. One in a car wreck, the other in a mountain climbing accident on the Jungfrau. The only one to survive until the age of forty was the second oldest grandchild, Angela Wolff."

"Why didn't he leave the collection to his own children?"

"He knew that, after the war, the children of Nazi officials would be closely watched for stolen war booty such as gold, art, and jewelry. He also believed that they would be stigmatized or even persecuted for the sins of their parents within the new post-war political structure. So he wanted to skip a generation and leave it to his grandchildren, whom he believed would be more distanced from the war."

"But what if you died? Who would leave it to the oldest surviving grandchild, then?"

"As I found out shortly after his death, I was not the only one who knew. Bernhard Heydrich, the son of Karl Wolff's German lawyer, was in on the arrangement too. He was the actual point of contact with the Wolff family as he was Angela Wolff's lawyer."

Lassiter looked at Pularchek. "So Heydrich was the one who told you about the art collection in Monsignor Hoess's possession?"

His father shook his head. "No, it wasn't Heydrich. But I did find out that Heydrich wanted to cut a deal with me for a fifty-fifty split in the treasures. He was aware of my reputation as a Nazi hunter, and he didn't want to have to look over his shoulder for the rest of his life. He even had a high-end but shady dealer in Paris who would handle the illicit sales of the various works. But as fate would have it, I managed to track down Monsignor Hoess here and seize the paintings first. Meanwhile, Heydrich was killed."

Lassiter was surprised. "You didn't kill him?"

"No, of course not."

"Then who did?"

"I don't know."

"But you do know who first leaked the word from Heydrich about the paintings. That was the person who told you that they were in Monsignor Hoess's possession."

His father smiled approvingly. "Very good, my son."

"So who told you that Hoess had the paintings, if it wasn't Heydrich?"

"I'm sorry, but that I can't tell you. That happens to be need-to-know, and until this operation is successfully concluded, you don't need to know. Such information could very well get you killed, and I can't allow that. After all, you have a honeymoon to return to with your sweet young wife."

Hoess was shaking his head in anguish. "I should never have vowed to keep this terrible secret and to pass along the *Schatzfund*. But I made a vow to God— and I could not break my sacred vow to the Almighty." He looked up towards the heavens and crossed himself. "Can you ever forgive me, Holy Father, for my sins and for causing so much death?"

"I wouldn't hold your breath, Monsignor," said Pularchek. "The Almighty's compassion only extends so far for a man of the cloth. I'm afraid you are held to a higher standard than the rest of us."

Lassiter thought his father was being unduly harsh given the monsignor's predicament at the time, but he said nothing. He wondered if he would have done anything differently, if he had been in the man's shoes. Ultimately, war was about making impossible choices. It was about being forced into painful compromises that could haunt you for life. That's precisely what appeared to have happened to Monsignor Hoess.

He ventured a question. "Why did you trust Wolff? As the head of the SS in Italy, he could easily have had you killed and simply seized the paintings. So why did you think you could trust him?"

"Because for all of his shortcomings, he was a man of honor."

His father shook his head sarcastically. "He was a Nazi, and Nazis have no honor."

"No, you must listen to me. I honored my promise to the *Obergruppenführer* and God for one reason and one reason only. Wolff was a man of his word, and I truly believed I would be saving more lives if I agreed to his plan than if I refused. It is only in hindsight that I have come to regret my decision."

"So how was Wolff a man of his word?" asked Lassiter, still unable to believe he was hearing firsthand such a remarkable wartime tale.

"There were three events that convinced me. The first was that Wolff, perhaps indirectly but nonetheless effectively, refused Hitler's request in the fall of 1943 to kidnap the Pope and seize the Vatican. He also later gave assurances to the Holy Father, in December of that same year, that as long as Wolff held his position in Italy, the Vatican and its occupants were safe from abduction. This made a powerful impression upon me as a young man, as it did to my mentor Father Pfeiffer."

"And the second?"

"At the request of Father Pfeiffer, who represented the wishes of Pius, Wolff used his influence to arrange for the release of a Roman leftist leader named Giuliano Vassalli. The young man was the son of a well-known lawyer and personal friend to the Pope, who had been arrested and sentenced to death. Acting as head of the German police in Italy, Wolff interceded and the young man was released to the custody of Father Pfeiffer within a few weeks."

"What about the third?"

"This story was the one that sealed it for me. A week after Wolff visited the Pope, I was told a story that Father Pfeiffer had heard from a Swiss businessman. Apparently, Wolff was in a restaurant in the city and he caught sight of a particularly appetizing woman, part American. Raising his glass, he sent across an officer with his card and a message saying that he would grant her three wishes. This playful Hans Andersen-type gesture was not spurned by the woman. She immediately asked for milk for her child, a permit to go to the country to get food, and the release of the painter Chicco Multedo, who was her close friend. Wolff granted her the first two, but said he had to refuse the last because he could not guarantee success. But he agreed to put in a favorable word."

"What happened to the painter?"

"Multedo's family was able to procure his release by paying a bribe to guards at the Via Tasso Nazi prison."

Lassiter nodded and looked at his father. He still looked skeptical.

"SS men like Wolff are not supposed to show mercy," said Hoess. "And yet, he did so on numerous occasions. I believed I was doing the right thing in trusting him, and I subsequently made my oath to him and to God."

They fell into thoughtful silence. Lassiter stared up at the Wiener-Neustadter altarpiece in the left chapel of the choir. Over one-half millennium old, it was one of the greatest artistic treasures in the world. Richly gilded and painted, it depicted the Virgin Mary between St. Catherine and St. Barbara, her expression one of pious submission before God. Glancing at Hoess, he saw the same penitent expression on the old man's deeply lined face.

But there was something else: a single wet tear.

CHAPTER 44

PRIESTING RIVER
SOUTHWEST OF VIENNA

THEY DIDN'T SPEAK at all during the forty-five minute drive to the river. Pularchek knew that his son needed some time alone with his thoughts, and he did as well. The motorized caravan wound its way southwest along the *Sud Autobahn*, E59. They stared out in silence at the green-forested *Urhauswald* on their right, and a series of small Austrian towns with red-roofed houses flanking the autobahn. Periodically, Romanowski gave him reports on his *Braciszku's*—and, therefore, Wolff's—movements through the GPS tracking beacon embedded in the neck of his double. Wolff and her BND entourage had just crossed the Austrian border and were heading south on the autobahn, a mere two hours behind him and his team.

Everything was proceeding according to plan. But Pularchek was still worried about his *Braciszku*. He had lost one Little Brother in America, and now another of his brave soldiers was risking his life for the Cause. He always felt a watery feeling in his gut when his operatives were at risk, as if he were right there alongside them, sharing the same dangers as they battled their common enemy. That was the way it was for him with all of his *Braciszkus*. The bond between them was like that between two identical twins; sometimes, it was as though he could actually feel what they felt, as if his senses were taking in the same sights, smells, sounds, and, especially, the dangers. The nexus between him and his Brothers was as strong as forged metal, and when one of his Brothers suffered or triumphed, he felt it too.

At the small town of Steinabrückl, they stopped and picked up some lunch supplies at a small Austrian deli. The caravan then drove to the nearby Priesting River, where Janu, Jerzy Gagor, Andrzej Kremer, and Rachel Landau put together an authentic Austrian picnic lunch of *Wurstsalat* sandwiches. Cold, thinly-sliced knacker wurst, Emmental and Gruyère cheeses, onions, tomatoes, sweet capsicum peppers, and chopped chives dressed with simple vinaigrette on crusty baguettes. They ate their picnic lunch and washed the meal down with Domäne Wachau Pinot Blanc from the Wachau Valley to the north, with the loner Skyler acting as guard on a small limestone knob to the west. When they were finished eating, Pularchek asked his son if he would join him for a brief stroll along the river.

"Sure," said Lassiter, and they headed west along a narrow footpath skirting the gurgling Priesting. The sky overhead was a milky blue, the sun a sulfur-colored tangerine. Oak trees and a smattering of green pines crowded the floodbanks. The serpentine river was running high with clear alpine water from the spring snowmelt.

"I know you have some questions, Nicholas," Pularchek began once they were out of earshot of his security team. "Maybe now, I can answer them."

"I thought you were holding off until after we've settled our score with the Germans. Remember, we were supposed to avenge our ancestors not with bullets, but with our brains. In the process, Angela Wolff and her storm troopers would get their comeuppance. And only then would you tell me what I wanted to know."

"I changed my mind. I am prepared to answer your questions now. I know you have many."

"You're right, I do. So let's start with this. Why do you kill Nazis?"

"You know why. I took you to the Polish resistance war memorial and Old Town in Warsaw. I took you to Auschwitz where my grandmother was tortured by the Angel of Death. And I took you to visit Monsignor Hoess at *Stephansplatz*. So you know why."

"So it's payback for what they did to your ancestors and the rest of Europe?"

"History tells us that the war ended more than seventy years ago. But I say it is still being waged today by the descendants, the profiteers and deniers who do not put a proper value on human life and doing what is right. These people must pay for their sins—and the sins of their ancestors."

"And what about Islamic terrorists?"

"What about them?"

"Why do you kill them? Is it because of what happened to your wife and daughters?"

"It once was, but not anymore. As I told Natalie at the safe house, it is to stop 'evil returned.'"

"What do you mean by *evil returned?*"

"Evil returned is what the Islamic extremists of today represent. They are the Nazis of the modern world, an entity so malevolent, insidious, and inhumane that they can only be understood as something beyond understanding. It was an American reporter named Richard Cohen from the *Washington Post* who coined the term."

"So you kill to eradicate this evil?"

He shook his head sadly. "No, there is no way to eradicate such evil. All I do is take a firm stand—however minor a pinprick my efforts may be in the end—against this evil. I see no way that humanity can survive if evil such as this becomes the norm among the world's supposedly civilized nations."

"But you're killing violence with violence. Is that really the best way?"

"I don't know, but it is *my* way. I am not Mahatma Gandhi or Martin Luther King. I do not believe in passive non-violence. Not against this kind of evil. Against this type of evil, I believe in pulling a gun when the other side pulls a knife, because that is the only thing that will get the attention of these monsters. I know it seems like I am playing God, that I am acting as judge, jury, and executioner. But I believe my way is the only way. I truly believe in the cleansing power of pure violence."

"So you kidnapped me and took me on this little road trip so I would see the light? Is that it?"

"No, I brought you on this journey so you could feel firsthand what your Polish ancestors felt. You may have been raised in America by your loving adoptive parents, Mikolaj, but the boy you were raised as does not truly represent who you are and where you have come from. You showed your Polish mettle last year when you went to New York and put away that crooked literary agent and that Russian mob boss. You are a stubborn man, Nicholas Lassiter. You are Polish-stubborn, and that is what makes you a survivor. We Poles are the most stubborn and defiant people on the planet. But we have always had to be, for the simple fact that we are a country that occupies the long-disputed territory between two ruthless conquerors: Germany and Russia."

They fell into silence as they stopped to watch the river swirling past. The water glittered in the early June sunshine. Pularchek could hear the pleasant burbling sound over the moss-covered stones. There were several shadow-striped riffles where the water tumbled into nutrient-laden pools that fed the lurking trout. He felt the coolness of the shade beneath the hearty oaks flanking the meandering water course.

"All right, I have another question. How many of you are there?"

"There is but one of me: Stanislaw Pularchek."

"I don't see how that's possible. I saw your clone pass from this world to the next before my very eyes."

"There are no clones, Mikolaj. That I can assure you."

"Come on, I know what I saw."

"And just what do you think you saw?"

"In D.C., I saw a man who looked exactly like you die before my eyes. And in Warsaw I saw, through a smokescreen, your men exchange you out for a man that also looked exactly like you."

"The smoke was thick at the safe house. How can you be sure there was an exchange?"

"Don't treat me like a child. I know what I saw."

"I'm just telling you that what you saw, and what you think you saw, may very well be two different things."

"You're lying to me and I want to know why. You said you'd answer my questions."

"I have answered your questions. I am telling you the truth. I have not cloned myself, Nicholas."

"But I saw you exchanged for an exact double, a clone."

"I promise you there are no Pularchek clones running around this world. Besides, no one has ever successfully cloned a human being before. It is a major criminal offense, prosecutable in every country on the planet."

"But you own a biotech company that performs cloning experiments."

"I own a lot of companies, Nicholas."

"Advanced Biosystems has successfully cloned Rhesus monkeys, chimpanzees, and a gorilla. Cloning advanced primates is illegal in every country in the world except for Poland—and that's because you petitioned the Polish government for a special exemption. I looked it up."

Pularchek saw that his son was becoming agitated. "I'm sorry that you don't like my answer," he said. "But it is the truth. Now, do you have any other questions because we do need to start back soon?"

They started walking again. "Okay, let's pretend for the moment that you're telling the truth. Even if that double I saw back there at the safe house wasn't a clone, how can you send him off with the enemy like that when you know he could be in harm's way?"

"Because we are an army and each of the soldiers in my army has a designated role."

"And these men have accepted the fact that they might die for you?"

"As I said, they are soldiers. They have come to terms with the possibility of death in support of the Cause."

They fell silent for a moment. His son's expression was thoughtful as they walked along the dirt path.

"I understand why you do what you do. In fact, I admire you for it. But you have to admit it is hard way. What happens if you're wrong about one of your targets and they're actually innocent of wrongdoing?"

"That does not happen. The men that I target are guilty. One hundred percent guilty. I make certain of that before lifting a finger."

"People and situations are seldom black and white. Just look at Angela Wolff's grandfather."

"Karl Wolff was evil."

"But not one-hundred-percent evil. He did a lot of good too, which is precisely why he wasn't tried at Nuremberg. I looked that up too."

"Many Nazis weren't tried at the Nuremberg Trials. That doesn't make them innocent."

"You're right, it doesn't. But there are different shades of morality and evil in the world. You, yourself, are a case in point."

"Duly noted and accepted as an indisputable fact. Any more questions, my son?"

"A few. Including one silly one. How did you get your middle name, Snarkus? Romanowski said your nickname is Snark. Snark Pularchek—what kind of crazy-ass name is that anyway?"

Pularchek grinned; it was nice to have a light-hearted question from his son. "My parents were devout fans of the Lewis Carroll poem *The Hunting of the Snark*. They gave a nod to the poem by naming me after the titular character, only they tried to make it more Polish by adding the *us*. It certainly isn't the first time that parents have bestowed a nonsensical name upon a child based on something they thought was amusing. Does that satisfy your curiosity?"

"Not quite, but we're getting closer. What about my mother? What was she like?"

"Her name was Rose. She was English. She was a beautiful and dedicated doctor with skin the color of alabaster."

"So you were madly in love with her?"

"No, Nicholas. The truth is I barely knew her."

"So I'm the product of a one night stand, is that it?"

"No, it wasn't like that. I cared for your mother. We met during the war in Lebanon in the 1980s. We were both aid workers. She was a doctor with *Médecins Sans Frontières*, and I was working for some international relief organization. I don't even remember the name because it no longer exists. The shells were coming down in the distance and we were isolated and all alone and it…it just happened. I had known her for about a week. Shortly afterwards, I was moved to another village and that was the last I ever saw of her. I'm sorry, Nicholas, truly I am. I wish I had a better story to tell you. But it is at least the truth."

They stopped again. His son bit his lip and stared off thoughtfully at the river, and Pularchek felt badly for him. It was not a very noble beginning, and seeing how sad the young man looked, he wondered if perhaps it would have been better to have made up a more glamorous romance and courtship story. Lebanon had been a hellhole, and though his time together with Rose had been passionate, it had been ridiculously brief. The simple truth was that he and Rose had been certain they were going to die and had made love as if it was their last moment on earth. In that context, perhaps their brief moment together had meant something after all.

"I want to know about your family that you lost: your wife and three daughters that died. That's the real reason you hunt down jihadis, isn't it? You say you do it to take a stand against evil, but isn't the real reason vengeance? I mean, look at what they did to your family. Personally, I would want my pound of flesh if that had happened to me."

When Pularchek spoke, he chose his words carefully. "I told you that vengeance is what drew me in at first, and that is one-hundred-percent the truth. When that suicide bomber in Madrid took from me Johanna and my daughters— Lena, Magdalena, and Zofia—I vowed to myself that I would wipe every Islamic terrorist off the face of the earth. But vengeance is not what drives me now, as I have told you."

"You truly want to wipe out evil?"

"I cannot just idly stand by in front of such a monstrous rejection of human dignity. If I could single-handedly kill off this curse, this plague on the human soul, spending every *zloty* of my money and dying violently in the process, I would gladly do it. We must rise up to fight this plague of international terrorism that has seized hold of our world. Do you see the nations of Europe, the Middle East, or the United States getting the job done? Do you feel as though we're winning the war on terror? I don't, and that is why I take the fight to these bastards. I have nothing against Islam, mind you, for Muslims are a glorious and generous people. I kill only those who financially support and promote terrorists behind the scenes: the men who delude themselves into thinking they are invisible."

They fell silent for a moment and stared at the river flowing past. The only sound was the gentle rhythm of the water rippling over the stones. Looking out, Pularchek saw the speckled silver-and-red flank of a trout swimming through the water. Near the bank it paused, and he stared down at its glassy eyes, fleshy mouth, and perforated gills as they opened and closed. Then it swam away and was gone.

Such beauty, he thought. *Such beauty and yet such evil in the world.*

He looked at his son. He genuinely loved the boy. He loved that he carried his flesh and blood, loved him for his steely resolve, loved that he had joined him on this dangerous journey into Austria to settle an old score with the Germans. He loved witnessing his offspring so strong and smart, and he felt a powerful kinship with him. At the same time, he couldn't help but feel a gulf between them. It was the violence. He should have known it would be hard to bridge the gap between the two of them, even though they were linked by blood and history.

"Nicholas, I know you are a little bit afraid of me, and I can't say I blame you. After all, I am a killer, and to kill is a sin against God. But now that I have found you, I want you to know how much I love you. The blood that binds us is sacred to me. Do you want to know why?"

Slowly, his son nodded.

"My wife and daughters have been killed and you and Natalie are all the family I have now. True, I have numerous relatives and loved ones back in Poland, but I do not have a son by my own blood line. You represent my seed that can live on and grow with that beautiful young wife of yours." He felt tears coming to his eyes and struggled unsuccessfully to hold them back. Embarrassed, he withdrew a handkerchief from his pocket and gently daubed his eyes. "Sorry about that. Regrettably, your father is an emotional man. I suppose it is the Polish way."

To his surprise, his son reached out his arms and took him in an embrace.

"I love you too...Dad," he said.

"You do? Really? You don't think I'm crazy?"

"A little crazy. But so am I."

They both laughed.

"I have just one more question. I need you to tell me one last thing."

"Yes, anything."

"You have to tell me how you plan to catch the bad guys. I know you have some big final showdown planned against the Germans, and I know you want me to be there to witness it. But I want to know exactly how you plan to pull this off without getting us killed. I'm secretly hoping that you have some clever trick up your sleeve."

Pularchek gave a knowing smile. "In fact, I do. But before I tell you about it, why don't we call your wife and father and bring them into the fold, so to speak?"

"I thought you'd never ask," and he pulled out his iPhone to make the call.

CHAPTER 45

LIECHTENSTEIN CASTLE
MARIA ENZERSDORF, AUSTRIA

PUNCHING OFF HIS SECURE CELL PHONE, Benjamin Brewbaker looked at his team. "That was Nick. We're all set," he said.

"Where are we going to meet them?" asked Natalie.

"At Bad Aussee. It's in the Salzkammergut lakes region, southeast of Salzburg."

"Salzburg? We're headed towards Salzburg?"

"Yes, ma'am. Is that acceptable to you?"

"Yes, I'm just surprised is all."

"Not as surprised as you two are going to be when you hear this," said Glover from the back of the van. "Langley just got back to us on the identity of that sharpshooter woman in the photos you took at the safe house."

Brewbaker looked at the techie, sensing that everything was about to become more complicated. "You're talking about the request I made to OTS and FACE?" he asked, referring to the CIA's Office of Technical Services and the FBI's Facial Analysis, Comparison, and Evaluation Unit. The Next Generation Identification, or NGI, database was used by OTS and the FACE Unit to identify and track criminals based upon thirty million mugshots and civil photos, as well as biometric data including fingerprints and iris scans.

"Yes, sir," said Glover. "They were able to obtain a facial match and ID the woman. There's no name though."

"I know. In the file, she's known only as Jane Doe."

"The file, sir?"

"The draft joint FBI and Secret Service report on the Kieger and Fowler assassinations. I read the draft report before it was redacted. She's a professional killer the FBI calls Jane Doe. They don't even have an alias."

"But I thought Kieger and Fowler were assassinated by Diego Gomez, the Spaniard? That's what it said in the final joint investigative report."

"Don't you believe in conspiracy theories, Agent Glover? You certainly can't believe everything you read in a government report."

They all seemed to agree with the basic premise and fell into silence. Brewbaker stared out the window of the control van at Liechtenstein Castle. Constructed of bright limestone and perched along a hogback ridge along the edge of the dense Viennese Forest known as the *Wienerwald*, the castle was built in the

12th century, destroyed by the Ottomans in 1529 and 1683, and remained in ruins until 1884, when it was rebuilt. He watched as a group of bicyclists peddled along one of the *wanderwege* trails cutting through the meadow on the castle's north side.

After a moment, Glover broke through his thoughts. "There's something else, sir. I believe the FBI special agent in charge of the case will want to talk to you. His contact information is attached to the file. He is to be informed immediately if this Jane Doe is positively ID'd. It's all in the case file."

Brewbaker turned away from the shimmering castle and looked at him. "What's our correlation coefficient on the facial match?"

"Ninety-eight percent."

"It's got to be her. And she's connected to Pularchek."

"How do you know?" asked Agent Webb.

"Because I saw a grainy photograph of that very same woman in the Pularchek case file. When I photographed her at the safe house, I knew I had seen her before. And now I know where. She was photographed by one of our field operatives leaving a building in Mosul shortly after the killing of Ahmad Monatzeri."

Natalie was looking at him. "Who's Monatzeri?"

"The terrorist leader behind the Madrid bombing that claimed Pularchek's wife and three daughters."

"So that's how this woman and Pularchek are connected?"

"Looks that way. Which means that we have a major conflict of interest on our hands. We need to call this special agent. What's his name?"

"Ken Patton."

"Give me the number."

Glover did. Thirty seconds later, Brewbaker had the senior FBI agent on the speakerphone of his secure cell and they had both verified, through official protocol, that they were who they said they were. Brewbaker quickly told him about the photos he had taken at the German safe house in Ursus and the results of the NGI facial recognition analysis. In return, Patton filled him in on what he knew about Jane Doe, which differed significantly from the official file Glover had downloaded since the CIA, Secret Service, and everyone in the FBI except Patton believed she was merely an accessory to the real killer, Diego Gomez. He found Patton a sharp, no-nonsense kind of guy, and in going over the case with the young head of the Denver Field Office Domestic Terrorism Desk, he couldn't help but feel the agent's theory was spot on and everybody else was wrong.

"So your theory, Special Agent, is that Gomez is actually Jane Doe?"

"Yes, and all of the facts back me up."

"So you're telling me the government's case hasn't actually been solved and the joint investigative report that came out two weeks ago is a sham?"

"I can't comment on the report. I only know what the evidence points to."

"Is the case still ongoing? I mean, if the official report is out, why are you still investigating?"

"I'm checking up on a few things. Call it final closure."

It sounded to Brewbaker as if Special Agent Patton wasn't able to let go and was acting on his own. Was he so obsessed that he was working on a closed case on his own time? "You weren't able to find out who Jane Doe, or Gomez if he's the shooter, were working for, were you?"

"Gomez wasn't the assassin. It was our Jane Doe. Gomez doesn't even exist. It's all a fiction. And yes, I do know who they were working for: the Christian leader Benjamin Locke. But unfortunately I wasn't able to prove it."

"So if you're right about your theory, Jane Doe killed Locke in addition to Presidents-Elect Kieger and Fowler and also Senator Dubois."

"Yes, that's true."

"Do you have any idea who trained this woman?"

"No. But Gomez has been linked to the communist terrorist group Euskara in Spain. Personally I think it's all a front. I believe that Jane Doe, or a control agent acting on her behalf, has for the past decade and a half been trying to deflect suspicion from herself to the fictitious Gomez. If I'm right, I consider it unlikely Jane Doe was trained by Euskara. In fact, she probably has no ties to the group."

"Then who trained her?"

"There are several possibilities. She could have been recruited by Russian intelligence or another Eastern European intelligence group. They were first to use female assassins on a wide scale. Or it could be one of the big terrorist groups in Western Europe or the Middle East. The Red Army Faction and Action Directe in Germany, the Italian Red Brigade, EXE in Israel, or a similar group. Most female operatives these days come from the former intelligence agencies in Eastern Europe, though. They've made career changes and become professional contract killers who sell their services to the highest bidder."

Brewbaker couldn't help but be intrigued by this most unusual contract killer. But could the sniper who had wreaked havoc upon the U.S. really be a woman?

As if reading his mind, Natalie said to him and the FBI agent, "If this Jane Doe is the actual assassin responsible for all these killings, this means the world's most dangerous sniper is, in fact, a woman. That's quite an embarrassing revelation for the macho international intelligence community, wouldn't you say?"

"You took the words right out of my mouth," said Patton.

"It also means that Gomez is nothing more than a phantom killer, a ghost of the files," she added. "Which to me suggests that Jane Doe is being protected by powerful people in the intelligence community."

"I happen to agree one hundred percent with that assertion as well," said Patton. "The French intelligence service has the most complete dossier on Gomez. I believe there could be someone high up in that body feeding Interpol and the world's law enforcement community false information. But there's a lot of people out there who don't believe me about any of this, so you might want to take everything I say with a grain of salt."

"Not a chance, Special Agent," said Brewbaker. "When I read your initial report, I couldn't help but feel it made a lot of sense."

"Yeah well, you were probably the only one. But that could change soon. I have a new lead down here in St. Croix. That's where I am now. I managed to track down a boyfriend of Jane Doe's during her time in the U.S. I managed to ID him from several CCTV camera feeds. He's a big shot Hollywood producer. Or at least he was a few years back. I don't think he was involved though. But he definitely knew her intimately. I questioned him thoroughly earlier today."

"What's his name?" asked Brewbaker.

"I'm afraid I can't tell you that, not yet anyway. Too many people think I'm a crackpot and I'm afraid I can't afford to give them any more ammunition."

"You want to catch her badly, don't you Special Agent?"

"That's an understatement." Brewbaker heard him take a lungful of air. "There's something else you should know."

"And what would that be?"

"I don't know if you've examined the Jane Doe file closely or not, but if you have you would see that access to the file was recently restricted."

He looked at Glover, who began typing at his laptop in the rear of the van. "What do you mean restricted, Special Agent?"

"I mean somebody high up has shut it down in just the last twenty-four hours. You can no longer access the Jane Doe file, only the Diego Gomez file."

"Then how did we get a match to the photographs from the facial recognition software?" asked Natalie.

"That's in the NGI database. I'm talking about the actual written text file. If you try to pull it up or download it, you'll see it's gone."

"Shit, he's right," said Glover, hammering at his keyboard. "I can't get in."

"Someone doesn't want us in there, Deputy Director."

Brewbaker looked at Natalie. "Who?"

"I don't know. The access was restricted by your people."

"It was Voorheiss, sir," said Glover. "It says that all inquiries must be cleared through him."

"Voorheiss," said Patton on the other end. "You mean Richard Voorheiss, the director of the National Clandestine Service."

"Yes, my boss."

"I'll leave it to you and him to work that one out, Deputy Director. Good luck."

"Thanks for your help, Special Agent. I have a feeling that you and I might be in touch again in the near future."

"I always wanted to have a high-level contact in the CIA, sir. Looks like today's my lucky day because you definitely owe me one after this call."

"I do indeed. But only if you don't get in trouble down there is St. Croix."

"Don't worry, I won't."

"Good. Have a conch fritter and rum punch for me, and be sure to go snorkeling out at Buck Island."

"Oh, I don't have time for Buck Island. Instead, I'm about to pay another visit to our friend the Hollywood film producer."

"Is that right?"

"Yes, sir. And it's time to turn up the heat."

CHAPTER 46

MAUTERN IN STEIERMARK
LEOBEN DISTRICT, CENTRAL AUSTRIA

ANGELA WOLFF—BND vice-president and granddaughter of the late *Obergruppenführer* Karl Wolff, the Highest SS chief of Italy—stared expectantly at her secure mobile in the palm of her hand. The phone's internal clock read 1409 hours. She had been expecting an important call nine minutes earlier, and it was not like her caller to be late. *Have I been double-crossed?* she wondered as she shifted her gaze from her phone to the green fields rolling past the Land Rover's passenger window. On her right, beyond the grassy alpine fields loomed the tidy, quaint Austrian town of Mautern in Steiermark. *Damnit, what is going on? Why haven't I heard from—?*

She jerked her head away from the window and looked down again at her phone: 1410 and counting. This was the tenth time she had checked the time.

Why the hell doesn't my phone ring?

And then suddenly it did.

She nearly jumped up from her car seat, as if a schoolboy had darted out from behind a wall and scared her. To settle her jangled nerves, she cleared her throat and smoothed her perfectly pressed gray business suit before accepting the call. She wanted to sound confident and relaxed, but at the moment she was neither. Fortunately, she only had to keep it together a little while longer. Then she would be rich and satisfied beyond her wildest dreams: a young woman of only forty with a handsome younger lover and not a care in the world. She and Dieter were going to be so happy together on the majestic Greek island of Skopelos.

"You're late, Richard," she said. "And you know I don't appreciate people who are late, whether for an appointment or a scheduled conference call."

"I got held up at the airport. It seems the Austrian Federal Police and Security Services have taken a sudden interest in me, despite my diplomatic cover. Why it's almost as if someone tipped them off."

"Well, it sure as hell wasn't me," she said to Voorheiss, struggling to control her irritation. "I've been above board with you on every aspect of the operation since the beginning."

"You've also managed to botch things at practically every turn."

"I have Pularchek, and soon we will have the merchandise. I don't know how you can consider that *botching* the operation."

"You've left in your wake a swath of blood and destruction."

"And you haven't? You're the one who killed Heydrich."

"I told you that wasn't me."

She looked at Dieter. He gave a nervous look as he took a bend in the road at high speed, causing the tires to screech.

"Then who the hell was it?" she demanded into her secure phone. "It certainly wasn't me or anyone from my service."

"Right now, it doesn't matter. The top priority is to get in there and secure the merchandise. But you are wrong to say that you haven't made a mess of things. The Polish president is meeting with your ambassador as we speak."

"But the meeting wasn't supposed to be until later today?"

"They moved it up. It's not my fault that our intelligence is better than yours, even in your own European backyard."

"I don't deserve that and you know it. You Americans are so rude. Why I'm beginning to believe that rudeness is in your nature."

"If that's the case, then stupidity is in yours. That damned witch-hunt magazine of yours—*Der Spiegel*—is stirring up controversy with a story about your drag race through the Tiergarten. You used to be a country of meticulous engineers and masters of espionage who kept the planes and trains running on time. Now you've become all sloppy and transparent like the damned Italians. My God, Angela, how can you ever expect to become president of the BND after this?"

"I don't want to be president." She made eye contact again with Dieter, who was gripping the steering wheel tightly as they accelerated into the next turn. "I plan on announcing my retirement and going on a nice, long vacation." She reached out and gently touched her lover's forearm, drawing a hint of a smile as he revved the engine and raced past a farmhouse on the left.

"Well, I'm planning on being the director of *my* agency. Which is why I refuse to tolerate any more of your blunders."

"You can't talk to me like that, Richard. I'm the one that brought you in on this deal."

His voice softened. "You're right—perhaps I have been too harsh. But we still have Pularchek's people and Brewbaker to contend with."

"Brewbaker? I thought you had eliminated that threat."

"No, he's still out there."

"And his son and daughter-in-law?"

"I don't care about them. They pose no threat."

She glanced at Dieter again as they passed another tidy, Tyrolean-style village on their right with white houses, red roofs, and timbered wood done in a faux-medieval style. He had been listening closely to the conversation and appeared skeptical of Voorheiss's motives.

She spoke again into her secure mobile. "What are you not telling me, Richard? I didn't trust you when you were head of Berlin Station, and I certainly don't trust you now. What are you up to?"

"If it's any consolation, I don't trust you either. But you have nothing to fear from me. All I want out of this is the spotlight on the big stage. Remember, you're getting all the money."

"I'll believe that when I see it."

"Just be in Innsbruck by midnight and we'll settle up. And you'd better have the merchandise in hand."

"Don't worry, I'll be there."

"How is the subject?"

"He's fine."

"You sure he hasn't double-crossed you? He's the one you should be worried about, not me."

She looked into the back seat. Handcuffed to the car door was Pularchek, who lay slumped in his seat fast asleep, his body covered with fresh new bandages. Yesterday's gunshots and the subsequent heavy travel and doses of pain medication and antibiotics had rendered him more and more exhausted as the day had worn on.

"He's sleeping like a baby," she said.

"You've seen no sign of his men?"

"No, none at all. Once we stripped him of his clothes and removed his tracking devices, we lost all pursuit from the Poles and Brewbaker's Americans."

"Don't let that fool you. Trust me, they're still out there. Keep a vigilant eye out and I'll meet you at the rendezvous as planned at midnight. There can be no more snafus. You need to get the merchandise out of there as quickly and quietly as possible and get to the rendezvous."

"And if for some reason one of us gets held up?"

"Don't let that happen, but on the off-chance it does, you know the backup plan. But don't even think of double-crossing me, Angela."

"Or what?"

"Or I will bring the full weight of the United States government down upon you and your countrymen. And that is something that you and your agency cannot afford."

"I don't appreciate being threatened, Richard. You don't have to bully me. I know how big and powerful the U.S. intelligence community is. You have nearly six million government employees and private contractors that hold security clearances giving them access to classified intelligence information. Nearly six million people. How do you keep all of them busy, Richard? That's what I'd like to know."

"We like redundancy. That and we only do big. Just remember, you will become a target with a bull's-eye, stalked and hunted down by a large number of highly committed professionals, if you don't come through for me. Like I said, I don't want the money. I'm looking to my future legacy."

"How very noble and altruistic of you."

"Watch your tongue, Angela. You're not out of the woods yet, and my presence is what gives you the cover with your people. I know that your boss, Walther Kluge, and the chancellor have ordered you to release Pularchek and return home to Berlin. And yet, you're defying them."

"Oh, so you've been busy eavesdropping on us again. Doesn't the CIA ever sleep?"

"As you said yourself, we've got nearly six million staff working for us with security clearances. That's a lot of people to keep busy doing something."

"Well, you have no reason to worry from my end. Personally, I'm worried about you. When it comes to the intelligence business, you Americans have a way of double-crossing even your most loyal NATO allies. Just ask my chancellor and the Turks."

"We have a history together, Angela, and I'm not going to double-cross you. I happen to believe that when spy agencies play nicely in the sandbox together, it can lead to diplomatic goodwill over the long term. That's you and I, Angela. Consummate team players who are smart enough to know that if we don't reach out and take a little bit for ourselves, somebody else will. But in your case, you also happen to be quite alluring to boot."

"Now you're trying flattery. You truly are a desperate man, Herr Director, if you believe that such a tactic will work with me."

"I'll see you at the rendezvous. *Auf Wiedersehen*, Ms. Vice-President. "

"Until then, Mr. Director. And don't you dare be late."

CHAPTER 47

MAUTERN IN STEIERMARK

AS SHE PUNCHED OFF, she made eye contact with Dieter and pointed up ahead to an abandoned, green-roofed Austrian-style farmhouse a half mile off the road. "Drive in there."

"What? To that old farmhouse?"

"Just do as I say. The others will follow."

Though skeptical, he did as instructed and drove up the dirt road to the farmhouse. There was no gate. The two Land Rovers and large lorries followed behind them along the dusty trail and parked next to a stone masonry farmhouse. The doors and windows were boarded up, and it looked as though it had been abandoned for years. The farmland all around had gone fallow, and there was no sign of anyone or any farm animals.

Wolff reached for her custom-fitted Brügger & Thomet baffle-type sound suppressor. The silencer would substantially reduce both the muzzle sound signature and ground echo of her pistol, so that no one from the neighboring farms or road could hear anything. With several quick turns of the wrist, she screwed the suppressor into the threaded barrel of her SIG-Sauer nine-millimeter backup piece that bore Pularchek's fingerprints.

"What the fuck are you doing, Angela? You can't kill Pularchek. We still need him."

"Wake him up and get him out of the car."

"I'm telling you we still need him."

"Don't worry. I'm not going to shoot him, Dieter. I'm just going to scare him to make sure he's telling the truth about the merchandise."

Reluctantly, Dieter Franck dragged Pularchek out of the vehicle as, one by one, the other car doors opened up and the team members stepped out of their vehicles. She crossed her hands behind her back, keeping her Walther concealed.

"What are we doing here?" asked Johannes Krupp, stepping towards her and the others. "Why are we stopping?"

"I just wanted us to get a chance to stretch our legs before we make the final push," said Wolff. "And to ask Herr Pularchek a few questions."

Krupp looked at his watch. "I don't think we have time for this. We're supposed to be there by five o'clock."

"Oh, I think we have time." She pulled the 9mm out from behind her back and pointed it at Pularchek, who gave her a sleepy-eyed look of surprise. "So tell me, Stanislaw, who ordered the killing of Bernhard Heydrich? It was the Americans, right?"

"No, as I told you before, it was someone *working for* the Americans."

Wolff pretended to play dumb. "Someone working for the Americans? You mean, someone working on behalf of the CIA?"

"Yes."

"Do you know who it was?"

"I don't see the relevance of this," interrupted Krupp. "We have to get to the mine, damnit. Time is running out."

"Keep quiet," snapped Wolff. Then to Pularchek. "My question still stands. Who ordered the killing of Heydrich?"

"I only know that it was someone close to you."

Wolff glanced at Dieter, who took an involuntary step backward as their eyes met. "How close?" she asked, covering Pularchek and her lover both with her pistol.

"Very close. Someone not just in your department, but working directly—"

"Okay, this has gone too far," cried Krupp. "He's making up tall tales to save his own skin."

She wheeled on him. "I thought I told you to shut up, Johannes!"

"But this is ridiculous. Here, let me put him out of his misery." He yanked out his Glock. "We're going to kill him anyway, damnit! We know where the merchandise is and don't need him anymore!"

She shifted her aim and leveled her Walther on Krupp. "No, it is you that we don't need anymore! You're the one who ordered Heydrich killed, Johannes! And you're also the one who is planning on double-crossing me with the Americans! What is their plan, Johannes? Tell me now, or die!"

"There is no plan, damn you!" He pointed his pistol at her as the rest of her team jerked out their own weapons. "Stop these accusations!"

"What did they promise you, Johannes?"

"They didn't promise me anything! I have not betrayed you! You have to believe me!"

"He's lying," said Pularchek. "I can see it in his eyes."

"I am not lying! Angela, you've…you've got to believe me!"

"How can I believe you when I know it was you?"

He looked around nervously at all of the semiautomatic pistols pointed at him. "Okay, everyone just calm down. We can make a deal."

"A deal?"

"It wasn't my fault. It was Voorheiss who approached me. I swear, I didn't…I didn't even want to do it. He…he forced me into it. You've got to believe me!"

"I do believe you. But that's still not enough, Johannes. Now tell me what I want to know."

"Everyone just stay calm," he said, keeping his gun on Wolff.

It was at that precise moment that Dieter Franck surprised everyone by dropping Krupp with a single shot to the forehead.

Wolff gasped in shock as her subordinate fumbled his pistol and fell to the ground with a dull thud. For a moment, she was paralyzed, unable to speak. *Lord, forgive me for what I just let happen. I have known Johannes for a dozen years.*

"There, it is done," said Dieter, leaning down and checking his pulse. "He was about to shoot you. I had to kill him." He gestured towards two of the other men. "Put him behind the barn. Quickly!"

As they lifted the body up and moved off, Wolff looked down at her gun hand and saw that it was trembling. It was one thing to shoot at a genuine enemy like Pularchek, especially if the gunplay involved only wounding him; but it was quite another to shoot a colleague you had known for a dozen years, or to watch as he was shot point blank in the head by someone else. All the same, she shouldn't have frozen up like that. But at least now it was over and she knew that it was Johannes that had betrayed her. He was the one complicit with Voorheiss. Now that she had uncovered the truth, she would have to be especially careful with the CIA man, who obviously couldn't be trusted.

She took a deep breath to steel her nerves. A voice called out inside her: *Get a grip, Angela! Don't lose sight of the objective!*

She immediately snapped to attention. "All right, let's get the hell out of here. We have a mission to complete."

Two minutes later, the team members had all crowded back into their vehicles and started off again on the road towards Salzburg. As they raced through the verdant Austrian countryside, Angela Wolff reached out and gently touched Dieter's hand.

"Thank you for that. I don't know what came over me, but I couldn't pull the trigger."

"Forget about it," he said, and he slammed his foot down on the accelerator. She wondered why he seemed to be angry with her when she was merely looking out for the whole team. "Let's just get the merchandise and get the hell out of this damned country," he added.

"I love you, you know," she said, squeezing his hand.

He reached up and stroked her fluffy blond hair. "I love you too. But I'll love you even more when this is all over."

"Skopelos. It's going to be so beautiful."

"Yes," he said. "It most certainly is."

CHAPTER 48

BAD AUSSEE
LIEZEN DISTRICT, CENTRAL AUSTRIA

AT PULARCHEK'S ALPINE CHATEAU outside the spa town of Bad Aussee, Skyler felt her coded mobile vibrate. Looking at the screen, she saw that the number was Anthony's. She glanced discreetly at Pularchek. Sitting on the spacious outdoor wooden deck, he looked like a wealthy Austrian landowner with his ruddy cheeks and authentic Tyrolean vestments.

"Go ahead and answer it, Skyler. I know your boyfriend is desperate to talk to you," he said with a conspiratorial grin.

Her eyes narrowed on him. "How did you know?"

"It's in my *interest* to know everything that goes on around me, especially love entanglements. Remember, I trust no one —not even you, my friend."

He gave her a mischievous wink. She smiled with grudging admiration in reply, rose from her seat, and took the call. "What is it, my love?"

"I've been trying to call you."

She started down the wooden stairs of the chalet. She could tell by the sound of his voice that something had happened and he had bad news for her. "I'm sorry, my phone was off for a while. What is it, Anthony? Is something wrong?"

"That guy came back to see me. Special Agent Patton."

She felt a sense of dread. "What did he want?"

"You wouldn't believe it. He told me the most fantastic story."

"He told you a story. What kind of story?"

"A story about you. At first, I didn't believe it because it was totally fucking outrageous and I didn't want to believe it. And then I realized that it made a lot of sense and he was telling the truth. And yet…and yet a part of me still doesn't want to believe it's true."

The phone went uncomfortably silent and she felt a sinking sensation. She braced herself for what he was about to say, but in her heart she already knew.

"He said that you're as assassin, Skyler. He said you're the one who killed President-elect Kieger, Fowler, and the others last fall. And he had the proof to back it up."

She gulped hard. "Proof? What kind of proof?"

"He showed me film footage of you in Denver and at various campaign rallies in California. And then he showed me footage of you and me together in LA. It was you, Skyler. It was you in all the videos. You were wearing several different disguises, but it was definitely you. He gave me a bunch of statistics on facial recognition analysis and shooting angles, and he gave me names and dates—and at the end of it all he said that you were a professional assassin."

She was unable to respond. Feeling her throat go suddenly dry, she took off towards the lake at a brisk pace, feeling a sudden wave of desperation. She couldn't believe the game was up, that she had been discovered by the one person in the world that she genuinely loved.

"Please tell me it isn't true, Skyler. Please. I don't want to believe it."

Feeling tears coming to her eyes, she paused a moment to stare out at the lofty mountains, thick pine woods, and intricate network of freshwater lakes of the Valley of Traun. Then, unable to say anything in her defense, she took a left onto a well-groomed hiking trail circumscribing the lake and marked with a green-and-white sign. The snow-capped peaks of the Totes Gebirge and the Dachstein massif loomed breathtakingly in the distance. Next to the lake, fields of narcissus burst into bloom, and the sweet smell of the alpine spring was in the air. She was in the "green heart" of the Salzkammergut. All in all, the scenery in every direction was picture-postcard perfect—and yet Skyler couldn't help but feel exposed and utterly doomed. She had been discovered and her wonderful life with Anthony was over, for she wasn't about to lie to him. Lying to the man she loved was beneath her.

"I love you, Anthony. I want you to know that," she said, tears streaming down her face.

"So it's all true? You're really an assassin?"

She couldn't bring herself to respond and wondered how Patton had figured it all out. Was it just the video images from the crime scene or had he somehow managed to collect DNA evidence from her shooting locations?

"I can't believe you've been lying to me all this time," said Anthony accusingly. "I was nothing more to you than a pawn. You just needed me for cover."

"You know that's not true."

"Then what is the truth? You've been a professional killer for how long?"

"You know I can't talk to you about any of this. Just know that my love for you is and always has been genuine. In fact, I have never loved anyone like I love you."

"That's it? That's all you're going to say?"

She didn't respond, just stared off in misery at the lake.

"Do you think I'm actually going to buy that?" he then asked, his voice quiet but incisive like the cut of a knife.

"I'm not going to lie to you, but I'm not going to give you the details, either. I care about you too much for that. Plus I would be putting you in danger."

"It's a little late. You've already put me in danger."

"I'm sorry about that. I never meant to hurt you."

"But you did. And now look at us."

Another awkward silence filled with unspoken emotion. She cursed herself for allowing her world to crumble around her once again just when she seemed to have found true happiness. Don Scarpello and Alberto couldn't have come up with a more ruthless and cunning ploy to destroy her. With the one person she truly loved taken from her, the nail had been driven decisively into her coffin.

"Now that I know, you're probably going to have to kill me, aren't you? That's how it works in your world, doesn't it?"

In your world. The words stung her, making her feel like a lowly criminal, a murderer instead of professional who, at least most of the time, simply rid the world of bad people. And yet, she couldn't help a little smile at his naiveté. "You've been watching and making too many unbelievable movies, Mr. Hollywood Film Producer. The real world isn't like that."

They both stopped talking for several anxious seconds, and all she could hear on the other end was his light breathing and the chirp of tropical birds. She pictured him pacing the wooden deck of their picturesque little tropical villa on the bay just east of Christiansted.

"Jesus Christ, this is insane," he said to finally break the tense silence. "Once again, I feel like we're Bogie and Bergman in Casablanca. As wrong as it sounds, I want to be with you, Skyler. I know who you are and what you do—and yet a part of me still wants to be with you. But how can that be when you've done these terrible things? You haven't admitted to committing these crimes—but you haven't denied responsibility either—so I know that Agent Patton is telling the truth."

"I don't know the answer to your question. All I know is that I love you."

"I can't believe I'm saying this, but I still love you too. That's how messed up in the head I am."

She felt suddenly lightheaded. She didn't want their relationship to be over, and was surprised that he seemed to feel the same way. Was there any chance that they could remain together, lead a normal life, and be a regular couple after this perilous moment in their relationship? Her brain told her that there wasn't a chance, but her heart told her something else entirely.

"You can never quit, can you Skyler? Whoever you're working for won't let you, will they? You're in too deep and that's why, after six months, you're back in the game again. Even if I could find a way to forgive you for your sins and take you back, I will always have to compete for your attentions. Once a killer, always a killer, right?"

"No. I can quit whenever I want."

"But you won't. In fact, you can't. Being in the game is like a drug to you."

"What makes you say that?"

"Because you tried to quit shortly after we first met last fall, but you couldn't do it. That phone call that night in LA…you got a call and then suddenly everything changed and we were on the run and Fowler was assassinated and you were shot twice. I nursed you back to health, Skyler. I was there. Isn't it all true? You wanted out, but you just couldn't do it?"

"Five years ago I made a promise to a very important man, a man that I respect and feel deep sympathy for."

"A promise? You made a promise?"

"A promise that if he ever called upon me, I would be there for him."

"You mean you would kill for him?"

"He is an honorable human being and the evil men he goes after deserve everything they have coming to them."

"My God, you really are an assassin. Don't you understand? This world of violence you inhabit is going to kill you. One day, someone's going to show up at your door and blow your brains out. One of your rivals, a government assassin, or some lowly gun for hire out to make his mark. A double tap and that will be the end of it. Well, I'm sorry but I won't be there for that. I'll miss that curtain call if you don't mind."

She felt the tears coming on again. "I'm sorry, Anthony. I'm truly sorry," was all she could manage to say.

"I'm sorry too," he said angrily. "I'm sorry I ever met you."

And with that he clicked off, leaving her to stare emptily at the frigid alpine lake below and wish that she was dead.

CHAPTER 49

BAD AUSSEE

AS BREWBAKER AND HIS CIA GROUP stepped from their van, Pularchek could tell Nick's father was agitated. But was it the operation or something else bothering him? A half hour ago, Pularchek had delivered a preliminary briefing to Brewbaker, Nick, Natalie, and the other members of the deputy director's team over a secure phone line about his risky plan to recover a dozen Italian Old Masters' paintings stolen by the Nazis, worth a billion dollars, and to take Angela Wolff and Richard Voorheiss into custody. It was a dangerous operation, with a hundred things that could go wrong, but as Brewbaker drew closer Pularchek realized that the CIA man wasn't actually worried about the operation. No, the cause of his agitation was Skyler. Pularchek could see it in the man's eyes.

As Brewbaker approached the chateau, his gaze narrowed on her and it was readily apparent that he recognized her. But from where? For more than a decade, her Diego Gomez cover had fooled everyone in the international intelligence community—until Special Agent Ken Patton of the FBI's Denver Field Office, the lead investigator in the Kieger and Fowler assassination cases, had figured things out. Through his team of expert hackers, Pularchek had acquired a copy of not only the U.S. government's draft report and final, mostly redacted report but Patton's internal FBI correspondence, and he had quickly realized that the Special Agent was onto something. And now it appeared as if Brewbaker, too, knew or at least strongly suspected Skyler's true identity. Not wanting to give himself away, the Pole pretended not to notice Brewbaker's suspicious expression and cordially waved him and his group forward, smiling the smile of a gracious Austrian host in his classic Tyrolean attire. He needed to take control of the situation quickly or the operation could be in jeopardy.

"Welcome, my American friends, to my alpine redoubt in the Salzkammergut lakes region of Styria. You happen to be standing on the precise geographical midpoint of Austria. Nicholas, why don't you take Natalie on a ten-minute walk along the lake. I'm sure you two newlyweds have some catching up to do. In the meantime, I will have a private word with your father and his two CIA colleagues, Mr. Webb and Mr. Glover. You can fill your lovely wife in on some of the additional details you and I discussed while your father and I have a pleasant visit."

He looked affably but forcefully at Brewbaker, instructing him with his eyes not to resist his peaceful overture. But as expected, the deputy director was not one to be even politely cajoled.

"If you don't mind," said Benjamin Brewbaker, "I'd like to say hello to my son first."

Pularchek gave a formal bow of acquiescence. "But of course, Mr. Deputy Director. My apologies." He backed up to give the two of them room.

ᴪᴪᴪ

After embracing and saying a few words to his wife, Lassiter pulled away gently from her and walked over to his father. He and his dad then took a few steps away from the others so they could be alone.

"Hey, Dad," he said, speaking into his father's ear in a low voice so the others couldn't hear. "It's good to see you."

"You all right, kiddo?"

"Yeah, I'm fine. I'm sorry about taking off like I did from the safe house."

"You didn't take off. Pularchek kidnapped you."

"Yeah, I know, but he had his reasons. Believe it or not, I think it was good for us to spend some time alone together. I hope you're not mad at me, but he wasn't going to take no for an answer. He is a very insistent fellow."

His father made a sardonic face. "You think? I'm just glad you're safe, Son. And Natalie too."

"Thanks. When you first got here, why were you looking at that woman like that? You looked like you recognized her."

They glanced discreetly at Skyler, who was calmly studying them from the deck. Lassiter couldn't help but feel vaguely threatened by her, as if he was in the presence of a stalking panther.

"Let's just say she's on our watch list. How long has she been with your group?"

"Right after the suicide bombing in Warsaw was the first time I saw her. She follows us everywhere. She seems to be watching over us, but I'm pretty sure she's on her own. She's something of a loner."

"You mean she's not with Pularchek's team?"

"I don't think so. But I'm not one-hundred-percent sure."

"What's her name?"

"They call her Skyler."

"Skyler. That's it, no last name?"

Lassiter nodded. "I'm sure it's just a code name. What's so important about her?"

"I don't have time to tell you right now. Just talk to Natalie while I meet with Pularchek. Suffice to say he and I have some issues to work out regarding this Skyler."

"All right, Dad."

"It's funny, but I still can't believe Pularchek is your father."

"You're my father too."

223

"Yeah, but now I have to share you just when you and I have gotten back together again." He pulled him closer and patted him on the back. "Like I said a moment ago, I'm just glad you and Natalie are both safe, Son."

"Thanks, Dad. I love you."

"I love you too. We'll talk in a few minutes."

ψψψ

As Nick and Natalie started down the alpine hiking trail, Pularchek motioned his Polish team, Skyler, Brewbaker, Webb, and Glover inside the chateau. Once inside, he led them to a large table in the drawing room bearing a series of color-coded maps and cross-sections. "If you would please step right up, ladies and gentlemen, I'd like to go over the final details of our little Polish operation. Seeing as you Yanks represent the world's largest intelligence organization, I'd love to get your professional input. But I'm afraid we don't have much time. The Germans and your lawbreaking American comrade, Director Voorheiss, will be here shortly. My team intercepted an encrypted cellphone communication between him and Angela Wolff not more than an hour ago. But before we make our final arrangements, I'm going to need a private word with you two."

He looked pointedly at Brewbaker and Skyler and then waved them towards a separate office on the north side of the chateau.

"I'm afraid I must insist," he added. "As I said, we don't have much time."

Brewbaker and Skyler both looked resistant, but after a moment of staring coldly at one another, they reluctantly acceded to his request. When they had all reached his private office, Pularchek closed the door behind them so they were alone.

"Listen to me very carefully, you two," he began in the tone of a lecturing schoolmaster, "because I am only going to say this once. I saw the way you two looked at one another when you first arrived, and I must say that I didn't like it one bit. I don't care what is going on between you two, but you are part of my operation now and will be acting under my orders. For the next seventy-two hours, you will do as I say and not take any action against one another or jeopardize the operation. I must have your word on this."

Brewbaker was shaking his head. "She's an assassin and just killed four prominent U.S. political leaders. She's going down."

It was as Pularchek had feared—Brewbaker had indeed managed to figure out who she was and what she had done—and the Pole knew he had to counter quickly and decisively. "Now listen here, your own official government commission headed by Senator Warren found that the responsible parties were the Spanish assassin Diego Gomez and several members of your own U.S Secret Service. So you can curtail your conspiracy theory speculation right here and now, Mr. Deputy Director. It has no basis in fact and we don't have time for this."

"She did it and I'm going to prove it."

"You can go ahead and try," said Skyler coolly. "But you may not live that long."

Pularchek held up his hands, calling a timeout. He realized that he had underestimated the extent of Brewbaker's knowledge and should have seen this potential intelligence disaster coming. The deputy director must have been in communication with Ken Patton. "Who told you all this? Have you been talking to Special Agent Patton of the FBI?"

Brewbaker's and Skyler's eyebrows raised at the same time. "How do you know about Patton?" asked Brewbaker.

"Don't insult the intelligence of me and my outfit. I know all about Special Agent Patton. In fact, I know he is in St. Croix this very minute harassing an American citizen without agency approval of his activities. It seems he's down there conducting an investigation on his own time without his superiors knowing. The case has been closed, and yet Agent Patton appears to be reopening it. I wonder what FBI Director Sidley would have to say about one of his top agents going rogue and embarrassing the U.S. by poking around and asking questions about a closed case. I must say this Patton fellow seems obsessed just like you. The next thing we know, you two will be planting evidence so you can secure a conviction."

"That's not funny."

"Actually, I think it's very funny," said Skyler. "You think you know me? You don't know the first thing about me."

"But I do," interjected Pularchek, "and I say she is under my personal protection until this operation is done and over. All I'm asking for is a seventy-two hour truce. Then you can draw pistols, step off twenty paces, and open fire on one another for all I care. But I need you to be mine unquestioningly for seventy-two hours."

"I don't trust him," said Skyler. "I don't trust anyone that works for the U.S. government."

Brewbaker's eyes narrowed. "Yeah, and so your answer is to shoot them?"

"You have no proof of that," she countered. "You're grasping at straws based on the ramblings of an obsessed agent that has gone off the reservation."

"And is about to become disciplined by his mandarin bosses in the Hoover Building for overstepping his authority," added Pularchek. "Once they find out what he's up to."

"You wouldn't dare alert them," protested Brewbaker.

"Oh, I absolutely will if you don't drop this matter and leave her alone." He looked severely at him, then at them both, making it clear that he would brook no further opposition. "Now you must stop this, the both of you. The job that I need you for right now is absolutely critical and has taken more than a year of planning. I don't care what you do after it is successfully completed, but right now I need you both to promise me that you will carry out the operation and not meddle in each other's affairs or threaten each other in any way. We are at the twelfth hour and I must have a unified team. Do I have your word on this?"

He continued to look hard at them. When they didn't respond, he laid into them again.

"What you do as far as politics goes once the op is complete is your own business. All I'm asking you to do is to put aside your differences for seventy-two hours and focus every ounce of your effort on the mission at hand. There are bad people that have done, and are continuing to do, very bad things linked to the Holocaust. We need to take them down. All of them. Can I count on you? Are you with me?"

The room went totally silent. Pularchek was worried that he might have overreached and become a little too preachy, but he could see that Skyler and Brewbaker were actually moved. They knew that they needed to put aside their differences if they were going to successfully complete the job.

To his surprise, Skyler was the one to step forward and speak first. "I am with you and will work with the deputy director. For seventy-two hours."

Pularchek looked at Brewbaker. "What about you?"

"Seventy-two hours or until the op is finished, whichever comes first." He looked hard at the beautiful Italian assassin. "And then I'm coming for you myself."

She gave a look of cool challenge. "Good. I will be armed, ready, and waiting. But I am warning you, it will be your funeral."

"I would not mess with her if I were you," said Pularchek. "But now that we've all aired our concerns, is there anything either of you would like to add?"

"Yes," said Brewbaker. "The next time you decide to steal one of my assets, you damn well better ask me."

"Is that all your son Nicholas is to you, an asset?"

"Right now—yes. And so are you, and so is she. So let's get this final briefing going because I happen to be out of work and I'm getting impatient."

"Out of work? What do you mean out of work?"

"Voorheiss fired me. I no longer work for the CIA."

"Oh, the plot just keeps getting thicker," said Skyler. "Somehow, Inspector Javert, I see a long vacation on your horizon with Agent Patton. You two can commiserate and work out your mutual obsession together."

Pularchek frowned. "That's quite enough, Skyler. We need to wrap up this mission quickly and successfully and help the deputy director get his old job back. That way you two can have your historic showdown at the OK Corral. But for now, let's get to work. Please follow me."

He led them back into the drawing room to the two teams hunched over the large color map spread out over the table. Pularchek's Polish brigade was dressed in marine-blue police raid gear. They had an arsenal of automatic weapons, various types of grenades, and explosive devices in the corner of the room. They looked like they were getting ready for World War Three.

"All right, ladies and gentlemen, the last GPS location of Angela Wolff was forty-seven miles east of Bad Aussee. Which means we have exactly one hour to prep."

"One hour?" snorted Brewbaker, looking at his watch. "Isn't that cutting it close?"

"Not really," said Pularchek. "Not when we have her."

He tipped his head deferentially towards Skyler.

"You see, she's our wild card. Our American friends will never see her coming."

Brewbaker stared at her, looking unconvinced. "So you're a magician, is that it?"

"No," said Pularchek. "She just knows how to pull off a little Hollywood misdirection."

Skyler smiled thinly. "Trust me, Deputy Director, you're going to like it."

CHAPTER 50

BAD AUSSEE

Once they were on the hiking trail and out of sight of the chateau, Lassiter took Natalie in his arms and kissed her like the sailor in the famous *V-J Day in Times Square* photo. She kissed him back passionately, and he felt his head spin. Pleasantly. My God, had he missed her! It was as if they had been separated for an entire lifetime instead of merely twenty-four hours! He drew her in close and they hugged and kissed again for good measure. Seeing the tears of joy spilling down her cheeks, he felt the power of their affection as well as the danger of their current situation. He was so excited to be reunited with her that he could scarcely breathe; and yet, he was fearful of the closing act in what had become a dangerous contest of international espionage, a modern spy game linked to the dark and deadly past of the Second World War.

After pulling apart, they walked down a narrow hiking trail towards a clear alpine lake, passing through fields of blooming narcissus. The snow-crested peaks of the Totes Gebirge and the Dachstein massif rose majestically in the distance. He took Natalie's hand in his and smiled at her as church bells rang in the nearby spa town. Here the local inhabitants, he had been informed by Pularchek, wore the traditional Austrian dress called *Tracht* on a daily basis.

He said, "I still can't believe this stolen Old Masters' art collection is worth a billion dollars. No wonder Pularchek's put together such an elaborate scheme to bring down Wolff and Voorheiss. The whole purpose of the D.C. and Berlin shootings was to shake things up and make them come after him. It was a well-laid trap from the beginning."

"He must have planned this for many, many months," said Natalie.

"But what Pularchek couldn't possibly have planned for was my presence on that rooftop terrace, or the suicide bomber trying to take him out in Warsaw. They threw wrenches into his plans, which is why his men had to make the exchange at the safe house. They couldn't let the real Stanislaw Pularchek be captured. They wanted the Germans to take a Pularchek prisoner so he could lead them to the paintings, but they didn't want it to be the real one."

"Have you found out if Pularchek has clones?"

"I don't think he does. They're definitely doubles, but I don't believe they're clones. He was very explicit about that when I asked him about it."

"Then what are they?"

"I don't know. But whatever they are, they are fiercely loyal and willing to die for him. He calls them his *Braciszkus*."

"What does that mean?"

"*Braciszku* is Polish for *Little Brother*."

"It sounds like something out of the Bible. But right now, I'm interested in hearing where these art treasures are hidden and how Pularchek intends to get them back. He didn't tell your father and me that part of the plan over the phone, but I presume he's told you."

"The paintings are hidden in a nearby salt mine, the Old Steinberg Mine. Pularchek owns it, and he put the entire Florentine Bellomo collection there. The paintings are undergoing restoration by a team of artists, technicians, and scientists. It's just a few miles from here in Altaussee. The goal is to lure the bad guys into the most famous repository where the Nazis once hid their stolen art collections. He's following in the footsteps of the Monuments Men and Austrian civilian miners who stopped the Nazi art looters."

"So he's making some sort of symbolic statement?"

"A big one. During the war, the salt mines at Altaussee served as the main repository for the art Hitler planned to use to fill his planned *Führermuseum* in his hometown of Linz here in Austria. The Führer's twisted plan was to stock the museum with the world's greatest works of art and showcase the superiority of Aryan artists over their supposedly 'degenerate' Jewish counterparts. It all started right here in the Austrian Alps. Within months of invading Poland in 1939, Nazi troops began seizing selected pieces—which eventually included paintings by Raphael, Da Vinci, Rembrandt, Michelangelo, Vermeer, and other Old Masters as well as Impressionists—from churches, museums, and private art collections throughout Europe. Until the war's end, they were hidden in the labyrinth of mines near here and in remote German and Austrian castles for safekeeping. Pularchek wants Wolff and Voorheiss to be caught stealing the paintings where the masterworks of European art were stored and nearly blown to bits by the Nazis at the end of the war. Paintings that were fortunately saved by the Austrian miners and the Monuments Men."

"Only this time Pularchek will be the one to save the day."

"Dudley Do-Right to the rescue."

"It's sheer genius. When Wolff and Voorheiss come to get their treasure, they're in for one hell of a surprise."

"Except they're not going to be arrested at the mine."

"What?"

"Pularchek doesn't want Wolff and Voorheiss taken into custody until *after* they've stolen the paintings and completed a sale to the actual buyers."

"So what is Pularchek's plan to catch them?"

"He plans to make the exchange for his double once they've stolen the paintings. He's then going to document the theft while keeping Voorheiss and Wolff under surveillance. My father—who is now unfortunately the ex-NCS deputy director—will be present as an official observer. Together, they will make the arrest following the authentication and sale of the paintings."

"So what are we doing here then?"

"Serving as eyewitnesses, like my dad. But Pularchek also has hidden surveillance cameras inside and all around the abandoned mine."

"I don't know about this. It sounds risky. And then there's that woman working with Pularchek. Did you know that she's a professional assassin known by the CIA and FBI as Jane Doe and that she's the one who killed Kieger and the others?"

"Jesus, I had no idea. Pularchek and his team call her Skyler. I wondered why my father was looking at her so intently. I had a feeling he knew who she was or there was some sort of history there. So you're telling me this woman is a professional assassin?"

She nodded. "She scares me. The look in her eyes is like a cold-blooded reptile."

"She doesn't say much, but I know Pularchek thinks highly of her. She's not part of his official team. She follows us around and keeps an eye on things from a distance. She's like an Indian scout."

"She's definitely a crack shot with that short assault rifle of hers. I saw her take down three Germans at the safe house in a matter of seconds. She's lethal, and this whole operation seems risky to me. I just don't see how we're going to get back a billion dollars' worth of Nazi stolen art without a major battle."

"I guess this is our D-Day."

"That's not exactly reassuring."

"Yeah, but it's the truth. Unless Pularchek, my dad, and that woman Skyler are coming up with a better plan right now, I'm afraid it's all we've got."

They stopped at the edge of the lake and stared out at the lush green valley and surrounding snow-capped mountains. It was a fairy-tale dreamland. Looking out at it, Lassiter found it hard to believe that the quaint little spa town had once been the last desperate refuge of fleeing Nazi officers and the hiding place of Europe's greatest stolen art treasures. He peered up at the towering backdrop of the Totes Gebirge and the Dachstein massif; he stared out at the flat-bottomed *Plätten* boats that had once been used in the salt trade; and he took in the fresh scent of the blooming narcissus in the nearby fields. Along the hiking trails, he saw locals bedecked in their traditional *Tracht* outfits. The women wore Dirndl-style dresses with fitted bodices and full skirts, while the men wore feathered felt hats, knee-length trousers of leather *Lederhosen*, rustic shoes and wool socks, and traditional gray loden *Steireranzug* jackets with green embroidery. The Bad Aussee area was one of the most beautiful places in all of Austria, and Lassiter could see why. And yet he felt a sense of unrest here, knowing the dark history of the Nazis that had cast their dark shadows on this majestic alpine valley.

"I just hope they have a backup plan in case everything goes to hell," said Natalie.

"Knowing my dad, I'm sure he's got one in place."

"I wasn't talking about him. I was talking about your other father, Pularchek. Are you sure you can trust him?"

"Absolutely not," he said. "Snark Pularchek is probably the most untrustworthy human being on the planet."

"Snark? What do you mean Snark?"

"That's his nickname: Snark. His middle name Snarkus comes from the Lewis Carroll poem *The Hunting of the Snark*. His parents were big fans, I guess, and his friends call him by the nickname. In fact, he told me to use it. Apparently, he likes it."

"Good Lord, Snark Pularchek? What has this world come to when it has a billionaire assassin named Snark Pularchek?"

Lassiter smiled. "I don't know. But I think I like the name."

"You would, you big dumb Polack." She pulled him close. "Now give me a kiss. This is supposed to be our honeymoon, and yet I feel as though this may be our last moment together on earth."

"Don't worry, we'll be fine."

"That's what you and your dad said last time. And then I got shot, remember?"

"You're never going to let me forget, are you?"

"Nope. Especially not on our action-packed honeymoon."

CHAPTER 51

OLD STEINBERG SALT MINE, ALTAUSSEE

"ONE FALSE MOVE—or the faintest sign of your men nearby before the paintings have been secured—and I will shoot you down like a dog," Angela Wolff warned Pularchek as they stepped up to the north entrance of the Old Steinberg Salt Mine. He glowered back at her and then, using his plastic zip-tie-secured hands, he quickly input a series of numbers to unlock the heavy stainless-steel door to the mine. Now that she was close to reaching her goal, she couldn't help but feel grudging admiration for a worthy adversary. It was almost a pity that it was all about to come to an end.

"Don't worry," he said as the door unlocked with a clicking sound. "Your instructions were made quite clear to my Operations-Security team. They are watching us at this very moment, but from a safe distance as you requested. And all of my restorationists and technicians have been quietly removed from the mine, so we are all alone here."

"Well, it had better stay that way. Now please lead me to *my* new art collection. After it's been locked away for three generations, I'm quite anxious to see it." She tipped her head towards the bespectacled man in the gray business suit with the Himmler mustache. "Once Dr. Bloeckler has verified the authenticity of the paintings and me and my men are safe, you will be free to go and we will notify your men to come get you."

"Where is Director Voorheiss? Isn't he going to be attending our little art exhibition?"

"I'm afraid he has other plans," she said, trying her best to conceal her own doubts. "It is late and we must get started."

"You don't trust him, do you? I wouldn't either if I were you."

"I don't trust anyone. That's why I always plan for the worst." She waved her arm forward. "Now lead the way, Herr Pularchek, and don't even think about trying to double-cross me."

"I wouldn't dream of it, Angela my dear."

He led the group into the salt mine. Inside the heavy stainless-steel door was a staging area with work lockers and a mining rack containing picks, shovels, coiled rope, work coveralls, jackets, and hard hats. They grabbed hard hats equipped with halogen lamps from the racks and donned them on their heads, though Wolff and her men also had high-powered battery flashlights. Having augmented and now consolidated her forces, she had twenty armed BND men in her detail, four of whom she had posted as guards outside the entrance to keep an eye out for intruders. All the same, she felt wary as she turned on the light on her hard hat and stepped through a second door into the main tunnel cut into the mountain.

Up ahead, she saw that the narrow passageway was well illuminated with electric lighting via extension cables. The walls were shored with sturdy wooden timber. With her and Dieter in the lead, Pularchek behind them, and two of her men covering the Pole with a pistol, the group started forward two-abreast through the narrow passageway, navigating by the headlamps, overhead halogen lighting, and flashlights. The air was musty and smelled of damp earth and brine. As they penetrated deeper into the interior, they encountered branching side tunnels that veered off to the east and west from the main passageway. She could see from the fresh footprints that the passageway had been used recently, and she could feel air whispering in from cracks in the salt rock.

The Altaussee evaporate deposits had originally formed in the Permian Period 250 million years before Hitler's *blitzkrieg* had swept across Europe. The world-famous accumulations of halite and anhydrite had slowly built up over millions of years, as an ancient epeiric sea had dried out during a major marine lowstand. The modern deposit mined for its valuable salt comprised the Permian Haselgebirge Formation, which had formed atop a dried-out sea floor before being buried under thousands of feet of sediment, uplifted, and wildly contorted in the later Cenozoic, the product of the immense forces between the colliding African and Eurasian plates. In the light of her bright halogen lamp, Wolff could see the S-shaped foliations and criss-crossing veins in the shimmering walls of multicolored salt-rock flanking the passageway.

The tunnel was an impressive feat of engineering. She could see why Hitler had made the caverns at Altaussee the repository for his looted art treasures. It was said that he and his Nazi henchmen had amassed over 6,500 art objects, worth upwards of 3.5 billion American dollars. She imagined the thousands of paintings, drawings, prints, sculptures, and tapestries that had been tucked away inside a labyrinth of tunnels just like this one, earmarked for Hitler's *Führermuseum.*

It struck her that she was doing virtually the same thing as the Nazi tyrant, but she was able to convince herself that her situation was really quite different. Her grandfather Karl Wolff had never been properly compensated for his courageous efforts to keep the Pope safe from the *Führer's* fulminous wrath and to end the war in Italy, thereby saving countless lives and preventing the costly destruction of property. No, she and her grandfather were no Hitlers. She was only collecting what was rightfully hers, what her flawed but nonetheless heroic ancestor the SS General had bequeathed her. She truly deserved this: her *Schatzfund.* Especially when one considered that the Florentine Bellomo family had acquired the bulk of their collection through questionable means, and the provenance of multiple pieces had been in doubt at the time her grandfather had seized the paintings. *If you're going to steal,* she thought with relish, *best to steal from a family of crooks.*

They took a short branching tunnel and came to a large, domed open space. A battery of high-powered halogen lamps illuminated a high-tech artistic work area. In the center of this large open space was an elevated concrete pad with mounted oil paintings, both large and small, arranged in neat rows on sturdy wooden restoration easels. She quickly counted the number: there were four rows with three paintings per row, for a total of twelve paintings. Among the paintings were various carts, trays, and storage lockers containing preservation, examination, documentation, and restoration equipment. This included jars of chemicals and varnishes, paints and brushes, canvasses, wooden supports, and gadgetry used for photography, microscopy, radiography, ultraviolet fluorescence, and infrared reflectography.

At the sight of her recovered art treasure, Wolff felt a tremolo of excitement rush through her whole body. Stepping up behind her into the large concrete-floored room with the raised pad in the center like a circus ring, Dr. Bloeckler was so excited that he stumbled and his wire-rimmed glasses flew off his head onto the hard floor.

"*Mein Gott*," exclaimed Wolff, unable to believe her eyes. "I can't believe this is really happening."

"The devil will make you pay for this, Angela my dear," said Pularchek. "You can count on it. The devil will make you pay."

But she was too transfixed to respond. She glided forward towards the center of the vaulted room. Bloeckler raced past her muttering in wonderment, his fumbled glasses perched back on his head. He strode quickly up and down the line of paintings, taking a quick inventory without even needing to check the affidavit signed by her grandfather and his official Vatican witness Helmut Hoess. The sheath of papers he had in his possession listed the full inventory and provenance of the twelve master works now unveiled and undergoing restoration in the high-ceilinged room.

She motioned Dieter. "Take two men and look around," she said. "Make sure we're alone."

"You think Pularchek's men are in the mine?"

"I don't know. But somehow this all seems too easy."

"What do you mean?"

"I don't know what I was expecting, but it wasn't this. I have the feeling we're being watched. I want you to check it out."

"I'll take care of it."

Suddenly, Dr. Bloeckler burst out: "They're all here—every one of them!" he cried, as if he couldn't believe it himself. "Da Vinci's *The Virgin and Child with St. Anne and St. John the Baptist*. Titian's *Perseus and Andromeda* and *The Sun Amidst Small Stars*. Tintoretto's *The Last Supper* and his lost series of three paintings depicting the legend of St. Helena and the Holy Cross. Botticelli's *Venus and Mars at Pompeii* and *The Madonna and Child*. And then there's Giorgione, Rubens, and Klimt. Good God, Gustav Fucking Klimt, the most famous painter of the Viennese Secession movement. They're all here. All twelve of them. It's unbelievable—they're truly all here!"

Despite her worries that this was all too easy and her suspicion that they were being watched, Wolff, too, could scarcely conceal her exhilaration. All her hard work, perseverance, and yes—controlled aggression and willingness to accept some collateral damage—had paid off. The eleven Old Masters' works and single Klimt painting were a spectacular sight, and she couldn't help but feel a shiver of jubilation as she gazed upon the breathtaking artistic wonders passed down to her from her infamous grandfather.

Bloeckler removed a high-powered digital camera so he could take photographs to verify the authenticity of the paintings. The camera was plugged into a portable laptop strapped onto his chest equipped with high-resolution black-and-white photographs of the original paintings and specialized digital image-analysis software. The original photos had been taken by Karl Wolff and his Nazi team in the spring of 1944 to catalogue the Bellomo collection and provide documentation of its provenance. Using his camera and portable laptop, Bloeckler swiftly but methodically took pictures of each of the paintings and ran his computerized image-matching software to compare the two images. The software was able to identify distinguishing characteristics in the original photographs and search for those characteristics in the color photographs, like matching two sets of fingerprints.

From Bloeckler's body language and occasional exclamations of delight, Wolff could tell that the matching process was going well. She was also impressed with the restoration efforts thus far. Though no art expert, she could tell that the restorers had already made considerable progress in less than a week's time. The restoration of oil paintings included many different processes: the removal of surface dirt and discolored varnish layers; the replacement of canvas or wood structural supports; retouching missing portions of the painting in strict imitation of the original by the use of similar pigments; careful restretching of the painted canvas if the painting had been removed from its mount; and removing fragments of sculpted or moulded areas in the paintings. It was a laborious process requiring extensive skill and patience, and by the looks of the paintings, the restoration process was well underway and had thus far been highly successful.

Dieter returned to her side. "No sign of anyone. But there are several hidden cameras along the cave walls and ceiling." He pointed up. "See that one there, and the one over there?"

"Are they surveillance cameras?"

"They could be just for documentation, or as a deterrent against theft for the conservators and technicians."

"Or, to watch and record us perhaps? See if there is a control room. They must run these cameras from somewhere."

As he shuffled off again, she stepped up to the Klimt. It showed a portrait of an alluring young woman and was titled simply *Marie von Brandauer*. The restoration revealed the beauty that lay beneath the veil of over seventy years of being locked away in a storage room. But to a great extent, she thought as she glanced around the room, that was what had saved all of these ancient wonders. Sunlight, fluctuating moisture content, dust, and the natural wear and tear of being put on display in a frequently used room were the worst culprits when it came to destroying priceless works of art.

Having finished his preliminary analysis, Bloeckler now returned to her side. "Master Klimt painted that in 1908," he said with pride. "It would sell for one hundred eighty million U.S. dollars if it were sold at Christie's or Sotheby's. These days the salacious Austrian outsells Picasso."

"You're sure it's an original?"

"It's Klimt all right. He paints like an erotic Samurai."

"And the others?"

"All the Old Masters on the list are here. They are all originals without a doubt. This collection makes the Uffizi look like child's play. It's worth *over* a billion dollars in my estimation."

"And the restoration?"

"Exquisite." He glanced at Pularchek, standing handcuffed ten feet away, gazing at one of the Tintorettos. "I don't know who his team of conservators is, or where they came from, but they are first-rate. He must have at least two dozen people working for him on these master works, and he must be paying them a small fortune."

"How far along is the restoration?"

"It varies from painting to painting. The Klimt, Da Vinci, two of the Tintorettos, and the Rubens could be shown at the Louvre tomorrow and no one would be able to tell the difference. But the others are a few weeks away, anywhere from twenty-percent to seventy-percent complete. As the late great restorer Francis Kelly once said, 'Every work of art starts out on the progressive path to destruction from the moment it is created. When the object passes from the artist's hands, he can but pray it will be well looked after.' To his credit, Pularchek has most certainly done that. He can afford to hire a very large team of the best and it shows."

"How much longer do you need to conduct your verification of the authenticity of the works?"

"I have completed my preliminary assessment. Final verification and pigment analyses through X-ray diffraction and infrared reflectography will have to take place at my private laboratory in Bonn. But I am already ninety-five-percent confident that this is the full Bellomo oil collection. And I will also tell you that this is the greatest private collection I have ever had the pleasure to feast my eyes on. Tell your men to start loading them onto the trucks now. Carefully, mind you. But my preliminary work is finished here."

"Very well." She turned to Erich von Hoen, her new second-in-command behind Dieter now that Johannes was dead. "Commence the loading. Dr. Bloeckler has completed his analysis."

"I'll see to it."

"I told you they were genuine, Angela my dear, but you didn't believe me," said Pularchek, stepping up to them with his hands bound. "Even if my men and I don't hunt you down per our agreement, you're never going to get away with this."

"I wouldn't bet against me if I were you."

"I would. In fact, I am right now. But in any case, your work is done here. Which means that I have met my end of the bargain and am free to go."

"It's true, that is our arrangement," admitted Wolff.

He held up his bound hands. "So can you please tell your lover boy to remove these? These restraints are beginning to irritate me."

She gave a bloodless smile. "I wish I could, Herr Pularchek." She pulled out her Walther. "But I'm afraid that's just not possible."

"Why the hell not?" he protested indignantly.

"Because I've changed my mind."

"Changed your mind?"

"Yes Stanislaw, my Polish adversary. In fact, I'm going to kill you."

CHAPTER 52

OLD STEINBERG SALT MINE

STARING THROUGH THE ONE-WAY GLASS MIRROR, Pularchek realized that he had indeed made a terrible blunder. His *Braciszku* had succeeded in his mission to lure Wolff into the trap, but now he was on his own and his life was in jeopardy. Pularchek had suspected that Angela Wolff might go back on her word even though the Monte Carlo statistical analysis based on her profile had put the probability at less than fifteen percent. But he had left the final decision of whether to proceed with the mission in the hands of his *Braciszku*, who had insisted on going through with it despite the inherent risk. But that didn't make Pularchek feel any better now as he saw Wolff pull out a 9mm with a silencer and point it at his loyal Brother's chest.

Only twenty feet separated him and his team from Wolff and his *Braciszku*, but it felt like miles. The surveillance and control room that he had constructed and outfitted in only the last month possessed not only a one-way reflective window, but a battery of closed circuit digital cameras, high-end microphones, and listening speakers. From more than a dozen carefully concealed cameras and listening devices, Angela Wolff and her team were being videotaped and recorded as her men loaded the paintings onto three heavy-duty, steel platform mover's dollies and began wheeling them down the passageway to the parked vehicles outside the mine. The audiovisual documentation that was being collected at this very moment would be enough to send Wolff and her team to prison for five lifetimes.

But it would not save his *Braciszku*. His son realized it too.

"What should we do?" asked Lassiter, standing next to Pularchek, Romanowski, and the rest of the Polish team as well as the American team of Benjamin Brewbaker, Natalie, Webb, and Glover. Skyler was not with them and had been posted outside the mine to monitor the situation and take appropriate action, as necessary. She was the wild card that Wolff and Voorheiss were unaware of. "Surely we aren't going to let Angela Wolff kill him."

"Don't worry, nobody's killing anyone," said Pularchek, listening to the conversation through the control room speakers.

"He knows the risks, Boss," said the Counselor. "We can't intervene, or it might jeopardize the operation."

"I know that," said Pularchek. "But Mikolaj is right. We can't just stand by and watch her shoot him."

"This is about the mission, Boss. You've always said the mission comes first."

He looked at his son and Natalie. Their eyes said it all about which choice they thought was the right one: they wanted the killing prevented even if it meant the objective would be compromised. Then he glanced at Benjamin Brewbaker, who was looking at him intently. For the CIA lifer, it appeared to be a toss-up.

"Boss, you've got to make a decision. She's going to shoot him any second."

"Just one moment. I'm thinking, damnit."

He wished he had prepared himself and his team better for this anticipated yet unfortunate turn of events. He took a moment to study Wolff's body language, wondering if she was truly willing to follow through with her threat. Her voice and that of his *Braciszku*, as they argued back and forth, thrust and parry, came through with crystal clarity through the overhead speakers in the sound-proofed control room. The conversation was being recorded, and an official transcript was being prepared by a computer and reviewed, word for word, by a stenographer. But a recording was not going to save his loyal comrade-in-arms, who truly was like a brother to him.

He winced as he saw Wolff step forward with her gun, pointing it at his *Braciszku's* chest. *My God, I've got to do something. But what can I do without blowing the op? The whole point is to let them take the paintings and think they got away with it!*

"We've got to do something," said his son with a note of urgency.

"He's right," said Natalie. "We can't just let them kill him."

"I know, I know," he said. "But we can't take Wolff out. We need her alive."

"Well, we've got to do something," said Lassiter. "She's about to pull the goddamned trigger."

O, kurwa. What should I do?

And then the decision was made for him.

One of the Germans checking the room with Dieter Franck pulled out his pistol and pointed it at the one-way glass window.

"What the hell are you doing, Otto?" Franck called out to him from fifteen feet away. "Put that thing away. A ricochet could destroy one of these priceless pieces."

"There's someone behind there, I know it."

"Okay, we'll check it out. But put that damned gun away."

"They're watching us right now."

"I'm not going to tell you again, Otto," commanded Franck, having drawn his own weapon now. "Put the fucking gun away."

But Otto wasn't listening. "There's only one way to find out if someone's in there," he said, pointing his gun at the window.

"No, Otto, stop!"

Suddenly, a female voice sounded from across the room. "What the hell is going on, Dieter!"

It was Angela Wolff. Franck wheeled around and, for the first time, he saw that she had pulled her gun and trained it on their Polish captive. Behind them,

Wolff's team had loaded the last two paintings onto a mover's dolly and had begun to wheel them down the narrow passageway.

"I should be asking you that question," said Dieter. "You can't shoot Pularchek. We need him alive."

"I'll be the one to decide who lives and who dies." She looked past Franck to his companion, who stood poised in front of the window with his semiauto. "What are you doing there, Otto?"

"I think there's someone behind the glass watching us. The doors are locked so I was about to shoot the window to find out."

"At least Wolff's momentarily distracted," whispered Brewbaker from behind the glass.

"Yes, but she's coming this way," said Pularchek, watching her closely as she prodded his *Braciszku* towards the one-way window with the nose of her pistol.

"The window's not bulletproof," said Romanowski. "What should we do, Boss?"

"Draw your weapons and take two steps back. I believe we're in for a bit of excitement."

CHAPTER 53

OLD STEINBERG SALT MINE

PEERING INTO THE WINDOW, Wolff saw her own reflection. Even she was shocked by what she saw: her eyes were pools of darkness, like lumps of coal, and her normally sensual mouth was set in a cruel line. In that illuminating instant, she saw herself as a murderous Nazi thug like the brownshirted hooligans that had aided and abetted Hitler in his rise to power, forever tarnishing her proud country's reputation.

What was she doing? What had she become? Since when had she developed an unshakable sense of murderous entitlement just like the Nazis? Where had she turned off the road of normalcy and allowed greed to take over her soul? Or was it even about greed? Was it power she sought? Or did she just want to retire in lavish comfort in Greece with her nubile young lover Dieter?

Suddenly, Otto's voice broke through her thoughts. "They're in there watching us, I know it," he said again, motioning at the window with his loaded pistol.

She stepped closer to the window. "How do you know?"

"Look at it. What else is it for except to watch what goes on in this room?" He pointed at the ceiling and along the walls. "It's the same with those cameras up there. I believe this whole thing was a setup from the beginning. And there's only one way to find out."

He pointed his pistol at the window.

"You're wasting your time," said Dieter. "It's probably bulletproof."

She pressed the nose of her Walther into Pularchek's ribs. "Is it bulletproof? Are we being watched?"

He said nothing.

"He's not going to tell us," snorted Otto disdainfully. "The doors are locked, and there is only one way to find out what's inside."

She pointed her gun at Pularchek's chest. "Tell me, damn you! Is someone in there or not?"

"No, of course not. It's just a control room."

"What kind of control room?"

"For the cameras and other monitoring equipment. Those paintings are worth a hell of a lot of money. I had to have some way to keep tabs on the restoration team. There are also elaborate controls for the temperature, moisture content, lighting, et cetera. It was installed according to the specifications of my chief restorationist. Plus the room holds the preservation and examination equipment, as well as all of the chemicals."

"Why does it have a one-way mirror?"

"How the hell should I know? I didn't design it."

"We should just get out of here, Angela," said Dieter worriedly. "We already have the paintings. We're just wasting time."

"No, I want to know if we've been had. Stand back!" She turned her gun on the window and opened fire once, twice, three times in rapid succession.

The glass exploded, producing a cascading waterfall of shards that fell to the floor of the mine vault.

Looking into the open window, she couldn't believe her eyes. Standing there pointing a gun at her face was a second Pularchek. A dozen men stood at his side, including Nick Lassiter, his wife Natalie, and Benjamin Brewbaker. They must have ducked down and shielded themselves when she fired, but now they were all standing there pointing guns at her. Jerking her head to her left, she looked at the man standing next to her. Which one was the real Stanislaw Pularchek?

"You bastard!" she shrieked as now both sides pointed their weapons aggressively at one another, but restrained from firing.

It was a Mexican standoff.

She grabbed the Pularchek standing next to her in a vise-like head clamp and dug the nose of her Walther into his neck, instantly taking him hostage. "I don't know which one of you bastards is the real one, but my men and I are getting out of here."

"You'll never make it," snapped Brewbaker, holding his pistol in a two-handed grip trained on her chest. "You might as well surrender now."

"Like hell we won't make it," she snarled back. "Now stay where you are in that room, all of you, or I'll shoot him where he stands."

She started backing up along with Dieter, Otto, and a third German intelligence officer. They kept their weapons locked onto Pularchek and the others inside the darkened control room. Behind the carefully retreating group, at the entrance of the passageway, appeared two members of her team who had just returned from transporting the paintings to the lorries. They immediately drew their weapons; one of them had a Heckler & Koch MP5 assault rifle and he aimed it quickly at the broken window.

"Cover us!" she called out to him. "We're coming to you and getting out of here!"

"*Jawohl*, Vice-President!"

"We're going through that passageway and I'd advise you not to follow," she warned Pularchek and Brewbaker. She was perhaps forty feet away from the tunnel entrance carved into the salt deposits. "Stay where you are, or I'll kill your double where he stands."

"Do what you have to do," said Pularchek. "He is a footsoldier in my army, and he understands that he may die at any time."

"You are fools, all of you," she said, trying to keep her voice calm despite her frantically beating heart. "This war you fight is a war you cannot win."

"That may be," he said. "But we will never sit by and surrender to the likes of a Nazi profiteer like yourself, or the Bin Laden's of the world. Your kind of evil must be met with force and death. That's the only language you people speak."

As he said this, he and his men began to enter the room from the two exit doors on either side of the window. Wolff and her team were badly outnumbered. She tried to steel her nerves: *Only thirty more feet,* she told herself.

"Give it up, Angela my dear," said Pularchek, stepping forward on her right along with Brewbaker and his son, Nick Lassiter. "Put down your weapon and surrender at once or we *will* shoot you."

He and his men continued to fan out until they had formed a semi-circle that enclosed the western half of the room.

"I told you to stop moving!" hissed Wolff, angry that she and her team were close to being surrounded and cut off.

"It's over, Angela." The Pole's voice was unnaturally calm and quietly commanding, like a career soldier. "Put the gun down and step away from my *Braciszku.*"

"He's not your brother, you bastard. He's your clone."

"If only it were true, Angela my dear. If only it were true."

"You created him in your laboratory. He's your Frankenstein."

"Wrong again, Mary Shelley. As I told you before, he is my *Braciszku.*"

She could feel her breathing accelerating and told herself not to panic; already she was halfway to the entrance to the passageway. *Only twenty feet further.*

"Tell your men to stop moving!" she commanded.

When he failed to do so, she let loose with a burst over his head. That brought him and his men to a temporary halt. She took the opportunity to quicken her pace towards the passageway entrance. She felt her resolve stiffen as she saw Dieter nod confidently to her on her left, his pistol trained on Brewbaker's chest. Then she chanced a glance over her shoulder at the passageway.

Only ten feet more. You can make it!

"You set me up, you bastard," she said to Pularchek. "This whole thing was a setup from the beginning. You lured me in like a fish."

"No, you lured yourself in, Angela, when you let your greed consume your life. You could have been the head of the German foreign intelligence service, perhaps even chancellor. But instead, you're going to go to prison for the rest of your life. And so is Director Voorheiss. My new friend here—Deputy Director Brewbaker—is going to see to that."

"I'm sorry to disappoint you, but that is not what is going to happen."

"Tell your men to drop their weapons now, or we will fire," said Brewbaker.

"No, you won't. Herr Pularchek loves his twin here too much to give him up. I can see it in his eyes. He would never let him die."

Pularchek strode forward and held up his hands, calling for her to remain calm. "You're right. I do care deeply about my *Braciszku.* But he is still a soldier and sometimes the individual soldier must be sacrificed for the greater good of the war. And that doesn't come from me. Ask him yourself."

"He's right, Angela my dear," said the double. "What you have always failed to understand in this contest is that I am willing to sacrifice my life in return for yours. In fact, I consider it a more than adequate swap."

"You are crazy, all of you!" she hissed.

She glanced behind her. *Five feet—just five more feet!*

"It's over. Put the gun down, Angela," said Pularchek. "You are surrounded and have nowhere to go."

"You double-crossed me, and for that I should shoot you and your double both. But you would just create more and more. How many of you are there? Or are you two the last ones?"

The Pole didn't respond. Instead, his team methodically moved in closer, tightening the noose. She glanced at Dieter. He looked on with tense anticipation like everyone else in the room as they each took another careful step backwards.

"Stop right there, Wolff," said Benjamin Brewbaker. "You're not going to get out of this mine alive. So tell your men to stand down and hand over their weapons."

She shook her head defiantly. Keeping her Walther pointed at her captive double's neck, she continued to back up towards the passageway entrance. Pularchek's team members shadowed her movements and began to accelerate their pace around her flanks, as if trying to block the entrance. But at this point, she and her cohorts were only two steps away and being covered by a light machine gun.

Two fucking steps! she thought. And then she told herself: *We're going to make it! We're truly going to make—*

The thought was cut off as suddenly her captive double twisted his body and jerked away from her grip. He tried to grab her Walther from her, but Dieter quickly stepped in and shoved them both into the passageway. Their comrade-in-arms at the entrance with the H&K opened up on the enemy with the light machine gun, mowing down Brewbaker's two CIA men and one of Pularchek's team members like a scythe. Out of the corner of her eye, she saw one of her men go down as he was drilled with small-arms fire. Then she was running through the darkened passageway, with Dieter up ahead prodding the double forward with his weapon and Otto behind her firing at the enemy as a rear guard. Behind her, she heard an explosion of gunfire and screaming and shouting as more men were hit, but she kept running.

The gunfire rippled through the echoing passageway like a roll of thunder, and she felt as though she was back in the Second World War.

And in a sense, she was.

CHAPTER 54

OLD STEINBERG SALT MINE

"QUICKLY, COUNSELOR, TAKE ONE TEAM and follow them. Jerzy, Andrzej, you and the rest come with me. We'll take the Hallstadt Tunnel and try to cut them off. Hopefully, we can drive them towards you. Or outside where Skyler is waiting for them."

"Got it, Boss! I'll see you on the other side!" said Romanowski. He and his team quickly reloaded, stepped over two fallen Germans, and dashed down the passageway in hot pursuit.

"Follow me!" cried Pularchek. He took off with his two bodyguards, Lassiter, Brewbaker, and Natalie towards the entrance to a second passageway on the east side of the room. They ducked into the narrow tunnel, followed it for perhaps one hundred feet, turned into a larger branch tunnel, dashed down it for a short distance, and linked up with another tunnel notched into the Permian Haselgebirge Formation. Turning left, they followed the passageway as the shooting resumed up ahead.

Pularchek saw a flash of gunfire and blur of movement at the far end of the tunnel. But he was too far away to make out who it was despite the halogen lighting along the salt cavern walls and ceiling. And then, the silhouetted figures disappeared amid a roar of gunfire.

"Who was that?" asked Lassiter as they paused to regroup.

"I don't know. I couldn't tell if they were friend or foe," replied Pularchek.

"Well, whoever is down that way, they're heavily engaged, which means we have to hurry."

"Where does this tunnel come out?" asked Brewbaker.

"Near the front entrance. It links up with the staging room where we grabbed the hard hats."

He waved them forward and they started off again. Soon, they came to a secondary passageway that split off the main tunnel and was poorly lit. He shined his headlamp at the salt rock walls and timber supports. The rock walls were more weathered and crumbly in this section of the mine, and the timber supports were old and rotting. But to Pularchek's relief, the passageway was reasonably well illuminated and appeared to be in working order despite the foul odor of mold and decay.

"Is it safe?" asked Lassiter.

"I don't know. We'll soon find out."

He motioned them forward again. They darted down the narrow passageway, using their miner's headlamps to guide them through the narrow corridor. Halfway down, they encountered a limestone unit interbedded within the salt deposits that had been partially leached away from groundwater infiltration, resulting in a localized roof collapse and sinkhole-type cave-in. Here the passageway narrowed to shoulder length, and they had to wriggle their way through the collapsed wall and blocky limestone obstructions. Once they made it through, they again heard the thud of boots and roar of gunfire up ahead.

They raced towards the sound.

The narrow passageway branched before opening up into a heavily-timbered, domed space next to the staging area. This portion of the subterranean labyrinth was not as big as the restoration room that had held the paintings, but it was substantial. Here they found Wolff's and Romanowski's teams heavily engaged, like a shootout in an old time Western. Startled by their sudden appearance, the Germans turned and opened fire upon them with a heavy barrage.

"Get down!" cried his bodyguard Jerzy Gagor.

Gagor and Andrzej Kremer knocked him to the ground as a hailstorm of bullets tore off shards and needles of salt from the crystalline walls where a moment earlier his head had been.

"Thank you, my Brothers."

"Don't mention it, Komandor," said Kremer.

"I wish I had protectors like that," said Brewbaker.

"Me too," said Lassiter as he and the others took cover behind a coral-head-like blob of slumped halite.

"Maybe I can arrange something in the future, my son," said Pularchek. "All right, let these bastards have it!"

Rising to one knee, he let loose with his semiautomatic pistol, and the others followed suit.

The Germans unloaded a return volley and then began an orderly retreat.

It was then that Pularchek saw his *Braciszku* shove Dieter Franck to the ground and try to make his escape.

"Run, my Brother, run!" he cried, and he provided quick supporting fire.

But his double didn't make it ten feet before Wolff gunned him down. The first shot blasted into his lower spine; and the second and third, delivered just as his body pivoted from the impact of the first bullet, tore into his jaw and throat.

Pularchek screamed. "Noooo!!!"

His *Braciszku* fell to the ground and didn't move.

"Brother, Brother!" he cried in stunned disbelief.

Enraged, he let loose with a blistering fire. Next to him, Nick, Brewbaker, Natalie, and his two bodyguards did the same with their weapons. The sound of the roaring gunfire echoed off the salt rock walls, as if it was 1945 all over again.

Just then Romanowski and his team drove in from the left, shooting from their hips with their semiautomatic weapons. The Germans had been reinforced with a dozen more men and they returned a crackling fire. To Pularchek's dismay, he saw first Romanowski then Rachel Landau go down.

My God, he thought, this is turning into a disaster. But you can't let them get away, damnit!

Popping in a fresh magazine, he charged forward with his Glock, yelling at the top of his lungs like a banshee. To his surprise, his son, Brewbaker, and Natalie jumped up and rushed in behind him, providing much needed suppressing fire.

Wolff and three of her men turned to resist, but they were too late. Pularchek fired his 9mm. His first shot missed, but the second dropped the man next to Wolff like a potato sack, striking heart and lung. The blood spattered her face as well as the window of the staging room behind her.

Pularchek then fired at Wolff.

The shot sailed wild, but again ended up striking her cohort next to her. The force of the impact knocked the German into a set of mining equipment lockers. His body bounced off the lockers and thudded hard onto the concrete, the blood from his chest quickly pooling out from his body like an inkblot.

This was too much for Wolff.

She turned and ran for the main mine entrance door just as Dieter Franck and several of her men managed to extricate themselves from the battle they were engaged in on the far side of the open cavern. Franck jerked open the door and the Germans disappeared from sight, leaving a dozen fallen from both sides behind along with a cloud of acrid gunsmoke.

Pularchek ran up to Romanowski just as Janu and four others from the other team came up and began checking the casualties.

"I'm sorry you got hit, Counselor. How bad is it?"

"The bullet's lodged in my thigh. I'll be fine, but I can't put any weight on it. You go ahead and get them."

"All right, but I'm leaving someone behind with you and the other wounded."

"I'm afraid they're all dead, Komandor," said Janu, kneeling down and checking the pulse of Rachel Landau, the former Mossad operative.

Pularchek looked at her body and then at his *Braciszku*. They were both covered in blood, not breathing or moving at all.

He shook his head sadly.

"Damnit, I'm the one to blame for this."

"No, Boss, no one is to blame. You must go now, before they get away."

"Yes, you're quite right." He turned to Brewbaker. "Benjamin, you come with me and my men. We're going after Wolff." Then to his son: "Nick, you and Natalie stay here and help the Counselor. He needs a dressing for that wound."

He handed his son a serrated military-style knife to use to make a field dressing.

"The Counselor can walk you through it. He's a soldier. He's done this many times before."

"Natalie and I will take care of it," said Lassiter.

"I'm sorry, everyone. I didn't want this to turn into a damned shootout, but that's precisely what's happened."

"Where will we meet you?" asked Natalie. "Outside?"

"No, you and Nick should go to the observation deck. That way if Wolff does manage to escape, you can see which direction she goes." He pointed to the left of the entrance at a circular stone staircase that spiraled upward to the second floor. "Take those stairs to the top. The door unlocks from the inside."

"Got it," said Lassiter. "Good luck."

"I don't believe in luck. I believe in training and preparation. Come on Benjamin, my new American friend, let's go get those damned Germans!"

He waved the team forward again.

They darted for the main entrance. But as Pularchek reached for the door handle, he prayed that the clever Angela Wolff hadn't laid some sort of trap.

CHAPTER 55

OLD STEINBERG SALT MINE

NICK LASSITER forced himself to ignore the gunfire and shouting voices outside the mine as he knelt down next to Pularchek's double and began to cut away a portion of his jacket. He would use the jacket strips to fashion an impromptu field dressing for Romanowski. He struggled not to gag at the sight of all the blood and meaty flesh that had been pushed aside by the gunshot entry wounds at the poor man's jaw and throat. The resemblance between the dead man on the cave floor and Lassiter's biological father was uncanny; the two men were identical.

Except for one very important detail.

Where the two gunshots had blown away part of the double's lower jaw and upper throat, Lassiter could see the effects of plastic surgery and a partially exposed metallic voice modulator. The outer layer was almost like a latex skin covering and had been blasted away and peeled back from the explosion of the bullets, like layers of the earth from a bomb crater. It was as if the dead man on the ground was not fully human at all, but rather some sort of hybrid between a living, breathing organism and a synthetic anthrobot. The double was not a clone, but rather a man scientifically manipulated to precisely resemble and talk like Pularchek. The voice device that had been surgically inserted into his throat must have allowed him to speak in precisely the same tone and cadence as his creator.

It was the strangest looking—and most terrifying—thing Lassiter had ever seen. Like something out of a science-fiction movie.

But it also meant that his father had been telling the truth.

And yet, who were these men that would sacrifice their lives for the Polish billionaire? Who were these soldiers that were willing to die so that he could continue to wage his war against Nazis, jihadists, and other evildoers of the modern world? Who were these Spartan-like militants willing to surrender their own individuality for their beloved Komandor? And what was so important about the use of doubles? Was it purely to send a message? Or did it allow Pularchek to confuse his enemies in case of attack since they would never know if they had the right target? Or was it to provide an alibi for the killings? Or was there some deeper, or perhaps darker, reason for their existence? Doubles had been used by military and political leaders since the ancient Egyptians, Greeks, and Romans, but he had never heard of anyone unleashing a small army of double-assassins. It was like a futuristic sci-fi scenario on the one hand—and a throwback to some sort of ancient warrior cult on the other.

Suddenly, Romanowski tore him from his thoughts.

"Well, Mikolaj, are you going to get me a damned dressing or let me bleed to death?"

"Sorry, sorry," he said, not realizing that he had drifted off momentarily into another world. He sliced away a final strip from the jacket. But just before he rose to his feet, he noticed one more striking detail. A colored contact lens had been dislodged from the double's left eye. The lens was blue, the color of the real Pularchek's eyes instead of the brown color of his doppelganger's eyes. So the man's eye coloring too had been modified to be in line with that of his master.

He went quickly to Romanowski's side. Natalie had propped his head onto a wooden pallet with his jacket and was carefully peeling away his pants from the wound so they could see the full extent of the injury. He could see the blood seeping through the torn pants, but it didn't look as though the bullet had struck an artery or that Romanowski would need a tourniquet.

Outside, the gunfire abruptly stopped altogether. Lassiter thought he could hear talking voices, muffled by the salt mine's thick walls, but that was all. But had his two fathers won or lost? Had Wolff managed to get away or not? The uncertainty made him feel a clinch in his gut and his heart ache. He didn't want Angela Wolff and her men to escape justice, and he most certainly didn't want his fathers—either of them—to die.

"The shooting's stopped," said Natalie. "Is that good or bad?"

"I honestly don't know."

"We need to get out there and see what's happening," said Romanowski, leaning up onto his elbows. "Hurry up and dress my wound, damnit!"

Lassiter wadded up the jacket, placed it against Romanowski's gunshot thigh with the soft inner part of the jacket facing downward against the wound, and began gently wrapping it with the strips he had cut out. Natalie took a strand from him and tied it off so that there were two ties in place to maintain gentle pressure on the wound. She then checked his circulation below the dressing to make sure that it was not too tight. Satisfied, she placed her hand on the dressing and gently pressed down.

"That's not half bad," said their patient, as if surprised.

Suddenly, a sustained burst of automatic weapons fire ripped through the air, coming from outside the mine. It was followed moments later by a single gunshot.

"Jesus, it's not over yet. I wonder what's going on?" said Natalie.

"I don't know, but we have to get out there right now!" exclaimed Lassiter.

"Yes, let's go! Quickly, help me to my feet!" cried Romanowski.

"But you're wounded!" protested Natalie.

"I can make it! They could be in trouble and we need to help them!"

"All right, you guide him to the front entrance," Lassiter instructed her. "I'm going to the observation deck like my father asked. Maybe I can stop them from getting away."

"Okay, but be careful."

"You too." He leaned down, picked up one of the Heckler & Koch MP5 assault rifles the Germans had discarded, and switched over the automatic lever so it would fire in machine-gun mode. "Here, let me help you lift him up."

"On three," she said. "You ready, Counselor?"

"Yes, let's go!"

"All right, one, two, three…"

CHAPTER 56

OLD STEINBERG SALT MINE

AS SOON AS STANISLAW PULARCHEK pushed open the mine door and stepped into the sunlight, he knew something was terribly wrong. Angela Wolff, Dieter Franck, Dr. Bloeckler, and the other remaining Germans had been rounded up and were being covered by a small army of hard-looking men in camo with M4A1 full-automatic-fire carbines. He knew who the new interlopers were: hired guns plucked from the ranks of the U.S. Special Forces, now paid twice as much money working as black op mercenaries as they ever had plying their military tradecraft for Uncle Sam's official army. They peddled their clandestine services to the CIA as its exclusive private military contractor, Blackthorn Security, Inc. He didn't recognize any of the men personally, but he knew the man in the crisp Brook's Brothers business suit commanding them quite well.

Richard Voorheiss.

"Tell your men to throw down their weapons," said the director of the CIA's National Clandestine Service in a stentorian voice. "And I'll let you all live."

Pularchek quickly scanned the enemy and the terrain, grappling for some way out of the trap he had suddenly stumbled into, but he saw nothing encouraging. They were surrounded and seriously outgunned. Resistance was pointless.

He looked at Benjamin Brewbaker, who was also studying the avenues of escape. "I'm sorry," he said to him. Then to his men: "Do as he says."

Slowly and reluctantly, Janu and the others dropped their weapons. But Brewbaker held fast to his weapon.

"You know the son of a bitch is just going to shoot us," he muttered in a low voice.

Pularchek shook his head. "No, he won't," he whispered back. "And remember, if all else fails, we have our contingency plan."

Brewbaker glanced at Dieter Franck then up above the cave entrance at the rocky bluff where Skyler was supposed to be dug in with her sniper rifle. "I don't like contingency plans. They tend to be unpredictable."

"Yes, well, right now it's all we've got."

"Did you not hear me, Ben? Put down the fucking gun!" shouted Voorheiss, breaking up their private conversation. "Unless, of course, you want to die a hero!"

With an expression of defiance, Brewbaker dropped his weapon. It plunked to the earth with a dull thud.

"That's better. Now where are your son and daughter-in-law?" asked Voorheiss.

"They...they didn't make it."

"I told you not to bring them overseas. But you wouldn't listen to me." He motioned with his gun. "All of you men keep your hands up and assemble with your German friends over there. You're going to form up in one nice little group."

Brewbaker was right—Voorheiss couldn't be trusted—but Pularchek gave a nod anyway to his men to do as instructed. Keeping their hands up, he and his group stepped over to where the Germans were standing. They were all now guarded by the soldiers in camo, clutching their compact M4A1 carbines on their hips, ready to fire in full automatic mode. Twenty feet away were the two lorries Wolff had brought to transport the paintings. Peering into the back of the vehicles, he saw that the paintings had been carefully covered and secured with padded bracing supports and were being fastened with ropes by several men.

"So, Mr. Director, you're planning on keeping all of these priceless works for yourself," said the Pole, standing at the edge of the group. "That's quite audacious of you, and despicable."

"I'm not going to keep all of them. I'm going to hold a press conference and announce to the world that the CIA, with invaluable assistance from a certain member of German intelligence, has recovered Leonardo Da Vinci's *The Virgin and Child* after more than seventy years. It will be the biggest coup of the last generation for the agency, and I'm going to be the one who made it happen."

"And the other paintings?" asked Brewbaker.

"Well, I'm afraid I'm going to have to keep them for myself. Come on, gentlemen, the remaining eleven works of art will fetch a billion or more dollars U.S. Surely, you don't think I'm so stupid as to give them up?"

Pularchek looked at Wolff. "So he duped you too, Angela my dear. Or are you the member of German intelligence who provided the invaluable assistance?"

"No, that would be me," said Dieter Franck, and he stepped away from Wolff and stood next to Voorheiss.

Pularchek had never before seen a face turn so ghostly white as he watched the color literally drain from Angela Wolff's face.

"Dieter, how could you?" she spluttered, her voice tremulous with the anguish of one who has been unexpectedly and devastatingly betrayed by someone close to them.

He said nothing.

"I am in love with you. We were going to retire in comfort to Greece together."

He laughed derisively. "Are you kidding me? You're an old bag. I'm only thirty-three and you're already forty. I would rather have my eyes poked out by a Cyclops than live the rest of my days with you on a Greek island."

She stepped towards him, arms out. "But Dieter, I love you. I have always loved you."

"That's funny because I never loved you."

She reached out to touch him. "No, Dieter, no...you can't do this to me...I...I love you."

He shoved her away. "Get away from me. I'm through with you."

"Dieter, no...tell me it's not true...tell me you don't mean—"

"You should have dealt with this, Franck, damn you," interjected Voorheiss angrily. "Now I'm going to have to do it for you."

In a swift motion, he pointed his pistol at her chest and squeezed the trigger. Wolff's face registered astonishment as a little red blot appeared on her white blouse beneath her Bettina Schoenbach designer blazer. He squeezed the trigger two more times and she grabbed her stomach, looking first at Voorheiss and then at Dieter Franck in disbelief. She stood there for what seemed like a lifetime before crashing hard to the ground outside the salt mine.

"Jesus Christ, why did you have to kill her?" protested Franck. "No one was supposed to die, damnit! That was the deal!"

Brewbaker snorted derisively. "My boss is a liar and a cheat, Agent Franck. Whatever made you think you could trust him?"

"He's right, you are scum Voorheiss," agreed Pularchek. "How can you call yourself an intelligence officer when you murder a woman in cold blood like that? She may have been morally bankrupt like you, but that doesn't give you the right to shoot her down like a dog."

Voorheiss turned and pointed the gun at him.

"Go ahead and shoot. But just remember, another one will just take my place."

The NCS director tipped his head towards his Blackthorn contractors in camo. "Commander Jacobs, kill them! Kill them all!"

Jacobs and his men just stood there. No one dared move a muscle; the grassy alpine hillside outside the Old Steinberg Salt Mine was shrouded in an anxious silence for a full fifteen seconds.

"Sir," said Jacobs finally, keeping his Glock pointed at the captives. "Deputy Director Brewbaker is one of ours, sir. He's American."

"Your job is to obey orders, Commander, not interpret them. And the director of the Central Intelligence Agency's National Clandestine Service in charge of this op just gave you a direct fucking order."

"Yes, sir, but..."

"But what, Commander?"

"But we don't kill Americans, sir. And besides, Deputy Director Brewbaker works for you. He's one of yours."

"Now you listen to me, you little weasel. I have just given you a direct order to shoot all of these...these enemies of the state. They pose a clear and present threat to the national security of the United States."

"We're not going to shoot the deputy director, sir. In fact, we're not going to shoot any of these men. They have surrendered their weapons."

"You dare to disobey a direct order from—"

They were interrupted by Dieter Franck. "We don't need to kill them all." He pointed to Pularchek and Brewbaker. "Just these two here. They're the only ones who are important to us. You want to kill the snake, cut off its head."

Pularchek watched what happened next unfold in slow motion like a strange dream as the German withdrew his Walther 9mm and aimed it at him and Brewbaker.

"If you're so squeamish about shooting Americans, Commander, I'll do the deed myself," said Franck. "Now you two, get over against the wall of the mine. This is the end of the line for you both."

"What, you're actually going to kill them?" gasped Voorheiss, appraising the German in a new light. "Now I am impressed."

Franck smiled harshly. "Dead men tell no tales. But there's no reason to kill any of the others. They're nobodies."

"All right, get on with—"

But Voorheiss's words were cut off as a sudden burst of unexpected gunfire crackled through the air and echoed off the rocky walls of the mine.

"There's the shooter!" he cried, pointing up to a silhouetted figure wedged in a crevasse cut into the salt rock above the mine. "Let him have it!"

Looking up, Pularchek saw Skyler pouring down from above. She was dressed in assault black and had disguised herself with a heavy fake beard and a cap to hold in all of her hair and make her enemies think she was a man. One of the American operatives in camo went down, then another and another. But the unit recovered quickly and returned a blistering fire, driving her back deeper into the seams in the rocks. With all of the gunfire, the Germans and Poles scattered.

At that moment, a pair of green-and-silver Porsche 911 police cars and a white ambulance appeared at the dirt road running along the base of the mountain. They were coming onto the scene fast.

"Damnit, the Austrian police are here!" snarled Voorheiss. He let loose with a burst with his semiautomatic pistol, taking down a Pole and then a German. "Get it over with and shoot those two, Franck!" he cried. "You've got ten seconds!"

Voorheiss started running for his black Mercedes as his team in camo made for their vehicles and the lorries packed with the art treasures.

"Don't you fucking leave without me!" hollered Franck. Then to Pularchek and Brewbaker. "Move it!"

From the bluff above, Skyler leapt up and opened fire again, her thick black beard clearly visible. Franck continued to move forward, using Pularchek and Brewbaker as human shields as the American mercenaries again returned heavy fire and drove Skyler back behind the rocks. Franck delivered a blow to the back of their heads with the butt of his Walther and shoved them to their knees. All around them automobile engines revved to life.

"Now, gentlemen, prepare to meet your Maker."

"You bastard," said Pularchek. "You fucking Nazi bastard."

"Shut up!" Franck whacked him in the back of the head.

"No, I will not shut up." He turned to his new American friend. "I'm sorry, Benjamin, but I'm afraid neither of us will be a father to Nicholas any longer."

"It's all right. It's not your fault. This op was FUBAR from the beginning."

"That may be, but it is still my fault."

"I told you that's enough!" roared Franck.

He put away his Walther and placed the nose of his SIG-Sauer backup pistol at the back of Pularchek's head.

"I'll see you both in hell," he said.

He started to pull the trigger.

But Skyler opened fire again from the rocky bluff, catching Franck in the left arm.

"God damnit!" He returned fire along with several of the American mercenaries, and they again forced her to take cover. When she no longer posed a threat, he returned his attention to Pularchek and Brewbaker.

"Now close your eyes you two. It will be over quickly."

He pulled the trigger once and then a second time. One shot to the back of the head for each man.

The last thing Stanislaw Pularchek saw was a blinding flash of white light. Then he saw nothing, nothing at all. But just before the tangible world disappeared, he did hear—or thought he heard—a primal scream.

It sounded like his son.

CHAPTER 57

OLD STEINBERG SALT MINE

SHOVING OPEN the stainless-steel door, Nick Lassiter dashed onto the observation deck above the entrance to the mine. Down below, he saw NCS Director Richard Voorheiss making a mad dash for a black Mercedes. And, in the foreground, he saw the German intelligence officer Dieter Franck—Angela Wolff's lover and number two—pointing a pistol at the back of his birth father's head.

He had to do something. But what could he do?

He pointed his Heckler & Koch MP5 assault rifle, set on automatic fire, at the German and squeezed the trigger.

But nothing happened.

He squeezed again.

Still the weapon didn't fire.

He looked with disbelief at the automatic weapon, wondering why, improbably, the fucking German hadn't been riddled with holes, or at least blasted off his feet.

Then he realized that the rifle had jammed.

That's when he screamed at the top of his lungs.

But it was not enough.

The first shot looked like it blew out a hole in the rear of Pularchek's skull, his entire occipital lobe dissolving in a ghastly spray of blood and tissue that rendered the alpine *terra firma* a shockingly vivid crimson color.

He screamed again and this time Dieter Franck looked up at him.

But that didn't stop the German from doing what he did next.

Now he jammed the nose of his pistol into the back of Benjamin Brewbaker's skull and started to pull the trigger.

"Noooo!!!" shrieked Lassiter.

He heard a gasp of shock and looked down at the entrance to the mine and saw Natalie and Romanowski standing there.

"Noooo!!!" he screamed again, his voice rising in the air along with his wife's and the Counselor's plaintive voices, but again their cries had no effect as the bullet ripped through the rear of his father's head. This time the blood and tissue spurted out from the head onto the ground along with a fine wet mist.

He couldn't believe his eyes!

In a cruel instant, both of his fathers were dead. He looked down at the blood and brain matter splattered everywhere on the ground, and he felt physically sickened.

He jerked back the automatic lever on his gun, took aim, and fired. This time the weapon bucked in his hands like a jumping deer and he saw a bullet strike Dieter Franck directly in the back. He was running for the black Mercedes that was pulling away along with a pair of lorries and several silver Range Rovers. But somehow the bullet had no observable effect except to make him run faster. Jesus, was Franck wearing a bullet-proof vest?

Damnit!

He let loose with another spray of gunfire, taking down a soldier in camo then another, as Romanowski and Natalie opened up with their pistols from the front entrance and Skyler, whom he could now see behind him and to the west, opened fire from a rocky crevice above the mine entrance. They poured into the retreating vehicles, blowing out two rear car windows and one side window, but they were unable to stop the enemy from escaping.

Lassiter shook his fist in the air. "Goddamn you! I'll get you for this!"

Tears erupted from his face as he looked down at the sprawled bodies of the two most important men in his life.

"No, no!" he cried, as if by shouting the words out loud he could miraculously take back the violence that had just transpired, and they would be given new life.

He threw his hand onto the deck railing and jumped over the side. He touched down with his knees bent to absorb the shock, but the landing was far from pillow-soft and he hit at an awkward angle, tumbled down the rain-pitted incline, and landed in a gnarly bush. Coming up limping, he hobbled to his two fathers, praying that by some miracle they had survived the gunshots. His wife came rushing forward, helping Romanowski along, as the fleet of police cars and lone ambulance screeched to a halt in front of the mine entrance.

"No, Boss, no! You can't be dead!" cried the Counselor.

But as Lassiter stood there clutching his wife and looking down at all the blood and splattered brain tissue on the ground, he knew it was not to be.

A moment earlier, he had had two fathers that he dearly loved.

Now he had none.

CHAPTER 58

SAFE HOUSE PIUS XII
VIA GERMANICO
ROME, ITALY

THE FOLLOWING NIGHT IN ROME, Skyler slept heavily for an hour once she slipped under the covers. But then the demons came on like a firestorm.

The nightmare was different than the others. First she saw Friedrich Shottenbruner, with a bright swastika painted across his forehead and reading a leatherbound copy of *Mein Kampf* as his melon-like head exploded from her gunshot outside the Berghain. Then she saw her father's business partner, Don Scarpello—"Yes I am going to hurt you, but you will like it"—gleaming in brutal triumph after taking her against her will when she was a girl. Next she saw her former lover Alberto—the Genovese freedom-fighter who had trained her and later ordered her death—cackling at her through clever brown eyes. Then she saw President-elects Kieger and Fowler as their knees buckled like stringless marionettes and they fell to the stage in Denver. Finally came all the other men she had killed over the years, one by one, standing before her as they had the moment before their unexpected demise. Their ghostly images were framed in her sniperscope, crosshairs centered on their faces. In the next instant, there was a little pop and their heads exploded like melons, one right after another.

She had now shot and killed a grand total of twenty-five men and one woman, counting those she had taken out at the Ursus safehouse and the Old Sternberg Mine in Altaussee. Before the last man in her nightmare fell to the ground dead, she jerked awake gasping for air. Touching her body, she felt sweat beneath her chin and arms. Her teeth ached from the grinding. As always, it took several minutes to bring her breathing under control and steel her shattered nerves. There was no hate for her victims; she felt only a profound guilt and hatred of herself.

She was tired of the killing and wished she had never complied with Pularchek's request and rejoined the game.

She went into the kitchen and fetched a glass of water. She gulped the entire glass down like a healing potion then poured herself another. Returning to her bedroom, she pulled a rosary with a small silver crucifix from her bedside table. For several seconds, she stared at the figure of Christ, nailed to the holy cross in humble surrender. Kneeling next to the bed, she clutched the rosary with trembling fingers, her lips quivering.

Then she said a prayer for every one of the people she had murdered. Her death toll was now twenty-six and counting and it took her several minutes.

When finished, she went to the French doors, opened them, stepped out onto the veranda, and looked up the street. The bright moonlight slanted across the roof of St. Peter's Basilica, spilling dazzling torrents of luminescence onto Bernini's colossal Tuscan Colonnade and the depraved Emperor Caligula's Egyptian Obelisk in the middle of the square below. On the wall of the hotel across the street, a giant colored banner displayed the white-robed, skull-capped figure of the current Pope, the Vicar of Christ, defender of the world's oppressed. He was speaking before a large crowd of his followers in the packed square below from the parapet of his central balcony at the Vatican. It was just an image on a banner, not the real thing, but to Angela Valentina Ferrara, a devout Roman Catholic, it was like gazing upon a beautiful garden in full bloom. On the banner, the massive crowd of supporters looked on in boundless wonderment at the Father of Rome, who shimmered in the late afternoon's transcendent golden glow.

After a minute, her thoughts turned to Anthony. It made her sad that they were lovers no more and she would probably never see him again. With Patton and soon perhaps others digging around and questioning him, she would have to go on the run again and return to a world of loneliness and constantly looking over her shoulder. God, how she longed to be nestled with Anthony back in their beachside plantation-style home outside Christiansted. But it was not to be and she would never again have a normal life filled with love and happiness. At this point, she would need to cease all contact with Anthony, have another round of minor plastic surgery performed, obtain new identity papers and credit cards, and go live in a remote region of Asia, the South Pacific, or South America. Those would be the safest places for her to live. It was true, she would live a life of luxury since she had over six million dollars to live on, but she would, once again, be all alone.

And yet…and yet she didn't want to just pack it in and inhabit a world of supreme loneliness again. She didn't want to live without Anthony. But equally important, she was sick and tired of the conflicting emotions, the surges of guilt and shame. She hated the ghosts of men she'd killed haunting her subconscious, coming at her in her dreams. Not just Kieger, Fowler, and Shottenbruner, but Don Scarpello, Alberto, and all the others she had murdered over the years. She didn't want to spend the rest of her life living like this—wandering around strange cities, biding her time until the next hit, surrounded by people she did not know or care about. Pularchek and his team were good people fighting on behalf of a worthy cause, but she was not one of them. She was and always would be an outsider, a hired gun.

It was time to quit the game for good, damnit.

Acting on her feelings, she went inside, grabbed her coded mobile, and called Anthony. He answered after the second ring.

"Skyler, is that you?"

"I don't want us to be apart!" she cried into the phone, feeling the emotions welling up inside of her, bubbling over. "I love you and don't want to lose you!"

The line was filled with silence, and she felt a sinking feeling.

"Anthony, did you hear me? Are you still there?"

Nothing. No response.

"Anthony?"

Finally, after several seconds, he spoke. "I don't believe I'm saying this, but I feel the same way as you."

She felt a flicker of hope. "You do?"

"Yes, but I can't be with you unless you quit the game for good. It's the only way, Skyler."

"I will quit! I will, I promise!"

"And I will never watch you die. I'm not going to be there for that."

"We'll go somewhere far away and safe. No one will know where to look for us."

"I know you want out. But can you really do it?"

"Yes, I can. For you I would do anything," she said, and she meant it.

"I know I've said this to you before, but I have to tell you again. The way I feel about you is like I'm in an old black-and-white directed by Billy Wilder. I've never felt so simultaneously scared and excited—in short, alive—as I have with you these past seven months. The truth is I like the rush of it all, the unexpectedness, the uncertainty. I like my stomach being twisted up in knots. I like waiting by the phone wondering if you'll call. I like not being able to think straight when I hear your voice. I like worrying about where you are and what you're doing even though I find it unspeakably immoral and repugnant that you take other people's lives. I'm telling you, it literally sickens me. And yet, I find the prospect of living the rest of my life without you even more terrifying. Now how can that be? How can a man be helplessly in love with a professional assassin?"

She felt tears coming on now and struggled to hold them back. "I will change for you. Please, just give me a chance."

"But is there something wrong with me? With us?"

Skyler was choked with emotion and tears now poured from her eyes. "Nothing is wrong with us. It is love—there is nothing rational or predictable about it. And that's what makes it so wonderful."

"So you don't think we're crazy to feel the way we do?"

"No, I don't. The only thing I know with any certainty is that I want to spend the rest of my life with you."

"Me too. I want to grow old with you and take care of you."

"I am yours then. We will be together."

"Yes, Skyler my love, we will be together. Because I don't want to live if I can't be with you."

CHAPTER 59

ALTSTADT
INNSBRUCK, AUSTRIA

THE NEXT EVENING, two full days after the Old Steinberg Mine shootout, Richard Voorheiss—the soon-to-be-billionaire director of the Central Intelligence Agency—brushed aside a piece of lint from his Brooks Brothers jacket and peered down at the group of international "high net worth" Old Masters' art buyers and their gaggle of expert consultants. He was standing at a mahogany auction podium in an upstairs parlor in Innsbruck's historic *Altstadt* district, preparing to give his introductory remarks while listening to polite patters of conversation in fluent English tinged with Russian, Arabic, Chinese, British, Hungarian, and German accents. They had just finished a three-course dinner of grilled Norwegian salmon béarnaise and herb-roasted lamb, and were about to begin the much-anticipated private auction.

Voorheiss gently tapped the wooden auctioneer's gavel onto the podium and cleared his throat to speak, instantly bringing a hushed silence to the room as the buyers picked at the last of their *marble gugelhupf á la sacher* and quietly sipped *café au lait*.

"Ladies and gentlemen, it is time now to turn our attention to the primary reason for our historic gathering. Our auctioneer, Mr. Grünewald, and his staff will now open up our phone lines to our remote participants all over the globe." He nodded towards the Swiss art dealer seated at the dinner table on the right, who would serve as both auctioneer for the stolen paintings and certifier of a "clean," or at least unchallengeable, provenance until the transactions were formally completed. "As you are all aware, this is no ordinary auction. What is about to be unveiled before your eyes is the greatest collection of Old Masters' paintings ever sold at any auction, public or private. All of these works were thought to be lost seventy-two years ago and have only recently been recovered. These works of art, long thought to have vanished from the world, will be yours, ladies and gentlemen, before the night is through. For a hefty sum of money, of course."

His words drew a chuckle from the gold-plated audience. They were more than ready for the contest to begin, a contest where a billion dollars was at stake and there would be definite winners and losers. The wealthy Saudi Prince Bandar al-Rashid Abdullah, as dashing as a young Omar Sharif, and British billionaire hedge fund manager Nigel Hawthorne were already giving one another the competitive eye, like a pair of jockeys jostling for position at the start gate. Like the other buyers in the room, they thrived on the exhilarating rush of attending auctions in person and meeting their opponents head on rather than the meekly anonymous competition of a remote phone line. This was perfect, thought Voorheiss: private auctions away from the public gaze typically fetched even more astronomical sums than highly publicized sales events at Christie's or Sotheby's, as private settings were smaller and more personal and the collectors tended to pay a premium for works prized for their investment potential as well as their aesthetic value.

He continued: "Through a combination of luck and determination, these long-lost works now all belong to me under Swiss law and the guiding hand of my official Swiss representative, Mr. Grünewald. What this means, ladies and gentlemen, is that my ownership cannot be challenged and restitution is impossible for any and all parties, including the Bellomo heirs. Now these works of art—my works of art, ladies and gentlemen—are being passed on to you with an unassailable provenance firmly established by the Swiss Confederation. Claimants have zero chance of success in Switzerland, and my dealer, the esteemed Mr. Grünewald to my right, is going to keep it that way until final payment is received and the works are securely in your hands. At that point, they will be legally and irrevocably yours."

He nodded towards the suave-looking Swissman, who was dressed in a slick gray suit, black silk shirt, and a shimmering silver tie.

"Without further ado, I'll now turn over the podium to our esteemed auctioneer, Mr. Grünewald."

Voorheiss stepped down as a round of light applause filled the room. While Grünewald took his place at the auction block, the CIA man returned to his seat at the dinner table in front of the stage where Dieter Franck was seated along with Commander Jacobs of Blackthorn Security, Inc.

"Ladies and gentlemen," began Grünewald in English laden with a heavy Swiss-German accent, his gunmetal gray eyes all aglitter now that the game was afoot. "Grab your paddles and get ready for the civilized world's oldest and most venerated blood sport. If you turn to your catalogues, we'll be commencing with Lot 1: the Giorgione." He feigned a sudden look of surprise, putting his hand over his mouth. "But wait, perhaps we can open with something a bit more, shall we say, sensational. You all like surprises, don't you?"

The buyers gave head nods and voiced their approval. Grünewald, ever the showman, beamed. Like a stage actor, he relished being in the spotlight.

"I thought so, ladies and gentlemen. That's why I selected something that is not actually included in your glossy brochure with which to inaugurate this historic occasion. What would you all say if we open the evening with Gustav Klimt's long-thought-to-be-lost *Marie von Brandauer?*"

The buyers, all knowledgeable art connoisseurs, emitted a collective gasp of surprise and jumped to their feet in unison. They stood there for several seconds pattering to one another and gawking in awe as Grünewald's two assistants carted out the painting and posted it to the left of the auction block. Then they broke into polite applause and exchanged a second round of glances at this most unexpected development. Grünewald continued to beam as the applause filled the room before lightly tapping his auctioneer's gavel upon the podium.

"Herr Klimt's last work sold at Christie's for one hundred seventy-eight million. The estimate for the *Brandauer* piece is comparable. Mr. Voorheiss has set the reserve at one hundred million so we will begin the bidding at seventy-five. Who wants to strike first blood?" He motioned towards an effeminate-looking German fashion designer and cosmetics baron named Wolfgang Svantz. "Wolfie, would you like to do the honors? You have been dying for another Klimt for years."

The German laughed good-naturedly and held up five fingers.

"Very good, we have Herr Svantz at eighty. Do I hear eighty-five?"

Lei Wenyin—the mobile phone and telecommunications tycoon who had enjoyed five consecutive banner years as the Republic of China's richest entrepreneur—discreetly touched his nose.

"I have eighty-five million dollars with Mr. Wenyin on the floor." Suddenly Grünewald was signaled by Siegfried Schmidt, one of his assistants. "Oh, now I have ninety on the phone. It's no longer with you, Mr. Wenyin, it's on the phone with Siggy. Do I have ninety-two million?"

Svantz held up two fingers.

"I have ninety-two million dollars U.S with Herr Svantz. Do I hear ninety-three or perhaps ninety-four?"

Saudi Prince Abdullah held up his paddle and smiled through perfectly stacked teeth the color of ivory.

"Lovely, lovely, we are up to one hundred million on the floor with Prince Abdullah. The price is one hundred million dollars U.S., ladies and gentlemen. Do we have another offer on the phone, Siggy or Gwyneth? No, nothing yet?"

Murmurs of excitement navigated through the crowd. Voorheiss felt a thrill of excitement ripple through his body like a generous shot of whiskey. He had no idea that an auction could be so exhilarating; it truly was like a football game, a see-saw battle of wills in the trenches, except that there was no physical contact. *Or at least not yet,* he thought with delight.

"I have one hundred million with the good prince. We have reached our reserve, ladies and gentlemen, I believe in record time. It's in the room, not on the phone with Siggy and Gwyneth. Do I have one hundred and one? Or perhaps one hundred and two?"

The Hungarian countess Erzsébet Szálasi touched her ear twice.

"I have one hundred and two million in the room. It's not with you, Prince Abdullah or you Herr Svantz, it's with the Countess Szálasi. No, wait a second. I have Gwyneth on the phone with one hundred and ten, ladies and gentlemen."

The British billionaire hedge fund manager Nigel Hawthorne raised his paddle.

"I have one hundred and eleven with Mr. Hawthorne in the room. Do I have one hundred and twelve million dollars now? *Ja,* who is with me?"

His assistant Siegfried Schmidt signaled him with another phone offer.

"It's no longer with you, sir or madame, it's on the phone. And the offer now stands at one hundred twenty-five million dollars U.S."

The Chinese, German, Hungarian, and Saudi buyers all jumped to their feet and emitted a collective gasp. To Voorheiss, it looked as though the auction had reached a frenzy point. And yet, if last year's Gustav Klimt had fetched nearly one hundred eighty million, this was just the beginning.

Suddenly, the auction turned even more thrilling as several telephone bidders stunned the room by quickly driving up the price to one hundred fifty million.

It was a *blitzkrieg*, the invasion of Belgium and France all over again.

"Bloody hell!" cursed Nigel Hawthorne, leaning towards his frequent fine art jousting partner, Wolfgang Svantz. "That's too rich for my English blood! I'm going to have to beg off."

"Don't worry, Nigel, I shall drive up the price," Voorheiss heard the German utter back to the Englishman through a heavy Frankfort accent. Then Svantz immediately raised his hand again, showing five fingers.

"I have one hundred fifty-five million in the room. No, it's not with you countess or you prince, though you must want a go at it. Hold on, Siggy is waving at me like an airport ground crew. I now have one hundred sixty million on the phone. No, make that one sixty-one, one sixty-two. I see you, too, Gwyneth my dear. Ladies it is now one hundred sixty-nine million dollars U.S. Now who wants to take a dare? I like round numbers—now do I have one hundred and seventy for the Klimt? Oh, thank you Mr. Wenyin…good to see the Chinese are still in the contest."

The bidding then stalled at one hundred seventy million. Grünewald enticed, cajoled, and finally begged the audience to up their ante to one hundred seventy-one, but to no avail. Then the Russian oligarch, Vladimir Blokhin, who had been surprisingly silent until now made the boldest move of the night. He rose to his feet and, in vodka-slurred but surprisingly fluent English, bellowed, "One hundred eighty million American dollars and that is the final offer. That is more than last year's Klimt at Christie's and it is mine." He gave a drunken grin. "Unless you want swords or pistols at dawn."

He then gave a debauched laugh, but nobody laughed with him.

"I think it's safe to say that our Russian friend, Comrade Blokhin—"

"Don't call me comrade."

"As I was saying, Herr Blokhin has made it quite clear where he stands in the bidding. But we are not done here, ladies and gentlemen, until the final bid is submitted. I'm giving you fair warning now. Is this the final offer? We have one hundred eighty million dollars U.S. with Herr Blokhin. Are we all done here?" He reached for his auctioneer's gavel. "This is the final chance. Going once, going twice—"

"Two hundred million!" screamed the Saudi prince, on his feet and waving his paddle like a madman.

A gasp of shock went up from the room, followed by a steady flow of stunned murmurs. Countess Szálasi fainted. As she fell like a dead weight towards the floor, she was deftly caught by the chivalrous and dashing Nigel Hawthorne, who gracefully guided her to her chair. When the noise refused to quiet down, Grünewald banged his gavel on his auctioneer's block with a plangent thud that echoed throughout the entire room. The crowd snapped silent. One of the countess's aides fanned her back to consciousness. Grünewald took a deep breath and stared down the buyers, withholding from proceeding until they had settled down and sat back down in their chairs.

"Ladies and gentlemen, please restrain yourselves from further outbursts and show this once-in-a-lifetime event the dignity and courtesy it deserves. Will this be the final bid then? Again, I must issue fair warning. Are there any further takers? All finished?"

No one said a word. At the phone bank, Siegfried and Gwyneth were shaking their heads.

"The legendary Klimt masterpiece—*Marie von Brandauer*—is sold to Prince Bandar Abdullah of Saudi Arabia for two hundred million dollars U.S."

He rapped his gavel on the podium. The crowd clapped and gave a cheer of jubilation that they had all survived the feeding frenzy. Several participants stepped forward to offer disingenuous handshakes to the Saudi monarch who looked like a young Omar Sharif.

"Again, congratulations your worship," said Grünewald unctuously. "Now, ladies and gentlemen, if we may move on to Lot 1 of the Old Masters—the Giorgione. My, my Herr Klimt is certainly going to be a hard act to follow, but I must say the game is truly afoot."

"My God," exclaimed Voorheiss to Dieter Franck. "Are art auctions always like this?"

"I don't know, I've never been to one before."

"Me neither," said Commander Jacobs. "But we're going to make a fortune."

"Yes, we are, gentlemen," said Voorheiss. "But I'll feel a whole lot better when the money is tucked safely in our Swiss accounts and we are out of this damned country."

"Me too," agreed Franck.

For the next three hours, the epic battle raged on. When it was over, Voorheiss couldn't believe that he had just witnessed the single most expensive art auction—public or private—ever held in the history of the planet. The eleven paintings, ranging from only partially restored to fully renovated, sold for an astounding 1.14 billion dollars. The art marathon smashed records for not only Klimt but Botticelli, Tintoretto, and Rubens, whose paintings sold for over $100 million. While Prince Abdullah had paid the top dollar for the surprise unnumbered lot, all of the other participants present in person had come away with at least one painting, with only Titian's *Perseus and Andromeda*, Tintoretto's *The Last Supper*, and the lone Giorgione going to phone bidders from three separate continents. None of the works were sold on credit and at the end of the night, as a fine Austrian moon shone down upon Innsbruck's *Altstadt* district, Voorheiss and his willing accomplices had received the down payments to their numbered Zurich bank accounts. The balance would be paid upon receipt of the paintings from Grünewald's art holding house, also based in Zurich.

With the auction completed, Voorheiss stepped again to the podium to issue his final remarks. He felt like a Medici, a member of the Italian dynasty of art patrons, after unloading all of the family's Renaissance paintings. "Thank you, ladies and gentlemen. This concludes our business transaction." His tone then turned cautionary. "Please remember that you still owe Mr. Grünewald the balance of your payments. Because he—and most assuredly I—won't forget. I'm giving you fair warning."

"What about the Da Vinci?" asked Prince Abdullah. "Are you sure, sir, that you do not want to sell it?"

"You're referring to *The Virgin and Child with St. Anne and St. John the Baptist*?"

"Yes, can we bid on it?"

"No, Prince, I'm afraid that tomorrow I will be reporting that the Central Intelligence Agency, working in collaboration with Swiss art experts and authorities, has located the lost Da Vinci and is prepared to return it to its rightful owners: the Bellomo family of—"

He stopped right there as suddenly more than a dozen armed men in uniform burst into the room, swept around the dinner tables, and formed a barricade around him and the art collectors, their expert consultants, and his two cohorts, Commander Jacobs and Dieter Franck. The penetration was so swiftly and precisely executed that they didn't even have time to draw their weapons.

And then, four people he recognized stepped into the room.

His jaw dropped.

He stood there, like a deer trapped in headlights, realizing that he was absolutely, devastatingly fucked and his short-lived life as a mega-millionaire was over.

CHAPTER 60

ALTSTADT, INNSBRUCK

AS NICK LASSITER stepped into the room with his two fathers—Stanislaw Pularchek and Benjamin Brewbaker—followed by his wife Natalie and the Austrian Special Police, he instantly felt a sense of triumph. Clearly, Voorheiss hadn't seen this coming. Just as he had been completely fooled by the trick Dieter Franck and Skyler had played on him with Pularchek and Brewbaker back at the Old Steinberg Mine. The contingency plan had worked to perfection. Using Hollywood-caliber special effects and Skyler's shooting from the bluff as a distraction, Franck had only pretended to shoot the two men at point-blank range and splatter their blood and brains everywhere, convincing Voorheiss that his two adversaries were dead when in fact their deaths had been cleverly faked. Now, tasting the twin fruits of revenge and deception, Lassiter had to admit they were delicious, despite the fact that he, too, had been fooled back at the mine.

"No, it can't be," spluttered Voorheiss, still in shock. "I saw you two die with my own eyes."

"Did you now?" Pularchek wondered aloud with a mischievous grin.

"It appears, Stanislaw," announced Benjamin Brewbaker with a sardonic expression, "news of our death has been greatly exaggerated."

"It would appear so, my American friend. It would appear so."

Lassiter couldn't help but crack a smile as he looked at Natalie and saw her raise an eyebrow. This was more fun than either of them had anticipated.

Voorheiss turned to Franck in desperation. "But I saw Dieter...I saw Dieter shoot you with his..."

He stopped right there before finishing as the German was up on his feet from the dining table and pointing a gun at him.

"Looks can be deceiving, Director Voorheiss," said Dieter Franck with a look of triumph on his rugged face. "And when you don't know where a man's loyalty lies, they can be very, very deceiving."

"Now that is something we can agree on, Herr Franck," said Pularchek, stepping forward with a pistol in his hand and still wearing his devilish grin. "My God, that's got to be the first time I've ever agreed with a goddamned German."

And probably your last, thought Lassiter as he discreetly studied the nervous faces of the billionaires in the room. They looked like they wanted to disappear into a hole; they knew their prodigious wealth was no guarantee to get them out of their current jam. Knowingly buying and selling stolen art was an international crime that carried stiff penalties.

"You're all under arrest," said Pularchek, and this was echoed in German by the plainclothed Austrian Special Police officer next to him.

"This is a private auction," protested Countess Szálasi. "You have no right to be here."

Pularchek's smile widened and he held up his gun, its silvery barrel glittering like a diamond in the light of the overhead chandelier. "Oh, we have every right, Countess. Don't we, Benjamin?"

"Oh yes, we most certainly do," said Brewbaker, his gaze fixed on his CIA boss.

Lassiter saw Voorheiss slump with resignation as handcuffs were slapped on him and the others in the room, one by one. They all looked exceedingly unhappy as the Austrian Special Police began reading them their rights under the law and they started to be escorted from the room to the waiting police vans. The two buyers of royal lineage—the prince and countess—were the only two to break down and cause a scene, but they were quickly brought under control.

"So what happens now?" asked Natalie, standing next to her husband, both of them mesmerized by the spectacle.

"I don't know. I guess we can finally enjoy our honeymoon."

"Yes, yes, that is a delightful idea," said Pularchek, coming up from behind them along with Brewbaker. "I'm sorry that I botched the affair the first time around."

Lassiter smiled. "Yes, well, no one can say that it wasn't exciting."

"Perhaps a bit too exciting," said Natalie.

Lassiter nodded towards Voorheiss. "What's going to happen to him?" he asked his father Brewbaker.

"He's looking at twenty years at least. The U.S. is going to want him back."

"So they'll extradite him?"

"Absolutely."

"Looks like someone I know is going to be getting his old job back," said Pularchek. "Congratulations in advance, Benjamin."

"My mother always told me not to count my chickens before they hatch."

"That's funny. My mother told me the same thing. That's why I have to ask you all a simple question. What makes you certain your Director Voorheiss is going to jail? I was thinking that perhaps he might receive some other form of punishment."

"Other form of punishment?" wondered Lassiter. "Like what?"

"I don't know. Perhaps a bullet to the brain."

His father was looking at the Pole funny. "Stanislaw, please tell me you didn't...I mean, tell me you're not..."

Pularchek held up his hands. "I'm sorry, my American friend, but those who choose to perform evil cannot be allowed to choose their own terms. They must pay the heaviest price of all—and that is to give up their own life."

"Are you telling me you have a shooter in play now? As we speak?"

"You can't do this," pleaded Lassiter. He looked towards the door for Voorheiss, but the Austrians had already taken him away. "It's not right. You can't play God. You have to obey the rule of law."

"You might have to, but *I* most assuredly do not."

"Oh my God, what have you done?"

"I'm sorry. It's out of my hands," said Pularchek. "Evil must be dealt with firmly but judiciously."

"But he's been arrested. The law is going to take its course and he's going to be prosecuted."

"Is that really enough after what this man has done? He murdered Angela Wolff in cold blood. Regardless of how bad she was, she was unarmed at the time and there was no reason for him to do it."

"And he will be tried for that," said Brewbaker.

Lassiter couldn't believe what he was hearing. "Jesus Christ, we have to stop this!" he cried. "Let's go, you two! We can't let this happen!"

Leaving Pularchek standing there, he tore out of the room with his father and Natalie. But they hadn't taken three steps when they saw the elevator doors close and a handcuffed Voorheiss disappear along with the Saudi, the Russian, and a detail of Austrian policemen.

CHAPTER 61

ALTSTADT, INNSBRUCK

THE FOURTH PULARCHEK peered through his pair of Leica range-finding binoculars at the front entrance of the art auction house. He could feel the anticipation building inside him. The light of the crescent moon bled down upon the city of Innsbruck, reflecting off the rippled surface of the alpine river that had given the Tyrolean city its name.

Soon, very soon, his three soft targets would yield to his crosshairs. His position at the second-floor window across the street provided a clear line of sight from the front door all the way to the waiting police wagons parked by the curb. Taking out three targets at once was definitely a challenge, but the odds were still strongly in his favor, provided that the targets were slowly escorted out of the building together. Of course, that had already been arranged with two members of the Austrian Special Police through a very substantial payoff, but circumstances could abruptly change.

With Angela Wolff extinguished, tonight's operation was the final and most important objective, the culmination of a full year of planning. All the sanctions during the past week had been conducted to bring about this climactic moment in Innsbruck. All along, the purpose of the selective program of revenge had been to draw two specific individuals out into the open so they could be terminated simultaneously. Wolff and Voorheiss were important in their own right, but the other two were even bigger fish. The German's and the American's crimes against humanity paled in comparison to those of the Saudi Prince Bandar al-Rashid Abdullah and the Russian oligarch Vladimir Blokhin.

For years now, Abdullah had been the proud financier of Islamic State, al-Qaeda, and two other Islamic jihadist groups to the tune of $80 million *riyals* per year, over $21 million dollars.

Blokhin was the son of the butcher Vasili Mikhailovich Blokhin, the Soviet Russian Major-General who had served as the chief executioner under Stalin. He had shot, by his own hand, 7,000 of the total of more than 22,000 Polish officers and political leaders murdered by the Russians during the Katyn massacre in spring 1940. That made Vladimir Blohkin's father the most prolific mass murderer in recorded world history. The son's crime was that, as a hard-line leader of the Communist Party of the Russian Federation, he continued to deny all Soviet responsibility for the massacre and his father's pivotal role in it, and to insist that the original Soviet version—the lie that the Polish prisoners were shot by Germans in August 1941—was the correct one. In vocal and outspoken fashion, he proclaimed that all released documents on the massacre were fakes. He routinely called on the Russian government to start a new investigation that would revise the findings of the 2004 investigation. The investigation had found, conclusively, that Stalin and his henchmen in the Politburo had authorized the mass killings to deprive Poland of a large portion of its military and political talent in post-WWII Europe.

The Fourth Pularchek's radio headset crackled to life. "The package is on the move. All three chess pieces are bunched together," he heard the Komandor say. "They'll be in your line of sight in two minutes."

"Copy that."

"Happy hunting, *Braciszku*. I'll see you at the rendezvous. Over and out."

Rechecking his distance to target, the Fourth Pularchek locked the laser ranging dot on his Leica binoculars onto the Austrian policeman standing to the right of the door. The invisible ray of laser light hovered on his simulated target's forehead, danced for a second, and bounced back its signal. He read the red digital readout in metric units in the upper right hand corner of the image.

Sixty-two meters.

The distance to the police vehicles on the street ranged from forty-eight to fifty-one meters so he had a kill zone of eleven to fourteen meters from the building entrance. Unfortunately, collateral damage was a possibility given all the people in close proximity to the targets, but the steep downward trajectory would help considerably.

He thought about his comrade-in-arms Pularchek. He liked the man and clearly understood and approved of his role as judge, jury, and executioner. There was nothing irrational or unfair about it: the men Pularchek killed on behalf of the Cause deserved to die, and the world was a better place without them. In that respect, reflected the Fourth Pularchek, maybe the Polish billionaire wasn't so different from the Islamic enemies he killed without mercy who dreamed of a Paradise filled with a harem of willing virgins in the name of Allah. Like them, Pularchek meted out his special brand of frontier justice in a world cast in simple black and white.

The Fourth Pularchek picked up his vintage Polish Bor-338 sniper rifle fitted with a Steiner 5-25×56 military scope. Slowly and carefully, he brought the weapon to his shoulder. The rotary bolt-action weapon was a man dropper. Chambered with specially designed armor-piercing, incendiary .338 cartridges, the rifle was equipped with a 27-inch-long barrel and fed from a detachable 10-round box magazine forward of the trigger.

He quickly sighted the weapon on the front door that any second now would open. There was no mystery to the shot: he knew the precise distance and had already computed the bullet drift and drop and zeroed the rifle. There was a slight easterly wind, but he didn't need to compensate for the windage in his hold since the distance to target was so short.

He took a deep breath to steady himself. These would be three of the most important shots of his life.

They were shots for Pularchek and his Cause.

The front door opened and he felt his heart rate click up a notch. A pair of Austrian Special Policeman appeared, scanned the area, and began leading the prisoners towards the police vans parked at the curb. Voorheiss was first, followed by Abdullah and then Blokhin, one right after another as planned, with the Austrian police on either side of the prisoners.

Each shot was clear. The kills would almost be too easy, like three dominoes lined up in a row.

He tightened the stock of the rifle against his shoulder and quickly sighted each of the soft targets' heads through the Steiner military scope. Voorheiss and the others started down the stone staircase in the direction of the awaiting vans, which were fortunately parked down the street so that they weren't blocking the front entrance.

The heavy black lines of the duplex reticle converged from all sides of his circular field of view. The thick lines pointed to a thinner crosshair centered on Voorheiss, who came through so clearly, the Fourth Pularchek could see loose strands of his silvery white hair fluttering in the light wind.

His right index finger slid forward and curled around the trigger. His hands were steady, his muscles tense but precisely controlled.

He felt the excitement pick up inside him as Voorheiss reached the third step. It was time to take the first shot.

The CIA man's image in the scope was unwavering, crystal clear. On the street below, the Fourth Pularchek heard a car engine turn over and the distant yap of a dog.

His throat went dry.

He calmly moved the rifle a fraction of a millimeter to his right until the burly chest of the NCS director was centered precisely within his crosshairs.

With the world-class discipline of his mentor and friend, Stanislaw Snarkus Pularchek, he summoned all his resolve, every ounce of concentration and professionalism he could muster, and channeled the energy into the shot.

His hold was perfect: no wobble, no tremor, not the slightest quiver.

There was no doubt in his mind that what he was doing was the right thing, the moral thing to do.

The field of fire turned preternaturally calm, utterly silent, as if he was in a cocoon.

Voorheiss's face through the scope was as clear as an alpine lake in mid-summer.

The Fourth Pularchek's breath came in a steady rhythm as his finger tightened against the trigger, slowly applying the pounds of pressure that would eventually result in bloody mayhem.

His mind was totally lucid and unencumbered: no fear, no guilt, no doubt.

There was only the rifle, his soft target, and the invisible arc connecting them.

"Evil must be snuffed out," he whispered under his breath.

He started to pull the trig—

Suddenly, he saw Nick Lassiter, Benjamin Brewbaker, and Natalie Perkins rushing out the front entrance just as Voorheiss descended the fifth step.

They signaled the Austrian Special Police by yelling and waving their arms.

"Komandor!" he cried into his radio mouthpiece. "Your son and his wife are down there calling to the police. Do you want me to still take the shot?"

"Yes, you are greenlit! Take the shot now!"

"But they're running down the—"

"Take the damned shot! That's an order!"

"But there could be collateral—"

"Take it, goddamnit! I want all three of them dead!"

"I copy, Komandor! I will kill them all!"

He quickly re-sighted the bolt action rifle. Then he squeezed the trigger, jerked back the bolt, and ejected the spent casing—not once but three times. Making three separate clean kills.

But what was most noteworthy was that the shooter wasn't a *he* at all, but rather a *she* who, with her clever mask and disguise, happened to look virtually identical to Pularchek.

When the first bullet hit, Skyler saw a tiny cloud of smoke from the incendiary, followed by a wet pink cloud of spurting blood, brain-matter, and bone as the head was literally pulped. The body was driven back, the arms flung out helplessly, and the victim tumbled down the steps. Then she saw the second and third bullets do their bloody, violent damage.

In less than five seconds, three bodies lay sprawled across the steps. Each one twitched for a moment before going totally still.

A great and heavy silence hung over the field of fire. Then she heard the Komandor again over her radio.

"It is done," said Pularchek.

"Three confirmed kills?" asked Skyler, the Fourth Pularchek.

"*Tak*, our work is finished here. The mission was a success. Now get out of there."

"It felt good, Komandor. I don't feel guilty at all."

"I know, my friend. With men like these, there is no reason to feel guilty. I will see you at the rendezvous to issue final payment. Then you will be free, once and for all."

"It feels good to know that."

"Our work together is finished. You must now live the peaceful life you always wanted and so richly deserve. I believe there is a man who loves you very much waiting for you."

"Yes, and I must try hard to make it work."

"I know you will succeed. You have always had goodness in your heart, Angela. Always."

EPILOGUE

TWO WEEKS LATER
STROMBOLI, SICILY

THE ISLAND'S INHABITANTS called it *"Iddu,"* which in Sicilian meant "Him." The bestowed title was a reference to the divine nature of the massive volcano most people knew as Stromboli. It took Nick Lassiter and Natalie over two hours to ascend the 8,000-foot mountain of solidified basaltic andesite—3,000 feet of which lay above sea level. By the time they reached the narrow ridge overlooking the volcano's crater and had cracked open their first bottle of Sicilian rosé, the sun's orange ball was sinking over the Tyrrhenian Sea, bathing the fishing boats far below in russet pink.

From their safe vantage point five hundred feet south of the volcano's rim, they watched the sunset against a backdrop of fiery explosions. The massive stratovolcano roared and rumbled, shaking the ground so violently that the black pyroclastic sand shifted beneath their blanket. As day passed into night, pockets of pent-up volcanic gas burst through magma-filled conduits and hurled basketball-sized volcanic bombs and smaller scoria fragments more than three hundred feet into the air in a psychedelic Fourth-of-July-like display. They kissed and sipped their wine as jet fountains of molten lava spewed out from the central crater in orange-tailed comets. In the night sky above, a brilliant Milky Way soon appeared and then disappeared, obscured by the smoke belching from Stromboli's magma chamber. On the sea far below, lights twinkled from boats as rivers of lava gushed down Stromboli's flanks in bright torrents and were funneled by the *Sciara del Fuoco*—the Stream of Fire—into the ocean.

"God, this is beautiful," exclaimed Natalie as a pair of volcanic bombs blasted up into the air in a fiery burst. "Quite a place to take a girl for her honeymoon. But do you think we'll survive the night?"

"I'd say the volcano is the least of your worries," said Lassiter. "Once we climb down off Old *Iddu* here, I plan to make love to you all night long on the beach. I'd say your chances of survival when I'm through ravaging you are fifty-fifty at best."

"Hmm, maybe we should climb down right now."

"If only we had a special raft, we could ride one of those lava flows. Then we could be on the beach in less than five minutes."

They both laughed and stared mesmerically at the "fountains of fire" erupting from the volcano. They were close enough to the volcano that they could actually hear the scoriaceous bombs whistling through the air. Then Natalie took out a tin of *aubergine caponata* from her backpack and, hungry from the climb up the mountain, they devoured it with *bruschetta*. They washed it down with rosé and then finished off the meal with a creamy ricotta cannoli.

When they were finished eating, Natalie said, "Have you thought any more about what we discussed after our Langley debriefing?"

"I don't want to talk about it."

"You have to, Nick. He's your father."

"No, he's not. No father of mine would kill three people after I warned him not to do it. And no normal person has an army of clones that have been artificially modified to look and talk like him and are willing to die for him. It's like some ancient cult."

"They aren't clones, Nick. They're German, Polish, Austrian, and Hungarian Jews whose ancestors died in the Holocaust. They are men who willingly choose to fight in Pularchek's war against evil. They are warriors who have been surgically altered and fight out of their own free will."

"It's still like an archaic cult. But that's not the problem I have with him. It's that he had to kill Voorheiss, Abdullah, and Blokhin instead of allowing due process to take its course. They would have all been tried and seen serious jail time if he had simply let the legal system prevail. When he ordered them killed instead of letting justice take its course, he proved that he's no better than them."

"Maybe that's what it takes to stop these kinds of extremists in the modern world."

"I'm not buying it, and I'm still angry at him. No matter how you slice it, he and that woman Skyler that works for him are still killers. My dad says that she may very well have been the one who actually pulled the trigger in Innsbruck. He wants her badly not just for Innsbruck but the assassinations in Denver. He's working with that Agent Patton with the FBI."

"I admit she's scary, but I don't see how that woman could be the one who shot down all those people in Denver. It just doesn't seem possible."

"Why not? Just because she's a woman?"

"Look, Nick, I understand that you're angry with Pularchek. But that doesn't change the fact that he *is* your father. One day you're going to have to accept that. You can't *not* talk to him forever."

He said nothing.

"Nick, he's written you five letters, called you a dozen times, and spoken to me and your dad three or four times. It's time you talk to him yourself. He's *your father*, Nick."

"I understand that. But I'm still mad at him. He shouldn't have had them killed right in front of us. Jesus Christ, you could have been hurt."

"Is that the real reason you're so angry at him? Because you believe that he put my life in jeopardy?"

"He could have killed you, Nat. Hell, he could have accidentally killed all of us."

"I was there too, remember? And I say we were never at risk. The shooter—whether it was that Skyler woman or not—wouldn't have taken those shots if they weren't clean."

"I don't know why you had to bring this all up on our honeymoon. We've just spent the last ten days getting grilled at Langley and now you're putting me through it all again?"

"This is different. This is about you and your father."

"Pularchek is not my damned father, okay? He's nothing but an accidental sperm donor. He had sex with an English girl he barely knew when they were both scared to death and under enemy fire outside Beirut. That doesn't make the son of bitch my father, all right?"

"Why not? He loves you and he wants you back in his life. That's what a father is: someone who loves you unconditionally."

"Look, I know what he does is morally justified. I just don't like that he completely ignored me when I pleaded with him not to kill them, and he put you, me, and my dad in danger. Of course, Blokhin and the others deserved to die. But no one, not even Pularchek, should be above the law. If you follow all the proper legal procedures and the system fails and still a guy gets off scot-free, well then, yes, by all means take the law into your own hands and kill the son of bitch. But if the system actually does what it's supposed to do and a person is put behind bars for a long time, then you should live with it. That's all I'm saying."

"You know you're just as stubborn as he is."

"I am not."

"Yes, you are. That's who you get it from. You're Polish-stubborn."

"So now you're quoting him. I told you I don't want to talk about this anymore. We're supposed to be on our honeymoon."

"He's your birth father, Nick, and whether you like it or not, you are very much like him."

The volcano erupted, lighting up the night sky in a colorful burst. He tried to keep himself from erupting too, but to no avail. "I may be like him, but I am not him. I would never do the things he does."

"Well, you still need to forgive him and accept him back into your life. He loves you, Nick."

"But why the hell did he have them killed when I begged him not to?"

"Because they were bad, bad men and they deserved to die. The whole setup with the stolen art was so he could get Abdullah and Blokhin. Voorheiss and Wolff were nothing but secondary targets all along. You've just got to accept it and move on."

"Jesus, he's reeled both you and my father in hook, line, and sinker."

"He's an amazing man, Nick. He does as much to fight terrorism as the United States, Great Britain, and Israel combined. He doesn't just play spy games, spend exorbitant sums of money, and blast away at low-level targets with drones or cruise missiles. He goes after the real money men and ideologues, and he takes them out. Quite frankly, I admire him—and so does your father."

"You know damn well that I admire him too. I just don't agree with his decision when all three men had already been arrested, handcuffed, and were ready to stand trial. A person can't just go around shooting handcuffed prisoners. It's not right. And neither is hiring professional hit women like that lethal Skyler to do your dirty work. No matter how you dress it all up, he's still a professional criminal who skirts the law and associates with criminals."

"Our government killed Osama bin Laden and Abdul Qader Hakim, and the Israelis kidnapped Eichmann and then put him to death. Tell me, what's the difference?"

"Eichmann was tried by an Israeli panel of judges, convicted, and hung for his war crimes. Pularchek disobeys the rule of law and kills the descendants of Nazis and Soviets, not the original perpetrators of the crimes. It's not the same thing."

"Sure it is. He takes out only those that have directly profited from their ancestors or are staunch deniers who refuse to admit what their ancestors did. He takes the battle to not only modern-day Islamic terrorists, but Holocaust and Katyn deniers. And as far as the jihadist financiers go, he terminates the actual bankrollers of mass murder today, not in the past. Your father and I are in agreement on that too."

"Great, maybe you should have married *him*."

"No, we both just happen to think that you shouldn't be shutting the door on Pularchek. He may be flawed, but he loves you as much as a father can love a son. You have to see things from his perspective."

"That's never going to happen."

"You have to admit that he stands up for exactly what he believes. He has a strong moral conviction that what he is doing is the right thing, and he refuses to back down despite what other people think."

"I'm tired of talking about this. I just want to drop it."

"Okay, I'm sorry," she said. "But I want you to promise me that you'll keep an open mind."

"I can't promise that."

"Come on, Nick. You can't be angry forever. You have to let go and take him back. He desperately wants to be back in your life."

"I don't care. He made his bed and now he's going to have to sleep in it."

"That's not fair. You have to give him a chance. Can you at least promise me that you'll try?"

He said nothing and stared out at the dark, mysterious sea as bright volcanic bursts flashed overhead.

"Just promise me that you'll keep an open mind."

"Okay, okay, I'll keep an open mind," he said reluctantly. "As long as you stop talking about it."

"All right, I promise."

Iddu erupted again, sending up another shower of fiery orange, the volcanic bombs whistling into the night. There was a hint of cacti, ginestre, and wildflower coming up on the sea breeze from the beach to mingle with the heavy smell of sulfur from the volcano.

"I love you, you know," he said after a moment.

"I love you too, Nick. But you have to admit, you're stubborn as hell."

"Yeah, I know. I'm Polish-stubborn."

"You most certainly are. And that's why I love you so much. You don't back down from anybody or anything. Plus you're a damned good kisser."

"Oh, I am, am I?"

"Yep, you sure are."

She snuggled up close to him on the blanket and they began kissing, slowly at first and then more passionately as the eruptions from the volcano picked up. *She's right—I need to keep an open mind,* he thought, as the sky burst with orange fireballs and he felt the power of his love for her seize control over his whole body.

Up here on the volcano, it was easy for him to see how everything in nature was spectacular and interconnected, how it was possible for love and empathy to conquer all. Up here in his wife's arms, on his honeymoon, he could see why the villagers referred to Stromboli as *Him,* as if it were a Deity. He felt something spiritual on this massive, erupting mountain of lava.

Up here, he felt the timeless power of forgiveness.

He decided that tomorrow, when they sailed to Cinque Terre, he would indeed extend an olive branch to his father.

He would call Stanislaw Snarkus Pularchek on the phone. And tell him about his idea for his new thriller.

AUTHOR'S NOTE AND ACKNOWLEDGEMENTS

The Fourth Pularchek, Book #3 of the Nick Lassiter-Skyler International Espionage Series, was conceived and written by the author as a work of fiction. The novel is ultimately a work of the imagination and entertainment and should be read as nothing more. Names, characters, places, government entities, religious and political groups, corporations, and incidents are products of the author's imagination, or are used fictitiously, and are not to be construed as real. Any resemblance to actual events, locales, businesses, companies, organizations, or persons, living or dead, is entirely coincidental.

To develop the story line, characters, and scenes for *The Fourth Pularchek*, I consulted hundreds of non-fiction books, magazine and newspaper articles, blogs, Web sites, and numerous individuals and visited most every real-world location in person. These principal locations included numerous physical settings in the United States, Germany, Poland, and Austria. All in all, there are too many resources and locations to name here. However, I would be remiss if I didn't give credit to the critical individuals who dramatically improved the quality of the manuscript from its initial to its final stage. Any technical mistakes in the facts underpinning the novel, typographical errors, or examples of overreach due to artistic license, however, are the fault of me and me alone.

I would also personally like to thank the following for their support and assistance. First and foremost, I would like to thank my wife Christine, an exceptional and highly professional book editor, who painstakingly reviewed and copy-edited the novel.

Second, I would like to thank my former literary agent, Cherry Weiner of the Cherry Weiner Literary Agency, for thoroughly reviewing, vetting, and copy-editing the manuscript, and for making countless improvements to the finished novel before I chose to publish the novel independently.

Third, I would like to thank Stephen King's former editor, Patrick LoBrutto, and Quinn Fitzpatrick, former book critic for the Rocky Mountain News, for thoroughly copy-editing the various drafts of the novel and providing detailed reviews.

I would also like to thank Austin and Anne Marquis, Governor Roy Romer, Ambassador Marc Grossman, Betsy and Steve Hall, Rik Hall, Christian Fuenfhausen, Fred Taylor, Peter and Lorrie Frautschi, Mo Shafroth and Barr Hogan, Tim and Carey Romer, Deirdre Grant Mercurio, Suie Tanner, Joe Tallman, John Welch, Link Nicoll, Toni Conte Augusta Francis, Dawn Ezzo Roseman, Will Nicholson, Brigid Donnelly Hughes, Peter Brooke, Caroline Fenton Dewey, John and Ellen Aisenbrey, Margot Patterson, Cathy and Jon Jenkins, Danny Bilello and Elena Diaz-Bilello, Charlie and Kay Fial, Vincent Bilello, Elizabeth Gardner, Robin McGehee, Bill Eberhart, and the other book reviewers and professional contributors large and small who have given generously of their time over the years, as well as to those who have given me loyal support as I have ventured on this incredible odyssey of suspense novel writing.

Lastly, I want to thank anyone and everyone who bought this book and my loyal fans and supporters who helped promote this work. You know who you are and I salute you.

ABOUT THE AUTHOR
AND FORTHCOMING TITLES

Samuel Marquis is a bestselling, award-winning suspense author. He works by day as a VP–Principal Hydrogeologist with an environmental firm in Boulder, Colorado, and by night as a spinner of historical and modern suspense yarns. He holds a Master of Science degree in Geology, is a Registered Professional Geologist in eleven states, and is a recognized expert in groundwater contaminant hydrogeology, having served as an expert witness in several class action litigation cases. He also has a deep and abiding interest in military history and intelligence, specifically related to the Golden Age of Piracy, Plains Indian Wars, World War II, and the current War on Terror.

His thrillers have been #1 *Denver Post* bestsellers and received national book award recognition. His first novel, *The Devil's Brigade* (formerly *The Slush Pile Brigade*), was an award-winning finalist in the mystery category of the Beverly Hills Book Awards. His follow-up *Blind Thrust* was the winner of the Foreword Reviews' Book of the Year (HM) and Next Generation Indie Book Awards and an award-winning finalist of the USA Best Book and Beverly Hills Book Awards (thriller and suspense). His third novel, *The Coalition*, was the winner of the Beverly Hills Book Awards for a political thriller and an award-winning finalist for the USA Best Book Awards and Colorado Book Awards. *Bodyguard of Deception*, Book 1 of his WWII Series, was an award-winning finalist of the USA Best Book Awards and Foreword Reviews Book Awards in historical fiction. His fifth book, *Cluster of Lies*, won the Beverly Hills Book Awards in the regional fiction: west category and was an award-winning finalist of the USA Best Book Awards and Foreword Reviews Book Awards.

Ambassador Marc Grossman, former U.S. Under Secretary of State, proclaimed, "In his novels *Blind Thrust* and *Cluster of Lies*, Samuel Marquis vividly combines the excitement of the best modern techno-thrillers." Former Colorado Governor Roy Romer said, "*Blind Thrust* kept me up until 1 a.m. two nights in a row. I could not put it down." Kirkus Reviews proclaimed *The Coalition* an "entertaining thriller" and declared that "Marquis has written a tight plot with genuine suspense." James Patterson said *The Coalition* had "a lot of good action and suspense" and compared the novel to *The Day After Tomorrow*, the classic thriller by Allan Folsom. Other book reviewers have compared Marquis's WWII thrillers *Bodyguard of Deception* and *Altar of Resistance* to the epic historical novels of Tom Clancy, John le Carré, Ken Follett, Herman Wouk, Daniel Silva, and Alan Furst.

Below is the list of suspense novels that Samuel Marquis has published or will be publishing in the near future, along with the release dates of both previously published and forthcoming titles.

The World War Two Series
Bodyguard of Deception – March 2016 – Award-Winning Finalist USA Best Book Awards and Foreword Reviews Book Awards
Altar of Resistance – January 2017
Spies of the Midnight Sun – January 2018

The Nick Lassiter – Skyler International Espionage Series
The Devil's Brigade (formerly The Slush Pile Brigade) – September 2015, Reissue April 2017 – The #1 Denver Post Bestseller and Award-Winning Finalist Beverly Hills Book Awards
The Coalition – January 2016, Reissue April 2017 – Winner Beverly Hills Book Awards and Award-Winning Finalist USA Best Book Awards and Colorado Book Awards
The Fourth Pularchek – June 2017

The Joe Higheagle Environmental Sleuth Series
Blind Thrust – October 2015 – The #1 Denver Post Bestseller; Winner Foreword Reviews' Book of the Year (HM) and Next Generation Indie Book Awards; Award-Winning Finalist USA Best Book Awards, Beverly Hills Book Awards, and Next Generation Indie Book Awards
Cluster of Lies – September 2016 – Winner Beverly Hills Book Awards and Award-Winning Finalist USA Best Book Awards and Foreword Reviews Book Awards

Thank You for Your Support!

To Order Samuel Marquis Books and Contact Samuel:

Visit Samuel Marquis's website, join his mailing list, learn about his forthcoming suspense novels and book events, and order his books at www.samuelmarquisbooks.com. Please send all fan mail (including criticism) to samuelmarquisbooks@gmail.com.

CPSIA information can be obtained
at www.ICGtesting.com
Printed in the USA
LVOW12s2306230817
546166LV00001B/83/P